American Lawyer Books

Simon & Schuster

New York London Toronto

Sydney Tokyo Singapore

Ann Woolner

Washed in
GOLD

The Story Behind
the Biggest
Money-Laundering
Investigation
in U.S. History

SIMON & SCHUSTER
Rockefeller Center
1230 Avenue of the Americas
New York, New York 10020

SIMON & SCHUSTER and colophon are registered trademarks of
Simon & Schuster Inc.

Designed by Karolina Harris

Manufactured in the United States of America

10   9   8   7   6   5   4   3   2   1

Library of Congress Cataloging-in-Publication Data
Woolner, Ann.
   Washed in gold: the story behind the biggest money-laundering investigation in
U.S. history / Ann Woolner.
      p.   cm.
   Includes bibliographical references and index.
      1. Money laundering—United States.   2. Drug traffic—United States—
Finance.   3. United States Drug Enforcement Administration.   I. Title.
HV6769.W66   1994
364.1'68—dc20   94-10614
                                                                                    CIP

ISBN: 0-671-74194-2

In memory of
Rosestelle Bach Woolner

Contents

Acknowledgments

The genesis of this book was a newspaper story I wrote about Operation Polar Cap in 1990 or, more specifically, the remarks it drew from my editor then, Steve Johnson, and my boss in New York, Steve Brill. First Johnson and then Brill told me they thought there just might be a book in Polar Cap, an idea that probably would not have occurred to me otherwise.

From that point and at critical junctures along the way, Steve Johnson gave me ecouragement and advice. Steve Brill offered me the way to turn the story into a book, as well as the benefit of his considerable editorial judgment.

At Simon & Schuster, I am grateful to Alice Mayhew for backing the book and for backing me. A special thanks goes to Marie Arana-Ward, whose enthusiasm and wise counsel saw me through the reporting and writing. I owe much to Bob Bender, who took over after Marie left Simon & Schuster, and who helped me to transform the manuscript into a book. Thanks also to my agent, Kristine Dahl, on whose persistence, advocacy, and good judgment I came to rely.

Even with all of that, this book would not have been possible if not for the encouragement and support of the management and staff of the *Fulton County Daily Report*. Thanks to Publisher Shayla Keough Rumeley and Editor S. Richard Gard for the generous and unusual leaves-of-absence they allowed me. And thanks to the editorial staff, who cheered me on while bearing the burden of my absences on top of already heavy workloads. I am grateful to Ed Wasserman, editor in chief of the *Miami Daily Business Review,* who offered insightful critical comment on my first draft, as did the aforementioned Steve Johnson, now executive producer of Court TV, and Steve Brill, chairman of American Lawyer Media.

I also owe a special thanks to Robert Lee Hotz, now of the *Los Angeles Times,* for his crucial early encouragement and advice, which continued throughout; and to Lee Smith of *The Atlanta Journal and The Atlanta Constitution,* who volunteered as a researcher, chasing down obscure bits of information. At CNN, I am grateful to Kathy Christensen and Frances Pici.

Still, this would have been a rather shallow story, indeed, had it not been for the patient cooperation of scores of local and state law enforcement officers and federal prosecutors, agents, and administrators in Atlanta, Los Angeles, New York, Washington, Panama, and Colombia. None was more generous with his time and his observations or more straightforward in recounting even the most embarrassing of events than Assistant U.S. Attorney Wilmer "Buddy" Parker. From the DEA, Albert "Skip" Latson, Cesar Diaz, and John Featherly spent countless hours answering my questions. They could not have done so, and neither could the other DEA personnel, if the Drug Enforcement Administration had not granted me access, for which I am thankful. William Ruzzamenti and Billy Yout were especially helpful. Thanks, also, to the Federal Bureau of Investigation, the U.S. Customs Service in New York, and the Internal Revenue Service in Los Angeles for giving me access to their agents.

I am also grateful to those people who had much to fear from this book, and who agreed to meet with me anyway. They know who they are, and to them I owe a special debt.

My family, friends, and neighbors suffered my absorption with this project while helping me to pull through it. They gave me shelter in my travels and a respite from my work. They acted as sounding boards for my ideas. I am especially indebted to my sister, Kay Brief, my lifelong friend and ally. As a youngster, her interest in the written word piqued mine. Throughout this project, she listened to my woes and shared in my excitement.

Lastly, I want to say a few words about my father, Charles Woolner, a storyteller and a lover of books, and my mother, Rosestelle Woolner, who was my first and best teacher. She cherished everything I did and believed I could do things I never thought possible. From the beginning of this book to the end, both of them were with me. To them, I am eternally grateful.

List of Key Players

The following list, while by no means comprehensive, gives the names and roles of the main participants in Operation Polar Cap. Pseudonyms or cover names are provided for those who used them. For a complete list, see the list of interviews at the end of the book.

Jimmy Brown: pseudonym for DEA-Atlanta Group Supervisor John Featherly.

Ron Caffrey: Special Agent; head of DEA office in Atlanta.

Alex Carrera: pseudonym for DEA-Atlanta Special Agent Cesar Diaz.

Ramón Costello (pseudonym; real name not available): informant for DEA-Atlanta.

Phil Devlin, Special Agent, DEA–New York.

Cesar Diaz (pseudonym: Alex Carrera): Special Agent, DEA-Atlanta.

John Featherly (pseudonym: Jimmy Brown): Group Supervisor, DEA-Atlanta.

Vincent Furtado: Group Supervisor, DEA–Los Angeles.

Ed Guillen: Special Agent, DEA–New York.

Elaine Harris: Group Supervisor, DEA–New York.

Russell Hayman: Assistant U.S. Attorney, Los Angeles.

Skip Latson (pseudonym: Allen Weston): Special Agent, DEA-Atlanta.

Orlando Lopez (pseudonym: Rolando): Glendale, California, police officer; later, Special Agent, California Bureau of Narcotic Enforcement.

Ralph Lumpkin, Group Supervisor, FBI–Los Angeles.

Kevin Mancini, Special Agent, DEA–New York.

Daniel Ortega, Special Agent, DEA–Los Angeles.

Michael Orton, Special Agent, DEA–Los Angeles.

Buddy Parker: Assistant U.S. Attorney, Atlanta.

Alex Romero, Special Agent, DEA–Los Angeles.

Francisco Serrano (pseudonym: Rubén Márquez): money launderer and cocaine broker based in Colombia.

Gail Shelby: analyst, DEA.

Bruce Stephens, Special Agent, FBI–Los Angeles.

Allen Weston: pseudonym for DEA-Atlanta Special Agent Skip Latson.

Fred Wong, Special Agent, FBI–Los Angeles.

Washed in Gold

1: Crossing Over

Ramón Costello was off on his own again, sulking. Trudging along the sandy coastline, he had a lot to think about. He had been charged with helping smuggle nearly half a ton of cocaine into the United States, and he couldn't expect to remain a fugitive forever. But turn himself in and live in some dismal penitentiary for God knows how many years?

A compact man of thirty-eight, with thinning black hair and intense brown eyes, Ramón had set off at dusk on a solitary hike, leaving behind the string of resort hotels that line the white sands and shallow, blue-green waters of Aruba's western coast. As he walked, he put more distance between himself and the federal prosecutor and drug agents who had traveled to this southern Caribbean island to meet him. They had come to bring Ramón over to their side—to torture him, so it seemed to Ramón.

Night had settled in and the beach had given out by the time he reached the northwest end of the island. He turned inland over desolate, low-lying sand dunes barely green with scruffy desert plants, and wandered east toward the island's other side. He bypassed the lighthouse at the northwest tip, where the shoreline cuts away and the water turns rough, and reached the rugged northeastern coast of Aruba where cliffs of rocky coral drop into churning sea.

He hated this place. It was arid enough for cactus to grow, and so windy and dry that the native divi divi trees grew stunted and twisted. The false glamour of the casinos and the bright lights of the resorts only made him feel more out of place. What had brought him to this terrible spot and this terrible moment?

What the feds were saying about him was true. It sounded as if they had him cold. An American living in Colombia, Ramón had helped some Colombians fly a couple of loads of cocaine to the United States. He had tried to hide, but the constant fear of discovery had made him paranoid and weary. He had longed for those he left behind.

No, he had to give himself up. But how could he possibly live for years behind bars? He was an adventurer, a lover of freedom, a man who preferred jungle hikes to city streets and fresh breezes to conditioned air. He couldn't survive caged.

He had to figure out a way to shave his prison time, or eliminate it, if possible. To do that, he'd have to plead guilty to his crimes, cross over and cooperate with the people who were prosecuting him. The thought repulsed him almost as much as the thought of prison. To Ramón, these people were the enemy and had been ever since his war-protesting, pot-smoking days in college up east. The idea of becoming one of them disgusted him.

And that wasn't the worst of it. If he had any hope of walking away from this thing without prison time, he would have to do more than admit guilt and rat on a few drug smugglers. That was clear. To do himself any real good, he would have to turn on former business associates and infiltrate the largest, most violent cocaine organization in the world. He would have to win and maintain the confidence of narco-terrorists and pretend to be their partner. All the while betraying them.

And if he could not play the undercover role convincingly, or if these federal agents whom he barely knew screwed up, he might well lose his life.

Ramón knew it could be dangerous, but he had no way of knowing what lay ahead. He did not know that, on behalf of the U.S. government, he would soon be planning a smuggling venture with Pablo Escobar himself, the most powerful of Colombia's drug barons, and one of its most ruthless. Neither could Ramón have guessed that even that would be dwarfed by a tip he would bring the feds. He would soon be pointing federal law enforcers to a gold mine: a billion-dollar money laundry, the largest ever uncovered.

Ramón did know from his dealings with Colombian drug traffickers that he would be their first suspect if anything smelled the least bit fishy. He was, after all, an American by birth and by upbringing, and Colombians trusted only their own. True, he had lived in Colombia for the better part of his adult life, spoke fluent Spanish, knew the culture, and had adopted a Spanish pseudonym for his first name. But he was still a gringo to them.

Yet, as dangerous as the assignment would be, and as distasteful as he found "weasels," as he called informants, Ramón saw few choices. That was why he found himself walking along the edge of this Caribbean island now, brooding on his unhappy predicament and angry at the people he would have to trust: government agents.

Ramón peered down into the black waves surging over the rocks below. They looked inviting.

One way or another, the life he had been living was about to end.

Back at the Concorde Hotel, a worried Wilmer "Buddy" Parker, a federal prosecutor from Atlanta, Georgia, downed a drink at the bar. Sitting there with Ramón Costello's lawyer and two federal drug agents, Buddy wondered about Ramón's whereabouts and his attitude. The tense, quiet man who had disappeared inexplicably hours earlier could be very important to Buddy's future. In fact, he could become the most useful informant Buddy had ever worked with. Was he about to back out? Was he a flake?

Buddy was having a hard time understanding this guy. They were so different, they even looked like opposites. Whereas Ramón was compact, dark and Italianate, with a downturned nose, Buddy's gangling frame stretched six feet tall, topped by a ring of straight, bond hair encircling a bald globe and Anglo features. While Ramón spoke with hesitation, almost with a lisp in his nervousness, Buddy's deep voice boomed across the room. Ramón could easily become inconspicuous, whereas Buddy Parker stood out wherever he went. Even his eyebrows stood out, so bushy and uncontrolled that stray hairs protruded into space.

Buddy had agreed to this strange meeting because Ramón Costello's criminal connections made him important. If Buddy could persuade Ramón to plead guilty in Atlanta to his past crimes—secretly, of course —and to work undercover in Colombia for the U.S. government, Ramón just might lead drug agents into the highest reaches of the cocaine trade. After all, here was someone who had personally met Jorge Ochoa, believed to be the number-two cocaine trafficker in the world. In fact, he had actually spent the night at one of Ochoa's ranches arranging a cocaine load.

This was heady stuff for a federal drug prosecutor living in Atlanta, far away from the major drug centers of Miami, Los Angeles, and New York. It was especially exhilarating for Buddy Parker, thirty-four, a former party boy from small-town Alabama, a tax prosecutor for five years, and a drug prosecutor for only three. Even coming down from Atlanta to a faraway island to persuade a cocaine smuggler to "flip"—in law enforcement vernacular—went far beyond anything Buddy had done before. Buddy did not know exactly where Ramón's cooperation would lead, but he knew it could transform him into a superstar drug prosecutor.

Ego wasn't all that had brought Buddy to Aruba. Fun as it was, and zealously as Buddy pursued it, prosecuting drug smugglers was more than a game to him. Nine years earlier, he had lost one of his closest boyhood pals, Jody Mills, a dentist's son, to heroin at the age of twenty-two. Jody now lay in a cemetery in Ozark, Alabama, a couple miles down the road from Squirrel Drive, the privileged enclave where the two of them had played together as boys. As an adult, Buddy had stood at Jody's grave, where the cold stone reads: *"His friends were his world."* And he had pondered what had put Jody below that stone, and what had kept him, Buddy, above it.

Jody's death made Buddy question his previously laissez-faire attitude about drugs. But it did not turn him into a fanatic about fighting narcotics. He had had a rather wild college career himself, and although he had preferred the liquid, foam-topped escape to the illegal variety, he never judged harshly those who made a different choice. Yet, harmless and free-spirited as drug use seemed then, the adult Buddy saw it as the fuel that fed a sinister criminal enterprise and took young lives like Jody's.

He did believe in what he was doing. But his main motivation was his passion as a trial lawyer. He loved the intellectual challenge of piecing together a complicated case and the strategizing required to prosecute it, and he loved the theatrics and quick thinking required to put it all to a jury. He had learned in his tenure with the U.S. Attorney's Southeastern Drug Task Force that the drug business was like any other multinational industry, only it operated in secret. Uncovering hidden nuggets of information in drug investigations thrilled Buddy.

He threw himself into his work—just as he threw himself into play. Sure, it bothered him when defense lawyers complained of overzealousness. A couple of high-profile cases in his past—a federal judge suspected of helping to launder drug money, and an Atlanta sportscaster charged with "distributing" cocaine by snorting with friends—had resulted in major embarrassments for the prosecution. But those cases had not dampened his enthusiasm or thwarted his drive. They merely taught him to avoid pitfalls while pursuing aggressive, creative prosecutions.

Buddy loved best the cases where he could begin with the investigation, watch it unfold, and help it progress. A sponge with facts, relentless in searching for connections between pieces of information, Buddy had been known to pull together a few clues himself.

Now, if Ramón would cross over, he could bring Buddy just that kind of case. Atlanta-based drug agents would devise a scenario: Ramón would work undercover with the agents and lure his contacts into the sting. Buddy would monitor the whole thing and, together, they might reel in major drug traffickers.

And the case would be Buddy Parker's to prosecute. But first, Costello had to agree to the plea bargain. He had tentatively said he would, but who could be sure?

Buddy ordered another drink.

Buddy's and Ramón's family histories were not in fact dissimilar. Ramón's father had been successful in business in the Northeast, while Buddy came from a well-educated family long prominent in the southeast Alabama town of Ozark. Both had been raised by mothers proud of family heritage, who taught their children the importance of doing things properly. As young men, each of them resisted the neat path his family laid out for him, albeit in different ways. Buddy's mother pushed her only son toward the best possible education, but instead he became a beer-guzzling, card-playing fraternity boy at one of the nation's top party schools, the University of Alabama. Despite his overindulgence, he earned a law degree and an MBA, yet he once had to sell his law books to pay off a football bet.

Ramón, on the other hand, studied economics at a well-respected state university in New England. Yet he did not perform as programmed, either. He shunned fraternity row to hop the anti-establishment wave sweeping the college campuses in the late 1960s, protesting the Vietnam War and partaking of illegal drugs.

Well suited to the times, Ramón played guitar with friends who specialized in Donovan and Dylan songs. He smoked marijuana and hashish and occasionally took hallucinogens. His left-leaning politics got him tear-gassed at a couple of demonstrations. He lived with a woman who considered herself a Maoist, and he would travel with her to Washington to protest the war.

The politics of the day seemed right for him: a distrust of government and authority, which peaked in his senior year, 1970, when the Ohio National Guard killed four anti-war protesters at Kent State University.

But Ramón was less interested in changing the world than in the adventure and experimentation the 1960s offered. A few months after graduation, he shrugged off the kind of future available to privileged young people. Long fascinated by Latin America, he headed south to travel the length of South America to its very tip, Tierra del Fuego.

He was looking, he says, for a "life experience."

His first experience was to run out of money at his first stop on the continent, Colombia. He took a cold-water apartment in Bogotá and a job teaching English to earn enough money to move on. But soon he was settling in, befriending Americans and other expatriates drawn to Colombia to sample a more exotic life. He fell in love with one of his students—and with the country itself. People lived passionately, and the place shimmered with color, sensuality, excitement. For adventure, he took weeks-long trips into the mountains or the jungles, where he learned to identify the local birds and animals.

At the same time, Ramón enjoyed something else Colombia had to offer. In the early 1970s, marijuana was everywhere; Ramón smoked it often. Only rarely did he use cocaine, which was new and unusual. But he would buy coke occasionally if a friend was coming down from the States. Soon he was smuggling small packages of cocaine for extra cash. By this time, he had well-connected Colombian friends who were also using and selling cocaine.

But eventually it got to be too much for Ramón. Cocaine was making him sick, and he became disgusted with himself for using it. So he stopped using drugs and moved back to the States in 1974 to find legitimate work.

Ramón stayed out of the drug business, although he associated with an American who arranged cocaine loads, Robert "Tiny" Dickerson. Ramón watched Dickerson lose huge sums of money on almost every cocaine load he brokered, giving the lie to a popular myth.

Except for an occasional marijuana joint, Ramón stayed straight even after moving back to Colombia in 1978, when he went to work as a consultant for European firms.

But finally a friend from the old days tracked him down and offered good money if Ramón would introduce him to the right Americans. His friend knew people who had "merchandise" they wanted to move north. The year was 1981, Colombia was awash with cocaine, and Ramón's friend was looking for U.S. pilots, airstrips, and offloaders.

Ramón matched him up with Dickerson and was back in business, only this time in a much bigger way than before. It took months to arrange, but he helped put together a 127-kilogram load—280 pounds —of cocaine air-dropped in August 1982 outside the rural community of Live Oak, in northern Florida. He cleared $80,000 for himself.

He agreed to help with another, larger load, which turned out to be disastrous. Weeks of delays and problems with law enforcement prompted the cocaine's owner, Jorge Ochoa, to question Ramón, who he suspected was a cop. Finally the plane took off from Colombia carrying 283 kilograms—more than 600 pounds—to an airstrip near St. Joseph, Tennessee, a small town near the Alabama border, where it crash-landed.

The loss of some of the load and a nose-dive in the price of cocaine left the Americans owing the Colombians something like $900,000. Of that amount, Ramón owed $200,000 and was responsible for seeing that his U.S. partners made good on the rest of the debt. Over the next two years, mostly through profits made on small cocaine importations, Ramón and his partners paid off their debt.

To conduct this illegal business while maintaining legitimate work, Ramón was living a double life, in fact, a multiple life. He had four passports for his "business" trips to the United States, as well as phony ID to back up the passports. He'd wake up in the morning and pick an identity for the day, as most people decide what to wear.

Ramón got a charge out of the intrigue. But when he paid off his debt in 1985 and cleared $200,000 to boot, he decided to get out of the business. It was simply too risky, and he wasn't out to make a million bucks, anyway. He had a comfortable home in Bogotá as well as a place in the country, and that was plenty for him. Besides, he didn't particularly care for most of the people he had to deal with. He especially disliked the Americans, who were young and wild and incapable of intelligent conversation. To help them understand Colombia better, Ramón had given them copies of a book he loved, *One Hundred Years of Solitude,* by the acclaimed Colombian writer Gabriel García Márquez. Not one bothered to read it.

Ramón quit the drug business in 1985 and relied mostly on legitimate work. But by this time, Atlanta-based agents of the Drug Enforcement Administration (DEA) had learned about him and his business associates. Some had been caught, had turned informant, and were working undercover for the feds. The resulting indictment came down in May 1986 in Atlanta, and listed forty-one people charged with bringing in a total of 3,800 kilograms (more than 4 tons) of cocaine over four years. It described four loosely connected smuggling rings. Named as the key broker in one of those groups was the man the Colombians knew as Ramón Costello.

With that indictment, federal agents swept through South Florida, where most of the suspects lived, and Atlanta, arresting some two dozen defendants and seizing property. Because he was in Colombia at the time, Ramón escaped the net. But his name appeared in news accounts of the sweep, and word quickly reached him that the feds wanted him.

He had been out of the business for months, but he had always known what he would do in this situation. He had assembled a "flee kit" containing $20,000 in cash, fake passports and identification. He arranged access to more money and set up specific days and times he would call his loved ones. On the morning after he heard he was under indictment, Ramón left Bogotá, thinking he would never return, and headed for Central America.

Ramón believed the U.S. drug agents looking for him were omnipotent, capable of listening in on any phone conversation they wanted, capable of finding any fugitive. Whatever thrill and adventure a fugitive's life might offer, he hated the paranoia and being cut off from everyone he knew and cared about. Fear made him do crazy things, like traveling to the next town and renting a hotel room to put in a single telephone call to Colombia.

He had been living like this for three months, while a relative in the States contacted lawyers and tried to persuade Ramón to give himself up. Finally, Ramón said he would think about it. He called a lawyer in his home state in New England, who referred him to a lawyer in Atlanta.

While fear of arrest had been following Ramón wherever he fled, the people capable of seeking his arrest had other matters on their minds. As the prosecutor in this mammoth case, Buddy Parker was too busy dealing with the suspects already arrested to be terribly concerned about the ones who got away. He and the main drug agents on the case fully intended to get the guy in Colombia; they just hadn't focused on how.

So when Atlanta lawyer Mark Kadish called and said Ramón might consider surrendering, Buddy was pleased to be relieved of one more worry.

Kadish wanted to know the strength of the evidence against Ramón and what kind of deal Buddy was offering. The prosecutor said he had plenty to win a conviction, including testimony from some of Ramón's former business partners who were cooperating with the government and who had helped drug agents infiltrate the conspiracy. He even had an incriminating videotape showing Ramón.

As for a plea bargain, Ramón would get the same deal his cohorts were getting for flipping: up to twenty years in prison. How much less than twenty would depend on how much help he gave the government. In addition, Ramón would have to give the government his drug profits.

Twenty years! The news further depressed Ramón's already low spirits. The lawyer told him he would probably serve six to eight.

"Are you crazy?" Ramón remembers telling Kadish. He couldn't stand being locked up that long. He had decided he could handle a couple of years, maybe three or four. But he was not about to spend six years of his life in a federal penitentiary. He asked Kadish what would happen if he stayed in hiding a few years and then turned himself in. Kadish said he had another client who had done that many years ago and was still locked up. You have to come in, Kadish told him. Come in and then talk to them about the possible sentence.

No way, said Ramón. The only leverage he had was his fugitive status, and he didn't want to give that up, only to be told he would have to serve a long prison term. He wanted to go home. What are the chances I could go back to Colombia and stay there while working for the feds as an informant? Ramón asked. It's not done like that, Kadish told him.

Before agreeing to plead guilty, Ramón wanted to know more about what he could get from a plea. What about meeting with the feds to discuss a plea, but doing it so that Ramón could walk away from the negotiating table without fear of arrest? Kadish said he'd check. They set a time for their next telephone conversation.

A few days later Ramón checked into another hotel for another phone call. I don't believe it, Kadish told Ramón. Buddy had said he would go along with Ramón staying in Colombia while cooperating with the government. And he had agreed to meet Ramón to talk about the plea before taking him to Atlanta for booking. They could meet some place where Ramón felt comfortable, South Florida, maybe?

No, Ramón insisted on meeting them off American soil, where U.S. agents had no arrest powers. Eventually they picked the Dutch-controlled island of Aruba, eighteen miles off the Venezuelan coast and almost that close to Colombia.

Through Kadish, Ramón extracted two promises: the feds would not arrest him in Aruba, and they would call off any arrest warrant they might have issued on Colombia. He could return to Colombia without fear of arrest while waiting for the meeting on Aruba. Never one to trust the government, Ramón didn't believe any of their promises, least of all their pledge not to arrest him in Aruba. He expected the prosecutor to show up with linebacker-sized agents to arrest him at their first meeting and haul him back to the United States in cuffs and leg-irons.

Ramón didn't know it, but the prosecutor he feared was uneasy, too. Buddy wasn't at all sure that Ramón wasn't setting him and the agents up for a kidnapping—or worse. He recalled that DEA agent Enrique "Kiki" Camarena had been tortured to death in Mexico the year before. And while Buddy knew Ramón's lawyer from previous cases in Atlanta, he was also aware that Kadish hardly knew Ramón.

So when these five men gathered on July 22, 1986, in a hotel suite several stories above sunbathing vacationers, they eyed each other with suspicion. Ramón was expecting to be arrested on the spot. The feds saw before them an incredibly nervous, tightly wound man.

They stood around awkwardly in the suite, where hot, tropical breezes blew through the open balcony door. Ramón hated air conditioning.

Kadish made the introductions, but he had already told Ramón about the men who had come from Atlanta to meet him. The older of the two drug agents, John Featherly, a crusty, upstate New Yorker who had spent most of his DEA career in Manhattan, was the more important of the two, because he was a supervisor. Featherly was the boss of the second man, Albert "Skip" Latson, the lead case agent in Ramón's case and a drug agent for sixteen years, mostly in Texas and South Carolina.

Scared as Ramón was, these agents nevertheless seemed smaller to him than the linebackers he had imagined. They were men of average height and everyday looks. Featherly, forty-two, had some girth to him and looked rather like an Irish precinct captain. Latson, a young-looking thirty-nine and a native Texan, was a cleancut, Boy Scout kind of a guy with a careful, quiet demeanor and deeply held but rarely mentioned religious beliefs.

The agents sat quietly as Buddy spelled out what everyone already knew, the reason they were there. He laid out the parameters of the plea bargain he and Kadish had discussed on the telephone: Ramón would plead guilty to one of the charges against him—cocaine-trafficking conspiracy—which carried a prison term of twenty years maximum. The government's recommendation on how much time he would serve would depend on how much Ramón helped the government. In addition, Ramón would forfeit all drug profits he had earned, and he had to agree to testify in court, if asked. Buddy told him that it was in the government's interest to keep him off the witness stand, but that might not be possible. If Ramón agreed to all that, the other charges against him would be dropped.

Buddy's booming voice and formal speaking manner brought home the seriousness of the situation. He told Ramón the agreement not only required him to provide evidence against the people already under indictment with him in Atlanta, it also required him to work undercover for the government. But Ramón had one big advantage over most defendants: he hadn't been arrested, and no one knew of this meeting on Aruba, so no one would suspect he was talking to federal agents. He could come to Atlanta and be secretly booked, his guilty plea sealed from public view, and he could return to Colombia with no one the wiser. Ramón could turn on his former business associates without their knowing anything had changed.

Buddy said he knew he was asking Ramón to undertake dangerous work. In fact, the five-page letter he brought with him detailing the plea agreement stated that Ramón "acknowledges that due to the inherent danger of the proposed undercover activities, there are risks to his life and safety which he assumes."

Of course, Ramón could walk away from the offer and return to Colombia. But if he did, Buddy said, he should know that the U.S. government would most certainly seek his extradition, and the Colombian government undoubtedly would track him down and turn him over. Although Colombia had suspended extradition of its own people, Ramón was an American and therefore subject to removal. What was more, if Ramón tried to remain a fugitive, he could never again see his relatives in the States without risking arrest the moment he set foot on U.S. soil.

Ramón knew all of this was true. He knew the Colombians could find him. In fact, he figured his fate could be even grimmer than Buddy's prediction. He figured he would languish in a Colombian jail for years before being flown to Atlanta for prosecution.

Buddy wanted Ramón to think about all of that before signing the letter he had brought. In the meantime, John Featherly and Skip Latson would debrief him. While Ramón had come to evaluate the proposed plea bargain, the feds had come to assess Ramón's value to them. Buddy told Ramón that meant figuring out what Ramón could do for them, and part of that involved assessing his trustworthiness. If Ramón lied to the agents—who already had information from former associates of his —the agents would know it, Buddy warned. Everything depended on Ramón's being straightforward.

Ramón was feeling worse and worse. He had told himself that if he crossed over, he would work hard to get as lenient a sentence as possible; in fact, he would try to avoid prison altogether. But he hadn't counted on working undercover. He had assumed he could simply act as a listening post and tell the Atlanta guys whenever he learned of a cocaine load headed north.

He didn't appreciate the warning about lying, either. But he would later concede it was probably good that Buddy issued it. Ramón hadn't planned on lying, exactly, but he hadn't planned on volunteering anything about his past, either.

Kadish called for a break so he could talk to Ramón privately to discuss what had just occurred. So the feds stepped out into the hallway, but were soon ushered back in. Ramón was ready to begin the debriefing.

The lawyers weren't needed for that, so while the two agents interviewed Ramón to begin the task of learning his past and testing his veracity, Buddy and Kadish left for the poolside bar.

Ramón, surprised he had not yet been arrested, sat down with the agents at the round table in his hotel room. Skip Latson asked him about his background and how he got into drug smuggling.

The feds had not intended to go very far into his criminal history that afternoon, because the first session was designed to put Ramón at ease and begin the difficult move to mutual understanding and trust. But for Ramón, the session marked a major turning point in his life.

He had begun revealing secrets he had been hiding for years, and he was disclosing these secrets to none other than government agents. He hadn't signed the agreement; but in his mind, he had crossed the line the moment he sat down at that table and the cleancut government agent took out his pen.

So, even though he had told them very little by the end of that day's session, in his own mind he had made a nearly irrevocable transformation. It seemed only fitting to him to go all the way. He pulled out a token of his transformation, an offering of himself to the government. It was a tape he had made of a conversation with a drug trafficker. Acting on his own, without any deal from the government, Ramón had taped a former associate discussing the cocaine trade. The man had stolen a kilogram and pinned it on Ramón, so there was an element of vengeance in handing over the tape. But at the moment, it seemed more like a sacrifice of his soul. The tape was worthless to the agents; to Ramón it represented the end of his former life.

*T*hat was what was on Ramón's mind as he stared down into the dark Caribbean. His conversion had begun just a few hours earlier. Sure, they said he could walk away from Aruba and try to run, but no matter what he told himself, he had obviously become a snitch. Suicide was the only other choice. Yet, lousy as he felt, Ramón saw adventure ahead, too; and besides, the suicide option would always be there.

So Ramón turned his back on the rocks and headed in the dark to his hotel—and the federal agents. He found the men at the Concorde bar and joined them, offering no explanation. None was demanded.

Buddy was happier to see Ramón than he let on. But he couldn't figure the guy out.

The more the feds tried to put Ramón at ease, the worse he felt. Sure, they were just trying to make him feel better, but how could he possibly feel good about this? You're doing the right thing, they kept saying. I'm doing the only thing I can do, and it's *not* right, he kept thinking.

Still, he went along on a sight-seeing venture, which they hoped would relax him and build rapport. They took him to a tourist spot, a natural bridge of coral worn through by the beating waves, where Ramón snapped photos of his three companions.

The feds seemed to enjoy Aruba's sites as well as its tourist resorts and casinos, but Ramón was put off by the glitz and the Miami Beach–style hotels he found so distasteful. He hadn't come to Aruba for fun, and he hadn't chosen his companions because he liked them. The feds, meanwhile, had reveled in the discovery of a moving Happy Hour where one hotel would have free drinks and snacks one night, and another would sponsor it the next. Buddy was the one most willing to take advantage of every opportunity for fun. Though happy in his two-year-old marriage to a petite Presbyterian minister, that didn't prevent him from harmless flirtations. At one point he won a free drink at a poolside dance contest for a wild bit of choreography performed with a woman he had never before met.

Buddy tried to tell Ramón that they weren't as different as he might think. He told him about going to a rock festival in Byron, Georgia, in 1970, sort of the Woodstock of the South, Buddy called it. He told him how he had watched Jimi Hendrix in the wee hours of July 4 play his unconventional rendition of "The Star-Spangled Banner" to thousands.

Ramón was hardly impressed that Buddy's big sixties experience had been a rock festival somewhere in Georgia. He wasn't warming up to any of these guys. But at least Featherly was somebody he could relate to. Both had a northeastern sensibility. And Featherly cultivated a sort of tough-guy image Ramón found intriguing.

The sandy-haired, rosy-cheeked Skip Latson was the hardest for Ramón to get a handle on. A Joe Friday kind of guy with softer edges, Skip was strictly business. He would patiently probe Ramón's memory, digging for more and more details and writing down everything in longhand hour after hour. Ramón didn't know it yet, but Skip would become the agent most important to him. He would become Ramón's chief contact with the government; his handler.

Slowly, as Skip debriefed him, Ramón became a bit more resigned to his situation. He initialed the plea agreement as outlined in the letter, agreed to give up $100,000 to the government, and his lawyer left Ramón to finish up the debriefings by himself.

Charlie's Bar sits in a formerly industrial part of the island, San Nicolas, amid bordellos and shabby casinos near an abandoned Esso refinery. A decent establishment in a rough neighborhood, it serves as a hangout for scuba divers who frequent the calm, protected waters of Aruba's southern coast . . . and for rougher types.

It was still daylight outside and warm inside when Buddy, Featherly, and Skip dragged Ramón to Charlie's for dinner and drinks one night. The four of them had been at the bar long enough to have had a beer or two when a boy walked up and offered to shine their shoes. Ramón told him he was asking too much. In Colombia, no one pays the first price offered for a shoeshine, so Ramón told him he should be charging half that price. Buddy says Ramón berated the kid, treating him like a street urchin and accusing him of trying to exploit tourists. The scene embarrassed and disturbed Buddy. But he wasn't the only person Ramón was offending.

Seated at a table close behind the Americans were several drunken, young, off-duty Dutch Marines who were stationed on Aruba, a common-wealth of Holland.

One of the Marines called for Ramón to ease up. Another chimed in something about ugly Americans. Soon, the drunken Dutch Marines were not only insulting these particular Americans but all Americans. This provoked Buddy, who wasn't entirely sober himself and decided to defend his country. No one remembers exactly what he said, but every-one remembers it was Buddy who got the Marines fighting mad.

Chairs scraped the floor and men jumped to their feet. Buddy turned on his bar stool and stumbled toward the floor, a move the Marines took to be a lunge. Featherly quickly stepped to Buddy's side. As one of the Marines started for Buddy, a loud crack sounded from the bar. The bartender had struck a baseball bat on the bartop to get everyone's attention. He told the Dutchmen to leave. What could have been a very nasty incident was over.

Starting a bar-room brawl would hardly inspire confidence in a man whose life would soon depend on the good judgment of the people involved. Yet suddenly the drug trafficker, the prosecutor, and the drug agents were all simply men about to be beaten up by loudmouths. The emotional and situational distance between the criminal and the feds had been completely unnoticed by these Dutchmen, who branded them all with the same insults. And inept though he was, the prosecutor had leaped to the defense of the drug trafficker.

Over the next few days, they would continue to meet in Ramón's hotel for debriefings and to throw out ideas for his undercover work. The DEA agents were becoming more comfortable with Ramón, realizing that despite his moodiness he had been honest with them. Before even getting to Aruba, they had known from previous evidence many details of his criminal past. They never let on which facts they knew so they could test his story against the evidence. It all matched.

The debriefings went on for three days, and Ramón felt emotionally drained but increasingly committed. He didn't completely trust the feds, even though he knew he would have to rely on them. On the day he watched the tiny island grow smaller from the window of a Bogotá-bound plane, Ramón still could hardly believe he had left Aruba of his own accord, instead of in handcuffs and leg-irons headed for Atlanta.

*I*t would be three months before Ramón would get to Atlanta, but when he flew in, he was hardly in chains. Eager to begin work, he came with several ideas about what he could do for the feds. Still, when no one met him at the gate, he considered taking the next flight out. But soon enough, the trio from Aruba showed up with a couple more agents to take him to his hotel.

The next day Skip picked him up and drove him the few blocks to the Richard B. Russell Federal Building, a twenty-three-story block of white concrete and smoked glass, circa 1979, housing the U.S. District Court, the Drug Enforcement Administration, and other federal offices. Ramón wore a hat pulled low over his face, and the agents took him on back elevators so he could be quietly booked and photographed. In an early morning proceeding, he pleaded guilty to conspiring to smuggle cocaine, and the papers were immediately sealed. The plea agreement, which had been initialed on Aruba, said Ramón faced up to twenty years behind bars, but he would await sentencing until his undercover mission was complete. And just in case Ramón was killed before that happened, Buddy took him to a grand jury to testify against his co-defendants.

Ramón had gone over to the other side.

2: Choosing Lures

Ron Caffrey had a plan in his pocket when he left DEA–New York and moved south. He and two of the agents in New York, where he had been second in command, had put together a blueprint for a money-laundering probe to be launched out of New York. Headquarters finally approved the idea, but then named Caffrey head of DEA's Atlanta office in 1985. He took his eagerness to go after drug money with him to his new assignment.

A tall man, with wavy salt and pepper hair combed high off his forehead Elvis-style, Ron Caffrey was the kind of boss who would always challenge agents to push their cases as hard and as far as possible. Don't stop at a simple buy-bust if persistence and a little creativity could lead to a regional cocaine distributor.

By the mid-1980s, Caffrey had been in drug enforcement for two decades and at DEA for one, mostly in New York, the largest and most competitive DEA office in the country. At thirty-five, he was ready for something new. Used to grabbing cocaine at some point in its movement from South America to users in U.S. cities, Caffrey now wanted to trace the route back. Nabbing drugs and the people who moved them was only half the picture. Caffrey wanted to follow the dollars as they moved from the pockets of American cocaine users to Colombian drug lords. He wanted to see how the drug barons' financial experts evaded cash-reporting laws and disguised the money's origins to slip it out of the United States.

The drug business generated far too much money—billions of dollars a year, mostly in small bills—for all of it to be smuggled out. It was too bulky and too tempting to the people hired to handle it. A million dollars in ten-dollar bills weighs as much as a hefty man and would fill several boxes. Besides, the traffickers used Colombian pesos at home, not U.S. dollars. Of course, some cash was flown out, but the preferred method was the same one legitimate businesses use: Deposit the cash into a bank account, where it is converted into innocuous numbers on a computer screen. From there, the sum can be quickly and cleanly wired to bank accounts down south, where U.S. dollars would be sold for pesos.

The problem for the traffickers was getting the money into the U.S. banking system undetected. Currency leaves no trail, but bank records do. And a large cash deposit generates more than the usual internal bank paperwork. Federal law requires bankers to fill out a form and send it to the Internal Revenue Service each time someone deposits $10,000 or more in currency. All transactions involving at least $10,000 —the purchase of a boat, a car, a house—are to be reported if conducted in cash. The law casts light on businesses trying to operate in the shadows. Nonetheless, millions of dollars in drug proceeds return every week to the men who sent the drugs to the States.

Caffrey's plan, a generic prototype aimed at no specific suspects, would pose agents as money launderers and move drug profits through U.S. banks to wherever the traffickers wanted the money sent. By providing that ongoing service, agents could infiltrate the drug cartels, gather intelligence, and ultimately seize huge chunks of drug profits and arrest the critical financial people. Caffrey didn't consider this a particularly radical idea. DEA and other agencies had begun doing similiar probes.

But at DEA, money-laundering probes clashed with the prevailing culture. This was a kick-down-the-door kind of agency, not a place where folks got their thrills from following numbers from one document to another. It was dominated by agents who believed the best cocaine investigations were the ones that put the most powder on the table. A DEA supervisor in New York expressed that commonly held view when, during a discussion of whether to launch a money-laundering investigation, he turned to an agent and asked him to pull out his credentials. The agent produced his badge and the supervisor read it aloud: " 'Drug Enforcement Administration.' Do you see the word 'money' on this?"

The traditionalists' main complaint was that money probes seemed to help the drug lords more than they hurt. With drugs, the agents tried to seize every load they helped arrange. Not so with money. Currency, after all, is perfectly legal until linked to illegal activity. Finding that link takes time. Law enforcers either must stand by and watch millions of ill-gotten dollars travel back to the kingpins, while they look for the crime that produced the cash, or—worse—help move the funds themselves, enabling the drug lords to get more money to ship more cocaine.

The Federal Bureau of Investigation had provided an infamous example of what can go wrong. In Operation Bancoshares, agents helped move more than $170 million in drug proceeds from the United States to South America. When it was over in 1981, they made few arrests and seized only $6 million in cash. The main thing they had accomplished was helping the bad guys get richer.

But Congress was constantly tightening the laws against money laundering, and Caffrey was convinced that, done right, a probe into how the traffickers make dirty money clean would lead to multi-million-dollar seizures and the arrests of important criminals. That would hurt the drug lords and their business a lot more than grabbing a few kilograms of cocaine, he believed.

Institutional reluctance at DEA had delayed headquarters' approval of Caffrey's plan until 1985, but Caffrey was now Special Agent in Charge of the DEA's Atlanta Field Division.

Although a regional hub, Atlanta hardly compares to New York as a center of finance and international business, legal or otherwise. And though it is a distribution point for drugs, Atlanta pales in significance compared to Miami or Los Angeles or New York. DEA had about ninety agents stationed in Atlanta in 1986, roughly a third the number in Miami. Only one Atlanta agent spoke Spanish. The Atlanta office wasn't expected to move so far into the cocaine trade that it would need Spanish speakers, and it rarely did.

None of that daunted Caffrey. He still wanted to oversee a money case, even from Atlanta. When he arrived, he called a meeting of DEA supervisors and told them to watch for the right circumstances. But he cautioned against jumping too quickly. "This has got to be a winner," he says he told them. "We've got to have one that works." He set up a class to teach Atlanta agents how to conduct such an investigation and brought in as a teacher one of the New York–based agents, Ed Guillen—himself a banker before turning cop—who helped design the prototype.

Like Caffrey, Skip Latson was looking to do something different. After sixteen years as a drug agent, Skip had been running increasingly more difficult and more comprehensive cases. Caffrey's idea intrigued Skip, and the class on money laundering challenged him. So almost every time a drug defendant in one of Skip's cases turned informant, he would tell the new snitch to watch for chances to offer money-laundering services to traffickers. None had found any. But none had been as well suited for this kind of case as Ramón Costello.

When they met on Aruba in 1986, Skip figured if any informant could pull this off, Ramón could. He had brains and education, and he knew Colombia as his home. His contacts reached high into the drug trade, and his reputation was good because he had paid off his debts to the traffickers. True, he hadn't done a lot of sophisticated banking or high finance, but he seemed to have an interest and an aptitude for it, having studied economics in college and worked for international businesses. Skip talked to his supervisor, John Featherly, about the possibility of a money case for Ramón.

Featherly did not immediately warm to the idea. He came from the traditional, powder-on-the-table school of drug enforcement. It struck him as just plain wrong for cops to help drug lords get their profits from narcotics. But Featherly did not nix the idea, either. After all, Caffrey was his boss, too. And despite the failed government money cases, there had been some successes. Featherly talked to an agent he knew in Miami, who told him about an investigation there that seemed to be working well.

Besides, no one was suggesting that Ramón limit his work to a money case. His main job would be brokering a load or two of cocaine to be brought into the United States with the help of Skip Latson, who would be working undercover. The agents wanted as large a load as possible, and they wanted Ramón to work his way up the drug hierarchy as high as possible. That was the sort of investigation most likely to produce results, and that was where Ramón would concentrate his greatest efforts.

But while Ramón was putting a load together in Colombia, he could look for opportunities to wash dirty money. So long as smuggling was Ramón's main focus, it wouldn't hurt to tack on this money thing.

So, at the end of the Aruba trip in the summer of 1986, the drug agents told Ramón to return to Colombia and bait two hooks. They told him to put out the word he knew Americans with access to a secure U.S. airstrip, where cocaine could be offloaded. At the same time, he would let it be known he also had other U.S. contacts who could move large sums of money discreetly.

In fact, no one was more eager for a case like that than Ramón, who says it was his idea to do the money probe, not theirs. He knew a money-laundering investigation would be long and hard, which suited him just fine. The longer it took, the longer he could stay in Colombia and out of jail. And the more difficult the task and significant the bust, the more he would impress the prosecutor and the sentencing judge, and the more time he could shave off a prison term.

He had no interest in a traditional drug case, helping to smuggle a load of cocaine to lure traffickers into the DEA net. The agents had told him they had to seize any drugs he brought in, which meant he couldn't do more than one or two loads without becoming an obvious informant. That would only take a few months. Ramón didn't say so, but he had no intention of wrapping anything up in a few months. Besides, that kind of case would not be impressive enough to keep him out of prison. So while the agents considered the smuggling venture his main goal, Ramón's hopes were pinned on the money probe.

After agreeing in Aruba to flip and before pleading guilty in Atlanta, Ramón sniffed around Bogotá and Medellín for possible DEA targets, looking up old drug contacts and offering both services. Some wanted help in transporting drugs. But it seemed to Ramón that everywhere he went, the Colombians most wanted some way to get their U.S. drug proceeds back home. He reported back to Atlanta that he thought he could do both the money probe and the cocaine venture.

So one day in the fall of 1986, more than a year after Caffrey had come to Atlanta and first asked the agents for a money-laundering case, Featherly and Skip walked into Caffrey's office, grinning.

"You want one of these things?" Featherly says he told the boss. "We got one of these things."

None of them realized that the case would lead them into a drug money laundry that was processing hundreds of millions of dollars each year, a case that would reach into the heart of the Medellín cartel.

Ramón knew what it would take to accomplish either of his two assignments. First, he needed a Colombian partner to vouch for him, a sort of human ticket to the higher echelons of the drug trade. For all Ramón's connections and experience, he was still a gringo, and he still would need a Colombian vouch. He avoided his closest friends because he didn't want to draw them into trouble. But he also avoided the more violent people in the trade, worried about the potential for vengeance.

In the weeks before his guilty plea, Ramón traveled to Medellín and knocked on the door of a former partner in crime, an affable, trusting lawyer of forty-one named Francisco Serrano. Short, rotund, cheery, with a mustache and a wreath of curly brown hair encircling his head, Francisco Serrano was perfect for the job. A man who eschewed violence, Serrano was well educated, articulate, and pleasant company. He was not one of the thugs who populated much of the Colombian drug trade and whom Ramón found so offensive. In fact, Serrano occupied a respectable place in Colombian society as well as in the drug world. He had real estate investments and other legitimate businesses, yet he also had important ties to traffickers in Medellín.

They had met years earlier through the drug business. In fact, Serrano had been in on the loads that had gotten Ramón noticed and convicted in Atlanta. When Ramón tracked down Serrano, looking for a vouch, Serrano greeted him like a lost brother. He threw his arms around Ramón and told him how happy he was to see his old friend.

This made it all the more difficult for Ramón, who knew he would eventually betray this likable, trusting man. Regardless of how it began, Ramón and Serrano would become pals as well as partners over the next two years. But their partnership would ruin Serrano's life. "It was hard. It wasn't easy at all," Ramón says. But he did it.

And he did it quite well, an embittered Serrano would later say. "He can take off your socks without removing your shoes."

It took little persuasion to bring Serrano in. When Ramón walked through the door, Serrano saw more than his old friend and former partner in crime. He saw a way to strike it rich. Serrano had suffered financial setbacks, and he needed money. He wanted to make himself, his infant son, and his twenty-five-year-old wife comfortable. Very comfortable. Ramón could help him do just that, because Ramón had friends in the States who could provide safe landing for cocaine planes, and more friends who could provide safe banking for cocaine funds. Ramón was saying they could keep 3 percent of all the money they moved. And with Serrano's contacts, they could move a lot of it.

Serrano and Ramón would act as brokers, connecting people with a need to people who could serve the need. Serrano liked the idea, and he told Ramón finding customers would be no problem. He knew men with money and men with drugs and men with both. Luckily for Ramón, the money part especially interested Serrano as a clean and easy way to get rich, less risky than dealing in drugs. Soon, Serrano was introducing Ramón around, and they found interested people. Some wanted an airstrip for their dope, others a laundry for their money. Ramón said he would take the news to his contacts in Atlanta.

He did just that when he traveled to Atlanta in October 1986, nervous but committed to his new role as an informant. On Wednesday, October 15, 1986, Ramón called Serrano from Atlanta to check on progress in finding customers for their new ventures. Serrano reported he had met with one of their potential money-laundering clients. "Everything is fine. We are going to do it with them," he said cheerily in Spanish.

Ramón told Serrano he was calling from Atlanta where he had been meeting with his U.S. contacts. What he did not say was that he was calling from the Richard B. Russell Federal Building, where he would become a convicted felon the next day by pleading guilty to cocaine trafficking. Agent Skip Latson taped this transcontinental call and would later have it transcribed and translated into English.

There was no hint of deception when Ramón told his new partner in

Medellín about the men in Atlanta: "I am telling you, I am with them and they are very enthusiastic, and they are ready!"

The next day, Skip officially opened the case. He named the primary target: Francisco Serrano.

*T*he Atlanta agents meanwhile learned to handle dirty money. They acquired a particularly useful technique from agents involved in the biggest money investigation around, Operation Pisces, a DEA probe in Los Angeles and Miami. Still ongoing, Operation Pisces was breaking new ground in drug enforcement. Pisces agents had concocted a solution to the problem of watching so much money—representing so much drugs—pass through before agents could make their case. In L.A., DEA agents had teamed up with a number of local and state law enforcement agencies to work surveillance. They would tail not only the main targets, but also the couriers who brought them money, and the people who had given the couriers money. By following everyone they could, the cops and agents would sometimes find a drug connection as they worked their way along the chain. They could learn when the lower-level people were likely to have drugs or money. They could then arrest those people on state charges and seize cocaine and cash from the organization without arousing suspicion further up the criminal chain. Sometimes cops would stop these people for an ostensible traffic violation; sometimes they would say a reliable tipster had given them cause for arrest, without revealing the tipster to be a DEA agent.

This technique dispelled the remaining doubts Featherly had about money-laundering cases. Although they would still be helping the traffickers wash drug proceeds, they would also be taking some away.

The DEA agents in Los Angeles were especially important to Atlanta not only for their experience in Pisces, but also because Atlanta would need L.A.'s help once the case got going. At least one of Serrano's potential laundry customers had dirty money in Los Angeles. So while the investigation was being run out of Atlanta, Atlanta agents would be coming to L.A. to pick up money and would need surveillance and other backup from DEA there. If the money pickups were frequent, L.A. would take over the job of handling them. The DEA office in Los Angeles assigned its Pisces team to help, including the local and state cops when necessary.

Alex Romero, a Pisces agent in Los Angeles, was named the lead DEA agent assigned to Atlanta's case and would serve as Atlanta's West Coast contact. At a case-planning session in Atlanta, he was struck by the enthusiasm shown by the prosecutor in the case, Buddy Parker, who sat in on some of the planning sessions.

Buddy was at least as gung-ho on the project as the agents. "He said if we could get these people, he would prosecute them and he would put them in jail for as long as he could," recalls Romero.

This was so different from Los Angeles, where assistant U.S. attorneys (AUSAs) were always reminding agents of all the precautions they needed to take. By comparison, "Parker was talking like a cop," says Romero. And it was clear he knew about money laundering—by this time, Buddy Parker had earned an advanced degree in tax law and had spent five years prosecuting tax cases for the Justice Department. Los Angeles had so many big cases that the average AUSA could not devote much time to a case like this, Romero says. Buddy Parker clearly would.

Caffrey and his former New York colleague, Guillen, had dubbed their drug money-laundering blueprint "Operation Fis-Con," for fiscal control. Guillen already had Fis-Con up and working in New York, where agents were drawing drug profits into it. Caffrey had him help the Atlanta agents set it up.

The DEA agents would pick up the money in Los Angeles—or wherever the customer had it—and take it to the DEA office for photographing and processing. Then an armored-car company would take it to a local cooperating bank for deposit into the account of a phony business. The L.A. bank would wire the funds from the West Coast to Atlanta, where another cooperating bank would receive it and thereby establish venue so the case could be prosecuted in Georgia. The Atlanta bank would then wire the sum to a New York account that DEA was already using for Operation Fis-Con. From New York, the money would go where the Colombians wanted it to go, most likely to Panama.

The undercover agents would charge a commission for their services, just as real money launderers would. But their cut would go into Fis-Con accounts to help cover the costs of the investigation. Drug money would be used to catch the drug traffickers.

The Atlanta agents weren't keen on New York controlling the bank accounts they were using. Guillen was giving them too much advice, they thought. Featherly didn't like being told how his agents should work, especially not by Guillen, whom he had known as a rookie in New York. Yet Guillen believed he knew better how to run a money case, and Caffrey insisted on plugging Atlanta into the existing Fis-Con framework. It would take forever to get another operation approved at headquarters, and Caffrey wanted to use the one he had already set up. He would act as referee.

At the same time, the Atlanta agents were roughing out and staffing undercover scenarios for both prongs of the investigation. Skip Latson, case agent over the whole thing, also would work undercover in the

more important smuggling scheme. He created an identity as a transportation expert named "Allen Weston." When Ramón brought him Colombians with cocaine to be brought into the States, Allen Weston would
show them airstrips in North Georgia where he could guarantee a landing safe from cops. He could also offer U.S. pilots and a plane, courtesy
of DEA.

For the money launderer, the Atlanta group needed someone credible as an experienced mover of dirty cash, someone the Colombians
would trust with their millions. Most of the Atlanta agents were so young
that Ramón complained whenever Featherly and Skip would trot out
some rookie to play the role. Do you want to get me killed? he asked.

Finding an older agent still doing street work wasn't easy. There was
Featherly, of course, but as a supervisor he wasn't supposed to be going
undercover any more. Yet, there was no one else to do the job. If DEA
could make an exception, Featherly could join the scenario as the top
dog in the organization. With a younger sidekick to do his legwork, the
head guy would only have to make occasional appearances. Skip spent
weeks working on it, and he finally won approval from headquarters for
Featherly to go undercover.

Ramón liked the idea not only because Featherly was middle-aged,
but also because he did not look like a drug agent. Traffickers believed
cops worked hard to stay fit so they could be ready for a foot chase,
Ramón had heard them say. Featherly was hardly a fitness freak. To
Ramón, Featherly looked more like a crook than a cop.

Featherly's assumed character, like himself, would be as a New Yorker
transplanted to Atlanta. In his undercover role, he would be an accoun-
tant-turned-businessman, a very successful, shady businessman. He
knew all about money, having moved illegal profits for "the Italians in
New York," as he would tell the Colombians. He could provide whatever
financial services were needed. He would tell them he bribed a well-
placed banker or two to bypass U.S. government requirements that large
cash deposits be reported.

For a name, Featherly picked "Jimmy Brown," naming himself for the
famous NFL and All-American football player at Syracuse University in
Featherly's hometown. It wasn't just the fantasy of a middle-aged football
fan that drew Featherly to the name. Featherly's twin brother was called
Jimmy, and Featherly had long ago learned to answer to that name as
quickly as his own.

For Jimmy Brown's sidekick, Featherly and Skip brought in the only
Spanish-speaking agent in the Atlanta office, Cesar Diaz. A handsome,
outgoing thirty-year-old, the Cuban-born agent would play the role of
"Alex Carrera," a cousin of Jimmy Brown's never-seen business partner,
a kid learning his way in the business.

Skip had no undercover role in the money laundry, although as case agent, he would direct both the laundry and the smuggling investigations. The trickiest part of his job would be handling Ramón. Skip was to be Ramón's contact with the government. When the agency wanted Ramón to do something, the directions came through Skip. When Ramón had something to report, Skip took the call. When Ramón came to town, Skip debriefed him, though other agents might be present.

Skip had managed confidential informants—or CIs, as they are called —before, and it was always a sticky business. These are, after all, criminals, and some secretly keep up their old line of work even while helping the government. Agents are taught never to trust a CI completely, and yet they have to rely on them. Criminals trying to work off a sentence teach law enforcers how the drug trade works, and it is often only through a CI that they can penetrate criminal organizations.

So, while the managing agent should listen closely to the CI's ideas and advice, the agent must remain in charge. He must not reveal more about the investigation than the CI absolutely must know. The agent cannot let the CI control the investigation.

In this case, managing the CI would be complicated by distance and by Ramón's temperament. He was on his own in Colombia, for the most part, with Skip more than 2,000 miles away in Atlanta. Ramón had already revealed his volatility and independent nature on Aruba.

Skip and Ramón were very different, though they were within a year of each other in age. While Ramón was living with a Communist and smoking pot up east, Skip attended Abilene Christian College, a small Methodist school where drugs were nonexistent in the late 1960s. And even though Skip opposed the Vietnam War and considered himself a "dyed-in-the-wool liberal," there was no obvious way to express dissent at Abilene.

Out of school and newly married, Skip toyed with the idea of government work and took an examination for federal law enforcers. But nothing came through, so he accepted a clerical job at a trucking company.

A year after Skip graduated, 1970, President Richard Nixon declared war on drugs. Virtually overnight, the number of U.S. Customs agents doubled. Skip got the call.

Soon he was ensnaring marijuana smugglers as an undercover agent working the Texas-Mexico border, a job he would love. The excitement hooked him, and he believed by fighting drugs he was making a difference. But in 1973 his job changed dramatically when Congress created the Drug Enforcement Administration to step up the anti-drug effort. With DEA getting the bulk of the narcotics work, Skip found himself chasing undervalued foreign goods dumped for sale in the United States. He missed the drug work.

So in 1974 Skip went over to DEA. He spent twelve years in San

Antonio, until DEA transferred him to Charleston, South Carolina, where he spent three years before moving to Atlanta in 1985. By the time he met Ramón, Skip, at thirty-nine, had spent the better part of sixteen years as a drug agent, going from simple busts to large conspiracies. He had been the lead agent on the massive, forty-one-defendant conspiracy case that had brought Ramón under indictment, a case that had its start because of a tip from a confidential informant. That CI had not only shown Skip how valuable an informant can be, he had also taught him to be wary. It turned out that the informant was doing a little freelancing, believing his work with the DEA would protect him. It didn't.

"No matter how much you start to like an informant," says Skip, "and how truthful you think they are about staying away from drugs, there is something in their personality that allowed them to do it the first time. And chances are whatever it was . . . is still there."

Getting too close to Ramón was hardly a problem at first. Skip was temperamentally shy and stiff with strangers, and Ramón didn't exactly yearn to become best buddies with a narc. Even under the best of circumstances, they were not the kind of people he would have chosen to hang out with. Ramón was a live-and-let-live kind of guy, whereas "they like to put people in jail," he says. Skip is so straight, Ramón would later say, that when he has a headache, he only takes one aspirin.

At the beginning of their relationship, says Ramón, "we had . . . very little rapport."

*I*n Atlanta, DEA agents were fashioning details of the investigation, setting up bank accounts for the laundry and checking out small airports for the smuggling. In Colombia, Ramón and his new partner, Francisco Serrano, were meeting with people who had money or drugs to move and were making plans to do both. Some medium-sized fish were nibbling. By the beginning of 1987, it was time to draw them to Atlanta to introduce the undercover agents to their targets and to establish venue.

Persuading these people to come to Atlanta was another matter. For drug traffickers, this was a backwater; few Colombians knew the first thing about Atlanta. While Atlanta's boosters called it the "New International City," a visitor would have to know where to look to find any Latin influence beyond Mexican restaurants. The only Spanish-language radio program drew most of its audience from the Mariel Cubans detained at the Atlanta Federal Penitentiary.

Others might hang back from Atlanta, but not Serrano. His eagerness to get the new ventures started propelled him to this strange, new place. By the end of January 1987, Serrano and Ramón had persuaded another Colombian, a man with lots of apparently dirty money, to come to Atlanta to meet a man who could wash those dollars: Jimmy Brown.

The Colombian, Jaime Parra, came from a wealthy, politically active family of cattle ranchers and businessmen. Serrano had known Parra's parents and some of his brothers for years, including one who was trafficking in cocaine. In his search for customers in his new venture, Serrano sought out Jaime Parra because he knew he would have cash in the United States that he needed moved to Colombia.

Drug money? "It could have been, it might not have been," says Serrano. "I wasn't going to ask."

Regardless, Serrano and his potential customer would come to Atlanta, where Ramón would introduce them to Jimmy Brown. They could finalize plans for moving Parra's money from Los Angeles through Brown's maze of bank accounts to Panama. On the same swing through Atlanta, Serrano would separately meet with another friend of Ramón's, Allen Weston (Skip), who would show them a couple of airstrips.

The prospect of the first undercover meeting with new targets—especially significant ones like Parra and Serrano—normally revs up agents to a state of nervous anticipation. There's the excitement of a new case with its unknown potential, the flurry of activity to set everything up, and the undercurrent of worry about what could go wrong. This time the meetings were preceded by a tragic reminder of the danger of undercover work. On January 20, eleven days before Serrano would come to town, a man with 8 ounces of cocaine to sell apparently realized his buyer was a DEA agent. In a parking lot shootout in a wealthy neighborhood of Atlanta, the man shot and mortally wounded thirty-year-old agent Raymond Stastny. A handsome, well-liked agent, Stastny never recovered consciousness. His death six days later devastated the Atlanta office, especially his close friend and neighbor, Cesar Diaz, his supervisor, John Featherly, and the Atlanta boss, Ron Caffrey.

As Skip and Featherly prepared to meet their Colombian targets, they told themselves their situation was completely different. This was not a drug buy from a street dealer, and their meetings would be in restaurants and hotels, not parking lots. Still, their colleague's murder reminded them that theirs was a serious business.

3: Going Under

On a Saturday night in a Holiday Inn on the edge of downtown Atlanta, Ramón introduced his old partner, Francisco Serrano, to his new one, "Allen Weston." There was no turning back now. As Skip shook hands with the primary target of his new investigation, he inaugurated his undercover identity.

As Weston, Skip was friendly but not gregarious, pleased to meet Serrano but quiet. Serrano says something about him made him uneasy enough to seek reassurances from Ramón. Ramón remembers none of that. He says Serrano never asked him about any of the undercover agents he brought into their partnership. If Serrano was worried, it did not stop him from talking about drugs with the undercover agent at the first opportunity. Serrano, in his manner and his dress, was a business-man, and he was eager to get down to business.

Inside a restaurant near the Holiday Inn, the drug agent, the drug broker, and the informant went to work. They talked about aircraft and airstrips and the per-kilogram cost of transportation. Serrano volunteered that he had helped arrange a 200-kilo shipment of cocaine several months earlier, only to lose it to cops in Santa Fe. Skip later confirmed that such a load had been seized.

Serrano showed no reluctance at all to work with Skip that night or the following day. He showed no hesitation the next morning when he rode out to a suburban airport to board a twin-engine plane, or when he flew with Skip, one of Skip's pilots (another DEA agent), and Ramón to a remote airport in the North Georgia mountains to check out an airstrip as a possible site for the offloading of cocaine. And everywhere they went, surveillance agents noted the time and place of their meetings.

The smuggling discussion went well for Skip. Next up was "Jimmy Brown," an experienced mover of vast sums of dirty money, played by John Featherly.

Under the DEA scenario, Jimmy Brown did not know Allen Weston, although Ramón knew them both. The agents had decided to keep the two operations separate, figuring more time would be needed to develop a strong money case than to bring in and seize a load or two of coke. If the same undercover agents were involved in both operations, the cocaine bust would expose the laundry as a government sting.

Jimmy Brown would make his first appearance at the Atlanta Marriott Marquis, one of the newer downtown hotels and an architectural landmark. Looking up into its atrium is like peering inside a giant cone with swirling sides. The open, balconied corridors at every floor form concentric curves, wide at the bottom and narrow at the top forty-seven stories up.

The bar offers a dizzying view of it all from one of the lower levels. At 6:10 P.M. Monday, February 2, Ramón and Serrano climbed the staircase up to the bar and waded through the Happy Hour revelers to the table where Featherly was waiting with a scotch. No beer for Jimmy Brown.

Featherly had the heft, the toughness, and the cool to be taken seriously. Besides, Serrano was so eager to set up this new money business, it never occurred to him to slow down and test his new partner's knowledge. Even though this meeting was intended as an ice-breaking session, it didn't take long for Serrano to begin talking money. Ramón acted as interpreter, as he had the previous day with Skip.

The laundry's first customer, Jaime Parra, was supposed to have been there, too, but Serrano explained that he had been delayed and would arrive the next day. In the meantime, he brought Featherly up to date on the arrangements he and Ramón had already made with Parra. Parra had money they would pick up in Los Angeles and move to Panama, where Parra had accounts. Parra would be a good customer, and one who could lead them to others. Between Parra's contacts and Serrano's, he told Featherly, he figured they would be moving about $50 million a year.

Featherly assured Serrano he could handle the business. He hinted at

Mafia connections to make it clear he knew what he was doing. But as much as he knew about money, Featherly said he knew nothing about the business that produced the cash his partnership with Serrano would bring.

The main thing to know, Serrano told him, was not to anger the Colombians. But he assured Featherly that his people would not have to deal directly with the desperados, or criminals. Serrano's people would buffer Jimmy Brown's people from that side of the business by picking up the money from the desperados and delivering it to Brown's people.

And don't worry about my people being stopped with cash, Serrano said. None would be carrying contraband; all would have documents showing a legitimate source for the money.

Featherly said he had read about someone who had been arrested in Miami because cops found cocaine on cash he was carrying. Serrano told him virtually all U.S. currency has at least traces of cocaine. If they could test it, Serrano said, they would probably find cocaine on the money in the cash register at the bar.

This went on for about an hour and a half. All the while a man familiar to Ramón, a DEA agent on surveillance, was sitting at a nearby table.

In his meetings with Skip and Featherly, Serrano's discussions of moving dope and dope profits began what would become extensive self-incrimination. Everything he said that was tinged with drug talk was going into DEA reports. But the best kind of evidence was taped evidence. And for that, the DEA rented a couple of rooms in Atlanta's finest hotel, the downtown Ritz-Carlton, where Jimmy Brown was supposed to be staying. Furnished in traditional style, with dark wood, this hotel and its rooms were designed to be backdrops for multi-million-dollar deals. That's what would happen this February afternoon.

Room 1107 was rented for the meeting, while the room next door housed the technical crew who would be watching through a camera hidden in a bedside lamp. Aimed across the bed, the lens framed a sitting area arranged in front of brocade curtains drawn shut across the room's bay windows. A loveseat faced the camera, and two chairs, one at each end of the loveseat, faced each other.

When Serrano arrived at 1:00 P.M., he had with him their customer, Jaime Parra, a tall, refined man not yet thirty. Despite his youth, Parra had the self-assurance of a frequent traveler, comfortable in new surroundings. Ramón met them at the door and introduced Parra to the man who would be moving his money, Jimmy Brown.

Featherly motioned the pair of Colombians to the loveseat while he and Ramón took the chairs on either side, Featherly sitting next to Parra. Featherly offered them drinks, snacks, and commentary on the weather, then quickly got down to business. He complimented Parra on his English. Serrano, whose English was less skilled, remained silent through most of the meeting.

First, there was the issue of the fee Parra would pay Jimmy Brown and his people for moving the money. Featherly quickly gave up his previous insistence on 5 percent, settling for 4.5 percent.

Parra said that as business got rolling, he would raise the fee to 5 percent. But that, he said, "depends on how fast this can be done."

They talked about how quickly the money would move, and where it would go. Jimmy Brown's people were to pick up Parra's money in Los Angeles, deposit the cash in a bank there, wire it to Atlanta, then to New York and on to Panama, which was where Parra wanted it sent.

Featherly said he figured he could get the money to Panama in two or three days. He didn't know what he was talking about.

But Parra did. "From our experience, let me tell you, I think it's five days," Parra said.

"I hope not," said Featherly, laughing. That seemed like a long time to Featherly, but within a year he would be wishing his laundry could move money in five days.

Parra told Featherly it was important to keep his organization informed of the money's movement through the system. Brown's group should notify one of Parra's people in Colombia of the time and day the money was sent to Panama, so they could be looking for it and, if necessary, pressure the bank for it, said Parra. This was a man clearly experienced in the matter of moving funds. But what kind of funds?

Featherly said he would telex a simple cryptic message. "We can do everything by coffee," offered Parra.

"Coffee. Okay. All right," said Featherly. "Do you want the amounts in bales of coffee, let's say? Let's say, 100,000 bales of coffee?"

"Sacks," Parra corrected.

"Sacks," repeated Featherly.

"Bales are something else," said Ramón, in an oblique reference to marijuana. Parra and the others laughed at that.

If things worked out, Parra said, he would put Brown's people to work picking up money in New York, too.

Featherly smiled at the mention of his former hometown, and at the chance to flesh out his undercover character.

"You know, I love that place," he said. He told Parra New York was his home. He said he still had contacts and business interests there. Although a CPA by training, Featherly said he made his money in investments, especially low-income housing in New York.

"You know, the financial world is my world, the business world," Featherly volunteered.

"Um-hmm," said Parra.

Featherly started to bring up his concerns about the source of the money when there was a knock at the door. Room service.

A waiter in a white jacket rolled in a table with a silver coffee service and parked it in front of the loveseat, leaving only the Colombians' heads visible to the camera. "Good afternoon, Mr. Brown. How are you?"

Featherly explained to Parra he had asked for coffee. He again offered to order sandwiches so they could eat there, but Parra declined.

The waiter apologized for bringing only two pots of coffee for the four men. As he arranged the table, he promised to come back with two more pots. No one dissuaded him. He left.

Featherly picked up where he had left off. He told Parra he understood the plan from the point where his people received the cash and move it through the system. "That I know," he said with a bit of a chuckle.

"The other part—how the money comes to my people—is unknown to me," said Featherly, fishing for a drug-related answer.

Instead he got a discussion about what sort of people Featherly and Parra had working for them. Both sides agreed to send only their most trusted employees for this assignment. They would be well dressed and professional-looking, the men agreed, and they would use the same one or two people for every money pickup.

Parra asked about the man Featherly intended to use. "Will you tell me his nationality?" Parra asked.

Featherly hesitated.

Ramón told him, "I think I mentioned that, you know, like, the Colombians don't like to deliver money to non-Colombians—or, to non-Latins."

"Well," Featherly said, thinking of Cesar, "my trusted associate here is Cuban."

Parra said nothing, then, "Well, uh . . ." He laughed nervously, and the others joined in.

"We can work it out," Parra finally said. "It will be no problem."

Another knock at the door. The waiter came in with two more coffee-pots. He rearranged the table—the cream, the sugar, the cups, the pots. He set one of the pots down in front of Parra, now blocking him from the camera altogether. While Featherly searched his wallet, the waiter talked to this odd foursome about the weather. Ramón complained about the cold and remarked to Parra and Serrano, "I think I'll move back to Cartagena" (a coastal town in Colombia).

The waiter acted as if this was a perfectly normal collection of businessmen. "Have a good day, gentlemen," he said as he left.

Ramón poured coffee for everyone.

Parra asked Featherly which Atlanta bank he would be using.

"I deal mostly with C&S," Brown said.

Ramón asked, "What's C&S?"

"Well, that's it, that's how they're—"

"No, but we have no idea what C&S is," Ramón repeated. "What does it stand for?"

Featherly paused momentarily, apparently drawing a blank on the name of this venerable Atlanta institution, Citizens & Southern Bank, which was cooperating with the DEA.

"It's, it's one of the largest banks in the South. It's, it's the Citizens South Bank." Close enough.

"It handles a lot of, uh, commercial accounts," Featherly continued. He told Parra that he worked through a banker at the main branch whom he bribed to help him evade the government's reporting requirements on large sums of money.

Featherly said he intended to use Brinks Armored Car Service to take the money to the bank. The funds would be deposited into the account of one of Jimmy Brown's businesses.

"What I'm trying to do, Jaime, is do this just like it's a regular business."

"That's because it is," said Parra. Everyone laughed at that.

They went over more details and then came to the delicate issue of counting the cash. What if Jimmy Brown's people count less money than Parra's people had counted? What if the bank comes up with a different sum? Which count is the real count—and who is responsible for making up any shortfall?

This is a tricky matter, Parra said, because the money he sends through Brown's organization will belong to different "providers." That is, the cash represents profits that are supposed to be returned to three or four people. If a discrepancy shows up in the total, he will not know how to distribute it.

This meant that Parra was moving money for several traffickers. Ramón and Serrano had reeled in a good one.

For starters, Parra said, the first delivery would be $100,000, to be repeated once a week for a month. But that would just be a test sum. If all goes well, Parra said, he would give Brown's people two deliveries a week, eventually three, and the amount of each delivery would grow. He was talking about bringing in more than $1 million a month, which represented a lot of cocaine.

Featherly again ventured into the illicit nature of what they were doing. "I know about money and things, but I don't know a lot . . . about the business here. And that's okay. I don't have a problem with starting slow and doing things right. I mean, none of us want problems—"

"No," agreed Parra quickly.

"—from the money, from the police, from anybody," Featherly went on. "I don't want to give up my life at the Ritz-Carlton," he said, laughing.

Parra didn't bite. But he did tell Featherly some of his concerns, too. He asked him not to move other people's money while they were working with each other. He had gotten into trouble in the past because a group he was using was also working for others.

At that moment, the phone on the bedstand next to Ramón rang. Everyone looked at it.

Ramón started to reach for the receiver but stopped. Featherly told him, "You get it," but stood up and walked over to get it himself.

"Hello," he said. It was a DEA agent on surveillance who was trying to reach the technical people next door. He had dialed the wrong room.

"Uh, he's not here. Guess you've got the wrong number," Featherly said flatly. He hung up and went back to his chair.

He turned to Serrano. "They're looking for you. Are you a bookie?" Everyone laughed.

Featherly sat down again. "I'm sorry," he said to Parra. "I lost my train of thought. Some people who were doing business for you were doing business with other people?"

Parra explained. "The other people had a problem. So the problem went from . . . them to us . . . without us having anything to do with it." Apparently Parra's people came to the attention of law enforcers because the laundry he was using had been noticed by cops investigating another group of customers.

"Their problem became your problem," said Featherly. "I see."

"So if there is anything you have to do with anyone else, please, don't use the same person we are using," said Parra.

"I do have some work for my people in New York," said Featherly. After all, he was supposed to have mob clients according to the undercover scenario they created. "When those people ask me to do it, I have to do it," he went on. "They don't let you not do it," he said, laughing.

That was okay, Parra replied. He explained that the exclusivity rule applied only to "anything that has to do with Colombia, or . . . something like that."

Featherly said that was fine. His only connection to Colombia was Ramón. "I know nothing about how the money is derived—that part of the business is nothing to me," he said. One more try.

"We all know that you don't pay me four and a half percent if it comes from coffee," Featherly said with a knowing smile. "I mean, we have to be realistic. We know, and that's the problem, you know what I mean."

He was edging closer.

"What I don't want—let me just quickly say—is that, I don't want any good deals being offered to my employees out there, where they can get a kilo or something—"

"No, no, no, no, no way," Parra interrupted. "Our people don't have any connection with that."

"Good," said Featherly.

"The other is completely separate," said Parra. "Of course."

"Good, good."

"Nothing at all," said Parra.

"Good, that's not our business," said Featherly. "That's not for me."

"Not for us," said Parra.

Then, from Featherly: "I'm not saying that after we've made a lot of money, that if we went to invest money in something that can double our money in thirty days—I'm not opposed to that. But I don't want to get involved in, whatever, what is it, sugar is it?" He chuckled.

"I don't need to know anybody like that," he continued. "I assume anybody you bring me—"

"They don't have anything to do with anything like that," said Parra.

Featherly rambled on about reputable people doing the work, and about how all of their meetings would take place in nice hotels or, perhaps later, an apartment if things go well.

Featherly was feeling good about his talk with this experienced Colombian money launderer, someone with significant drug dollars and several clients. While he hadn't gotten him to admit the money was drug profits, the illicit nature of the business seemed obvious. There had been some awkward moments, but Parra seemed not to notice. And, barring some technical glitch, it was all captured on videotape.

"How 'bout some lunch?" Ramón asked.

"Yeah," Featherly said. "How 'bout maybe we go downstairs, have a little lunch and celebrate a little bit?"

The men were discussing cuisine as they walked out of camera range. But they weren't off the scope. When they showed up at the Ritz-Carlton's restaurant, one of the finest eating establishments in the city, surveillance agents marked the time—2:00 P.M.—and watched them eat, celebrate their new venture, and plan the next steps.

Their first pickup would happen within a week. Parra would fly to Los Angeles that evening to get his people ready, and they would contact Serrano when the time came. Serrano would see that the money got to Jimmy Brown's people, and the Brown organization would move the money from Los Angeles to Panama.

And when the meal was over and it came time to pay, Parra insisted on putting it all on his American Express card.

At his office at DEA just a few blocks from the Ritz-Carlton, Cesar Diaz picked up his phone and called Los Angeles. With Jaime Parra headed toward L.A., Cesar wanted surveillance and help in picking up the money Parra was pledging to give them.

Ever heard of a guy named Jaime Parra? Cesar asked the agent in Los Angeles assigned to help Atlanta.

Jaime Parra! Agent Alex Romero knew all about Jaime Parra. Parra was a target of the most significant money-laundering investigation DEA had going at the time, Operation Pisces. Romero knew that Parra headed entire networks of money couriers and drug distributors in L.A. Pisces agents had spent countless hours surveilling him, but during the year and a half Pisces had been running, they had met Parra face to face only once, for a single money delivery. And now he had turned up in Atlanta, of all places.

Sure, I've heard of him, Romero told Cesar. He's a very significant Colombian, a bona fide trafficker and a big-time money launderer. He was high enough in the drug trade to be in direct contact with the world's top traffickers, according to another Pisces agent. As Romero told Cesar, "He's a good shot."

Romero's reaction thrilled Cesar. Their first time out, the Atlanta agents had reeled in someone big enough to impress the Pisces team. This investigation was off to a promising start. As a confidential informant, Ramón looked golden.

*L*ess than six hours after finishing his meal at the Ritz-Carlton in Atlanta, Jaime Parra stepped off an Eastern flight in Los Angeles just before 6:00 P.M. local time. He was stepping into an elaborately engineered surveillance operation organized in part by a co-worker of Romero's, an agent still peeved that Parra had vanished from Pisces's sights months earlier. That agent, Dave Hansen, was a friend of Alex Romero's who had razzed him that the man Hansen had spent so much time surveilling for Pisces—a man who had slipped from view—had suddenly turned up in a case from Atlanta. At least Hansen had Parra under his scope once again, and this time he would not let him get away.

Over the next three days, Hansen and more than two dozen other officers from four local, state, and federal agencies would take turns watching Jaime Parra. That evening, they watched as he deplaned, followed him through LAX, and saw him phone for a room at a nearby Sheraton. They were there when he stepped off the curb and hopped the hotel shuttle bus, and when he checked into the Airport Sheraton. They saw him go for dinner at the hotel restaurant, and they knew when he made a pay phone call afterwards and then retired to his room.

They kept an eye on his room through the night, and recorded it when he arrived at the hotel restaurant for breakfast at 8:00 A.M. When he walked up to the Hertz stand in the hotel lobby and rented a black Thunderbird for a week, they saw that, too. As usual, he put the rental charge on his American Express card.

And when Parra got into the Thunderbird, at least five undercover police cars were ready to follow him. Communicating by radio and switching off among themselves to evade discovery, the cops watched as Parra drove from suburb to suburb in the San Fernando Valley on the northern edge of Los Angeles. From the time he rented the car at 9:30 A.M. until he returned to the hotel twelve hours later, they followed him to each place of business he went, to each home and apartment he visited, to every shopping center and to each of the many pay phones he used. They noted when he picked up his cleaning and when he stopped for lunch. They wrote down each time he met someone, that person's description, and where they met. Later, they would return to those places and those people to continue the watch and try to determine whether these were cash or drug houses, and whether the other people were couriers.

Wherever Parra went, a school of police cars followed. While one cop was tracking him from behind, the others would be traveling on parallel streets or would park up ahead, listening by radio to be told where to pick up the tail. In this way, Parra would see different cars in his rearview mirror, and the cops could better withstand his efforts to shake him.

L.A.'s thick traffic makes it hard to stay with a suspect, and Parra's erratic driving made it trickier. A master at countersurveillance techniques, Parra tried every tactic criminals use to throw off a tail. They dart into cul-de-sacs, they make sudden U-turns. They accelerate into high speed, only to brake quickly and slow down. They zip in and out of traffic, and they run red lights. On city streets, they might back up in the middle of the road. On an interstate, they'll exit only to loop around and rejoin it.

When they drive like that, they might be trying to expose a tail, or they might be trying to shake it. It's almost impossible to know when the suspect believes he is being followed and when he is simply being careful. Sometimes a surveillance cop is convinced he's been spotted, only to watch the target then drive somewhere to conduct a major drug deal. Sometimes the target does a deal even after confronting the cop watching him.

Sometimes the "crooks"—the suspects, or "bad guys," in cop vernacular—make a game of it. Says DEA agent Hansen, "If you don't know the area, you might follow someone into a cul-de-sac, and he's waiting at the end of it," with his car facing yours. "He'll smile at you and wave, and then take off. It's their way of saying, 'I see you.' " Sometimes, says Hansen, the crook will lead the cops on a wild ride to nowhere.

During the three days Parra was in Los Angeles, Hansen was totally focused on him. On the third day, a Friday, Parra checked out of the Airport Sheraton at 11:00 A.M., put his bags in the Thunderbird, and started on the day's errands. Parra's driving was worse than usual this day. "We were afraid we were going to lose him," Hansen says. To keep up, "some of us got pretty close to him."

By 1:00 P.M., Parra had led the cops to the suburb of Culver City, not far from the airport. Parra stopped at a Mobil station; a surveillance car pulled in to a convenience store next door. While waiting, the cop was radioing another car when he realized a young Latino who had just come out of the store and walked by his car now was strolling over to Parra. Then he got into Parra's car. The guy had been close enough to the surveillance car to hear the distinctive static of the police radio. Chances were good Parra now knew he was being followed.

Even so, there was no backing off. Tipping off the suspect is part of the risk and happens with some regularity no matter how careful the cop. Still, when on surveillance, "you have to stay with what you've got," says Hansen. Parra could be on his way to a meeting that could lead the agents to a crucial piece of evidence.

Parra and his passenger traveled a bizarre route through Culver City, driving into quiet neighborhoods where any car was noticeable. He would slow down for green lights and speed up for yellow ones. He'd bypass a red light by driving through a corner service station. But the cops still were watching when Parra dropped his passenger off at the same Mobil station ten minutes after picking him up.

Did Parra know he was being followed? Hansen thought it was possible. Regardless, Parra was now about to lead his watchers into the desert. He turned his Thunderbird onto Interstate 10, and pointed it east. He zipped past the southern edge of L.A. and kept going while the exits named town after suburban town: San Gabriel, Rosemead, El Monte. This was not Parra's usual territory. West Covina, Covina, Ontario.

"We thought, 'Where is he going?' " says Hansen.

Well east of downtown by now, Parra exited I-10 and turned north onto Interstate 15, five cop cars trailing.

Hansen figured Parra was going to one of two places: a remote place in the desert (a clandestine landing strip perhaps?) or else Las Vegas. Hansen hoped it was the latter. Maybe Parra would meet an important criminal there, perhaps a casino operator who laundered cash, someone they had never seen him with before. Yes, it was beginning to look like Hansen's job was taking him to Vegas, which was bound to offer some fun on the side—a payoff in Hansen's mind for the grueling Parra watch.

Parra was driving carefully now, no speeding, no tricky stuff. That stretch of road was notorious for state troopers, and Hansen figured Parra had abandoned countersurveillance in favor of avoiding the highway patrol. But did he know that cops already were watching? When Parra stopped at a roadside café, the surveillance crew waited outside, posted at various spots from the restaurant parking lot to expressway entrance ramps down the road. When he returned, the cars took turns keeping up with him as he led them along the Mojave Desert, through mountain passes, and into Nevada. For five and a half hours—for 300 miles—they tailed Parra into the evening, until he finally pulled into Las Vegas at 7:00 P.M., drove down the garish neon strip, and stopped at Caesars Palace.

Yes! Sometimes this job does have unexpected benefits, Hansen said to himself. He hoped Parra would rent a room there, because wherever the crook stayed, the cops stayed. Hansen wouldn't mind a night at Caesars Palace.

Parra bypassed the registration desk, headed into the casino, bought some chips, and strolled up to a blackjack table. The cops took positions around the casino, trying to blend in with the tourists who filled the place. Hansen bought quarters and started feeding them into a slot machine that offered a clear view of Parra.

Parra appeared to be losing at his game, but he didn't seem to mind. Neither did he appear aware of his watchers. Not once did he glance over his shoulder or scan the room. Showing no signs of self-consciousness, Parra calmly played blackjack, staying focused on his game. Maybe he hadn't seen them, after all, Hansen thought. Hansen was wrong. In retrospect, Hansen says Parra probably felt no need to look for them because he "was confident that we were there with him."

After an hour or so at the casino, Parra left Caesars Palace, to Hansen's disappointment. He drove out of the casino district a few miles to the Sheffield Inn, a rambling motel done in southwestern motif. Parra registered to stay for two days and went to his room.

The five cops and agents followed suit, each of them taking a room as close to Parra's as possible. "We had him surrounded," says Hansen. Each of them had a view of the parking lot and Parra's rented black Thunderbird.

Some of them—the guys more experienced at surveillance and its surprises—kept bags in their cars with a change of clothes and basic toiletries. The others called a cop back in L.A. to go to their homes and gather key belongings to bring the next day by plane. In the meantime, they set up sleeping shifts to ensure that Parra's room and car would be watched at all times. And they all planned to be up by seven, because they knew Parra's habits well enough to know he'd probably be out by seven or eight.

When Hansen woke up that Saturday morning and peered out his window, Parra's car was still there. He and the others coordinated their shower schedules. They cleaned up; they dressed; they packed their gear; they prepared to leave. And somehow, while all that was happening, whoever was supposed to be watching the car must have stepped away.

At 7:30 A.M., one of the cops looked outside and saw to his horror that the Thunderbird was gone. The cops scrambled to their cars and quickly mounted a search. The streets were deserted. The black Thunderbird had vanished.

They called in the local police, who helped them check hotel after hotel. Finally, that afternoon, they checked Hertz's airport office and discovered Parra had returned the Thunderbird that morning. He had driven straight to the airport from the Sheffield. A check of the airlines revealed he had bought a ticket to Miami. By now, he could be anywhere.

When their co-worker arrived that afternoon with their belongings, the cops had to tell him they had lost Parra's trail.

They could not be certain they had spooked Parra. But that was how it looked. If Parra was spooked badly, he would never return, and the Pisces agents could forget about arresting him. Later the cops would learn through American Express that Parra had paid an extra $250 to drop the car off in Las Vegas instead of returning it to Los Angeles. It was unlikely Parra had done that for an hour at a blackjack table.

And if Parra believed his new friends in Atlanta might have sent the heat, "Jimmy Brown" and his guys could lose their first customer, and a significant one at that. Before his sudden jaunt to Las Vegas, Parra had started arranging a small load of dirty money for the Atlanta laundry. That was what he had been doing when he led the surveillance crews throughout greater metropolitan Los Angeles before leading them into the desert. Serrano and his American friends would be in Los Angeles soon, and Parra had been preparing for their first venture.

A couple of days after the Las Vegas fiasco, John Featherly and Cesar Diaz flew across the country to get their laundry going, unaware that Parra might have been scared off. The L.A. office had reported that surveillance had followed Parra to Las Vegas and lost him just before he caught a plane to Miami. Why speculate on whether he had "made them," or spotted his watchers?

In fact, if Parra was worried about his new Atlanta connection, it didn't stop him from sending word to Serrano to be ready to pick up cash in L.A. Serrano passed this along to Ramón, who notified the Atlanta agents, which was why Featherly and Cesar were headed to Los Angeles. Featherly, as Jimmy Brown, would oversee the inaugural pickup, and Cesar would debut as Alex Carrera, sidekick to the big man. Skip Latson stayed home because this trip involved money, not an Allen Weston cocaine venture.

The team in L.A. told Featherly he should stay home, too. In real life, the head man of an organization the size of Jimmy Brown's would never participate in a money pickup, especially one as small as this was supposed to be, says Tony Ricevuto, supervisor of DEA-L.A.'s money-laundering group, known as Group 6. "We said, hey, John, you got people working for you, our agents, who are used to doing these kinds of things. Let them do it." But Featherly insisted. "We thought it was sort of comical," says Ricevuto.

At the western edge of downtown Los Angeles, shiny office towers bear the names of banks and a maze of pedestrian overpasses and multi-layered roadways link high-priced hotels and glistening high-rises. A blend of glitz, well-tended greenery, and glass and concrete structures, this part of downtown serves as a hub of finance and commerce for the western United States.

Here, too, DEA had offices in a medium-rise office building named the World Trade Center. Unlike its famous namesake in New York, this World Trade Center is no landmark. Not even the taxi drivers know it by name. With a ground level of sandwich shops and yogurt stands, the building features a stylish, two-story atrium, but upstairs the DEA offices appear to be standard government issue: large rooms with messy, battered desks and file cabinets.

Across the street from the World Trade Center and connected to it by pedestrian overpass, the Sheraton Grande made for a convenient location for undercover DEA meetings. An open, airy lobby with contemporary furnishings holds a sunken conversation area: an escalator runs up the middle to conference rooms upstairs, while elevators at a corner take guests to their rooms. The hotel bar is tucked away in another corner.

It was after 9:00 P.M. on a Tuesday night when Cesar Diaz, as Alex Carrera, strolled into the Sheraton Grande's Tango Bar, making his entrance into the undercover case. Furnished in white and rattan, the Tango Bar reverberated with live, Top 40 music. On this particular night in February, only a smattering of customers had gathered, leaving plenty of empty overstuffed chairs and two-seater sofas arranged around little tables.

Featherly had already joined Ramón and Francisco Serrano around a table in the corner, which Cesar spotted as he entered the noisy bar. The agents had decided to let Serrano get comfortable again with his new partner, Jimmy Brown, before introducing him to yet another partner. They needn't have worried. Serrano instantly warmed to the outgoing young man introduced to him as Alex Carrera. Happy to be doing business with a fellow Latin, however Americanized, Serrano took an immediate liking to this Cuban-born gringo, with his friendly manner and his dark, handsome looks. New in the business, "Alex" seemed eager to learn and pleased at the chance to work with someone of Serrano's background.

Cesar was, in fact, quite eager. With less than four years at DEA, he was a virtual rookie, having handled mostly 2- to 3-kilogram cocaine cases. The Colombians he had helped bust were grunts compared to Francisco Serrano. Now Cesar found himself working undercover in one of the major drug distribution points in the country. Here he was, linking up with a guy from Medellín who was casually discussing his previous smuggling ventures with Jorge Ochoa. Cesar was definitely moving up, and into something very different. No blue jeans for this assignment; Cesar was wearing a gray suit. Like the others around the table, he was dressed as a businessman.

His ability to charm Serrano was testimony to his skill as a salesman, because at the time of this meeting, Cesar was going through one of the most troubled periods of his life. He had just buried his best friend at the agency, Ray Stastny, whom he had met when they were at DEA school at the federal law enforcement training center in coastal Georgia. In Atlanta, they had lived back to back to each other, and they knew each other's families. When Cesar's mother came up from Florida, she would cook for Ray. When one of Ray's parents came to town, Cesar would visit. They partied together. They had Thanksgiving dinner together.

This was not the first time a criminal's bullet had killed someone close to Cesar. When Cesar was fifteen years old in high school in Miami, a robber killed his father, who was working part time as a security guard at a plumbing company. Now, with his close friend dead, too, Cesar was having a hard time coping with his grief and his fear. Undercover deals frightened him as never before. His widowed mother and his dead friend's family members fanned his fears by continually admonishing him to be careful.

Cesar intended to be careful, but if he took too much care he could not do his job. And he never considered quitting drug work. If anything, Stastny's death reinforced his determination. He had always believed in the importance of going after the big guys. But when his friend was shot dead by a street dealer with a lousy 8 ounces of cocaine, Cesar decided it was important to go after the little guy, too. And he figured somebody needed to find a way to cut consumer demand for the drug. American hunger for the stuff was what kept the little guys and the big guys in business.

Cesar was battling his sorrow and his fear when he walked into the Tango Bar that night. But none of it showed. He came off as open and personable, sincerely interested in the person he was meeting, and quick to make everyone comfortable. His dark, curly hair was beginning to show early signs of silver, but this only added glamour to his appearance. Given to Miami-stylish clothes, Cesar worked out to stay fit and looked exactly like someone involved in either drug trafficking or drug enforcement.

Now, Serrano was chattering away in Spanish with his new friend and partner, the only other native Spanish speaker at the table. And when Serrano discussed their new venture, Cesar and Ramón would translate for Featherly.

Serrano told them he had recently talked by telephone to Parra, who was back in Medellín after his trip to L.A. But Serrano mentioned nothing about Parra being tailed, or about his jaunt to Las Vegas. He told them he would have Parra's money for them the next day. It would be only a small amount, a test run to build Parra's confidence in his new U.S. partners. Serrano expected that once things got rolling, the Atlanta operation would be handling more than $1 million a week.

The number sounded impressive, and certainly Parra had that kind of capability, according to the Pisces agents. Plus, Ramón and Serrano had been lining up other customers for Jimmy Brown's laundry, too. But $1 million a week? Did Serrano really believe he could do that, or was he bluffing? So far, the laundry had not handled a single dollar. That was about to change.

At 7:00 P.M. the next evening, a team of L.A.-based surveillance agents watched through the darkness as Ramón and Serrano left the Hilton, where they were staying, a few blocks down from the Sheraton Grande. They saw the pair slide into Ramón's rented Cutlass Ciera and head onto U.S. 101, the Hollywood Freeway. They followed them north out of downtown, past the glamour of Hollywood and Universal City and west into the San Fernando Valley. As cops watched the automobile zip through L.A.'s suburban sprawl, they realized they were back in the neighborhood where they had watched Jaime Parra just a few days ago.

Ramón finally pulled the Cutlass onto Victory Boulevard, a wide, palm-lined roadway traversing middle-class apartments and commercial development. He parked at the curb outside a Spanish-style townhouse complex and let Serrano out. Serrano walked through a narrow courtyard and entered Apartment 131. That same unit had been one of the places the Parra surveillance team had watched the previous week. They had been led there by two Latinos who had met with Parra. Apparently, this was a stash pad for cash.

Serrano stayed in the apartment for quite some time. When he emerged, he was carrying a plastic grocery bag containing some sort of box. He walked up to the Cutlass, and Ramón got out of the car to open the trunk. Serrano put the bag in the trunk and closed it. The pair climbed back into the car.

They had just picked up their first load of dirty money. Serrano told

Ramón none of it appeared to be counterfeit. They talked about finding the fastest way back to downtown, and pulled out the maps that had helped them find their way in the first place.

They needed to turn around. Ramón drove off and decided to circle back on the side streets rather than drawing attention with a U-turn on the boulevard. He turned right, and right again. Suddenly, they found themselves in a cul-de-sac.

Chagrined, Ramón glanced in his rearview mirror and spotted a car he had seen following him on Victory. It was pulling into the cul-de-sac, too. Strangely, as Ramón traveled around the circular end of the street, the car following him did the same. It was a distinctive car—a Mercury with an exterior light mounted on the vinyl between the front and rear windows.

Those stupid cops, Ramón said to himself. How could they be so obvious? He hoped Serrano didn't see the car, too. To divert Serrano's attention, Ramón cursed his wrong turn and told Serrano to look for house numbers—as if that would help get him headed in the right direction.

Ramón needn't have worried. Francisco Serrano was not looking for trouble. He was looking to get rich. He never even noticed the Mercury.

The pair showed up at the Sheraton at about 9:00 P.M., Serrano carrying the bagged box under his arm. They strolled into the Tango Bar, where Featherly was drinking with one of "Jimmy Brown's" employees, a red-haired rookie named Jack Harvey, who had come from DEA-Atlanta to help.

Featherly greeted Ramón and Serrano and asked whether everything went as planned.

Yes, everything was fine, a smiling Serrano told him. He tapped the shoebox-sized object wrapped in the plastic bag to show that all had indeed gone smoothly. He then took the bag out from under his arm and thrust it toward Featherly.

No, no, no. Featherly shook his head angrily. A man in Jimmy Brown's position never handles this stuff, and Featherly made sure Serrano knew that.

Don't ever give me anything like this, Featherly told Serrano, refusing to touch it. The idea that he had brought that box into a public place at all was totally unacceptable.

Take that upstairs, to Alex's room, Featherly insisted. He introduced Serrano and Ramón to the red-haired man with him at the bar, Harvey, and said he would take them up to Room 524. Harvey stood to escort Serrano and Ramón upstairs, stopping on the way to the elevator to call the room and alert Cesar Diaz.

Waiting upstairs with Cesar was one of Jimmy Brown's West Coast employees, "Rolando," whose real name was Orlando Lopez, an officer with the Glendale, California, Police Department—one of the local agencies assisting DEA-L.A. Like Cesar, Orlando Lopez was Cuban-born, young, and athletic.

When the knock at the door came, Cesar welcomed Serrano and Ramón, and Harvey left. Cesar introduced the two men to "Rolando" as someone who would be making money pickups in the L.A. area for Jimmy Brown's organization.

Now it was time for the transfer to take place. Serrano and Ramón, who acted as go-betweens, had picked up the package from Parra's people and were about to hand it over to Jimmy Brown's people, the undercover DEA agents. Serrano opened the plastic bag and removed a shoebox. He lifted the lid to reveal bundles of U.S. currency.

I have some very expensive shoes here, Serrano joked. He said it was $90,000, plus $4,050 for the commission of 4.5 percent, as Parra and Featherly had agreed.

Neither Cesar nor Lopez had seen that much cash before. The sight of it stunned them. They could hardly believe that this virtual stranger had simply handed over a shoebox full of cash. It made them nervous to be handling it.

Cesar set up an automatic money counter, which he had borrowed from the DEA's L.A. office the day before. He had also gotten a quick lesson in how to use it. Now, he was putting it on a small table while Serrano unloaded stacks of money from the shoebox. Lopez removed the rubber bands from the currency and handed the cash to Cesar.

Serrano said he had already counted it, but the count continued, anyway. Stack by stack, Cesar laid the currency flat onto a tray at the top of the money counter. With a flip of a switch the device whirred. Mechanical fingers grabbed the bills, sent them through the body of the apparatus, and spat them out into a vertical stack below. At the same time, a digital display on the front of the machine tallied each piece of paper, spinning into higher and higher numbers as the whirring continued, counting the number of bills without regard to denomination. Cesar had to be sure each stack being counted contained bills of the same denomination, or else the count would be meaningless. This haul included bundles of fives, twenties, all kinds of denominations, and took about a half hour to count. The sum came to $94,050. Not much by Colombian standards, but it was a start.

It was certainly a lot to Cesar, who was used to receiving drugs, not money. It struck him as bizarre that a man he had never met before the previous night had just handed him more money than Cesar would make in years. Serrano asked for no receipt, no merchandise in return, nothing. And Serrano seemed so happy about doing it, too.

Serrano told Cesar he expected to pick up more money the next day. In the meantime, the important thing was for Jimmy Brown's people to get the money to Parra's account in Panama as quickly as possible.

When that happened, there would be trust, Serrano said.

Cesar bundled up the cash. He called yet another DEA agent who was waiting next door to come and get it. The agent whisked the money away.

Serrano told Ramón later he thought it was strange that Jimmy Brown had sent so many people to handle so little money. But as numerous as Jimmy Brown's people seemed to be, they were just a fraction of the agents and cops on hand for this transaction. Next door to the money counting, in Room 526, more DEA agents were listening to the conversation in Room 524, which had been outfitted with a hidden microphone.

When he returned to the Tango Bar downstairs, Ramón noticed that three guys at a nearby table had been there for forty-five minutes, yet their beer glasses were still full. It irked Ramón that the surveillance team was so obvious.

As for the shoebox, the agent who carried it away from Room 524 took it to DEA offices across the street to photograph and store it overnight. The next day he would take it to the Sanwa Bank, where DEA had an undercover account, to start it on its long journey. The Sanwa Bank, which was cooperating with DEA, would count the cash and wire-transfer the sum to C&S in Atlanta, which would wire it to New York, where agent Ed Guillen had opened an account at Chemical Bank for this purpose. Chemical Bank, which was cooperating with Fis-Con, would then wire $90,000 to Panama, where Parra had an account at the Banco de Occidente, a Colombian bank with a branch in Panama City.

The $4,050 in "commission" would wind up in another account in Chemical Bank in New York, to be used by the DEA to further its investigation.

But before all that happened, there was a celebration to be had. While drug agents next door to the Sheraton were processing the cash as evidence in a new case, Serrano, Ramón, and Cesar went downstairs to meet John Featherly and Jack Harvey for dinner at the Ravel, an intimate —and expensive—restaurant off the Sheraton's lobby. Pleased with the success of the day—although for different reasons—the five men chatted amiably as they savored their dinners. Serrano said he planned to become a millionaire through this new venture. He told them about his beautiful young wife, Sol, and how that would please her. The men brought out cigars, ordered brandy, and began toasting each other. A happy Francisco Serrano toasted the rich future they would all have together.

And when they were finally done at twenty before eleven, a surveillance agent marked down the time and followed Serrano and Ramón to their rooms at the Hilton.

4: Testing Ramón

Eight days after that first money pickup, a crew of cops tailing one of Jaime Parra's couriers spotted something unexpected. On surveillance on the western edge of the San Fernando Valley, parked across the street from a Denny's restaurant on Ventura Boulevard, Mike Ferrari peered through his binoculars to be sure.

Ferrari and about five other West Covina cops assigned to DEA-L.A. had followed the courier to this Denny's, which was jammed into the parking lot of a phonily rustic Vagabond Inn along a mostly commercial strip. What surprised him was that when the guy came out of the coffee shop, he was with Ramón Costello, Atlanta's CI. Surely Cesar or Skip would have told the guys in L.A. if they had known their informant would be meeting with this suspect, Jorge Mario, one of Parra's couriers. Was Ramón conducting a little freelance business on the side, as plenty of CIs do?

Ferrari studied them in the binoculars as the two men walked over to a car parked in the lot shared by Denny's and the Vagabond Inn. Mario opened the trunk of the car. The way Ferrari remembers it, Ramón reached in and pulled out a manila envelope. He folded it up under his shirt, as if to conceal it, while Mario shut the trunk. Ramón then walked up to one of the motel rooms, unlocked the door, and went in.

It didn't look right to Ferrari. He didn't know what the envelope contained, or whether anything illegal was going on. It probably wasn't drugs, but it could be some sort of paperwork, or it could be money. All he knew was that the CI was somewhere DEA didn't expect him to be, having a meeting with someone linked to illegal activity, and acting as if he had something to hide. Ferrari reached for his car phone.

That evening, Ramón spotted a familiar car driving through the parking lot of the Vagabond Inn: a Mercury with an exterior light between the side windows. He recognized the driver as the man he had seen following him and Serrano into the cul-de-sac. He was being watched.

The next morning, Ramón called his contact at DEA-L.A. to report that the money pickups weren't going too well. He had been meeting with couriers he had hoped would have money, but instead they gave reasons for delays. The agent told Ramón he should call Skip Latson in Atlanta. Ramón said he had planned to call him the following day. No, you'd better call him now, the agent said. In fact, you should plan to leave L.A. for Atlanta as quickly as possible. Ramón then called Skip, who told him to come back to Atlanta. The money pickups wouldn't happen until next week, anyway, so come on back, Skip said.

Ramón didn't know why he was being yanked out of L.A. But things got stranger once he reached Atlanta. Skip and an agent Ramón didn't know picked him up at the airport, took him to a room at the Days Inn downtown, and told him to open his suitcase.

Puzzled, Ramón unfastened the bag. Skip told him to move the contents around so he could see them better. Maybe they have to do this every now and then, Ramón told himself. But why now and not when he came up from Colombia? Ramón picked up the suitcase and dumped the contents onto the bed. He had a couple of girlie magazines he handed to Skip. Skip put them down. He told Ramón to open up the shaving kit and other containers. Ramón, getting peeved, complied.

The search complete but still unexplained, Skip told Ramón to come to the office in the morning.

On DEA's main floor in the Richard B. Russell Federal Building in Atlanta, a receptionist behind a heavy, Plexiglas window speaks to visitors through a microphone. She monitors television screens displaying various places within DEA where cameras are mounted. Electronically, she operates the locked door leading from the windowless waiting room to the hallway and offices beyond.

Down the hallway, behind one of the doors, a large room dubbed the Group 1 room was where John Featherly's agents worked. A maze of clutter and battered, government-issue office furniture, the room offered individual work spaces separated by six-foot, fabric-covered room dividers where agents had tacked up cartoons and posters and newspaper clippings. A long window with a view of downtown lined one of the walls. Skip had his cubicle in a corner, next to the window.

On this particular morning, Ramón was standing around in Skip's work space when Featherly and Skip walked in and came up to him. Ramón gave them friendly greetings, but they were not particularly cheerful in return. Featherly, the tough guy, signaled for Ramón to come with them.

Ramón followed them out, down the hall to a small, bare conference room.

We want to know what happened in L.A., Featherly told him.

What do you mean, what happened in L.A.? Ramón asked.

What did you do in L.A.? Featherly wanted to know. What did you do on the first day, the second? He led Ramón through each day he had been in Los Angeles, through each hour, through every ten-minute interval, it seemed. What did you do then? Why did you go there? Who were you with?

Ramón had no idea where this was headed, but he was certain Featherly and Skip were unhappy about something important. He answered the questions, describing everything he could remember about his recent trip to Los Angeles. I went to this place; I met this man; we called Jaime Parra at this time. He didn't mention anything about a bag or an envelope.

Featherly asked about the day at the parking lot of the Vagabond Inn. What were you doing with Jorge Mario?

I was making arrangements for a money pickup.

What did Jorge Mario give you?

Nothing.

What about a bag? (In DEA-Atlanta's version of the L.A. parking lot episode, Ramón had received a bag, not an envelope, from Jorge Mario.)

What bag? Ramón didn't know what they were talking about.

The bag he put in the trunk of your car.

Featherly told Ramón agents had seen Jorge Mario put a bag into the trunk of Ramón's car. What was it? Was it drugs? Was it money?

Ramón said he remembered no bag. Really, he didn't.

Two agents saw you with it, Featherly insisted. What was in the bag?

Maybe he bought something Mario was holding for him—a snack, some small item—but he didn't think so. Maybe it was trash. Ramón had absolutely no memory of the incident.

Skip, taking a less accusatory tack, told Ramón that whatever the truth was, it would be easier to handle than a lie. Lying would jeopardize the entire operation because it would throw doubt on everything Ramón did or said. The only way he could answer their questions wrong would be to lie. Just tell us what happened, Skip said. Whatever it is, we'll straighten it out.

I told you what happened, Ramón insisted. He swore he was telling the truth.

Look, we're not going to arrest you, Skip told him. We're not going to put you in jail. We just want to know what you did out there. And we don't want to have to learn the truth from a polygraph examiner.

A visibly nervous Ramón, eyes down, stammered and fidgeted but kept insisting he was telling the truth. He was feeling smaller and smaller. Nothing had happened in L.A. If Jorge Mario had given him something, it was so insignificant that Ramón could not remember what it was.

Featherly had been through this before with CIs, grilling them to fess up to criminal activity. Some confess, some don't. It's certainly easier when suspicions are confirmed by something concrete, like evidence. But the guys in L.A. had not stopped Ramón to search him, to see what had gone into the trunk.

Ramón was sticking to his story, and after about twenty or thirty minutes the agents figured it would do no good to keep up the interrogation. They were inclined to believe Ramón, but they needed to be sure. If Ramón was doing drug deals on the side, the whole investigation would be ruined. They had to know whether Ramón could be trusted to tell the truth. So Featherly and Skip said he would have to take a polygraph test. They arranged for a DEA polygrapher to test him the following evening.

The polygraph detected no lies, and Ramón was declared to be truthful in his claims that nothing out of the ordinary had gone on in the parking lot that day.

Featherly was satisfied. Ramón had held up through the questioning, and he had held up on the box. Skip, too, was convinced his CI was clean. From that point throughout the rest of the case, Skip would defend Ramón against any hint of dishonesty. But in Los Angeles, the DEA supervisor helping Atlanta continued to doubt Ramón's veracity. The polygraph, says Tony Ricevuto, "doesn't mean a thing."

For his part, Ramón was angry for the humiliating interrogation Featherly had put him through. Skip had gone easier on him, but Featherly had been relentless in his disbelief. He told himself he would never forgive Featherly.

And he was fed up with the agents and cops in L.A. Their surveillance crews were easy to spot, and now they were accusing him. His work was dangerous, all right, but not because of anything the Colombians might do. Ramón figured his biggest risk was that the agents would screw up, especially the guys working out of DEA's Group 6 in L.A., the money-laundering team assigned to the Atlanta case. Ramón gave it a new name: "Group Sick."

Once he got back to Colombia, Ramón learned that Parra had burned the surveillance cops. In a meeting at his office, Parra told Ramón that on the day he was planning to leave L.A., he spotted someone following him. He had tried to shake the tail, but couldn't. He told Ramón he had driven all the way to Las Vegas, and still had been followed.

One of his couriers, Jorge Mario, had also spotted a tail during the same period and would not return to the United States, Parra told Ramón. For himself, Parra said he might make an occasional business trip to Miami, but never would he go to Los Angeles again.

U.S. cops weren't all that was hampering Parra's business activities. He told Ramón that the black market exchange rate for cashing in dollars for Colombian pesos was too low. He was postponing all U.S. money pickups.

Ramón reported all of this to Skip Latson. Eventually, word would get to the Los Angeles DEA that Parra knew he had cops in his dust when he drove to Las Vegas. They had suspected this, but had no way to be sure. It pleased Ramón that he had been the bearer of that piece of news. The cops and agents in L.A.—the same group whose suspicions had led to his humiliating interrogation—learned through this same informant that their surveillance had scared off an important suspect. Although agents insist that even the best surveillance teams sometimes get burned, Ramón believed he was doing his job better than they were doing theirs.

Without Parra, the Atlanta money laundry was in need of a customer. Serrano and Ramón quickly drew in another large family—the Ospinas —who had lots of money in Los Angeles to be cleaned and wired to Panama. And the Ospinas didn't feel the need to bother with some paltry sum as a tryout.

On March 13, Juan Ospina's couriers delivered to Francisco Serrano a plastic grocery bag containing bundles of cash, each bundle encased in heat-sealed plastic. In a Safeway grocery store parking lot, Serrano handed the money over to Jimmy Brown's men—undercover agents from Group 6 in Los Angeles—and they all went to a Comfort Inn to count it. The total came to $291,555.

That money was whisked away to the nearby Glendale Police Department for photographing and processing, and then deposited. From the undercover account at the Sanwa Bank, it was wired to Atlanta, to New York and on to Panama.

It was still in the laundry's pipeline when, ten days later, Serrano beeped Cesar Diaz in Atlanta to tell him he had another load of Ospina's money ready to be picked up in L.A. Again, an undercover DEA agent met Serrano at the Safeway, where, in broad daylight, Serrano handed him an oblong box. Inside was $257,540 in cash—the third load for the Atlanta laundry.

Ten days after that delivery, on April 2, Ospina reported he had yet another load of money for Serrano: $350,000. This would bring to nearly $900,000 in three weeks the sum of money this one organization had sent through the Atlanta laundry. The money represented roughly 65 to 90 kilograms of cocaine, or nearly 150 to 200 pounds.

But on the day of the third pickup, something went wrong. Serrano kept delaying his meeting with the undercover agent, Alex Romero, who was supposed to get the money from Serrano for Brown's laundry. Finally, about 6:00 P.M., Serrano told Romero by telephone he still did not have the money. Serrano said he was worried. Ospina's couriers had borrowed his rental car to fill the trunk with cash, but they had not come back with it. He was stranded at the Promenade shopping mall, he couldn't find his car or the $350,000, and he had a plane to catch. He was heading back to Colombia that night.

The surveillance cops could see the car, a white Toyota, parked exactly where Serrano had left it in the mall lot. They also figured Serrano suspected something because he had wiped the steering wheel clean of fingerprints before abandoning the car, according to one of the surveilling cops, Mike Ferrari of West Covina P.D.

The cops reported the car's position to agent Romero, who would be meeting Serrano undercover.

When Romero showed up at the mall, Serrano was visibly distraught. The guys who were supposed to fill his car trunk with cash still had not returned. He didn't know what had happened to the car or the money, and he had to get back to Colombia.

Romero offered to drive Serrano around the parking lot to hunt for the car, according to the agent.

No, it's no use, Serrano said. I've looked all over.

Let's just take a quick look and see what happens, Romero recalls saying. You might have missed it.

No, Serrano said, I have to get to the airport. Serrano had already made arrangements for a friend to pick him up and take him to LAX.

Serrano left, and the cops called Hertz to report the abandoned car. When the rental car people came, they gave the agents permission to look in the trunk.

The trunk came up, revealing a bloated duffel bag. It looked like the money had been delivered, after all, and the scatterbrained Serrano had simply left it. Finding the cash like this would be better than laundering the money, because the agents could intercept it and use the money as evidence instead of wiring it back to drug traffickers.

The agents opened the duffel bag. To their shock, there were no bundles of money in this bag. Not even a dollar bill. The bag was full, all right. But it was full of Mickey Mouse toys.

Oh no, Ferrari groaned.

What's going on here? Romero wondered. This was like some scene out of *The Twilight Zone.* "We were super depressed," says Romero. "Why would anyone want to put a bunch of toys in a car?" Was it some sort of decoy?

And where was the $350,000? The cops had tried to watch it all, but somehow in this shell game, the cash had not gotten to the shell where they expected to find it.

Meanwhile, other surveillance crews had followed two Latinos Serrano had met earlier in a restaurant—men believed to be Ospina money couriers—to a house on the western edge of the San Fernando Valley on Llano Street in the suburb of Woodland Hills. Given what the cops had seen and what they knew about Serrano's line of work, they figured this would be a good place to search for the $350,000.

But before they hit the house, they watched it. They saw people leave and followed their car to a place in West Los Angeles on Manning Avenue. The car pulled into a private, secured parking lot, and one of the Glendale cops climbed up a fence and watched the suspects take what looked like cocaine from one car trunk and put it into the trunk of another car. Bingo!

The cops and agents hit both houses. Seventy-five kilograms—181 pounds—of cocaine came out of the car trunk and out of the Manning Avenue house. The agents raiding the Llano Street house found what was clearly an office, complete with plenty of paperwork. They arrested six Colombians and seized four vehicles. But they didn't find the $350,000 they were looking for. The only cash they found was $10,000.

Still, what they did find showed they had come across a very successful enterprise. The ledgers they confiscated indicated a multi-million-dollar business. In one of the client's accounts alone, the ledger showed $2.5 million had been moved over a ten-day period in December.

The ledger did not give the full names of the clients for whom the money was being moved, of course. Some were first names, like Raul, and some were nicknames. A few listings seemed to be in some sort of code. Three entries attributed the $2.5 million to something listed as "Mina 30" (in English, Mine 30), as in a salt mine or gold mine. The cops didn't know it at the time, but the Mina 30 entries would turn out to be gold. And those few pieces would lead them into a very large mine indeed.

*I*n Colombia, the incident left Ospina steaming. He called in Ramón and Serrano and blamed them for bringing heat to his couriers. He didn't tell them the couriers had been arrested, but he said they had spotted men watching them and decided against delivering the money to Serrano. Serrano swore he was not to blame. He hadn't seen anyone following him, he insisted. If the couriers were being watched, it was their fault, not his. Serrano did not want to lose this important client. Ospina could easily send $1 million a week through the laundry.

But Ospina had been shaken by the surveillance. He told Ramón and Serrano he'd have money for them in New York in a few weeks, but he wouldn't give them any more business in Los Angeles, not until things cooled down, anyway.

It looked like the Atlanta laundry had lost a chunk of business. The luckless Serrano was doubly disappointed. He had also lost a bag of toys he had bought for his young son.

*T*he Atlanta investigation kept sputtering and stalling on all fronts in the spring and summer of 1987. Parra and Ospina were both too nervous to send money. And the smuggling probe was stuck, too. Sure, the L.A. teams had seized cocaine and money as a direct result of the Atlanta probe—nearly $533,000, 209 pounds of coke, and thirteen Colombians had been taken in by early April. But the investigation wasn't moving into new territory. Every time the case jumped forward, it hit a wall.

Nonetheless, Ramón and Serrano kept fishing for customers, and it seemed they had a big one in April. A Colombian said he would soon have $9 million in drug funds to be picked up in New York, where a 15,000-pound marijuana shipment would be landing. He said half the pot was going to the Gambino crime family, which would pay on delivery. But that fell through, too, because the Gambino family turned out to be DEA agents in New York pretending to have mob ties. They seized the huge shipment.

As bad as business was for the Atlanta laundry, it got worse in May when Attorney General Edwin Meese announced the culmination of Operation Pisces—the biggest money-laundering case ever, with more arrests and seizures of cocaine and cash than the feds had ever before accomplished. Among the people indicted was Jaime Parra, a fugitive.

"There will be no safe haven for drug money," Meese had said in a story carried around the world on CNN. "We're going to find it. We're determined to take it when we do find it," he added. Pisces made traffickers and launderers plenty nervous, not only in the United States but also in Colombia and in Panama, where millions had been seized from bank accounts.

The smuggling part of the Atlanta probe was sputtering, also. Ramón and Serrano would meet again and again with people, but nothing ever seemed to firm up.

Finally, in June, they found a guy who wanted to go to Atlanta to meet Allen Weston (Skip Latson) and check out airstrips for a possible cocaine load. His name was Carlos Restrepo, and this Colombian seemed to have access to lots of cocaine.

Restrepo said he had to go to Miami, anyway, so he and Ramón could meet there and discuss the Atlanta possibilities. In Miami, they met at the elegant Mayfair Hotel in Coconut Grove, where Restrepo was staying. Restrepo agreed to go with Ramón to Atlanta to meet with Skip and look over the airstrip. But first, Restrepo had business to finish up in Miami. He told Ramón to wait a couple days and they would fly to Atlanta together.

On Friday, June 12, Ramón was holed up in his hotel room at the Airport Marriott in Miami, the television on, waiting for Restrepo's call, when a story on CNN caught his attention. Attorney General Meese was announcing yet another major money-laundering case, Operation Cashweb-Expressway, a three-year, $200 million probe in eight cities. The feds had arrested people in Miami and all over the place. A closeup on the criminal complaint was clear enough for Ramón to read the first names. The fourth was Carlos Restrepo.

"These cases provide bad news for the drug kingpins," Meese was saying. "Now they'll never be certain they're not handing the cash over to undercover federal agents."

Great.

Ramón walked out of his room and left the hotel, crossed LeJeune Road, and kept walking until he saw a pay telephone three blocks away.

He called the number he had for the cellular phone Restrepo carried in his briefcase. No answer. He called Restrepo's hotel room. No answer there, either.

He called Francisco Serrano in Colombia.

In cryptic terms, Ramón told Serrano they had lost another customer. Your friend has gotten sick, he said. He has a cold, a bad cold. A real bad cold. In fact, his friend is so sick he's in the hospital.

I can't believe your luck could be that bad, Ramón told Serrano.

Ramón didn't know what to do at that point. Should he go back to Colombia? Should he go to Atlanta? He kept trying to reach Restrepo because, as clear as it was, he couldn't quite believe that the Carlos Restrepo he had been meeting was the same Carlos Restrepo who had just been arrested. It was just too weird. He decided to wait until the next morning and see if there were more details in the *Miami Herald*.

"FBI Arrests 41 in Drug Money Sting," read the headline on the front page of the local news section that Saturday morning. Ramón scanned the *Herald* story. Among those arrested in Miami: Carlos Restrepo.

That was it. He called Skip at home.

Our man got busted, Ramón told him. Do you believe this crap? I don't know what to do. He told Skip about the story on CNN and in the *Herald* about the FBI case.

Skip had known nothing about this case, and it troubled him that his informant had been meeting with a man the FBI had been watching. For all the FBI knew, Ramón Costello was what he appeared to be to Restrepo: a man trying to help bring a load of cocaine into the United States. He feared the FBI would pick Ramón up next.

Skip told Ramón to get out of there. Come up to Atlanta as soon as you can, Ramón remembers Skip saying. If FBI agents knew you were talking to Restrepo, they might decide to pick you up. Leave Miami as soon as you can. We'll be able to protect you in Atlanta.

That the FBI could be watching unnerved Ramón. He said he'd be up to Atlanta that day.

But just to make sure the guy the FBI arrested was the same man he had met, Ramón called the Mayfair. The hotel operator said Restrepo was no longer there. Ramón left a message that he had called. Then he began throwing his clothes into his suitcase.

Ramón checked out of the hotel, all the while uneasy. He glanced into one of the multiple mirrors decorating the hotel lobby—mirrors that reflect each other's reflections—and spotted a plainclothed, straitlaced kind of guy watching him. Ramón was certain it was the FBI.

He took a taxi to the Miami airport, headed to the Delta counter, and bought a ticket for the next flight to Atlanta. Ramón figured if the feds were going to pick him up, they would have done so at the hotel, not the airport.

He relaxed.

As soon as Skip hung up after talking to Ramón, he turned on CNN and called Buddy Parker at home to tell him about Restrepo.

Buddy asked Skip whether Ramón had been reporting his dealings with Restrepo. Was it possible Ramón was doing something illegal behind Skip's back?

Ramón wasn't calling as often as he might, but he was keeping Skip informed. Skip knew he had gotten Restrepo interested in bringing cocaine through Georgia. In fact, the two of them were supposed to arrive in Atlanta that day to check out an airstrip.

Was there an arrest warrant out for Ramón? A law enforcement officer couldn't help a suspect evade arrest, after all. Skip knew of no warrant for Ramón's arrest, although he hadn't exactly searched high and low for one. Interagency protocol prohibited Skip from calling the Miami FBI to find out what was happening, but Buddy could call the prosecutor there.

In the meantime, Buddy agreed Ramón should come to Atlanta, soon. If Ramón were jailed in Miami with Carlos Restrepo, they probably would have to surface Ramón as an informant and spoil the investigation.

"We had to get him out of Miami," Buddy would later say. "We had to get him where we could deal with the legal issues." If a warrant for his arrest turned up, Buddy would take it to the federal judge in Atlanta who had been dealing with legal matters arising out of Atlanta's undercover case.

And if the problem was worse—if Ramón, indeed, was freelancing and deserved to be arrested—then the Atlanta agents should be the ones to do it.

It didn't take many calls to learn that the FBI had been watching Ramón. In fact, the Bureau had audiotape of Ramón conspiring with Restrepo to import cocaine, just as Ramón had told Skip he was doing. Yes, the Bureau was watching Ramón; but, no, he was not wanted for arrest.

Ramón had slipped safely through once again. The case was intact.

5: Glimpsing a Gold Mine

Finding crooks not already under investigation proved to be quite a task for Ramón Costello. Finally, in the summer of 1987, Serrano introduced him to an old acquaintance in Colombia with a promising proposal. He wanted to use Allen Weston (Skip Latson) to help move a load of cocaine through Georgia, and the negotiations were leading Ramón up the ladder in the Medellín cartel.

Stepping up a rung, Ramón met Nicolás Ramírez, a former manager of an important city club in Medellín who boasted of high-level connections in the cartel. A partner in the proposed shipment, Ramírez told Ramón the air route the coke would travel had to be approved by a cousin of Pablo Escobar's, Gustavo Gaviria, who Ramírez said was Escobar's man in charge of cocaine distribution for North America. Gustavo Gaviria was no petty crook, and Nicolás Ramírez knew him personally.

But Ramírez didn't just talk about Gaviria: He took Ramón to meet him. In June 1987, the two men drove up the hills outside Medellín to a well-guarded house that had been converted into an office. This appeared to be one of the so-called brokerage houses traffickers used to negotiate and plan drug loads. Ramírez went there seeking Gaviria's approval for the cocaine route; Ramón went looking for anything he might use to impress the boys in Atlanta. But when they arrived, they were told Gaviria was out of the country. A few days later, Ramón got word that Gaviria had approved the route.

It looked like the load would fly, so in July, two of Ramírez's Colombian partners traveled to Atlanta, where Ramón and Serrano introduced them to Allen Weston and to the airport the DEA had selected.

As it turned out, the Colombians had an American partner in California who had not traveled to Atlanta but who was calling regularly for progress reports. And, as it happened, the California partner was recording the calls because he was a San Francisco–based DEA agent gathering evidence against the two Colombians as well as Ramón Costello, Francisco Serrano, and their American partner, Allen Weston.

The Atlanta load fell through, and DEA–San Francisco soon learned the truth about Serrano and the Atlantans. The two Colombians were arrested in San Francisco in short order and charged for conspiring with the San Francisco agent to arrange another cocaine shipment.

The resulting case did not focus on the Atlanta proposal, but the tapes could have exposed Ramón and Skip as DEA operatives. Buddy Parker worked with the prosecutor in San Francisco to make sure that didn't happen. It seemed to Buddy his main task in life these days was keeping Ramón out of jail and undercover. Now he was also protecting Serrano, who had proven himself invaluable as the DEA's unwitting birddog.

Serrano and Ramón, meanwhile, continued to scheme in Medellín with Nicolás Ramírez. He assured them he was still interested in doing business with them, apparently figuring they had had nothing to do with the arrests of his friends.

At the same time as they were courting Ramírez for a cocaine shipment, Ramón and Serrano were trying to crank up their preferred line of work, picking up and washing dirty money. They were getting some nibbles again, and it looked like the money would be showing up in New York.

That was what led them to the Sevilla restaurant in New York City, a dark and intimate place at the corner of Charles and West 4th streets in the West Village, amid bakeries and curio shops. Plants line the windows, making the room inside cozier, with its high-backed booths of deep, dark wood and its white tableclothed tables. Among the bullfighting posters, a banner declares: *Te Amo Julio Iglesias*.

John Featherly knew the Sevilla well. He could not have worked in New York so long and loved food so much without learning that this was the place for paella. In fact, the Sevilla had been something of a DEA hangout during Featherly's years in New York. Serrano loved paella, too, so when it appeared they would have business in New York, Featherly brought Serrano, Ramón, and Cesar Diaz to his favorite place.

On this particular August afternoon, the cool, dark restaurant seemed the perfect place to get out of the city heat and talk business. Traveling in separate cars, Featherly and Cesar would meet Serrano and Ramón there. At 3:00 P.M. on a Tuesday, the place should have been empty—except that two dozen drug agents and DEA office workers were holding a going-away party for an agent and a retiring DEA secretary.

When Featherly and Cesar walked through the door, the celebrants recognized their old friend and former co-worker and welcomed him. Featherly was not nearly as happy to see them, of course. Serrano would be coming through the door any moment. Pure luck had allowed Featherly and Cesar to find a parking space first.

Cesar stepped outside to intercept Serrano and Ramón while Featherly explained the situation to his former co-workers. By the time Serrano and Ramón walked in, the DEA contingent had become apparent strangers to Featherly.

The foursome took a booth away from the group. With that constant reminder of their duality, the agents nonetheless dropped into their undercover roles. They remarked on the grand old time the group of partyers was having.

Over an excellent paella, Serrano was trying to explain why the money-laundering business had slowed to a halt. It had seemed so promising at first, but all the U.S. arrests and the freezing of Panamanian bank accounts had scared the traffickers and their bankers.

Serrano felt terrible about not being able to bring Jimmy Brown more business, he told them. He had promised to send him $1 million a week, yet he hadn't found a single dirty bill for months. But now the dry spell was ending, he was sure. Business was getting back to normal, and Juan Ospina had money he wanted them to move.

Serrano explained whose money it would be. Ospina, he said, was moving money for Nicolás Ramírez. This was the same Colombian who knew Escobar's cousin, Gaviria, and who wanted to fly a load through Atlanta, although Serrano did not mention that to Jimmy Brown and Alex Carrera, who were money movers, not cocaine smugglers. He did explain, however, that Ramírez was close to the big guys in Medellín. He said any money Ramírez gave them in fact belonged to the Ochoa family. He expected to pick up and deliver some of that money in New York, and he expected it to happen quickly. He then excused himself to make several telephone calls.

When Serrano returned, he said he wanted to tell them a few more things, but he didn't want to talk in the restaurant, where they could be overheard. "The walls have ears," he said, unaware that his problem was the people in the booth with him.

The foursome paid up and took a walk around the West Village. In what areas of New York would they like to do the work? Serrano asked.

Cesar told him either Queens or Manhattan. They agreed on Queens, and Serrano said he'd call Cesar as soon as the money was ready.

Two weeks later, that call came. Serrano had $241,800 in New York for Jimmy Brown's laundry. DEA–New York sent undercover agents to receive the money from Serrano, skim off Jimmy Brown's commission for the DEA, and pump the rest of it into DEA's complicated pipeline of banks. The Atlanta laundry was back in business.

Two weeks after that, Cesar and Ramón made the next pickup, this time in the basement of a house in a quiet, middle-class neighborhood in Queens. As the obese Colombian who lived there watched, Cesar and Ramón opened cardboard moving boxes heavy with cash, unloaded and unbundled stacks of bills, and fed them into a money-counting machine. Then they rebundled each stack with a rubber band and recorded the count. The counting was slow because the machine occcasionally threw out a bill, causing them to redo that stack. Too, the denominations were relatively low—tens and twenties. For three and a half hours they counted. Finally, they had a total: $615,555. The laundry had its biggest load yet.

Like the previous delivery, this one was taken to New York DEA agents, who processed the cash for evidence, took out DEA's cut, and deposited the two sums into separate bank accounts. The larger chunk was sent through Atlanta's multi-cycle laundry to make its way to Panama.

The laundry was still churning away on that load when, six days later, Juan Ospina's people sent another one through: $377,260. New York DEA agents assigned to help Atlanta picked up that load, posing as more of Jimmy Brown's helpers.

In five weeks, Juan Ospina had delivered more than $1.2 million to the undercover laundry. It still wasn't $1 million a week, but the DEA's job was to gather evidence, not wash as many drug dollars as possible.

Jimmy Brown's laundry was great at picking up money, but it was lousy at moving it quickly. The longer it took the money to get to Panama, the angrier and more nervous the customer became. The reason was that once the cash got into the hands of Jimmy Brown's people in the States, the middleman who had hired them—in this case, Juan Ospina—had to dig into personal funds and hand over the same sum to the drug trafficker who had hired *him*. And as long as the drug money was in the hands of the middleman's subcontractor—Jimmy Brown's organization —the middleman, not the trafficker, was out the cash. It was one of the many ways the drug lords made sure that if anyone lost money in this tricky business, it would not be them.

So, while the drug proceeds were winding their way through bank after U.S. bank, the middleman was anxiously wondering whether he would ever see his money again.

"The clock is ticking against him" while the money is in the pipeline, explains Skip. From the drug baron's viewpoint, "that money is technically in his custody. And all the days it's not in the bank, he's losing money on the interest."

The Atlanta laundry was taking a week, two weeks, sometimes longer —an interminable length of time for the middleman to be short such large sums.

Under the best of circumstances it takes drug agents longer than real money launderers, and in Atlanta's case, there was an extra wash cycle or two that slowed things down further. The money had to go through Atlanta for venue purposes, and for L.A. deliveries, the funds had to travel through a local bank as well as Atlanta and New York banks.

Skip explains what the agents did with the cash in Los Angeles, where most of the money pickups happened: First, "they'd take it into the office and secure it in a safe, and then start trying to do the paperwork" to get it to the bank the next day. But often some emergency would arise, and they would get called onto some other case.

"Maybe it's the second day that they finally call Brinks or some other armored-car service to pick it up, take it to the bank," says Skip. This means if the agents picked up the cash from the "crooks" on Thursday, it wouldn't get to the bank until the following Monday. "You've already gone almost four days."

Skip continues: "Busy banks in big cities don't always have cashiers to break loose to count . . . $500,000, if you're bringing it in every other day. The bank may not get to counting it until the following day. . . .

"So they count it, say, the following day, on Tuesday, and you have a record of the deposit. They cannot make a wire transfer until after two o'clock in the afternoon. So if they don't get it counted and all the paperwork done by two in the afternoon on Tuesday, they can't wire-transfer it until the next day. They get it out by two o'clock on Wednesday, but by that time the banks are closed in New York [and in Atlanta, where it's three hours later]. So there's no record of it arriving in New York or Atlanta or wherever it's going to go until Thursday."

By this time, a week has passed, and the money has just arrived at the second of three or four U.S. banks through which it must travel before hitting Panama. After it reached Atlanta, the money had to be wire-transferred to New York to one of DEA agent Ed Guillen's Fis-Con accounts. Along the way, the banks had no incentive to move fast because they make money by keeping large sums as long as possible.

Meanwhile, the laundry's customer was calling Serrano or Cesar to ask where the hell the money was. " 'Where is it, where is it?' and we're all pushing along the way and making everybody mad at us," says Skip. He could hardly give the customer the bottom-line explanation: "That's just the way Uncle Sam works."

Real money laundries, if they are big enough, do not have to wait for the money to travel from bank to bank before giving the customer the sum. According to Guillen, a real laundry would simply open an account in the country where the customer wanted his money sent and keep a reserve of, say, $1 million. So, when the launderer's people picked up a load of cash in the United States and confirmed the amount, the launderer could immediately tell his bank overseas to make that same sum available to his customer—perhaps in the form of a cashier's check, perhaps in the form of a wire transfer.

But at DEA, "we couldn't at the time open up an account and have a million-dollar reserve just floating around to make it available to wherever these people might happen to want it on that particular day," says Guillen.

They certainly couldn't seek the cooperation of the banks in countries like Panama, where agents believed that bankers' loyalties to their big customers, including drug traffickers and money launderers, would make it hard for them to keep the DEA's secrets.

"That was why we could not compete with these people," says Guillen.

Juan Ospina was plenty hot about how long it was taking, as Serrano told Featherly and Cesar when they met for dinner and drinks at the Sheraton Grande in Los Angeles in September. In addition to the normal slowness, one of the wire transfers had been sent out of New York with the wrong account number—a zero was missing—further delaying the transfer.

Featherly told Serrano that even if the account number had been slightly off, the Panamanian bank had enough correct information about the money and the names of the account to process the transfer. The banks were just manipulating the situation to make more money off the float, he said, trying to deflect Serrano's anger.

Serrano said he had smoothed things over for now with Ospina, telling him that it might be slow, but the Atlanta laundry was reliable, the money always got where it was supposed to . . . eventually. Nonetheless, Serrano urged Featherly to speed things up. The customers would not tolerate these delays, Serrano told him. Ospina had lots more money he could send their way, but only if they improved service.

The following month in Medellín, Ospina wanted to meet with Serrano and Ramón. So on a weekday in late October, the pair got a ride from their friend Nicolás Ramírez to the modern, high-rise office building north of downtown where Ospina had told them to come. When they arrived, they told Ramírez to wait downstairs in his car; they didn't expect to be long.

It was after working hours and before dinnertime when they rode the elevator up to the designated suite, a small collection of offices with modern paintings and tasteful decor. The receptionist and other workers were gone for the day. They were greeted by Ospina and someone they had never met before: a handsome, dark-haired man in his mid-thirties with a broad, athletic build. He was Eduardo Martínez, and this was his office.

Ramón and Serrano had heard of Martínez, a black market money exchanger whom the top traffickers in the Medellín cartel reputedly hired to move dirty money and to transform U.S. dollars to Colombian pesos. Black market money exchanges were big business in Colombia, where the government imposed strict limits on the amount of foreign currency its citizens could hold. Though illegal, these money exchanges were allowed to operate in Colombia without interference from law enforcers.

Martínez in turn had heard of Ramón and Serrano, as well as their friend in Atlanta, Jimmy Brown. He wanted to know whether Brown's organization could handle money for him.

Yes, Serrano said, he thought they could work together. Serrano knew enough about Martínez to believe he could send a lot of work their way. The more gifted negotiator of the pair, Serrano did most of the talking: the commission . . . the logistics. They began working things out.

Martínez said he wanted to send money through this laundry, but he was worried about how long it would take. Ospina had told him how slowly the Atlanta group worked, and he knew these things simply did not have to take that long. He knew, Martínez told them, because he was using a group in Los Angeles that moved money from there to Panama in forty-eight hours. Two days, compared to the two weeks that Atlanta was taking. These were not small sums, either, Martínez added. Within the past month alone, this group in Los Angeles had moved $12 million for him.

This was a lot of money, representing a lot of cocaine. Only the world's biggest traffickers would have that much cocaine to sell. Twelve million dollars a month. At the wholesale U.S. price of $14,000 a kilogram, that would be nearly 860 kilos, or 1,885 pounds. Close to a ton.

It seemed incredible that anybody could handle $12 million in cash in a month's time, and take only forty-eight hours between pickup in L.A. and delivery in Panama.

Perhaps sensing disbelief, Martínez pulled out a ledger and showed it to Ramón and Serrano. The ledger indicated the L.A. group was picking up money with remarkable frequency and handling impressive sums. Ramón was amazed that one money ring could make that many frequent money pickups.

The group, said Martínez, was called La Mina, Spanish for "The Mine." As in gold mine. It was something for Ramón to remember to tell the boys in Atlanta.

As good as La Mina was, Martínez didn't want it handling all of his business. So he told Serrano and Ramón he'd like to try them out. He gave them the names and account numbers for four accounts at the Banco de Occidente in Panama City. He told them he would need money picked up in Los Angeles and New York. And he told him he was partners with Juan Ospina and his cousin, Ivan Ospina. In fact, Martínez was more than partners with the Ospinas. He was family: Martínez was married to Ivan Ospina's sister.

In a half hour to forty-five minutes, the meeting ended cordially, with the clear sense that they would be doing business soon.

Ramón and Serrano accepted Martínez's offer to drive them where they were going, forgetting that Ramírez was waiting for them downstairs.

The information Ramón took out of his meeting with Martínez thrilled Skip. Martínez was precisely the kind of crook the agents had hoped to bring into the money sting when they set it up. He claimed to handle millions in U.S. drug proceeds a week, and he was based in the right place—Medellín—to do it. Best of all, he had books to prove he wasn't bluffing. As for the CI's credibility, by now Skip trusted Ramón's word, and he instinctively believed Martínez's revelations, too.

Skip showed none of the excitement he was feeling. He knew everything Ramón said would have to be investigated and corroborated. Agents are trained not to tell CIs how important their leads may be. So when Ramón called to tell him about Martínez, the $12 million, La Mina and its ability to wash millions in forty-eight hours, Skip did what he usually did when Ramón called with information.

"I'd say, 'It sounds good . . . What else happened?' "

Nonchalant as he was, Skip recognized Ramón had just turned this meandering, mixed-bag case into a potential blockbuster.

6: Meeting the Men at the Top

Nicolás Ramírez was steaming with anger when he realized Serrano and Ramón had abandoned him in the parking lot of the office building in Medellín. How many ways could they humiliate him in one night? First, they cut him out of the meeting upstairs. Then he had been left to wait for the pair, who had forgotten his very existence. And now his partners had met a key source of dirty cash without any help from him.

Ramírez knew everyone of importance in Medellín. It embarrassed him that his partners had made this connection without him. Well, Eduardo Martínez isn't that important, anyway, he later told Ramón. Martínez is nothing compared to the men I can introduce you to, he said. Ramón and Serrano might be able to meet middlemen like Eduardo Martínez without him. But, by God, he would take Ramón to the men whose money Martínez moved. He would take Ramón to the people who *ran* the cocaine business.

True, nothing he had tried to do with Ramón had gelled yet. But it was time to change that. It was time to visit the compound outside Medellín again where he had taken Ramón months earlier to meet Pablo Escobar's cousin, Gustavo Gaviria, who had been away that day. As the man in charge of Escobar's cocaine distribution in North America, Gaviria could surely send some cocaine through Ramón's Atlanta contacts. When it came to the drug world, Martínez was nothing compared to Gustavo Gaviria.

On Wednesday, October 21, two days after Serrano and Ramón had stood him up, Ramírez came to fetch Ramón at the Hotel Inter-Continental. This was something he was doing for Ramón alone; Serrano knew nothing about it. In fact, he would be angry if he learned Ramírez and Ramón were doing a load without him.

They drove in Ramírez's white Toyota 4Runner out of downtown Medellín and high up into the hills, above even the best neighborhood in Medellín. Up there you could look out and see the city crawling up the mountainside. Soon Ramírez pulled up to the same walled compound they had come to before. As before, the guard at the iron gate recognized Ramírez, opened the gate electronically, and waved them through the 12-foot-high stucco walls topped with barbed wire.

The walls enclosed about five acres of rolling, partially wooded land. A mountain stream tumbled into a lake where ducks glided. Beyond the lake and the stream stood a modest, two-story, Spanish-style home with a veranda around much of it. The whole scene was idyllic—except for the men with pistols in their belts and machine guns in their hands.

Ramírez parked the Toyota in the lot, and the pair walked over a bridge that crossed the moatlike stream. At the house, Ramírez told a man he had come to see Gustavo.

The two were led through what was once a kitchen but now appeared to be a snack bar, then into a large open space that seemingly had served as dining room and living area at one time. It held a pool table, some chairs, a couple of other tables. Aside from a large still-life hanging over a sofa, the only "art" was a series of posters of buxom women in bikinis posing alongside fast cars.

The two set in for the wait. A half hour, forty-five minutes dragged by. Ramírez's nervousness was visible in the constant shaking of his foot, which had a way of relaxing Ramón. Other people's fear tended to calm him because it made him feel more in control. So Ramón, who had considerably more to fear than Ramírez, calmly memorized everything about the place so he could describe it and draw it later for the boys in Atlanta. About a dozen armed men milled about, some carrying walkie-talkies.

Then Ramón, looking through a window, saw five or six cars drive up to the house and park. Out of a green Renault emerged Gustavo Gaviria and his cousin, Pablo Escobar, the man himself. Escobar, Gaviria, and the men with them walked onto the porch and into the house.

For Ramón, this was serious business. An informant for the DEA, here he was in one of the inner sanctums of the world drug trade, waiting to discuss cocaine smuggling with a top trafficker so he could inform on these very dangerous men and help get them indicted for their crimes. Still, Ramón says he felt no fear.

Finally, about fifteen minutes later, an hour after they had arrived, they were told to go upstairs. Gaviria would be with them soon.

The pair climbed the steps in the middle of the house. On the second floor at the head of the staircase stood a large, hexagonal conference table surrounded by chairs. On each side, an office ran the length of the house. They were led into the office belonging to Gaviria.

In walked a short, overweight man with wavy hair whom Ramón recognized immediately. It was Jorge Ochoa, reputedly the second most important man in the world cocaine trade.

Ramón had met Ochoa twice before. He had stayed overnight at Ochoa's hacienda, had even been questioned by him about a load of cocaine that had gotten wet while in Ramón's care. In fact, Ramón's ability to get to Ochoa had been the chief reason prosecutor Buddy Parker and the DEA had been so eager to flip him. That was why they had agreed to the unusual meeting in Aruba in the first place. But at this moment, Buddy Parker, now Ramón's protector, was thousands of miles away.

A smiling Ochoa walked up to Ramírez and shook his hand, saying he had spotted him across the hall. Ramírez greeted Ochoa warmly, if nervously.

Nodding to his associate, Ramírez said to Ochoa, This is Ramón. You might remember him from business dealings you had with him.

Ochoa offered his hand and looked into Ramón's eyes.

I don't remember you, he said.

He doesn't remember you, an edgy Ramírez repeated. It was at this point that Ramón, too, started getting nervous. Ochoa would be angry if he sensed that Ramón was not the man Ramírez thought him to be. And Jorge Ochoa was not someone Ramón wanted to anger.

Ramón searched his brain for references, people who would assure Ochoa that he could be trusted as a cocaine trafficker. He sped through the possibilities, eliminating one because he was angry at Ramón, another because he was too minor a figure, a third because he was dead. He just had not come prepared for this, he thought, as he kept trying to think of someone to vouch for him.

Hardly a second had passed when Ramón abandoned the exercise. Instead of offering a name, he tried to refresh Ochoa's memory of their previous meetings.

I had long hair and a beard at the time, he told Ochoa. That was years ago. I arranged the transportation and distribution of two loads of merchandise, he said.

Ochoa was still holding his hand, still staring into his eyes.

I still don't remember you, he said.

Ramírez repeated, He doesn't remember you, as if Ramón hadn't heard. Maybe Ramírez figured Ramón had lied about having done business with Ochoa.

Finally, Ochoa let go of his grasp and his stare. He said he would talk to them later, and then he walked out.

It was impossible to know whether they were in danger, but both men were shaken by the experience.

Minutes later, Gaviria came into the office, a thin man of thirty-three. The pair waiting for him was ready to get down to business and to get out of there.

Ramírez introduced Ramón, who laid out the proposal: Ramón and Ramírez would provide the air route and the plane, and their contacts in Atlanta would provide a secure airstrip in North Georgia. The Atlanta guys would meet the cocaine there and deliver it as far away as Miami or New York, but would charge more for delivery beyond. For those services, the basic price would be $2,800 per kilogram, up to 700 kilograms, Ramón told him. They discussed the details of the plan. And then Gaviria asked Ramírez about Ramón.

How long have you known him?

Ramírez had only met Ramón a few months earlier.

Gaviria turned to Ramón. Who's your Colombian partner? He wanted to know who could vouch for him.

Ramón paused a half a beat and then said, Francisco Serrano.

You come back with Francisco Serrano and we'll sit down and talk, Gaviria said. Come back tomorrow.

In twenty minutes, the meeting was over. They all shook hands, and Ramón and Ramírez left Gaviria in his office.

Outside, at the head of the staircase, the large table that had been empty before was now surrounded by six men, two of whom Ramón recognized. One was Ochoa, and one was Pablo Escobar.

Ochoa told Ramón once again that he did not remember him.

The deals were in 1982 and 1983, Ramón told him. They were overseen by Jesús Gómez, or "Chuco," he said, finally coming up with someone who knew Ochoa.

Ochoa said he'd ask Chuco about Ramón. And then he introduced him and Ramírez to the men around the table, including Escobar. After the formalities, Ramón and Ramírez walked down the stairs, out of the house, and into the Toyota.

Now Ramón knew he was in trouble. Serrano would be so angry he might never forgive him; he had made it very clear to Ramón that he did not want to involve himself with the highest levels of the drug trade. It was too dangerous, and it was unnecessary. Almost as bad was the fact that Ramón was doing business with Ramírez on the side. They had been planning a load without Serrano, and now they had to tell him. It was either that or never go back to Gaviria. But to stand up Gaviria would be to earn the distrust and risk the wrath of some of the most violent and unforgiving men in the world.

On the way back into town, Ramón and Ramírez settled on a story to tell Serrano. They would say Ramón had never intended for any of this to happen. Ramírez had simply run into Ramón in the lobby of the Inter-Continental and taken him for a ride, without saying where they were going or why. Ramón was surprised to end up at the Gaviria-Escobar compound and had done the best he could under the circumstances. Yeah, that might work. Ramón promised to call Serrano after dinner. Ramírez dropped him off at the hotel.

Ramón did not want to call Serrano. He had dinner and took a walk. He walked through Medellín's northern edge, all the way downtown. He turned around and walked back. In his room, he was still putting it off, wondering what to do, when the phone rang. It was Ramírez.

I haven't called Serrano yet, Ramón admitted.

I'm right here at his house now, Ramírez said. He knows.

Serrano got on the phone. This is not good, he said.

Ramón told him the story he and Ramírez had concocted. I didn't even know where I was going, Ramón said. But now, we're committed.

It's stupid to go up there, Serrano replied. Those people are dangerous. Not only that, there are spies up there. The DEA has people up there.

"He just ranted," Ramón recalls.

"I said, 'Frank, we have to go up. We have to do what we'd said we'd do and go up.' "

Serrano didn't want to go, and he certainly didn't want to negotiate any cocaine loads directly with those people. These are dangerous men who could have them all killed, he told Ramón.

Ramón said they didn't have to actually consummate a deal; they were free to reject anything Gaviria offered. But they had to act serious about negotiating one.

"We gotta go," he says he told Serrano.

Serrano was very angry and very nervous, but he agreed to meet Ramón the next morning at the Inter-Continental. Over breakfast at the poolside restaurant, Ramón tried to reassure Serrano on several fronts. No, he and Ramírez were not cutting Serrano out of cocaine loads; no, this whole event would not interfere with their money laundering; and, lastly, if Serrano didn't want to cut a deal after seeing Gaviria, Ramón would tell Ramírez that he and Serrano had decided it was not in their interest to pursue the matter, and that would be that. On the other hand, if Serrano wanted to do a load with these guys, he would get a cut of the commission, Ramón said.

Serrano insisted the whole thing was stupid. These people are hot, he told Ramón. They are dangerous. We don't need them to make money.

Ramón pleaded with him: If you won't do this for me, do it for our friend, Nicki Ramírez. Ramírez had been cut out of lots of deals that Serrano and Ramón were working, and Serrano knew how much Ramírez hated to be left out.

Finally Serrano agreed, and Ramírez picked them both up at the Inter-Continental. On the way up through the mountains, Ramón explained the details of the proposal to Serrano, who was still very nervous. Within ten minutes, they had arrived at the compound and the guard was waving them through the tall, thick walls.

Again, they were told to wait downstairs. Only this time, Ramón had two nervous Colombians on his hands as he tried to concentrate on the details of the compound. After forty guards, he lost count. But still, he was thinking that the place wasn't all that secure. It wouldn't be too hard to storm it.

The men were offered drinks, and Serrano was brought a very cold soda.

Again, they waited about forty-five minutes. Then, a man posted by a telephone at the stairway called to Ramírez that they could go up. They went into Gaviria's office, where he was waiting for them.

The men shook hands, and the three visitors took seats facing Gaviria, who sat behind a desk. As Ramón was about to begin, Gaviria stopped him. He said he wanted someone else to hear the proposal and left the room. Moments later, Gaviria came back with his cousin, Pablo Escobar.

Escobar shook their hands and sat down in a chair near Gaviria's desk, facing the visitors.

Ramón detailed the proposal, laying out what he and his people in Atlanta could do. Gaviria kept asking why they couldn't do things differently: Why was the price so high, he wanted to know. Couldn't they take a smaller load for a smaller charge?

Ramón hesitated before answering, trying to decide whether the agents in Atlanta would go along with Gaviria's suggestions. He had to consider DEA rules as he knew them, and he had to consider whether Gaviria's suggestions would take the profit out of the venture and make it look like a phony operation. Skip had worked out all the numbers; could Ramón deviate from them? It was a lot to consider as he tried to answer Gaviria. He could tell he was pausing too long, too often. He was aware that his performance was having an unsettling effect, but somehow he couldn't answer any faster, and his explanations were not getting any clearer. Things seemed to be falling apart.

Excuse me, Don Pablo, piped up Serrano, who was facing Escobar.

With that, Serrano started explaining the arrangements with amazing clarity, according to Ramón. For someone who didn't want to be there, who feared for his life, Serrano was remarkably calm as he answered all of their questions. Serrano the lawyer, the skilled talker and experienced negotiator, had taken over. A born dealmaker, Serrano just couldn't let this one go.

Ramón sat back and said to himself, Thank you, Francisco Serrano.

Serrano now says that Ramón did most of the talking. Serrano insists he merely vouched for Ramón's trustworthiness.

But in the account Ramón gives, the version now part of the court record, Serrano explained the package deal to Escobar and to Gaviria. He told them Ramón and his partners would charge $2,800 per kilogram up to 700 kilograms. The price would cover the plane, the pilots, the secure landing site in North Georgia, and distribution as far as New York or Miami.

Maybe it would be better, said Escobar, to use a plane registered in Colombia. The American pilots could come to Colombia, pick up the plane loaded with cocaine, and fly it to the site in Georgia. That way they wouldn't have to fly their U.S. plane to Colombia to pick up the merchandise, they could simply fly commercially.

No, that would not do, Serrano replied. If the American pilots used a Colombian plane, they would have to return it to Colombia. It made more sense to use a U.S. plane, Serrano insisted.

What is your minimum load? Escobar asked.

Three hundred and fifty kilograms, said Serrano.

Escobar and Gaviria wanted to see the route. They pulled out a map of the southeastern United States and laid it on Gaviria's desk. Now, where is this airstrip? Escobar asked Ramón.

The primary landing spot is here, said Ramón, pointing to the Franklin County airport in the mountains of North Georgia, the foothills of the Smokies. As backup, he indicated another North Georgia site, then one in South Georgia and one in East Tennessee. All were available through his contact in Atlanta, who could ensure security at each of them, Ramón explained.

Serrano added that he had seen the primary landing site—the one Skip had shown him back in February—and it looked good to him.

Escobar turned to Ramón. Who is your American partner? he asked.

Allen Weston, Ramón answered, thinking to himself, Skip, I hope your alias is clean in Medellín. My life depends on it.

Escobar showed no reaction to the name. He wanted details of the route from Colombia to North Georgia.

Ramón told him the plane would fly over the Gulf of Mexico through the oil rigs of Louisiana to avoid radar detection. If refueling was necessary, the pilots would stop in Belize or Costa Rica.

Escobar put the map away. He was done with the questions.

We can send a lot of merchandise, he told them. But he wanted to start slowly. He wanted to send only 300 kilograms.

Serrano explained that Weston's transportation costs were fixed at $750,000, whether Escobar sent 1 kilogram or 700. He and Ramón could not pay Weston's fee and clear a reasonable profit for themselves if only 300 kilograms went through.

Escobar made a counter offer. What if he provided the plane and paid Ramón $300,000 for the pilots, the airstrip, and the distribution?

No, that is not acceptable, said Serrano. Weston's package included a plane, and they had to transport at least 350 kilograms to make a profit. But if this deal didn't work, they could talk later about others, everyone agreed.

Escobar and Gaviria stood to leave, and Gaviria asked Ramírez to come with them. After a few minutes, Ramírez returned and reported that Escobar and Gaviria had nixed the deal because they believed the charge was too high.

That this package was rejected didn't mean they couldn't come back with another in a few months. And even though he'd rather walk away from that place and never return, Ramón knew he'd come back if the boys in Atlanta really wanted him to. If anything would keep him out of prison, surely it was risking his life to make a case against the biggest cocaine trafficker in the world.

All the way back to town, Serrano was saying, This is terrible. This was stupid.

Look, Ramón said to him, I know you don't want to do a deal with those guys. If you don't want to, you don't have to. You get first refusal. But be fair to Nicki Ramírez.

If Nicki can put something together, I'd like to do it, Ramón told him. You can refuse, but let Nicki and me go ahead if we want to.

Ramírez wasn't so eager, either, but Ramón figured he might be willing to go back to the compound in a few months.

Ramírez dropped them off at the Inter-Continental, where Ramón again tried to reassure Serrano he was with him 100 percent. He wasn't trying to cut Serrano out of anything or force him into anything, either. Dealing with Serrano was tricky at times, because he was so quick to anger, easy to hurt and hard to soothe.

Finally, Serrano went home. It was time to notify Ramón's chief partner.

He hopped in his car and traveled to a place south of town where the national telephone company had public booths for people with no phones. Here, he could call Atlanta without fear of being heard.

Ramón had come here so often that the round woman behind the counter greeted him by name. Don Ramón, she said. Atlanta again?

He gave her the number and waited for her to make the connection. Soon she called out his name and directed him to the booth where his call was ringing.

The conversation started as usual, with his managing agent, Skip Latson, saying, How'd it go today?

Okay, Ramón answered.

Got anything for me? Skip asked. He knew the answer. Ramón never called without news.

Are you standing up or sitting down? Ramón asked.

Aw gee, Skip said. Ramón liked these games, but they irritated Skip. I'm sitting down, he said.

You want the good news first, or the bad news? Ramón asked.

Why do you always do this to me? The good news.

Well, Skip, said Ramón, I'm still alive but the bad news is . . . and then he told him about meeting Pablo Escobar, Jorge Ochoa, and Gustavo Gaviria. Ramón spoke cryptically, using a code he and Skip had worked out but which neither of them remembered exactly. Skip kept asking questions to be sure he understood this rather astounding development. He did.

That sounds like good news, said the agent.

It could be bad news for me, the informant replied.

Risky as his work had been, Ramón's life now clearly depended on keeping his cover intact.

7: Revelations

Skip flew Ramón up to Atlanta for a full debriefing. Ramón poured out everything he could remember: the height of the walls, the number of armed men, the layout of the grounds, the house, the offices. He sketched drawings, he recounted conversations, he described the men he'd met. He brought a map of Medellín and showed the agents where he'd been.

Skip wrote it all out in a report that Atlanta boss Ron Caffrey believed was too sensitive for general distribution within DEA. Caffrey knew he had a potentially huge case on his hands. When it came to protecting the people under his watch, Caffrey was an "old lady kind of guy," as he describes himself. He cared that his agents took no unnecessary risks, and he worried about his confidential informants, too. Especially this one.

Caffrey knew that only one U.S. government informant had penetrated that far into the Medellín cartel while working for the government, and he was dead as a result. Flamboyant, Louisiana-born Barry Seal, longtime pilot for the Ochoas turned DEA informant, was killed by a hitman for the cartel in February 1986—twenty-one months before Ramón traveled up the hills beyond Medellín to meet Jorge Ochoa and Pablo Escobar.

Caffrey was especially familiar with Seal's story because, as chief of DEA's cocaine desk at the time, he had monitored Seal's undercover work and briefed high-level administration officials. Caffrey knew Seal had been plotting to lure Escobar and Ochoa into Mexico to be arrested when Seal's cover was blown—apparently by officials outside the DEA.

Caffrey figured Ramón would be rendered useless—not to mention endangered—if too many people knew what he was doing. So, while he would brief the head of DEA, Administrator Jack Lawn, on Ramón's trip to the compound, he would not allow the report to travel in the usual broad circles within DEA.

Caffrey called in Buddy Parker to talk about the legalities of keeping the report that secret. Buddy, who had already been told about Ramón's chat with Escobar, was in a state of disbelief that his CI should be involved in a case of this magnitude. But if Buddy doubted it, Caffrey was there to confirm it.

Ramón noted the excitement his trip to the compound had generated among the agents in Atlanta. It made him rather uneasy. He told them if they thought it was so much fun, why didn't they come along next time?

Featherly says he wanted to do just that. True, Ramón had talked only about cocaine with these guys, but maybe next time he could offer laundry service, too, and maybe offer to introduce his new associates in Medellín to Jimmy Brown. But boss Caffrey refused even to consider the idea. It was too dangerous to send a DEA agent into the heavily guarded house without surveillance, and it was too dangerous to send surveillance. Forget it, Caffrey said.

Still, the agents wanted to confirm Ramón's story. They believed him; but without corroboration, it was simply the unsubstantiated word of a former drug trafficker trying to stay out of prison. Skip suggested Ramón go back into the house with a microphone hidden in an arm cast and pretend he had broken his arm. No way, Ramón insisted. The cast would draw attention and suspicion. Skip trusted Ramón's judgment would keep him from doing anything stupid. He knew Ramón was willing to take risks, so he never pushed the informant to do anything Ramón considered too dangerous.

With or without a microphone, now that Ramón had the ability to go into the house above Medellín and talk with Escobar and Ochoa, he might be able to bring them into a scheme that would lure one or both of them out of Colombia—where arrest and extradition were virtually impossible—to a place where they could be nabbed. Over the next few months, the agents, Ramón, and Buddy would think up all sorts of scenarios to try to lure the kingpins out of Colombia.

For Buddy, this probe was drawing him way beyond his traditional duties as an assistant U.S. attorney. Now he was not simply wrestling with mundane questions like what's admissible in court and what charge fits the evidence. Now he was plotting to use a government spy to snare two of the world's most wanted and most dangerous men.

He says, "It's like when you get so close to history that the history is just the people," and, strangely enough, some of them were people he knew. "When you get close to it, you—you're taken aback by it."

At last, the slow, frustrating work of the previous months was paying off. By early November 1987, the case was leaping ahead on all fronts. Ramón had gained access to the top drug lords; Skip was talking to a Colombian about helping him ship 16,000 pounds of marijuana to the Georgia coast; and Jimmy Brown's new customer, Eduardo Martínez, was promising to send $1 million a month through the Atlanta laundry. Ever since the Pisces takedown in May, the money business had been sporadic at best. But now, Serrano was so certain of Martínez's business that he suggested to his American partners that they open some sort of business—a florist shop, anything—with a private, rear parking entrance, a back room for money counting, and, perhaps, an underground safe.

As Serrano and his partners at DEA readied for a surge in business, an event in Colombia stirred the Atlanta investigation even further. In an ostensibly routine traffic stop one late November Saturday outside Cali, two policemen arrested Jorge Ochoa. He tried to bribe them, and they took him in.

The United States wanted Ochoa for prosecution on a variety of drug, racketeering, and murder charges. The chance for extradition was slim, because the drug barons had terrorized and corrupted officials into lifting the extradition treaty with the United States. Still, the mere possibility sent U.S. Justice and State Department officials scrambling for the most incriminating information they could get to persuade Colombian authorities to send Ochoa to the United States for prosecution.

While Buddy Parker was pulling together information on Ochoa to relay to Washington, Serrano was in Los Angeles getting money to feed into Jimmy Brown's laundry. It was the Monday after Thanksgiving and two days after Ochoa's arrest that Serrano handed over to undercover agents what would be the first of many loads of Martínez's dirty money: $145,800. Two days later, another $597,000 came through. A week after that, Serrano had a third load—$116,600—to wash. It would go on like that for weeks.

But even with this big new customer, Serrano was not a happy man.

Jimmy Brown's laundry was just too slow, Serrano complained to John Featherly and Cesar Diaz when they met at a hotel bar in L.A. in early December. Brown's people in L.A. were not calling Serrano back quickly enough after he paged them for the pickup. Some days they refused to pick up money at all. And after they got the cash, it took forever to get it to Panama. Not only that, but the last load was short $5,000 by the time it got to Panama.

They simply had to learn how to handle this money better, Serrano stressed. The trickle of money was a stream now, and they had every reason to expect the flow to get heavier and steadier, but only if they removed the impediments by improving service.

Featherly told Serrano that things should work more smoothly now because one of the pickup guys Serrano trusted—"Rolando"—would be back on the job after some months' absence. As a Glendale police officer working with DEA, Orlando Lopez had acted as one of Jimmy Brown's West Coast staff at the beginning of the case. When Cesar in Atlanta got word that Serrano was ready to send money through the laundry, Cesar would call "Rolando" Lopez in California to collect the cash and set up surveillance. But Lopez had left his job as a cop to become an agent with the California Bureau of Narcotic Enforcement (BNE). Now that Lopez was finished training for his new job, he was again available to work with DEA. Serrano had missed him. When he had asked about his whereabouts, Cesar explained that Rolando and Jimmy Brown had had a falling out. Now, it seemed, they had resolved their differences.

The news pleased Serrano. He told Featherly and Cesar that if they could make their business more efficient, the timing was perfect for the laundry to take off. Martínez was capable of sending them $1 to $2 million a week, and he would need them more now than ever because of the Christmas season.

Their biggest competitor, Serrano told them, was La Mina. And like many Latin businesses, La Mina was shutting down for a month, beginning December 15. Already they had stolen some of La Mina's business by nabbing Martínez as a customer. Now, if they worked through the holidays, they could score really big. And if they could become more efficient, Serrano told them, they could keep some of Martínez's business after the holidays, too.

They were on the verge of something big. Why, just recently he and Ramón and Nicolás Ramírez had met with Pablo Escobar and Gustavo Gaviria. Serrano didn't say he had been dragged into this meeting. Serrano recounted the story to impress his American business partners with his contacts in Medellín. But in so doing he was corroborating Ramón's story, unwittingly making it all the more useful to the DEA.

They talked about Ochoa's arrest, and then Featherly jumped into the opening Serrano's boasting had created.

Who handles the money for Escobar and Ochoa? he asked. Serrano told him that those two got part of all profits from Colombia's cocaine.

Featherly asked, Do you mean that they get a percentage of the money we handle for Ospina, Martínez, and Parra?

Yes, they get a cut of all of the money, Serrano said, giving the agents more evidence that the Atlanta laundry had been cleaning the drug lords' money all along.

I'd like to handle all of Escobar's and Ochoa's money for just one year, said Featherly. Not a little bit of it, all of it. After one year of doing that, Featherly said, they could all retire as very wealthy men.

Featherly told Serrano he knew Ochoa was in jail and not available at the moment, but he'd like to meet Pablo Escobar and explain how he could launder his money.

Serrano smiled. He said he and Ramón would be meeting again with Escobar in January and could tell Escobar about Jimmy Brown's laundry. This was apparently more bragging on Serrano's part. Ramón says they had no plans to go back, and certainly, Serrano had no desire to.

Serrano was using Featherly's interest in Escobar to underscore his main point: the need to speed up the laundry. If Brown wanted to launder money directly for Escobar and Ochoa, then he needed to become more efficient, Serrano told him. And if he wanted Serrano to talk up his laundry with these important men, then he needed to go into that meeting with a reputation as a good, fast money mover.

No matter what Serrano said, no matter how much the Atlanta agents tried to speed up the money washing, service barely improved. Still, the money kept coming. Every few days for the last six weeks of 1987, Serrano and undercover cops and DEA agents in L.A. would pick up money for Martínez and Juan Ospina in sums as small as $100,000 and as large as $1 million. Fifteen times during those six weeks, Jimmy Brown's people picked up bundles of cash, photographed them, wrote reports about them, and sent them through the DEA's multiple wash cycles to accounts at Banco de Occidente in Panama. Martínez constantly complained about how long it took, but he kept sending money. During those six weeks, the DEA laundry washed nearly $4.7 million for Martínez and his clients, some of the biggest drug lords in the world.

Serrano loved getting all that money. During an especially large delivery, while his favorite pickup man—California agent Orlando Lopez—was counting out $974,000, Serrano boasted that he had personally met three of the world's wealthiest men.

Yes, these men—customers of his—were even listed in *Forbes* magazine as among the world's richest, Serrano told Lopez. Serrano didn't name them, but *Forbes* had just come out with its annual survey of billionaires, listing Escobar, Ochoa, and José Gonzálo Rodríguez Gacha, among others.

Serrano kept bragging as the counting machine whirred through nearly $1 million in a room in a Holiday Inn. He told Lopez that with the volume of money he expected to handle, he could retire in a year and live comfortably for the rest of his life.

Though outwardly cheerful, agent Orlando Lopez was not as happy as Serrano. These sums coming through DEA were incredibly large. And the more drug dollars cops wash, the greater service they are giving the criminals. The whole point of the exercise was not to please the customer, after all. As Lopez put it, "Our goal was to identify the source of the money and put those people in jail." To do that, the L.A. agents and cops were watching everyone involved in each of these transactions. And whenever they figured they could knock off a sizable sum without making the laundry look suspicious, they did.

Lopez wanted to stop dope distributors and money movers operating within U.S. borders. He cared little about working up yet another indictment of the faraway Colombian kingpins.

But in Atlanta, Buddy Parker wanted all of it—and so did the DEA agents working the case. They wanted not just to make a case but to make history. Featherly's initial qualms about washing money for traffickers were soothed by the money seizures. But by this time, he says, "the people who brought the money were of no interest to me. I wanted to meet the men at the top for evidence against them—indictment. Maybe we could get an arrest."

Of course, at the time, there was already an arrest. In the United States, federal officials were preparing for the possibility, however unlikely, of Jorge Ochoa's extradition. What evidence did the various prosecutors around the country have against him? Could that information be used to persuade the Colombian government to extradict him?

High-level Justice Department officials wanted to hash out all of that with the prosecutors and drug agents with evidence against Ochoa, including those in Atlanta. And because of its location and its easy air access, Atlanta was picked as the place for this meeting.

For Buddy, the meeting confirmed his ascension up the ladder of drug prosecutors. He found himself at a conference table with the nation's top drug agents and prosecutors—men and women who had transformed drug cases into vehicles for uncovering and shutting down whole networks of international criminals.

The Pisces prosecutors and agents from Los Angeles were there. From Miami came Assistant U.S. Attorneys Dick Gregorie and Mark Schnapp, two of the architects of the most comprehensive indictment ever brought against the cartel leaders, the 1986 indictment that first identified and defined the Medellín cartel and its breadth. By depicting drug trafficking as international organized crime, "Dick Gregorie, more than anyone else in the country, changed the way drug prosecutions were going," says Schnapp, his co-counsel in the cartel indictment.

As impressive as the cartel indictment had been to Buddy, he learned while socializing with Gregorie and Schnapp outside the meeting that they were working on an even more remarkable case. They were preparing to ask a federal grand jury in Miami to indict a foreign leader for conspiring to traffic cocaine—Panamanian dictator Manuel Noriega. Yes, Buddy Parker from Ozark, Alabama, was in rarefied company, indeed.

In all, about twenty DEA agents, assistant U.S. attorneys, and Justice Department officials were gathering in the conference room in the Southeastern Drug Task Force where Buddy and his boss, Craig Gillen, worked. This was the Atlanta group's chance to lay out Ramón's evidence to see what the experts thought. Buddy figured it was good stuff, of course, but he worried that if it was too valuable, he would lose control over the case to the Justice Department in Washington.

With that many egos and that many important prosecutions represented in the room, there were other undercurrents, too. Gregorie and Schnapp, for example, wondered uneasily why anyone would doubt their right to have dibs on Ochoa. "We were thinking we would really be surprised if [Ochoa went to a] jursidiction other than Florida, because we had the most comprehensive case," says Schnapp. They feared this meeting could be an attempt to take the Ochoa prosecution away from them.

The focus of their uneasiness was Charles "Chuck" Saphos of Justice, who had organized the meeting and who headed the Narcotic and Dangerous Drug Section of the Criminal Division, overseeing major drug prosecutions. Before landing the job in Washington, Saphos, a lanky man with piercing blue eyes and rugged good looks, had worked as a special drug prosecutor in Miami. Ever since he left Miami for main Justice in Washington, "Dick [Gregorie] was always concerned that Saphos would try to screw us," says Schnapp.

"It's unfortunate if Miami had that feeling, because it's not true," responds Saphos. If anything, Saphos's stint in Miami had predisposed him to favor South Florida, he says.

The gathering point for this high-powered group was a long table in a windowless conference room buried deep within a warren of generic government offices and hallways.

Saphos and others from main Justice talked of Ochoa's arrest and the chances for extradition, which were slight. Still, the United States was preparing an extradition request, which should include the heaviesthitting evidence the U.S. government could bring together. Justice wanted to know what each of them had.

Atlanta was first up. Featherly gave the group an overview of the case, beginning with the original two cocaine loads that had brought in the confidential informant, and ending with the possibility of the CI and Serrano meeting again with Escobar and Gaviria.

The evidence Atlanta had against Ochoa was this: for starters, the CI had named Ochoa as the owner of much of the cocaine the CI had helped bring to the United States in 1982 and 1983; secondly, the CI had met with Jorge Ochoa, Pablo Escobar, and Gustavo Gaviria just six weeks earlier while trying to arrange a drug load; and lastly, in an undercover meeting in Los Angeles eight days ago, Featherly said, the CI's partner, Francisco Serrano, had confirmed that part of the $4 million in drug proceeds the Atlanta laundry had washed to date belonged to Ochoa and Escobar. It wasn't much compared to the case Miami had built. But it had gotten Atlanta into the discussion.

Miami's case against Ochoa was far more sweeping. The indictment said he was one of the leaders in the largest cocaine-smuggling operation in the world, the Medellín cartel. It linked Ochoa and the other cartel members to the production of 58 tons of cocaine between 1978 and 1985, and it said the cartel used murder and bribery to protect its business. Miami's star witness would be a high-level, Miami-based cartel member who had been arrested in the United States two years earlier, Max Mermelstein.

Miami's case was quite impressive. And unlike the Atlanta case, Miami already had an indictment and witnesses available to testify.

But as Saphos pointed out, Atlanta's information was a lot more recent. It could be used as part of the continuum, to show that Ochoa was still involved in drug trafficking, Saphos suggested. What about using the Atlanta information—along with the Miami evidence—in the extradition petition? he asked.

"I went berserk," says Buddy. Disclosing in Colombia that the U.S. government knew about the meeting Ramón and Serrano had had with Escobar and Gaviria would identify Ramón as an informant and would kill the case or the CI. The government wasn't ready yet to move Ramón to the States for protection, Buddy said. And even if he could do that, it would mean the end of the investigations Ramón was doing.

Atlanta didn't even have an indictment against Ochoa, Buddy pointed out. No, Buddy vehemently insisted that the CI was too important for Saphos to surface for the slim chance that doing so would persuade Colombia to extradite Ochoa. No other government operative had access to the cocaine bosses. And the CI also was working a very important money-laundering case, Buddy added.

This was the opening to disclose Ramón's amazing find: La Mina. Skip and Featherly told the group Ramón had met a major money launderer

for the Medellín cartel, who had described an L.A.-based money laundry that was washing $12 million a month in drug funds. The CI, who had met with Martínez again, had seen ledgers that showed $47 million going through La Mina in four months.

From the Los Angeles delegation—the Pisces experts—came skepticism. A laundry moving $12 million a month would be so big that surely the government would already know about it. Either Martínez was blowing smoke, or the CI was, the L.A. group said.

No, the money launderer had shown the CI ledgers, the Atlanta agents said. Besides, Serrano had confirmed La Mina's existence in conversations with undercover drug agents. In fact, Serrano had called La Mina the single largest drug money-laundering operation in the United States.

By this time, the Atlanta group was certain of Ramón's veracity. Not only had he passed the polygraph in the earlier incident, but everything he said that could be corroborated had been—often through Serrano. But around this table sat agents trained to be skeptical of CIs at all times. Among them was Tony Ricevuto, the Group 6 supervisor in Los Angeles and one of the Pisces architects. Ricevuto believed nothing Atlanta's CI said. Polygraph notwithstanding, he believed Ramón had lied about what had happened in the Denny's parking lot and lied about meeting Escobar and Ochoa. "This guy wasn't well heeled [enough] to be talking to all these big people as much as he said he was," says Ricevuto.

The Atlanta delegation sensed condescension from the big-city delegates' suggestions that perhaps the Atlanta guys had been suckered by a skilled CI. Buddy wondered whether the L.A. contingent was trashing Ramón out of jealousy, at least subconsciously. After all, Ramón had shown up the L.A. office by bringing to the United States one of the Pisces targets, Jaime Parra, only to have L.A. agents and cops scare him back to Colombia.

It did seem to Buddy that the prosecutors and agents from the country's drug centers—Miami, Los Angeles, and New York—assumed Atlanta's team was inexperienced in big-league investigations and was too easily impressed with the claims of informants and crooks.

But Buddy was sure of Ramón and believed his information on La Mina. Skip described it further, just as Eduardo Martínez had described it to Ramón: The money laundry imports gold from Uruguay to the United States and overstates its value as a cover. Gold and jewelry stores in L.A. serving as fronts use the documentation from those exaggerated gold sales to cover the movement of large sums of drug profits from L.A. to South America.

The idea of gold imports from Uruguay induced laughter from another side of the room, Buddy remembers. The DEA attaché to Panama, Alfredo "Fred" Duncan, square-jawed and self-confident, said the whole

thing was preposterous. There *are* no gold mines in Uruguay, said Duncan. He knew this because Uruguay had been part of his territory when he was stationed in Argentina. Duncan says he remembers none of this discussion, but Buddy, Skip, and Ricevuto recall Duncan's laughter at the story of La Mina. Your CI is taking you for a ride, they remember him telling the Atlantans.

Nobody seemed particularly impressed with the information from Atlanta. Gregorie, who had heard evidence from the government's top witnesses against the cartel (Mermelstein and Barry Seal) had never heard of Eduardo Martínez. As for the CI's access to Escobar and Ochoa, it would be wonderful to use that for arrest purposes, says Gregorie. But as evidence, it was superfluous.

"If we could put them in a position where we could put our hands on them, great," Gregorie said later. Beyond that, it seemed to him that Atlanta's CI "couldn't do more than what was already done. . . . We already had an indictment."

Not only that, Gregorie was another one who hated the idea of cops laundering money for drug traffickers. He simply did not believe government resources should be used to serve the drug trade. Gregorie says he did not denigrate Atlanta's investigation. He just did not see how he could help the Atlanta agents, or how they could help him. Besides, at that point, he had his hands full with Noriega.

Even if the Atlanta group didn't inspire awe, neither was anyone eager to surface Ramón for the purposes of Ochoa's unlikely extradition. Saphos dropped the idea. Ramón could continue working the case. And while nothing specific was decided, the sentiment at the meeting favored Miami getting Ochoa if extradition worked.

Skip and Featherly say it was all rather interesting and friendly, and they were satisfied with the outcome. "I didn't get any bad vibes from it," says Featherly.

Schnapp says he and others at the meeting left wondering why it had even been called. "It was really a non-event," he says.

But to Buddy it was a big event, because it introduced him to the country's top drug prosecutors, and they had offered their readings of Ramón's findings. Despite their skepticism, he figured Ramón was onto something bigger than these guys had given him credit for.

Besides, the Atlanta group knew firsthand that Martínez had access to incredible sums of drug money. The Atlanta group was washing about $1 million a week for him, and they believed Serrano's assertions that this was money from the sale of cocaine sent over by Escobar and Ochoa. Nobody but the leading drug traffickers could have that much dirty money.

· · ·

*I*n the investigations department of the Wells Fargo Bank in Los Angeles, a woman new to her job as a troubleshooter was having a similar thought: only drugs could produce such large sums of cash.

A banker for twenty-seven years, Drusilla Leightner had been in investigations only a month when a friend of hers, a loan officer in the suburban Monterey Park branch, called her in early January 1988 with an extraordinary complaint.

Several days a week, the loan officer said, men who worked for one of the bank's commercial customers were bringing in suitcases full of cash, dumping the money on the counter, and asking that it be deposited to the company account. This upset the loan officer greatly because it posed a security risk. Moreover, sometimes the money came late in the day, forcing the branch to keep more cash overnight than bank rules allowed. The loan officer wanted to know what she should do about it.

"I said, 'What do you mean by suitcases full? . . . A hundred thousand, two hundred thousand?' " Leightner recalls asking.

"And she says, 'No. About a million a day.'

"And I said, 'What!' "

The loan officer told Leightner the customer was a wholesale gold jewelry business in L.A.'s jewelry district downtown, and all its sales were conducted in cash. The loan officer simply wanted to know from Leightner what to do with all this currency. Ever since the account opened three months earlier, this one customer would regularly bring in all that money, forcing bank personnel to stop everything else to count the cash. The loan officer said she feared having that much money at the branch, located so close to a freeway.

Leightner asked whether the customer ever deposited checks. Her friend, according to Leightner, said, "No, it's all strictly cash. Every day they come in, two or three of them, with suitcases full of money."

Leightner told her no legal business would generate that much cash, and any legal business would have checks or other types of receipts to deposit. The loan officer said she had checked with the branch manager, who assured her it was all legitimate. The manager knew the owners of the company and knew their business to be legal.

"I said no, no. Can't be," Leightner says. She asked for the name and number of the account. The loan officer refused, fearful the branch manager would disapprove. Leightner could find out the hard way, if necessary, she said, and the loan officer could wind up in trouble for withholding the information. Think about it, Leightner said. The next day, the loan officer called back.

Andonian Brothers Incorporated (ABI) was the name of the business. She gave Leightner the account number.

Leightner called up the account's most recent monthly statement on her computer and saw very large sums of money coming in and going out of this gold and jewelry company she had never heard of before. On most days, the account showed hundreds of thousands of dollars in deposits. The computer didn't indicate whether the deposits were in cash, checks, or what, but most of the deposits were in even amounts— no change. Leightner reasoned those had to be cash. She ordered copies of statements for the three months the account had been open. She saw that Andonian Brothers had started out with deposits of a few hundred thousand dollars at a time and had just recently begun making million-dollar drops.

She called her friend and asked for more details on the deposits.

Sometimes they brought other containers, but mostly they brought suitcases and emptied them onto the counter, the loan officer explained. Out would come strapped bundles of currency. Apparently, someone had already counted it.

"I said, 'How did they count this, by hand?' " Leightner says.

No, they have a money-counting machine at the business, said the loan officer. She had been to the business with the branch manager and had discussed it all with the owners.

Leightner pictured employees running stacks of cash through a money counter. "I said, 'Don't you think that's kind of funny?' I mean, this girl was thirty-two, thirty-three, at the time, and I said, 'Don't you think that's kind of funny, having that much cash?' 'Oh no. Not at a place like that,' " her friend replied.

The showroom at Andonian Brothers was full of gold jewelry, the loan officer said. And the owners had invoices showing gold and jewelry sales sufficient to account for the deposits. This was a legitimate business, all right, the loan officer insisted.

Leightner gave up trying to convince her friend, but she knew that a wholesale business sells to other companies, and no business makes large purchases in cash. Business people in Los Angeles do not carry around hundreds of dollars in currency for wholesale jewelry purchases.

And why would anyone drive all the way to Monterey Park from downtown, a distance of ten miles, with $1 million in cash? Why not use the closest bank? Or an armored-car service?

Even though she was so new to her job in investigations that she did not yet have a desk, Leightner was sure the whole thing stank. A tough, hardworking woman in her late forties, Leightner had no more than a high school education. She believed college-educated people often lack the common sense and independent thinking skills necessary in banking. She knew banking well, not only through her own career but through her husband, who worked at another bank. And when she was sure of something, she was certain. In recent years, she has taken to wearing a small gold chain around her neck with a gold charm that reads: "DAMN I'M GOOD."

No, Drusilla Leightner didn't need an MBA from Harvard or years as a bank investigator to tell a legitimate customer from a crooked one. She believed she knew the true business of the Andonian Brothers. "Where else could they get that much money, except from drugs?" she asks.

And Drusilla Leightner hated the business of drugs. So when she learned that millions of dollars in cash were traveling through a small jewelry wholesaler each week, she knew two things: "This is drug money, and I have no use for drug money."

Leightner took the matter to her boss in the security department. She showed him the monthly statements, and she told him what the loan officer had said about the cash deposits. He told Leightner to check with the district office to see what should be done.

The woman in the district office said she was already well aware of the situation. Another bank investigator had already checked out Andonian Brothers and had learned the cash deposits were legitimately earned.

So Leightner went to talk to the investigator, an ex-cop. "I said, 'You cannot tell me that the business is going to be legit and just accept cash.'" But he defended his position, which was based on an interview with the branch manager. So Leightner went back to her boss.

He told her that if she felt that strongly about it, she should get more documentation.

Leightner hunted down copies of deposit slips, and almost all of them showed cash. A few checks turned up, but very few. In all, the documents showed that in the three months that Andonian Brothers had had the Wells Fargo account, $25 million in cash had traveled through it.

When Leightner showed her boss the findings, he agreed it looked fishy. "He said, 'Do whatever you want. Call DEA or the IRS, the FBI, whatever.'

"I said, 'Which one of them do you want me to call?'

"He says, 'Call all three of them and see if any of them want it.'"

The telephone message, as DEA agent Dave Barkett remembers it, gave the name of the Wells Fargo investigator, her bank, her phone number, and the nature of the call: "Re: possible money laundering." The message went to Barkett because it happened to be his week to serve as "duty agent," answering all incoming calls.

Over the phone, Leightner told Barkett what her research had shown. She told him about the suitcases full of bundled money and the $25 million in cash deposits.

Recalls Barkett, "She said something was wrong. It just didn't seem right that these people were walking in the door . . . on a daily basis, dropping anywhere between five hundred thousand to two million in cash a day in suitcases." And all the denominations were fifties or less.

She told him that bank managers had visited the store and were shown invoices showing jewelry and gold sales made in cash. But she believed that was just a cover, and Barkett was inclined to agree. "I certainly felt that a jewelry store couldn't generate that kind of cash," says the agent.

Barkett soon learned from a legitimate businessman with a jewelry store about the size of the Andonians' that the most in cash he would generate was about $9,000 a week—a fraction of the Andonians' deposit.

"We knew right away we had stumbled onto something."

Dave Barkett had never heard of La Mina or Eduardo Martínez or the investigation in Atlanta that had uncovered them. He worked out of a different group—Group 1—from the agents from DEA-L.A. who had heard La Mina described the previous month in the meeting in Atlanta. Some of the members of Group 6, which had been working with Atlanta's Operation Fis-Con, had been told that this money launderer in Medellín was using a highly efficient, L.A.-based laundry that used phony jewelry and gold sales to cover the movement of astounding sums of drug proceeds, generated for the benefit of the Medellín cartel.

They had been told, but they hadn't believed the story.

8: A Million-Dollar Ticket

Eduardo Martínez was sending so much money through the Atlanta DEA laundry in late 1987 and early 1988 that sometimes it came in faster than the agents could count it. Three days before Christmas, for example, an agent was counting cash in a hotel room in Torrance, south of L.A., with one of Serrano's assistants when the assistant was beeped to come get more money. So they crammed the boxes and duffel bags full of cash into the bathtub and drove off to the Orange County suburb of Costa Mesa—more than an hour away—where they met a man with a half million dollars.

By the end of that day they had counted out $1,035,425. All this money was beginning to numb Orlando Lopez, "Rolando." He had been awed by the first pickup in the case, a measly $94,000. Now the sums were simply too mind-boggling to be real. It came in boxes. It came in bags. It came in every kind of container. And it just kept coming. The same thing was happening in New York, though to a lesser degree.

The team in Los Angeles was thirsting for a seizure. Nearly a year had passed since they had brought in any big money in the case, and they didn't want simply to help launder drug funds. Now that the money was flowing through them like a river, they needed to dip in as big a bucket as they could.

There was no need to check with the guys in Atlanta first; Featherly and Skip had told their L.A. counterparts they could move on any money or drugs they wanted so long as they kept the seizures far enough away from the main targets not to spook them and burn the undercover investigation.

The chance seemed to come on January 5, 1988, in the early afternoon. On that day, agent Lopez was sitting in a motel room on the Pacific Coast Highway in Redondo Beach south of the city counting money with another undercover cop posing as his helper, and with Francisco Serrano's assistant, José Britto. Britto, a tall, distinguished-looking, older man, was filling in for Ramón during the holidays so that Serrano could be in Colombia with his family.

The three men had spent the morning picking up money at various locations in suburban Los Angeles. Usually, a courier would meet them at a restaurant and lend them his car, which contained a box or a bag of cash. Britto would drive the car to a mini-warehouse he had rented in Torrance, just east of Redondo Beach, unload the goods, and return the car to the courier.

On this day, Britto and the two undercover agents had picked up cash from four different customers this way. After the fourth, they went to Britto's storage locker, pulled out the bags and boxes he had left there from the three earlier collections, and brought them all to the room Lopez had rented at the Redondo Pier Inn Hotel.

With money counters whirring, they began assessing the morning's haul. One sports bag yielded $400,000. A box that once had held a small kitchen appliance now contained $185,000. Before they could get to the rest, Britto's beeper went off. The same man in Costa Mesa who had brought half a million dollars into the laundry on December 22, Rodrigo Alvarez, had an even bigger load of dirty cash to be picked up. This time, he had a million.

Britto told the money courier he and his partners would meet him at a fast-food place, Carl's Jr., in Costa Mesa, more than an hour away. They would call him when they arrived.

After Britto made those arrangements, Lopez broke free to make a few of his own. This was a perfect opportunity for a seizure. It was a lot of money, and the cops already knew this courier, Rodrigo Alvarez, from the December 22 money delivery. They knew where he lived, too.

Politically, the timing couldn't have been better. DEA Administrator Jack Lawn happened to be visiting Los Angeles that week. "We wanted to knock off a good one in front of him," recalls DEA agent Romero, the top West Coast agent in the case.

Lopez called the lead man on the surveillance team and told him their plans. By the time the trio arrived at the restaurant and Britto had called Alvarez to come over, a surveillance crew was in place outside Alvarez's home in the suburb of Garden Grove, watching him leave his house and drive to the Carl's Jr.

When he arrived, Britto asked him, How much do you have?

"Just over one," came the answer. More than $1 million.

Alvarez said the money was back at his house, so they lent him Lopez's rental car, a black Cadillac, so he could go load up the trunk.

When the courier left the restaurant, Lopez alerted the surveillance team. The cops posted at Alvarez's house watched as he arrived home at ten minutes to five, pulled the Cadillac into his garage, and shut the door. Five minutes later, they saw the garage door open, and they saw Alvarez back the Cadillac out. Although the car looked the same, it was now worth $1 million more than it had been moments before.

The Cadillac headed back toward the Carl's Jr., cops watching. Among them was a uniformed Garden Grove police officer, on hand for the occasion. The drive from Alvarez's home to the restaurant wasn't far, but it didn't take long for Alvarez to give the uniformed cop reason to stop him, according to the resulting police report. Officer John Enriquez said he spotted the Cadillac speeding in the rain-slicked road. He tried to follow the car to stop it, but lost it momentarily in traffic. When he spotted it again, it was traveling within the speed limit. But then the Cadillac changed lanes so abruptly that a small car had to brake suddenly to avoid hitting it. "I therefore stopped the Cadillac to advise him of the lane change and the need for safe driving, especially under these adverse weather conditions," Enriquez's report states. He describes the adverse weather conditions as light rain.

The officer asked the man for his driver's license. Alvarez said he did not have it with him, an arrestable offense. In fact, he had no identification at all.

Whose car is this? the officer wanted to know.

It belongs to a friend, Alvarez said.

The officer asked for the registration and proof of insurance. Alvarez fiddled with the glove compartment, but the key he had wouldn't open it. He gave the key to Officer Enriquez. He couldn't get it open, either.

Enriquez asked for permission to look inside the trunk.

"*Sí*. No problem." the cooperative driver said.

Inside the trunk the Garden Grove officer found two cardboard boxes taped shut. He asked Alvarez whether they were his boxes. Alvarez said they were not. They must belong to his friend, he said.

Officer Enriquez punctured the tape on one of the boxes with the car keys he still held and ripped the box open. It was full of cash. Stacks and stacks of it. He tore open the second box. Again, the carton was nearly overflowing with U.S. currency. A later count would reveal the total: $1,004,955. Just over one.

Alvarez insisted he knew nothing about the money. It wasn't his. He didn't know how it got there. Maybe it belonged to his friend who owned the car.

It didn't matter. The cop seized the money and arrested Alvarez for driving without a license. At the station where he was booked, Alvarez filled out a disclaimer saying the money was not his but belonged to Ramier Restrepo, his imaginary friend.

Back at the Carl's Jr., Britto was starting to worry. His two partners, the undercover agents, acted worried, too.

The trio waited for an hour and a half and finally left in Alvarez's car. Customers were waiting, Britto told Lopez.

Indeed, from the time they left the restaurant at 6:30 P.M. until about 9:00 P.M. that night, the threesome drove to restaurants and shopping centers in the suburbs south of Los Angeles, meeting money couriers, picking up boxes and bags of various sorts (most of them heavy) and taking them back to the hotel room. They resumed the counting they had started earlier in the day, adding it to the evening's receipts.

When the counting was done for the day, the total came to $1,134,187.

As big as the Garden Grove seizure had been, it reduced Britto's intake that one day by less than half.

That the cops in L.A. had taken $1 million from one of Martínez's couriers struck Ramón as very bad news. It seemed so incredibly stupid. Just when the laundry was cranking up, "Group Sick" had given the customers something to worry about, maybe even reason to suspect him and Serrano. It's so hard to build trust with these guys, and so easy to lose it, he thought. At least the cops made it look like a routine traffic stop. Maybe the whole thing could be pinned on the courier's bad driving.

To the agents in Atlanta, the seizure offered a chance to learn more. Skip figured someone was bound to scream ouch after a million-dollar pinch, and he wanted to know who. Martínez had sent the money to the laundry, but it didn't belong to him. It belonged to the traffickers who had hired Martínez to get the drug proceeds to Colombia clean. Who were they?

At 1:00 P.M. on the day after the seizure, with Ramón on another phone patched into his, Skip dialed Francisco Serrano's home number in Medellín. From the DEA office in Atlanta, Skip recorded the conversations that followed.

Francisco wasn't home, his wife told Ramón, but he had called and left a number where Ramón could reach him. Ramón wrote down the number, 32-44-67, thanked her, and hung up.

He dialed that number, and a woman answered.

"May I speak to Francisco Serrano?" Ramón asked in Spanish.

"Just a moment, please," she said.

After a pause, a man came to the phone. "Hello."

"Who is this?" Ramón asked.

"Chucho," said the man, giving a common nickname.

"Chucho, look," said Ramón. "I am looking for Francisco Serrano."

"Who is this?" Chucho asked.

"Ramón."

"Brother, I don't know who Francisco Serrano is, nor do I know who Ramón is."

"Well, I was given this telephone number to reach Francisco Serrano," Ramón said.

Chucho asked him to wait. Ramón could hear him shout Serrano's name.

Finally, Serrano came to the phone.

"How are you, man?" Ramón asked.

"Look, it's just that . . . it's just that," Serrano stuttered. "There's a small problem over there—"

"Listen, where are you?" Ramón asked.

"—Fortunately, it's not with us, right?" Serrano said.

"Where, where, where?" Ramón asked impatiently.

"Look, I . . . talk to Don José," Serrano said, referring to his assistant in Los Angeles, José Britto.

Ramón realized Serrano was not answering his questions. It was as if they were in separate telephone conversations. It was as if someone whom Serrano feared was listening in the same room with him. Serrano was trying to signal Ramón that he could not be candid.

"This is what happened," Serrano said finally. "The kid over there who was going to do the round with us yesterday was in an accident."

"Injured, or what?" Ramón asked.

Serrano laughed. "No. He's already out of the hospital."

"Ah, but the car?" Ramón asked.

"We were very concerned," said Serrano. "We were very concerned for Rolando. . . ." Serrano said he was halting all activity in Los Angeles as a result.

"Was in an accident, huh? Really?" asked Ramón.

"No, no, no, no," said Serrano. "Call me tonight and I'll tell you about it calmly."

Ramón said he had talked to José Britto, who had told him to call Serrano. From the tone of their conversation, "José had me scared," said Ramón. "He had me scared because I thought he was sick." In the code Ramón and Serrano used, "sick" meant arrested.

"No, no, no," said Serrano. "It's one of the kids who was going to do the round with us."

"Oh, okay, fine," said Ramón, finally seeming to understand. "Thank God there's no problem with us, right?"

"No, not with us, no," said Serrano.

"It doesn't have anything to do with—nothing to do with us?" Ramón asked again.

"Nothing."

Serrano asked Ramón about other business. And then he said, "When you call me again, always ask for Rubén, man." That was the name Serrano used in the drug trade—Rubén Márquez. Which was why the man who answered the phone—Chucho—had never heard of Francisco Serrano. Until now.

That night on the phone, Serrano explained to Ramón that he had been at the office of the owner of the money. He did not name him. But Ramón realized that at the moment he called Serrano "he was on trial for his life," Ramón says.

And Skip was beginning to get the answer to his question about whose money it was.

Serrano had been Skip's unwitting scout, tracking down the answer to this question, whether he wanted to or not, unaware it was even being asked. It was a question that would take Serrano several unpleasant days to answer.

The first reaction in Medellín to the Garden Grove incident came from Eduardo Martínez, who called Serrano into his office the morning after the seizure.

He wanted to know what happened and how. Somebody had to make good on that million, because in this business, the men at the top always get paid. Whoever screws up pays for it. If someone Martínez hired lost a million, Martínez would have to make up the difference.

"He had to answer for that money," says Serrano. He had to face the money's owners and either own up to his responsibility or persuade them it was not his responsibility at all. The main thing Martínez wanted to know was whether the money had gotten to the launderers—to Serrano's man, Britto, or to Jimmy Brown's man, Lopez—when it was seized. Martínez had hired those organizations, and if the money had been seized while it was in their possession, Martínez would have to answer for it.

The courier, on the other hand, worked for the traffickers, not for Martínez. If the money had been with the courier when it was taken, Martínez could not be held accountable. Neither could Serrano or Jimmy Brown.

Normally, it's perfectly obvious when money changes hands from the people who collected it from drug dealers to the people who will launder it and move it to Colombia. This is a critical juncture in the cycle, a point where the responsibility moves from one organization to the other. It is the point in the circle where the drug side of the business meets the money side, and where the path begins to curve south again toward Colombia.

In each of the other pickups that Britto made that day, for example, the moment of transfer was clear. Not so for the $1 million that the collector Alvarez was supposed to give to the launderer Britto. At the moment the Garden City cop interrupted the cycle, the money had been in Alvarez's custody—but it was in the trunk of a launderer's car. Alvarez's defenders in Medellín claimed there must have been something wrong with the car that attracted the cops. The people who hired Alvarez didn't want to take responsibility. But Serrano insisted the problem was with Alvarez, not the car.

For Martínez, this fine point determined whether he would have to give up $1 million to the traffickers who were his clients.

Beyond the matter of who owed whom, placing blame was important in answering another question: How reliable was Jimmy Brown's laundry? Service was maddeningly slow, but Brown's people always answered that at least the money got to its destination. Not so now.

Martínez seemed more worried than angry when Serrano went to see him. Serrano, who had learned of the seizure from Britto in an early morning phone call, was worried, too. If he and Ramón were held responsible, they would have a hard time paying off $1 million—especially if the laundry had no customers. And he knew Martínez's clients were dangerous men who would expect to be paid.

Serrano told Martínez what he knew about the million-dollar loss, that the courier had been stopped by a cop for a traffic violation; it had happened before his people even saw the money.

When Martínez was done questioning Serrano, he asked him to come talk to some other men, men who worked for the money's owner. Serrano had no choice but to allow Martínez to drive him across town to meet these other people. It was about noon when Martínez took him to a two-story building. The lower floor looked unfinished, like a warehouse that also served as a parking area for the people who worked in offices on the second level.

Martínez left, and Serrano was led to an office belonging to the owner of the money, who was not there. This was when Serrano called home and gave the phone number to his wife, telling her to give it to Ramón if he called. Under the circumstances, it was acceptable to do that, because Ramón was his partner in the matter that led to the inquiry. "We needed to find Ramón," says Serrano. "I was authorized by them" to make the call, he says.

But mainly he did it for himself. He says he left the number with his wife "as a measure of safety, so that if I were to disappear they would know that I had been in that place."

He had no way of knowing that the number, this crumb he left in his path, would wind up in a DEA report just like everything else he did with Ramón. And he had no way of knowing that this small morsel would help lead federal agents to a gold mine: a criminal enterprise of mammoth importance.

Nor could he have imagined the significance of a diploma he noticed hanging on the wall of this office: an engineering degree awarded to someone named Geraldo Moncada. At least, that's the name Serrano would later recall; it sounded like one he had heard before. "Many people in Medellín had heard it before," says Serrano. Moncada was a trafficker rumored to be as rich as Pablo Escobar, but much more elusive. Escobar made sure the world knew his name, while Moncada used many names.

Here in Moncada's office, Serrano faced two interrogators, men in their mid-twenties, while another two or three men paced about. Their clothing bulged, indicating they were armed. They never told Serrano their names or the name of their boss, only that they worked for the owner of the $1 million. And they never threatened Serrano. They didn't have to.

They wanted to know exactly what happened, and Serrano told him what he knew. They wanted to know about his gringo partners. How well did Serrano know Ramón? Was it possible that Ramón stole the money? Serrano told them he could vouch for him completely. What about Jimmy Brown? Alex Carrera? Serrano told them everything he knew about the money launderers, and that they could be trusted. The loss had nothing to do with any of those people, Serrano said. It was a fluke, an accident. A loss to be written off. Maybe the courier took the money.

The men kept asking the same questions over and over, looking for contradictions, for changes in Serrano's story. For an hour they went on like this, when they were interrupted by Ramón's telephone call.

Finally they declared an end to the inquisition and drove a weary Serrano back to his apartment. They did not say whether they believed him or not.

A couple days later, Martínez called Serrano again. This time he wanted to take Serrano to meet the owner of the money.

Hardly pleased at the prospect, Serrano nonetheless took this as a sign he was not being blamed for the loss. Otherwise, "they wouldn't have introduced me to anyone. They would have taken me for a ride. One way."

Martínez took Serrano to a different location this time, an apartment building under construction in El Poblado, a trendy area on the south side of Medellín. The two went into the construction office, where they met the man Serrano took to be the owner of the $1 million. He went by the nickname "Chepe."

The man who stood before Serrano appeared to be in his mid-thirties. Slender and somewhat short, Chepe had thinning brown hair and a small mustache. This was a man said to be Escobar's equal in drug profits?

Serrano had heard only wisps of rumors of the man. But judging from the sums of money Chepe was sending through Martínez, Serrano believed the rumors to be true. Chepe was either trafficking a lot of drugs himself, or he was handling business for Escobar or Ochoa. Or both. He had too much dirty money to be a peon.

As the men talked, construction workers roamed around them, seemingly oblivious to their conversation. Again, Serrano was asked what happened to the $1 million. Again, the smooth-talking lawyer explained how the money had never gotten to his people. The courier had been stopped because of his poor driving, Serrano told him. It was an accident. Nobody's fault.

"The thing is, we never received the money, and that's the point I based myself on so that I wasn't responsible for the money," says Serrano. "If we received the money, we would answer for the money."

His meeting with Chepe lasted only fifteen minutes, and Serrano was uneasy throughout. Even when it was over and they let him go home without threat or injury, Serrano continued to worry. He appeared to be in the clear, he says, but "you just never know when things are going to flip."

*L*osing $1 million was not something Eduardo Martínez could shrug off. The whole episode gave him qualms about the Atlanta laundry, now not only slow but unreliable. Even though he couldn't pin the blame on Jimmy Brown's people, the fact that it was their car blurred the issue. At least they could try to help him retrieve the cash. Martínez asked Serrano to hire a lawyer in Los Angeles who could find out what had happened to the money and how to get it back.

Martínez wanted more than that, though. Given all the problems with the Atlanta laundry, he wanted to meet the men behind the business. He wanted to meet Jimmy Brown and Alex Carrera, he told Francisco, who passed the word along through Ramón.

This struck the agents in Atlanta as good news and bad news. Until now, no DEA agent had met Eduardo Martínez; all their evidence against him came from Ramón and Serrano. Getting credible evidence against criminals was the whole point of the operation. If they ever brought Martínez to trial, they'd stand a better chance of conviction with an agent's testimony than with uncorroborated statements from a confidential informant. No matter how reliable, a CI is a criminal trying to minimize his time in prison. He is almost never as believable to a jury as an officer of the law.

On the down side, Martínez was obviously displeased with the way things were going with Jimmy Brown and his laundry. What would he do about it?

Meeting in Colombia was out of the question because of the potential danger to the agents. Instead, the men picked a spot next door to Colombia, a place appropriate for the business at hand. They picked the destination for the millions of dollars the laundry was washing, the point on the map where Jimmy Brown's responsibility for the money ended: Panama.

The business meeting was set for Monday, January 18, 1988. Everyone would be arriving the day before and staying at the Caesar Park Marriott in Panama City.

Though thrilled by the potential for hard evidence against important criminals, the potential for danger concerned the agent in charge of the Atlanta DEA office, Ron Caffrey. "I was worried," Caffrey says, "because there was trouble down there. . . . We knew they were annoyed because of the loss of money, and there was some explaining to do. We were kind of walking into some things that we didn't know about."

It was a volatile time in Panama. A grand jury in Miami was poised to indict General Manuel Noriega for drug trafficking, for money laundering, and for turning Panama into a free zone for the Medellín cartel. Noriega and his police were still ostensibly cooperating with the DEA, but were they also on the traffickers' payroll? In Panama at that point, a drug agent could never be sure where the ground was solid.

If Caffrey was going to send agents into all of that to meet an operative of the Medellín cartel who was angry at them, there would have to be backup. DEA had an office in Panama, but it had only a few agents, who were usually busy with their own cases or with the multitudes of other visiting DEA agents with Panamanian connections to their cases.

Skip wanted four or five agents for the assignment, including himself as case agent. Caffrey pleaded with Washington to give his agents what they needed. He pushed the request up to the number-two man. This would be a major meeting for a big case, and Panama was too hazardous to put undercover agents there without backup, he argued.

Washington saw it differently. No money or drugs would change hands, so how dangerous could it be? This was simply an informational meeting. The agents stationed in Panama could offer backup if necessary, headquarters said. In addition, another group of agents would be in Panama for training at that time and could be called if help was needed.

Two agents only, came the word from Washington, one undercover and one backup. Two agents: if Atlanta could only send two, one would be Cesar Diaz, as Alex Carrera, Jimmy Brown's sidekick, Skip figured. Cesar not only could discuss the laundry, but as a Latin and an outgoing follow, he could put Martínez at ease. Moreover, Cesar had developed a good relationship with Serrano, who would be there, too.

But Cesar was still green, had never traveled on assignment before, had been an agent for less than five years, and knew virtually nothing about banking. How could he calm their concerns if he had only a rudimentary knowledge of how to move money?

Caffrey worried about Cesar for another reason, too. In the year since agent Ray Stastny was killed in Atlanta, Cesar's friendship with his dead friend's wife had grown into a romance. They were getting very serious about each other, and Caffrey knew a tragedy involving Cesar would devastate Stastny's young widow, as well as Cesar's widowed mother.

Caffrey told Cesar he did not have to accept this assignment. We can tell Martínez to meet us some other time, some other place, he said. But Cesar wanted to go.

For the other slot, Skip would go, even though he could not meet Martínez undercover, and even though Martínez was expecting Jimmy Brown/John Featherly. But Featherly had been transferred out of Atlanta, and it was tricky getting him back for this assignment. If Washington had allowed even a third agent to go, Caffrey would have tried to spring Featherly loose.

There were only two slots, however, and it was important for Skip to be there. Since he was case agent, this whole thing was his responsibility to oversee, and this was a critical event in the case. He couldn't work undercover, because Serrano knew him as Allen Weston, cocaine transportation expert who had nothing to do with Jimmy Brown. In fact, Cesar and Skip could not be seen together in Panama, because they were not supposed to know each other.

But behind the scenes, Skip could direct Cesar and Ramón, help them sort through events, act as backup, and coordinate with the local DEA office. They could contact him on the sly to get grounded, to get help if need be. Skip would be their anchor, their security.

An agent working undercover needs to come out from the deception as quickly as possible. Cesar says it's like running through fire—you don't stay there any longer than you have to. For this assignment, Cesar and Ramón would be undercover for days, never knowing who was watching. Skip's presence would give them someone safe to talk to, a way to cool off after a run through the fire.

Still, it was a dangerous situation for Cesar. "Usually when you do undercover work, you do the best you can to create an atmosphere where it'll be safe and you can control what happens," says Skip. But with only two agents in a faraway place, there was no way to control the situation or to make it safe. Skip believes they should have had surveillance agents, and they should have had Featherly. "Caffrey fought for all of that." But when Washington said no, "it was a matter of either making the meeting with what we had and what we were given, or not having the meeting at all."

For Ramón, the trip to Panama was not much different from what he did all the time in Colombia. And while it was true that he took no unnecessary chances, it was also true that he welcomed a certain level of danger. He liked the intensity of it, the adrenaline surge, the sharpness of mind it required.

"You see this," Ramón would say years later over a drink in a near-empty bar, holding his hands in front of his face and pulling at the skin. "What is this worth?" still tugging at his skin, his eyes intense. Do you know what this is worth? Until you risk losing it, Ramón goes on, you can't know the value of your own skin or appreciate the richness of life. "You have to risk life to live it."

No, the danger of the assignment did not concern Ramón. Besides, he loved Panama. He loved its international sophistication, softened and sensualized by a Latin sensibility. Like Ramón, Panama had been Americanized more than its soul wanted to admit. Sterile high-rises puncture the sky, in contrast to the bright displays of moving Panamanian folk art that chug through traffic-clogged streets below: the multi-colored public buses painted in whimsical swirls, magical birds, and—on the rear panels—portraits of celebrities. Graceful neighborhoods, lush with banyan trees and palms, border busy, dirty thoroughfares lined with boxy concrete and glass office buildings and fast-food places like Mr. Pollo.

As a crossroads for international business—legal or not—Panama was a place of high intrigue and easy flexibility, where a certain degree of lawlessness was part of the draw, even while a strong-arm regime ruled. Things were seldom as they appeared to be in Panama. And this was fine with Ramón, who was seldom what he appeared to be, either.

He knew the place well. He had traveled there often enough to know the best restaurants and most secluded beaches, enough to have friends there. Because of that, and because no agent would be working undercover with Cesar, Cesar would be relying on Ramón in ways that make drug agents squirm. Even though Ramón had shown himself to be a reliable confidential informant, "you never trust a CI one hundred percent," Cesar explains. He therefore found it unsettling that for a mission as risky as this, his own safety was tied to a CI's trustworthiness.

9: Panama

It was night when Ramón and Cesar reached Omar Torrijos Airport in Panama on Sunday, January 17, 1988, and began a long, dark ride into the city, with Ramón in charge of logistics. He rented and drove the car. He knew the way. The dimly lit road took them through impoverished but lively neighborhoods, where people come out of the darkness to converge on sputtering buses or to congregate at open-air cafés or other establishments whose business is undiscernible in the dark.

Even knowing the way, a stranger feels lost en route to Panama City, Ramón would say later.

Finally, after the outlying neighborhoods gave way to the city, and luxury apartment towers mingled with rundown shacks, the two came nearly to the water's edge. There, the top of a concrete and glass structure glowed with the words "Marriott Caesar Park Hotel," a beacon for foreign travelers seeking American-style cleanliness and efficiency in Panama. The Panama Hilton was closed at that time, so everyone of any means stayed at the Marriott—bankers, businessmen, flight attendants, undercover drug agents. Providing familiarity and therefore security, the Marriott also offered a taste of intrigue. The lobby's white stucco walls and wrought-iron accents give a sense of place, while a sense of the world is offered by the clocks behind the registration desk showing the time in Tokyo, New York, Los Angeles, London, as well as Panama. Fashionable guests from faraway places meet in this lobby, with its polished, earthen-tiled floor and its centerpiece Spanish fountain, sur-rounded by plants overflowing their pots.

It was also where the DEA put up its visiting agents, as a rule, and many drug traffickers knew that.

When Cesar and Ramón walked into the Marriott at nine forty-five that Sunday night, they did so in their undercover roles. From the time they stepped off the plane, they behaved with the understanding that some-one could be watching them.

In fact, when he and Ramón walked into the Marriott, Cesar noticed two men standing just inside the plate-glass doors, facing the people who came in and out of the hotel's main entrance. Cesar had never seen either of them before, but he soon learned that one of them was Ed-uardo Martínez. The men did not rise to greet them, though Martínez had surely recognized Ramón. He only watched as the pair made their way into the lobby, passed the fountain, and walked up to the registra-tion desk below the clocks.

Ramón and Cesar checked into rooms on the fifteenth floor. Up there, the view was dark, as their rooms overlooked the vast Bay of Panama. After dropping off his bag, Ramón called the desk for the room number of Francisco Serrano, who had arrived earlier. He reached Serrano in Room 1018, and Serrano invited him to come down.

Ramón was walking down the corridor to the elevator on his floor when he saw two men he recognized: one was Martínez and the other Martínez's brother-in-law, John Jairo Ospina.* Their sudden appearance on his floor surprised Ramón.

The men exchanged greetings. Ramón could see they were both on edge. They told him they were looking for "Rubén," the name Serrano used with them. Where's Rubén? they wanted to know.

Ramón told them he was on his way to see Rubén now. Why didn't they come along? The three men headed for the elevator together.

Who are you with? Martínez asked Ramón.

I'm with a guy named Alex, Ramón said, giving Cesar's undercover name. He's Cuban. Speaks Spanish, Ramón said to reassure them, as they seemed so uneasy.

The guy with black hair? Ospina asked.

Yeah, that's him, Ramón said, realizing they had been watching.

Who was this guy, Alex, Ospina wanted to know.

Ramón told him Alex worked for Jimmy Brown.

They probably had expected to see an older, more Anglo-looking man, because they were expecting to meet Jimmy Brown. When they

---

* Ospina also went by the name Juan Jairo Ospina. However, he is not the same Juan Ospina who previously moved money through the Atlanta laundry, but a cousin of his.

saw Cesar instead, "I think they thought we might have brought some muscle or something," says Ramón.

The trio arrived at Room 1018, where Serrano, surprised to see Martínez and Ospina, opened his door. He welcomed them in and soon was talking about what had brought them all there, the problems with the Atlanta money laundry, which still had nearly $7 million that Martínez had sent through it.

Ramón promised to trace the funds the next morning, but for now he was too tired to talk business. Let's relax and save that for tomorrow, he said, figuring he wanted Cesar to be in on whatever business discussion ensued.

Besides, it *had* been a very long day. It was ten thirty, and Ramón and Cesar had to be "on." If it had just been Serrano, it would have been easier. But their main target, Martínez, had suddenly appeared, and there was no mistaking the undercurrent of tension.

The subject changed, and the four men started trying to settle in with each other. Ramón told them Jimmy Brown had decided not to come. He didn't want to meet any new people right now, plus, he had other business to tend to. The explanation seemed to suffice. Ramón had brought Brown's assistant, Alex, to answer their questions.

As the tension among them eased, Martínez said to Ramón, Why don't you call Alex to come join us, and we can all go for a drink?

Ramón rang Cesar's room. I'm with Rubén and some other people, Ramón told him. Come down to Room 1018.

When Cesar showed up at Serrano's door, Serrano threw his arm around him. He then turned to make the introductions. Indicating Martínez, he said, "This is Edmundo," using the code name Martínez had used in his wire transfers.

The handsome, stocky man stretched out his hand to Cesar and corrected Serrano, offering his real name instead of his code name. "Eduardo," he said. "Eduardo Martínez."

Cesar had had no idea he would be meeting the main target the first night. He cursed to himself, irritated that he had to go to work. But he extended his hand and greeted Martínez warmly, making a mental note of his height, his weight, his coloring, his Polo knit shirt. These were the two guys he had spotted in the lobby, who had been sending him nearly $1 million a week in drug proceeds, and who weren't too pleased with the way things were going.

Outside the lights of Panama City flickered. Cesar began by telling them he was suffering from a very bad cold, which was obvious. But he then headed into the reason they were all there. Everything seemed to be moving a lot more smoothly now, Cesar said to Martínez. He hoped Martínez and Ospina were happier with the way things were going.

Serrano volunteered that things were not going well enough. As the middleman between Martínez's organization and Jimmy Brown's, Serrano's job was to keep each side satisfied, a difficult task. Relating Martínez's concerns, he told Cesar the money still moved too slowly and there were problems picking it up in Los Angeles.

Martínez remarked that perhaps they should not get into all of this now since Ramón had suggested they put off the business discussion until the following day; Cesar agreed. Meanwhile, however, he did want Cesar to know the nature of his problem with the Atlanta laundry.

Martínez reminded Cesar that, without even meeting him or Jimmy Brown, he had handed millions of dollars over to them. Normally, he knows the people with whom he does business, and they know him. He travels to Uruguay and Chile to meet business associates, and they come to Colombia, Martínez said. They introduce each other to their wives and children. They show each other their businesses, their farms. If I do anything wrong, Martínez said, people know where to find me. It's a way of gaining trust.

But in this case, he hears all about Alex and Jimmy but he doesn't have the slightest idea who they are. Martínez kept harping on how he had entrusted all this money to people he had never met. Nearly $7 million. And he made it very clear he was unhappy with how they handled it.

Martínez was firm but diplomatic. "He was in a double dilemma," says Ramón. "He wanted to make a point, that this thing is dangerous, but he didn't want to wake up the next morning and find out we'd gone." Martínez told them he had a lot more business to send their way —three times the business, he said. But he was holding back because the service was so poor.

Serrano agreed. He complained that Jimmy Brown's people in Los Angeles would only pick up money on Tuesdays and Thursdays. Just two days a week! And even then they were not necessarily available on the specific Tuesday or Thursday that the money was ready, Serrano said. In fact, DEA in Los Angeles was deluged with money and was trying to limit the frequency of pickups. Each pickup required so many agents and cops and so much work that it nearly overwhelmed the people assigned to the case, who didn't want to be that useful to the traffickers, anyway.

But Martínez wanted to send more business. If they could improve service, he told Cesar and his partners, he would have some "big ones" for them in New York. Instead of delivering a few hundred thousand dollars at a time as was his usual practice, Martínez would send between $1 and $2 million with each New York pickup.

Cesar told Martínez that the problems all stemmed from Jimmy Brown's bank connection. The banker was limiting the days and times he could accept the cash. This was something Jimmy will have to deal with, Martínez replied. Maybe the banker would do more if he is paid more. Cesar didn't know, but said he would tell Jimmy.

The main issues now in the open, the atmosphere lightened. They would talk more business the next morning, Martínez said. For now, he suggested they go downstairs for a drink. Serrano and Ramón held back to talk to each other privately for a moment while the other three headed out.

In the elevator down, Martínez complimented Cesar on his good Spanish. Where are you from? he asked. Cesar told him he was born in Cuba but had left as a boy. This would be the only time Martínez questioned him about his background, and it was hardly an interrogation. "If he had any doubts, or if he had any concerns about me, I did not see them," says Cesar. He sensed no personal tension between them. It seemed they were getting along just fine. And even though Martínez must have been uneasy about the situation, he was nonetheless socially personable. "Martínez is a very charismatic kind of guy," says Cesar.

Downstairs, they waited in the lobby for Serrano and Ramón. Martínez turned to Cesar. In confidential tones he told him to be careful at this hotel. The DEA, the FBI—they're all over the place, Martínez warned. Watch what you say over the hotel's telephone system. All calls are monitored, he said.

When the other two joined them, they proceeded down the hall to the main bar at the Marriott, Mi Rincón (My Corner). A long, deep room whose plate-glass windows overlook the lighted swimming pool and surrounding palms below, Mi Rincón is dark and intimate, decorated in muted colors and furnished in cushioned rattan.

The group took one of the tiny cocktail tables near the entrance and crowded around. They ordered drinks, and for the next hour and a half the banter may not have been business to the Colombians, but it was definitely work for Cesar and Ramón.

"You're trying to relax and be yourself," Cesar explains later. He was telling himself, "Be a person, do not be a machine, because they pick it up . . . especially Latins. Latins, you talk, you talk loud, you talk with your hands . . . you're very opinionated." If he was too stiff, they might be wary.

"So you're trying to play that role, and at the same time you have to focus in on what this man is saying. And in between all the B.S. stories, there is evidence coming out. And you have to capture that," explains Cesar.

In fact, they talked about Jorge Ochoa's arrest, and about the recent bombing of one of Pablo Escobar's buildings. Martínez blamed U.S. lawmen for both.

Cesar kept listening for inside knowledge from Martínez, indicating close ties to drug lords. Was he merely recounting gossip or news accounts? Still, the conversation kept returning to drug-related topics. And Martínez clearly had criminal contacts. He told of parties he attended with major traffickers; Ospina boasted that his cousin arranged entertainment for traffickers' parties, bringing in such stars as Madonna and Julio Iglesias, he claimed.

Ramón was impressed with the level of gossip. It was the sort of thing he heard all the time in Colombia, but he generally let it slide. He was wondering how much of this Cesar would remember later.

By now, Cesar and Martínez were bemoaning the fact that with all their money, Jorge Ochoa and Pablo Escobar could not spend it in the United States for fear of arrest. As for extradition—the main fear of Colombian drug traffickers—Martínez told Cesar he had just learned over the Christmas holidays that the justice who broke a tie on the Colombia Supreme Court and voided President Virgilio Barco's extradition treaty had sold his vote, holding out for a large sum of money. According to Martínez, who gave no names, the traffickers spent a lot to kill the extradition treaty, and would have spent more, if necessary.

The talk went on like this, with Martínez discussing new government restrictions on Colombian bank accounts, the banking turmoil in Panama, and the like. He mentioned he had been in banking at one time, himself. And he mentioned that his parents did not know the true nature of his business. Martínez also informed them he had checked out Ramón through a contact Ramón had given him, a trafficker with whom Ramón had done business in his pre-CI days.

Martínez grew more gregarious as the evening wore on, and when he spotted a familiar face at the bar, he greeted the man like a long-lost friend. A former general manager of Banco de Occidente's Panama office who had been transferred back to the home office in Colombia, the banker sat down and chatted with Martínez and his drinking companions. Martínez teased him about how lousy his bank was.

Banco de Occidente was the bank where Martínez had directed Jimmy Brown's people to send the cleaned money.

Your bank is no good, Martínez told the banker. These people here are telling me your bank is holding my money. We're going to change banks and go through Morgan instead, Martínez said.

You're wasting your time, replied the banker.

As Sunday night turned into Monday morning, Ramón and Cesar said they wanted some sleep. Martínez told them they would meet the next morning and then go to Banco de Occidente. There, they could talk business.

Ramón, Cesar, and Serrano left them at the bar about 12:30 A.M., and the long day was finally over.

It was still dark when Cesar and Ramón slipped out of the Marriott the next morning to meet Skip at the Holiday Inn. Although only a couple of miles away, Ramón steered the rental car through a long, tortuous route to elude anyone who might be watching.

Skip had spent the night in the high-rise, bayside apartment of DEA's attaché to Panama, Fred Duncan, the same agent who had laughed at the idea of gold mines in Uruguay at the meeting in Atlanta the previous month. Duncan's place was not far from the Holiday Inn. Although he didn't stay there, Skip kept a room at the Holiday Inn, where he met Cesar and Ramón.

Cesar, still sick with his cold, wanted to pour out everything he and Ramón could remember from the night before, and Skip wanted to know how it was going. The three men huddled around the micro-cassette recorder Skip used to record his notes, and for the next half hour recounted their meeting with Martínez and his sidekick. They told Skip how Martínez had said he was holding back the big money because the laundry was so slow; they told him about meeting the banker; they related everything Martínez and Ospina had said about Pablo Escobar, Jorge Ochoa, the extradition treaty, even about Madonna and Julio Iglesias performing for the traffickers. Cesar told Skip he thought noteworthy that Martínez had mentioned traveling to Uruguay and Chile to meet with business associates, an apparent reference to the competing laundry.

Skip pressed for anything Martínez might have said to link him unequivocally to the drug trade.

From their conversations, "you could tell he was in the business," Cesar responded. This was the underlying assumption of everything that transpired.

"It was right away, 'This is drug money and we're laundering and it's illegal.' There was no question whatsoever," said Cesar.

But specifics? "All this stuff was general," he said.

Skip suggested that at their meeting later that morning Cesar should try to draw Martínez out. Aim for the kind of admission Serrano had made the previous month in Los Angeles, that all the money they washed ultimately belonged to Escobar or Ochoa, Skip said.

Cesar said he'd try.

As they contemplated what had already happened and what was about to transpire, Cesar said, "Ramón thinks that by the end of the day today, he'll be inviting me down to Medellín."

The trio paused to consider that prospect. As unsettling as it was to do business in Panama, Medellín was out of the question.

"Do another meeting here," Skip urged, "or maybe some place like Aruba."

Skip also told Cesar not to even try to answer all of Martínez's questions. Cesar shouldn't pretend to know more about banking than he knows, so he should simply promise to take their questions to Jimmy Brown. This would give them all another reason to meet.

Cesar said that one of the things he wanted to do in Panama was meet the Banco de Occidente banker who handled Martínez's accounts, Clara García. Cesar wanted to be able to contact her directly later, to call her on the phone from the States. They wanted to be able to prove that she knew, if she did, exactly what kind of money she was helping Martínez move. As with Serrano and Martínez, whose phone conversations with Cesar and Ramón had been recorded, it would be good to capture Clara García on tape.

Another thing Ramón needed to do that day was track Martínez's money that was still in their laundry. Ramón had promised Martínez he would call the banks in the States to do so.

"I need figures today," Ramón said.

"Jesus, today's a holiday," Cesar said.

A holiday? What holiday? Ramón asked.

"Martin Luther King, a federal holiday," said Cesar. U.S. banks would be closed; this had not occurred to them.

Cesar and Ramón were late getting back to the Marriott, where they were supposed to have met Serrano and the others for breakfast. A furious Serrano wanted to know what the hell was going on.

Ramón went on the offensive. He told Serrano he and Cesar had gone for a long walk that morning because Ospina had said insulting things to them the night before, and they wanted to talk about it.

This lie rang true because, in fact, Ospina countered Martínez's charm and refinement with belligerence and vulgarity. Short, dark, and crude, Ospina clearly had been brought there to act as Martínez's heavy. He was a natural for the job.

"That Ospina guy was saying a lot of crap," Ramón says he told Serrano. "We don't like him; we don't like his attitude. Alex [Cesar] is all pissed off," Ramón remembers saying.

Serrano bought this explanation. And even though the two gringos had missed breakfast, they hadn't missed the main event of the day.

In Panama, international banking ranks as perhaps the country's most important business. Secrecy laws, Panama's use of U.S. dollars, and the international trade spawned by the Canal and Panama's free-trade zone in Colón had brought to this small nation of 2.4 million people more than a hundred banks from twenty-seven countries with assets of some $40 billion in the late 1980s. Panama's proximity to Colombia and Noriega's welcome mat to the drug trade pumped billions more into Panamanian banks. Panama City's skyline was defined largely by bank towers. The smaller banks had taken over a lovely old neighborhood, dominating it with one- and two-story contemporary office buildings.

"The banks run Panama," says prosecutor Buddy Parker. "I mean, if ever there were a concept of international corporations controlling the economies of the world, here's a prime example. Because they're not just Colombian banks. They're American banks. They're German banks. They're Japanese banks."

A longtime Panamanian banker put it this way: "The banking system has always been treated with, let's say, respect."

Like most of the banks in Panama, Banco de Occidente's home office is elsewhere, in this case, Cali, Colombia, but its Panama branch was an important outpost. An unimaginative box, the Banco de Occidente building in Panama City stands about a dozen stories high on a busy four-lane commercial strip amid restaurants, boutiques, and other midrise bank buildings. Next door a laundry bears the name Lavandería California.

When Eduardo Martínez strolled into the airy bank lobby with his four business associates at about ten thirty that January morning, tellers, secretaries, and bank officials dropped what they were doing to shake his hand and welcome him. The banker they had all met the night before at the Marriott bar was on a telephone and waved a greeting. There was no doubt that Martínez was a favorite customer here.

Martínez introduced two of the fawning bankers. One was the woman Cesar had been wanting to meet, Clara García, the branch's commercial manager; the other was the branch general manager, William Guarin. Both were dressed conservatively and in businesslike taste; she was in her early thirties, he a few years older.

Martínez told them they needed a place to meet, so the pair led the five men into a glass-walled conference room with a circular table. Coffee, juices, and water appeared; the two bankers left the room and shut the door.

Martínez explained he had wanted to meet because several aspects of their business together troubled him. He had questions about their operation, and he wanted to offer his help in straightening out the kinks. Ospina was here, Martínez said, to advise him and to look after his interests.

Martínez said he was disappointed that Jimmy Brown had not come. Cesar told him that given the atmosphere in Panama, security considerations had kept Brown away.

He had been in their line of work himself, Martínez continued, but had quit because he had lost a lot of money. Despite those losses, his experience and knowledge could be useful in working out their current problems, but he had to know more about the Atlanta operation to help.

He informed them that his partner, the man whose money they were laundering, had hundreds of millions of dollars to wash. He looked at Serrano, who was seated to his left, and said he was referring to someone Serrano had met. Cesar took this to mean Pablo Escobar.

Martínez didn't name him, but he said this man was one of his customers. These customers call him when they have money to be picked up in the United States, he said, and he arranges for that to be done by one of the organizations he uses, such as Jimmy Brown's. Once the money changes hands in the States, Martínez moves the same sum from his own working capital to an account belonging to his customer. Martínez was betting his own funds that the launderers would do what they promised.

This meant that the longer it took to get the money from the United States to his accounts in Panama, the longer Martínez was without the use of his money, and the more interest he lost on it.

And if his customer's money gets lost, Martínez went on, the customer will want to know why, and Martínez will have to find out what happened. In the case of the recent $1 million loss, Martínez had no one to question except Serrano, he pointed out, because he had never met Jimmy Brown or Alex Carrera.

This is how it works, Martínez told them. First, the customer—the owner of the money—sends people to question Martínez. Martínez, in turn, sends people to question his contact, in this case, Serrano. Serrano then must question his contact, Ramón. And this would go on until the questioning got to Jimmy Brown. During all that time, everyone along the chain would keep each other informed until the owner eventually gets the answer to what happened to the money.

In somber tones, speaking mainly to Cesar, Martínez continued: These men with whom he does business count on others to keep their word. As long as you keep your word and show good faith, they cause no problems. But if you break your word, it will come back to haunt you sooner or later.

These men would retaliate simply to prove their point so that others would learn to keep their promises, Martínez told him. So when a problem arises with these men's money, it puts him under a lot of stress.

Cesar told Martínez he understood. Indeed, there was no mistaking the message.

There is no room for error, Martínez stressed. Ramón said risk always accompanies this type of business. Martínez responded that it would be best for everyone to eliminate all possibility of error. Ospina agreed.

Toward that end, Martínez asked Cesar for details. How does the money leave the United States undetected by authorities? What sorts of accounts were they using? How does the system work? He said he wanted a general knowledge so he could help find ways to safeguard it.

Cesar said he would tell him what he knew, suddenly wishing he did know something about banking. Jimmy Brown, Cesar began, had worked as an accountant for the Italian Mafia in New York for several years and had developed banking contacts in New York and Atlanta. Through these contacts, he could move lots of cash into corporate bank accounts without the usual paperwork the government requires. The types of businesses Jimmy Brown used as fronts—mainly chains of supermarkets and gas stations—were exempt from the IRS reporting requirement on cash transactions of $10,000 or more. So the IRS never looked at them, Cesar explained.

Cesar said that was all he knew about Jimmy Brown's system.

Brown must use foreign banks to move the money, Martínez said.

Ramón said Brown had some accounts in Hong Kong.

How did the money leave the United States? Martínez and Ospina wanted to know. How much money would Jimmy Brown guarantee, and how? Would it be in cash or other assets? Cesar couldn't answer these questions, but he promised to ask his boss. Martínez suggested he write down the questions.

Until he got answers, and until he got the rest of his money, Martínez said, he would send them no more. And even then, he would give their laundry only as much money as Brown could guarantee.

At that point, Serrano, the lawyer, set in. He said their business comprised three separate phases. With that, Serrano drew three circles on a piece of paper. Phase one, he said, is the selling of the merchandise in the United States. In phase two, the proceeds are moved outside the United States. And in the last phase, the money gets into the owners' hands. Each of these is separate from the others, even though they are all the same business.

Martínez drew circles on a piece of paper Cesar had given him. It was a piece of stationery Cesar had ordered for Jimmy Brown's fake business in Atlanta. With Cesar's poor spelling, the letterhead called the company "INTERGRADED FINANCIAL GROUP." Martínez laughed at the spelling and wrote a thick T over the first D as he doodled. (But he didn't catch the rest of Cesar's error, the extra R.)

While Martínez sometimes displayed good humor, Ospina always played the heavy. How secure was the money as it went through Jimmy Brown's organization? Ospina now asked Cesar. It's very secure, Cesar said.

Martínez couldn't understand why it was so hard to track its route. Each time money is delivered, a message comes with it indicating who had brought the money, how much, and who should get it.

Yet, after going through Jimmy Brown's organization, some of the money was coming by wire into the bank in Panama without any information at all, not even an account number. When that happened, the bank returned the money to the United States.

Cesar said he would locate the problem.

Martínez and Ospina said they were very concerned that their accounts had received nothing from Jimmy Brown's organization since before January 5, thirteen days ago. Since then, Jimmy Brown's group had received $6.7 million in seven pickups in New York and L.A. for Martínez, but none of it had reached them.

Where is this money? Ospina kept asking. Where in their system was it now? How could it possibly take this long?

Cesar couldn't say. Today is a federal holiday in the United States and the banks are closed, he told them. He could find out tomorrow. As for questions about the system itself, Jimmy Brown would have to answer those.

They told Cesar to call Jimmy Brown as soon as possible and get reference numbers from the banks in New York so they could trace the money. Martínez gave Cesar the dates and sums involved in those seven pickups.

Perhaps the U.S. banks were holding the money, Martínez said. The only way to trace it is with the reference numbers from New York, he added.

Maybe Jimmy Brown's laundry could learn something from another money-laundering group Martínez was using in the United States, La Mina, he then said. It was run by Argentinians and had been operating for years, using international gold trading as a front.

Martínez explained that La Mina would send a certain amount of gold from South America—Uruguay or Argentina (Cesar and Ramón would have different recollections later)—to the United States and exaggerate its value on the accompanying documentation. The inflated figures allowed La Mina to wire large sums of money back to South America, ostensibly to pay for the gold, thus creating the cover they needed.

La Mina had gold stores all over the United States, he said. And it only took forty-eight to seventy-two hours from the time La Mina received the money until it showed up at his bank in Panama. In that time—only two or three days—La Mina would deposit the money in the United States, wire the sums to Uruguay, and then back up to Panama.

Two or three days. The DEA laundry was taking two or three weeks. Martínez said La Mina used codes to track its customer's funds. His own account was numbered Mina 30.

Their system is foolproof, Martínez said. La Mina is so good that it has been investigated by the IRS, by U.S. Customs, by all sorts of cops, but always eluded authorities.

That statement grabbed Cesar and held him momentarily, so that he lost whatever it was Martínez said next. He wondered to himself whether La Mina could really be that good, or whether Martínez was making the whole thing up.

And he also wondered whether he could remember everything that was being said. He was amazed at all the evidence Martínez was giving him about his own activities as well as La Mina's. Cesar was trying to remember all of it while remaining calm in the face of apparent threats. As for Ramón, he was mostly trying to keep warm in the icy air conditioning. Martínez's threatening tenor was no different from what he heard all the time in Colombia.

At this point, Martínez said they would bring in the two bankers, Clara García and William Guarin, to answer any questions Cesar and the others might have, and to help figure out how to speed things up.

Clara García told Cesar she did not understand these delays in getting the money to Banco de Occidente. Once the cash is deposited, the original bank might keep the money for two, possibly three days. But after that, it's all a matter of wire transfers, which take no time at all. A couple of days, tops, she said.

She suggested that each bank along the way telex her when it received and wired the money, so she could track its progress. Each telex would give the account names and numbers and instructions for transfer, which would not only speed things up but also identify snags.

What about Banco de Occidente opening an account at an Atlanta bank? she asked Cesar. That would speed up things considerably, because once Cesar's group wired the money to Atlanta, Occidente in Panama could move it immediately into Martínez's account there. Cesar said he would check into that.

Serrano told Martínez and García he wanted to open a new account at Occidente—an account with his, Ramón's, and Martínez's signatures on it. It should be called Integrated Financial Group, and any funds that went into it would be moved immediately into Martínez's own account.

García instructed a secretary to type up the necessary papers, including a letter stating that all funds received by Integrated Financial would be credited to Martínez's account immediately. Serrano and Ramón signed the letter.

García and Guarin gave him their business cards—which would soon be labeled as evidence—as well as an account book for the fake business in Atlanta, Integrated Financial.

Then García turned to Martínez and told him she had been worried about him. She had heard that "Don Pablo's" office building had been bombed, and she knew Martínez worked in the same building in Medellín. And when Martínez had not shown up in Panama the previous week as he had said, she was concerned.

Martínez assured her he was fine.

Cesar noted that García had called Escobar "Don Pablo" and, at another point, "Don Pablito," indicating not only respect for Escobar, but also familiarity and fondness.

As a gift, García then gave each of the five visitors a coffee-table-style book of photographs of Colombia, where Occidente is based.

Martínez told Cesar he and Ospina had more business to conduct at the bank and would meet them later at the hotel. Cesar, Ramón, and Serrano said their goodbyes and headed out the bank's double glass doors.

"Oh, man," Cesar would later remember. "I felt good that it was time to go, believe me."

Mentally exhausted, tired and jittery, Cesar was also excited. As the three men drove away, Serrano said he believed the meeting had gone smoothly. But, he stressed, they absolutely must locate Martínez's money. And they must move it faster. Serrano was very worried about this and told Cesar to get those bank reference numbers as soon as possible. Cesar said he would try to call Jimmy Brown from the hotel that day.

Ramón and Cesar dropped Serrano off at the hotel, telling him there was someone they wanted to see. Cesar had been cool enough in the meeting, but now that he could let his guard down, he was obviously shaken. "He was very tense after that meeting," says Ramón. This surprised Ramón, because Cesar had performed so calmly at the bank.

What had rattled Cesar was the threatening tone of the meeting, and the fact that he had gone in there with virtually no banking knowledge and no DEA backup. They had scored big on evidence, but it had been one of the most difficult meetings of his young career.

He and Ramón wanted to talk to Skip, the sooner the better. They needed to pour out everything that happened, sift through it and get it in perspective. And Skip was waiting anxiously at the apartment of DEA's number-two man in Panama. But several other visiting DEA agents were there, too, and they kept tying up the phone.

Ramón drove Cesar around town, stopping at pay phones every now and then and taking erratic turns to make sure they weren't being tailed. Some of the phones were broken; when they did work, the line was busy.

Finally, it rang, and Skip came on the line, irritated that he hadn't heard from them sooner but relieved to hear Cesar's voice.

"We gotta talk," Cesar said. "We've got to get together."

Ramón named the place: Fort Amador, a U.S. military installation near the Canal, on the causeway.

Ramón drove Cesar westward out of the city. He pulled into Fort Amador and drove past the cream-colored stucco and cinder-block buildings, the well-manicured lawns with their palm trees painted white at the base, the deep green golf course. They followed the main road onto a narrow finger of land with benches and palm trees on either side of the blacktop strip.

As they drove out the causeway, to their left was the Bay of Panama, with the skyline of Panama City off in the distance. To their right, the Bridge of the Americas spanned the mouth of the Panama Canal. Huge vessels just lowered to sea level were making their way beneath the bridge at regular intervals, past the lush green hills on the other side of the bay, headed into the Pacific Ocean.

Ramón drove the length of the causeway, a mile or two, to a hilly peninsula which lay in the water like a balloon tethered to the mainland by the causeway. He parked, and the two of them got out and sat on a bench, watching pelicans and viewing the distant skyline of the city across the bay.

Out here, Panama felt more like Miami than a foreign land, which was why Ramón chose to bring Cesar here. In Panama, Cesar seemed to feel as if he was in enemy territory. "He was out of his element," says Ramón, who wanted Cesar to relax and appreciate Panama as he did.

They had been in enemy territory at the bank, and Cesar wasn't certain who had won. He knew he had gotten plenty of evidence, and he seemed to keep their cover intact, but he couldn't be sure of the nuances. Aside from Serrano, Cesar had had few dealings with Colombians. Ramón was much more experienced.

Even when crooks act as if everything is normal, they may have an unspoken, nagging suspicion. "They won't say anything, they will continue on [as if] everything's fine . . . but that will be the last time you'll ever see them," says Cesar. Perhaps Ramón had picked up on something Cesar had missed.

Ramón considered Cesar's performance fine and was upbeat after the meeting. Even so, the CI worried that the investigation was on the verge of collapse because of DEA's inefficiency at washing cash.

Out on this strip of land, away from everyone else, they had begun assessing the morning's events when Skip arrived.

You look tense, Skip said when he saw them. What happened?

We were threatened, Cesar said.

We were? Ramón asked Cesar. When? I don't remember that.

Cesar recounted Martínez's references to the trouble they could cause by breaking their word or losing the money.

Oh that, Ramón said. I hear that kind of thing all the time and never consider it to be a threat. In the Colombian drug trade, "every conversation—in Medellín especially—is peppered with talk about killing," Ramón explains. He had grown callous to it and was surprised that Cesar had taken it so seriously. In Colombia, he told them, a threat is when someone points a gun at your head and says he will kill you on the spot if you don't do what he wants.

As Cesar and Ramón recounted the details of their meeting, Skip could see it had been successful beyond expectation. Through Martínez, an obviously important customer to the bank, the DEA had met Panamanian bankers, who had eagerly explained how to move money better. It was no smoking gun, but García had shown herself intimately involved with Martínez's business and eager to make it go more smoothly.

"Had we gone into the bank ourselves [without Martínez's introduction], we would never have been received as well," says Skip; and they would never have gotten so much evidence, he adds.

Martínez had not only given them the bank, he also was giving them more information about La Mina, and this time in the presence of a DEA agent. This was no fantasy invented by a CI, as some of the agents at the meeting at Atlanta had implied. Now they had an agent to corroborate Ramón's story.

Cesar was back in his room at the Marriott when there was a knock at the door at about 6:00 P.M. It was Ospina, who invited him to join him, Martínez, Ramón, and Serrano in Serrano's room. There was no getting away from these guys for long.

This time the subject was the $1 million seizure. Martínez had been pressing Serrano and Ramón to send an L.A. lawyer to question the guy who had been picked up with the money. Cesar told Martínez that he had, in fact, gotten a lawyer to look into the matter. Cesar recounted the details of the arrest as he had learned them, ostensibly from this lawyer. The only lawyer Cesar had actually talked to about how to get the money back was Buddy Parker.

The money was still with the government, because the Colombian who had been arrested had disowned it. The problem with retrieving it, Buddy had told Cesar, was that someone would have to claim a legitimate business reason for stashing $1 million in cash in the trunk of a car. A simple claim of ownership would not do, because whoever made that claim would immediately be investigated by the police as well as the IRS. And even if the claimant could stand up to that scrutiny, it would take years to retrieve the money, Cesar told Martínez.

Martínez asked what would happen if the police stopped one of Jimmy Brown's people who was carrying cash.

Yeah, what would happen? Ospina chimed in. He wanted to know about Serrano's people, too. He stood up and walked over to Serrano to see what he had to say about it. What would his people say, Ospina wanted to know, if a cop stopped them while they were carrying Martínez's money?

Ramón told Ospina to back off with the interrogation. He objected to the threatening tone. That's okay, Serrano told Ramón. He would like to answer Ospina's questions. He said to ensure security, in the future he'll make sure that no money is picked up in New York or L.A. without two people involved: someone from his own organization, and someone from Jimmy Brown's. So at the point that Serrano gets the money, Jimmy Brown will, too. And when Jimmy Brown gets it, he will protect it. Brown has corporations to lend legitimacy to the cash and the mechanics in place to retrieve the money, Serrano said. Their cash is perfectly safe once it gets into his hands.

Cesar agreed. This was how it was usually done, anyway, with Jimmy Brown's people helping Serrano or his workers with the money pick-ups.

Martínez returned to the question of the $1 million. Even though it might be hard to accomplish, he asked Cesar to contact several attorneys. The owner of the money would pay up to half the amount—a half million dollars!—to get it back.

He and Ospina told them that the owner, a man named Chepe, had been so concerned about this loss that he had sent an Aero Commander airplane to Martínez's farm to pick him up and bring him in to answer questions.

Cesar said coming up with a legitimate claim to the money would be difficult. But he said he would try to find an attorney who could help. That subject exhausted, the men planned to get together for breakfast the next day. Yet another difficult meeting was adjourned.

Ramón took Cesar to one of his favorite restaurants that night, El Panamar, a few blocks from the Marriott. Situated by the water, El Panamar offered elegantly prepared seafood and a bayside patio with palm trees, potted plants, and white tablecloths. The two men relaxed for the first time that day, to the soft sound of lapping water and the feel of a tropical breeze. The air was damp from an afternoon rain.

Ramón was doing one of his favorite things, dining outside at night in the tropics. Cesar felt calmed by the setting, too. He felt as if he could float away on the warm breeze.

Since the opening of the case, this was the first time Cesar and Ramón had simply relaxed together by themselves. Both of them now knew the bank meeting had gone well, and they savored that fact along with their sumptuous meal.

Still, Ramón was upset about other aspects of the case, and he wanted Cesar to know how he felt about the investigation. He told him he was angry at the agents in L.A. who kept blowing surveillance, and he was disturbed at how long it was taking money to get through the DEA laundry. And while he didn't blame Cesar or Skip, "I really felt the government was screwing up."

And he was concerned about going to jail. Cesar tried to allay his fears, but he understood that the case was hard on Ramón—harder than it was on him. He knew Ramón had a lot more to lose. "I wasn't in his spot, never been in his spot," says Cesar. "Here's a guy that's facing all these years, he's been indicted, and now he's doing undercover work for the DEA, and you know, what can you say to somebody like that? I'm not in his shoes."

And while Ramón never talked about it, Cesar sensed he felt ashamed for drawing the too-trusting Serrano into all this. "I just had the feeling that he felt bad for what he was doing," says Cesar, who believed Ramón had done the only thing he could do when he decided to work for DEA, and only Serrano was to blame for getting himself so deep into the drug trade.

Once the case was over, Cesar assured Ramón, he could eventually settle down to a quiet life in the United States under government protection. Ramón told him no, he thought he would go back to Colombia a year or so after the end of the investigation. Cesar didn't believe that, but Ramón insisted it was true.

"You gotta be crazy," Cesar told him. It would never be safe for him to return to Colombia once his role as a CI was known. It was pure insanity for him to want to return under those circumstances.

Ramón insisted he would return.

The empathy Cesar was feeling, and Ramón's sharing his concerns with Cesar, recalled to Cesar Ramón's first weeks with DEA when he was full of distrust and resentment toward the guys at DEA-Atlanta. Now they were a seamless team. Cesar had depended on Ramón to guide him through the mirrors and shadows of Panama, and Ramón had pulled them through. And despite the circumstances under which they met, Ramón seemed to have learned to like his partners in DEA.

You must be feeling pretty good about us, Cesar told Ramón.

Cesar didn't realize that even as he felt closer to Ramón, Ramón was working harder at keeping his emotional distance.

I hate you, Ramón replied. I hate you all.

I don't believe you, said Cesar.

I hate you all, Ramón insisted.

Ramón knew how to get along, how to be charming, how to kowtow. And yes, he had, in fact, teamed up with these guys. But his partners were, after all, narcs. And even though he was now one, too, he still resented being in this position. True, these fellows were not the evil men he at first assumed they would be; in fact, they had treated him with decency and were actually sort of likable. But he still didn't want them as pals.

"I made an effort not to like these guys under any circumstances," says Ramón.

It was all strictly business, he kept telling himself.

Everyone else was staying, but Cesar wanted to get out of Panama as soon as he could do so gracefully. "I was so paranoid," says Cesar. "I was seeing shadows." He arranged to leave the following afternoon, saying he would return to Atlanta to check on Martínez's money. The five men agreed to have breakfast together Tuesday morning.

That morning, Cesar and Serrano went to Ramón's room before breakfast. Cesar said he had felt threatened by Ospina and Martínez, and he hadn't appreciated it. Serrano said they were simply trying to explain the business to Cesar and to stress the importance of keeping one's word. But he would have a word with Martínez about it.

Serrano repeated to Cesar the need for him to get the money moving and the urgency of getting the bank reference numbers so Clara García could trace the funds. Serrano repeated that Martínez was understandably anxious, and Cesar should get the answers to Martínez's questions as soon as possible.

Serrano told them he needed to speak privately with Martínez and Ospina, and that they would all meet for breakfast at the restaurant at the top of the Marriott.

Once they all reconvened, with a panoramic view of the city fifteen floors below, it was clear Serrano had passed along Cesar's concerns. Over fresh papaya, Martínez apologized if he had sounded threatening; he had simply meant to educate Cesar. Ospina was more subdued, too. At breakfast, and later that morning in Serrano's room, Martínez told Cesar to talk to Jimmy Brown as soon as possible. If Brown's answers were satisfactory, Martínez would resume business. But it still concerned him that so much of his money was in their system.

Cesar promised to meet with Brown immediately on his return, and he was sure his group would be doing business with Martínez for a long time to come.

Martínez reminded Cesar to look for lawyers to check into the $1 million. As for banking in Panama, Martínez said Clara García could help Cesar with anything he needed.

Martínez told him that if he wanted to open an account in his name or in the name of some fictitious corporation, she could help him with that, too. It would take only a few minutes. If Cesar wanted to open an account today and needed money to do it, Martínez offered to lend him some. Not today, but Cesar said he might open one in the future.

Martínez and Cesar traded telephone numbers, and the meeting broke up. Cesar checked out of the hotel, and Ramón drove him to the airport. In the daylight, on the way out of town, the ride was not nearly as mysterious as it had been on the way in.

Cesar left Panama eager to go but pleased with the way his first overseas assignment had gone. And when he reached Miami, he felt like kissing the ground.

Ramón and Serrano—and Skip, too,—were just as happy to stay on in Panama for a few days. But by Wednesday or Thursday, Ramón was ready to leave. He told Serrano he was going back to Medellín.

You can't do that, Serrano told him. Martínez wants us both to stay until his money comes. A little of it had trickled in since the meeting Monday at the bank, but not much.

Ramón looked at Serrano. He had no intention of waiting around in Panama, and Martínez couldn't make him, he said.

They went to see Martínez in his room. Martínez wrote down the sums of money that were still outstanding and said he was waiting on them to show up in Panama.

Ramón told him he was leaving Panama for Medellín.

You can't go, Martínez said. You have to wait here until the rest of the money comes through.

If I am being kidnapped, tell me I'm being kidnapped, Ramón told him. I'm going to Medellín.

No, you've got to stay, Martínez said again.

The money is coming, Ramón said, and my being here is not going to make it come any faster. I have an appointment in Medellín, and I intend to make it. I'm not going far, and if you want to reach me, you can reach me in Colombia.

Serrano said he would stay. This seemed the right thing to do, whether he liked it or not.

Martínez was satisfied with keeping Serrano as hostage. Soon after Ramón left, most of the money arrived in Panama and Serrano was free to go, too.

The question then was whether Martínez would do business with them again.

10: Surfacing the Mine

In the three weeks following the meeting at the Panama bank, Eduardo Martínez sent $24 million in dirty money through U.S. laundries, he claimed, but none of it went through Jimmy Brown's people. That was more than $1.5 million for every banking day, and most, if not all of it, went to La Mina. Serrano desperately wanted to get back on track with Martínez, and the DEA desperately wanted to keep its hook in this man who could tap such incredible sums of drug money.

Martínez had lots of work waiting for Serrano in New York, he told him. But first he must get the answers to the questions he had posed in Panama. Jimmy Brown was working on that and had been traveling to New York to straighten things out with the bank, Cesar told Serrano, for him to pass along to Martínez. Serrano wanted to talk to Jimmy Brown himself, face to face.

Getting John Featherly to Atlanta for an undercover appearance proved to be a lot easier than winning approval to send him to Panama. So in mid-February, Featherly met Serrano, Cesar, and Ramón in Atlanta, where they hashed out their problems over dinner at a trendy seafood restaurant, and the next day at the Marriott Marquis downtown, where Serrano and Ramón were staying.

If they could clean up their system, Serrano told them, Martínez would have lots of money to throw their way. He told them they still had a shot at him, and it was good that Martínez had met Cesar.

But Martínez still wanted to meet Jimmy Brown, and he wanted to do so within the next couple weeks. Serrano suggested they all convene in the Dominican Republic, where he said that he could introduce Brown to two contacts who might help their business: the country's finance minister, and a Kuwaiti banker located there. These men might enable them to do in the Dominican Republic what they were now doing in Panama, Serrano told them.

Featherly was intrigued at this suggestion and told Serrano the Dominican Republic sounded like a great place to meet.

In the meantime, Featherly said, he was straightening out their banking problems. But he still couldn't believe that anyone could move money as quickly as Martínez had said La Mina did—forty-eight to seventy-two hours. It just wasn't possible.

Serrano assured him that it was.

Featherly said he'd like to send some money through La Mina just to see. Maybe they could use La Mina as a backup to their own system, or to impress a new customer, Featherly suggested.

Or, more important, to make a case against the people in it, Featherly figured.

Serrano didn't respond to Featherly's idea of sending money through La Mina. Instead, he said they needed to get their own business in order; they needed to run money through their own laundry a lot faster and a lot more efficiently. Pay your bankers more, Serrano told Featherly. Don't be so cheap, he teased, and they will perform better.

Featherly pressed on. How does La Mina do it? he asked.

La Mina deals in gold, Serrano told him. The organization sends gold from Uruguay to its chain of jewelry stores in the United States. La Mina's people claim to import more gold than they actually do, using the exaggerated gold sales to explain the large sums of money.

He used to use La Mina himself, Serrano said. He sent cocaine proceeds through an account labeled "Mina 77." The money went from the United States to Montevideo by wire and then on to Panama.

Cesar asked whether La Mina could pick up money anywhere in the United States. Anywhere, Serrano replied. La Mina charges 8 percent for the money it launders. The Atlanta laundry was now charging 7 percent: 4 percent for Jimmy Brown's group and 3 percent for Serrano and Ramón.

Turning the conversation back to their own business, Serrano said he had an idea about a new service they could offer. Why not fly the money from the United States to Panama? Their main customer, Martínez, had suggested this because sometimes he had a lot of money stockpiled in the United States. Martínez was willing to pay 10 percent of the sums flown and would take delivery at the Panama City airport, Serrano said.

Featherly said he could provide a plane and a pilot, but what about the Panamanian side of the transaction?

Martínez would take care of that, Serrano said.

Why would Martínez want his money that way instead of by wire, as they had been doing it? Featherly asked.

Because it's quicker and safer, Serrano replied. In a matter of hours, Martínez could get his money, instead of the many days, sometimes weeks, it took to squeeze money through Jimmy Brown's organization.

Yes, it could probably be done, Featherly told Serrano.

What they didn't say was that Martínez must be truly big league if he had stockpiles of cash lying around in addition to the millions he was sending through Atlanta and through La Mina.

And if Martíncz could guarantee security in Panama, it meant he could lead them to corruption there. Noriega was already under indictment at this point. But why not see where Serrano would lead them? So far, he had served unwittingly as an amazingly valuable bird dog for the drug enforcers.

Big cases, big problems, goes the saying at DEA. Little cases, little problems; no cases, no problems. Atlanta clearly was onto a big case. The agents had evidence of a bank's complicity in drug money laundering —no small accomplishment; they had a major launderer on the line; they had access to Pablo Escobar and Jorge Ochoa; they had information of a money laundry washing millions of dollars each week in drug funds for the Medellín cartel; they had Colombians who were pointing them toward criminals all over the United States and Latin America.

Some $12.8 million in drug proceeds had been delivered to their rickety laundry, of which about $1.7 million had been seized. That was admittedly a low ratio, but spinoff investigations had brought in more than 760 pounds of cocaine, thirty-one arrests, and nine trucks and cars.

Big cases, big problems. The Atlanta agents had to speed up their own laundry, but they had little control over what went on in L.A. and in New York, where virtually all of the Stateside laundering occurred. As for La Mina, so far no one in Los Angeles was willing to admit the possibility of its existence, much less get involved in its investigation.

It was time to try to hash things out. On Tuesday, February 23, 1988, some two dozen prosecutors, DEA agents, and supervisors from Los Angeles, New York, Atlanta, Washington, Panama, and Colombia again gathered around tables arranged in a huge rectangle in the Drug Task Force office in the federal building in Atlanta.

Speeding up the laundry was easier said than done. In Los Angeles, the agents had been drowning in Martínez's money. A single pickup would tie up agents for days, and it wasn't even their case. "I was on the

L.A. end seeing all the problems that we had to straighten out in order to get this money processed, documented, counted by the bank and sent, and actually wired out," says DEA agent Dan Ortega. "It was just a lot to have to do, and it never seemed to get done within a forty-eight-hour time frame."

Even after it left L.A., the money seemed to crawl. Winding it through all those banks took time, no doubt because no one wanted to give up that extra day's interest on it. The DEA sent it from one cooperating bank to another, from L.A. to Atlanta to New York, but only Chemical Bank in New York had agreed that DEA would take precedence over other customers. From Chemical Bank, the money had to be transferred to Manufacturers Hanover in New York, because it had a correspondent relationship with Banco General, the Panamanian bank that was the money's point of entry there.

"You can see how that wire transfer from L.A. via Atlanta to New York . . . would literally take seven days," says Ed Guillen, the New York DEA agent in charge of the Fis-Con banking.

Just getting the money to Panama wasn't the end of it, either. Banco General was holding it for days before transferring it to Banco de Occidente.

So, at the February meeting, the Atlanta contingent wanted to coordinate and streamline this ungainly operation while seeing where the new information on La Mina might go.

The Atlantans believed the heart of the problem was that they were working the case by remote control: their informant worked in Colombia; the Colombians' cash was picked up in New York and Los Angeles; the money had to be handled by New York and then wired to Panama; and La Mina was apparently run by Argentinians and Uruguayans through jewelry stores in Los Angeles.

To keep jurisdiction, the Atlantans had to coax Colombians to meetings there, divert their dirty money through an Atlanta bank, and persuade the drug traffickers to bring their cocaine or marijuana loads to Georgia landing strips or harbors.

To make this case, the Atlanta agents had to rely heavily on scores of DEA agents and local and state cops in Los Angeles and New York. And while the cooperation was generally quite remarkable, each of the jurisdictions chafed at times over doing so much work for a case over which they had so little influence.

"You know, it's a difficult situation where you've got a case of this magnitude that's not being prosecuted out of your division," says Dan Ortega, who was coordinating the L.A. part of the case. "It's sort of a territorial thing in that you want to be more in control of the case."

That was never clearer than at this meeting. Each jurisdiction told the others how to do the job better, with none conceding the potential for self-improvement. From Los Angeles, Group 6 supervisor Tony Ricevuto said the problem was not with L.A. but with Atlanta, which promised more than could be delivered. He says, "I always told the guys in Atlanta not to commit to too fast a schedule because there were always delays."

And when the agents in Atlanta told Ed Guillen to speed things up in New York, Guillen told them there was an easy way to shorten the money's trip: cut out the Atlanta wash cycle. Buddy Parker argued that would weaken Atlanta's jursidiction over the case, but Guillen countered that venue had already been established through the other transactions.

"Atlanta is complaining about the speed and trying to do everything quicker in L.A. and New York, and they're not willing to bypass Atlanta, which was the only thing we had control over," Guillen says. He says he told them, "Why don't you give an inch instead of telling us to adjust everything we're doing by a yard?"

Guillen, a former banker and one of DEA's chief money-laundering experts, kept reminding the Atlanta agents that their job was not to please the drug traffickers and money launderers. So what if it's a little slow? "The government does not want to become the most effective money launderer," says Guillen. Although the agents had to keep the customer satisfied, their job was to help the bad guys as little as possible while gathering evidence to jail them.

Moreover, making the laundry too efficient would make eventual arrests and seizures harder, Guillen told them. Once it's time to take down the operation, the government will want to have as much money in the pipeline as possible so it can be seized. If they sped up their laundry now only to slow it down later to get ready for seizures, the targets might become suspicious and disappear. It's important to be consistent, even if it means being consistently slow.

Skip disagreed. Atlanta's goal of getting Ramón high up into the Medellín cartel would be more easily accomplished if the Atlanta laundry worked more smoothly.

Guillen had never liked having Atlanta run the undercover part of the investigation while he controlled the purse strings, and he still didn't like it.

"I think Atlanta just wasn't aware of the nuances of trying to do what they wanted to get done," says Guillen. He didn't hesitate to instruct them.

If *he* had been in Panama, Guillen says, he would have told Martínez it was safer for the money to come in dribs and drabs than in large, conspicuous sums. He would have stressed how safe Martínez's money had been in Jimmy Brown's laundry, even if it was slow. As for the $1 million seizure, Cesar could have turned that to the government's advantage in dealing with Martínez. He could have told Martínez that the $1 million would have been safe if it had been in the hands of Jimmy Brown's people. He also could have offered to pick up money directly from the drug courier to make the process safer and quicker and to get the DEA closer to the drug side of the business.

But instead of answering Martínez's complaints on the spot and turning them into opportunities, Cesar simply came back to the States to deliver Martínez's marching orders to the rest of DEA.

The Atlanta group bristled at Ed Guillen's attitude. So what if they had never done a money-laundering case before? They were doing this one, and it had led them a lot further into the Medellín cartel than Guillen had ever reached. They were tired of Guillen's advice and suspicious of his motives.

"The bottom line was, we were meeting Eduardo Martínez and we were getting evidence on the Medellín cartel and we were picking up their money," says Cesar. "You can say anything you want about it. Maybe we were stupid. Maybe the little scenario that we told Martínez, maybe that was dumb, and maybe Martínez should have been smarter, or had us checked out. But does that matter? No. He fell for it. . . .

"Bottom line: We were there because Eduardo Martínez trusted what Francisco Serrano and [Ramón] had told them, and finally when he met me, and finally when he met Jimmy, he trusted us," says Cesar.

As usual, Ron Caffrey, Atlanta's Special Agent in Charge and a man admired by Guillen as well as the Atlantans, played referee. He made sure that each side of the debate took the other side seriously. In Atlanta, says Caffrey, "we had not done this before, so we needed that area of expertise." Besides, he didn't want to alienate the New York office, because Atlanta needed New York agents to help pick up the money. "One guy has to scratch another guy's back."

In that spirit, the Atlantans laid out their latest information on La Mina, the ring Martínez had said was running drug money through jewelry stores in Los Angeles. They wanted to know whether anyone had come across anything that could be La Mina.

The people around the table talked about the name, "The Mine." To what did it refer? "There was all kinds of speculation," recalls Bruce Stock, head of DEA's office in Colombia. In Chile and Argentina La Mina is slang for a good-looking woman, so perhaps a woman is involved in this somehow, one of the agents from South America suggested. From New York, one of the higher-ups said he knew of a Colombian mining company that used jewelry businesses in New York and Los Angeles to launder drug funds. Was that La Mina?

Whatever the name, this thing was big. Real big. Martínez had told Serrano that $24 million had gone through La Mina during the three weeks since their meeting in Panama. That was $8 million a week.

But instead of piquing the interest of the other agents, the alleged La Mina sums brought more skepticism, especially from Los Angeles, where the biggest money laundering case to date—Pisces—had been made. Ricevuto stated emphatically that no $8-million-a-week money laundry could possibly be operating under their noses without the DEA in Los Angeles catching a whiff. They had never heard of it before, so it could not be true. Period.

The Los Angeles contingent and the New Yorkers told the Atlanta group not to swallow so much hype. A fissure had developed at the meeting, with Atlanta on one side and everyone else on the other. Atlanta kept insisting on the value of its information and its informant, while everyone else—chiefly Ricevuto from Los Angeles and Guillen from New York—kept saying they shouldn't take as gospel the word of drug traffickers, money launderers, and informants.

"The Atlanta division had some good information," says agent Ortega from Los Angeles, but the others at the meeting "weren't probably giving it the attention it deserved."

He recalls, "They had a lot of people that were not going along with the program at that meeting."

The La Mina story did not surprise the man prosecuting the Pisces case, thirty-two-year-old Russell Hayman, bright, driven and number two in command of the narcotics section of the U.S. Attorney's Office in Los Angeles. Years afterwards, the boyish-looking Hayman would insist he didn't doubt the information Atlanta was offering at the meeting, he just didn't have any use for it.

From Pisces "we had a concrete suspicion that there were one or more money-laundering entities operating in the jewelry district in L.A.," says Hayman. In fact, he says, Pisces agents had watched a suspect head into the Jewelry Mart Building with a suitcase, spot the surveillance, drop the bag, and run. The suitcase contained about half a million dollars in cash.

But neither that incident nor Atlanta's La Mina story was particularly useful, says Hayman. "There are literally hundreds of business entities in that area . . . literally, hundreds, and . . . they're constantly changing. People leaving, going in and out of business. New ones coming in. Without further information it was impossible to pin down."

Apparently no one at the Atlanta meeting realized it, but DEA-L.A. was in fact homing in on a possible money laundry similar to the one Martínez called La Mina. L.A.-based agent Dave Barkett had been working with his tipster at the Wells Fargo Bank for a month at this point. He had the name—Andonian Brothers—the location and bank account number of a jewelry store he was convinced was washing huge sums of drug money.

It wasn't as much as the figure Martínez had given; it was $25 million over three months. But Andonian Brothers was a jewelry store in the L.A. jewelry district, and the money came in as cash. Barkett was operating on the belief the money came from drug proceeds, but he knew nothing about the information Cesar Diaz had brought back from Panama. He knew nothing of Eduardo Martínez or La Mina. Although he worked out of the same DEA office as the L.A. agents who attended the Atlanta meeting, he worked out of a different group.

Just as the Atlanta agents were having a hard time convincing others of the importance of their discovery, Barkett was having trouble getting the resources he needed to investigate the laundry fully.

At 4:30 A.M. on Sunday, February 21, at the DEA offices in midtown Manhattan, agent Phil Devlin kept thinking this was too strange to be happening. Three Colombians had walked into DEA headquarters on West 57th Street to tell whoever would listen that they had been working for a man bringing 2,000 kilograms—more than 2 tons—of cocaine a month into the city.

But what the informants—Devlin calls them Larry, Curly, and Moe— really wanted to talk about was not the dope but the money. They wanted him to know what they did with the cash. They told Devlin they had been taking the proceeds to a business called ABI, located in a seventh-floor penthouse office at 1200 Sixth Avenue, just around the corner from West 47th Street, the heart of New York's diamond and jewelry trade. The Colombians would take the cash there to be counted and then would call Colombia and report the delivery. Then, ABI would see that the money got to where it was going.

It was all part of a larger operation, the informants told Devlin. The whole thing was run by Argentinians, they said. And it was called "La Mina."

Devlin wasn't sure what he had, but rarely do Colombians show up on DEA's doorstep. And these three seemed awfully determined. They came, they said, because they owed $300,000 to the boys in Medellín and had no way to pay. They were hoping their information would be worth money to DEA. Devlin got them because he happened to be the only Spanish speaker in the office when they had first shown up on Saturday morning as he was getting off his midnight to 8:00 A.M. shift on "base duty." He couldn't talk with them then because he was about to go out on a bust, he says. He asked them to return later when he was back on base duty. So there they all were at 4:30 A.M. on Sunday. Devlin split them up for individual interviews and got help so that he wouldn't be outnumbered.

"I was wary of them," says Devlin. He pumped them for more information about the drugs and the money, information he would try to corroborate to test their veracity. The early morning meeting would be the first of several debriefings. Over the next few days—during the same week that some of Devlin's fellow agents from New York were meeting in Atlanta—the informants told Devlin this account:

A man they knew only as "John" had been giving them 20 to 40 kilograms of cocaine at a time to sell on consignment. The coke was owned by a Colombian who went by the nicknames "Chepe" and "Quico," as Devlin spelled it. They did not know his real name, but they knew his organization was shipping cocaine from Miami to New York behind false walls built into trucks.

As for their role in his organization, once the trio sold their portion of the merchandise, they were supposed to take the cash to the seventh-floor penthouse office on Sixth Avenue at 47th Street. "John" had given them telephone numbers in Colombia to call once the money was dropped off, so that Chepe's organization would know the amount and be credited with it. They would leave the money there in an office equipped with little more than a couple of desks, a safe, a fax machine, some telephones, a kitchenette, and a terrace.

One other thing. When they dropped off the cash and notified Colombia, the trio said, they were supposed to use a code name for the account into which the money would go. That code, they said, was "La Mina 30."

Packed into one block of 47th Street between Fifth and Sixth avenues in midtown Manhattan, the New York jewelry district is a world unto itself. Jewelry is everywhere, and everywhere are the people who make it, sell it, import it, weigh it, appraise it, broker it, size it, buy it. There is gold, silver, diamonds and emeralds and rubies. There is cut glass, too. At street level, jewelry exchanges contain hundreds of businesses squeezed into small booths. Upstairs, where the public rarely goes, in the dingy back shops of the district, men and women bend over battered tables equipped with the paraphernalia to make and perfect small objects with big prices. Hasidic Jews, with their thick beards, dark hats, and long coats, people this block of 47th Street, brokering diamonds and crafting ornaments as their ancestors did.

At most any hour of any work day, armored cars virtually line both sides of the block, dropping off boxes, bags, and buckets, and picking up parcels, too. Drug and Customs agents say the jewelry district offers the perfect camouflage for money laundering. The legitimate business looks a lot like the illegal business, with valuable goods delivered and picked up regularly.

On Sixth Avenue around the corner from 47th Street, an inconspicuous glass door stands open beneath the numbers 1200. Inside 1200 Sixth

Avenue, a guard sits at a modest desk next to the building directory, a hodgepodge of names and suite numbers punched into vinyl strips and attached to the wall in mysterious order.

After their visit from Larry, Curly, and Moe, Devlin and other DEA agents began watching 1200 Sixth Avenue and, sure enough, began seeing men drive up and—with the help of others who would come down to meet them on the street—unload bags and boxes and heavy-looking suitcases. These would be taken upstairs. Some time would elapse before one of the same men who had taken the containers up-stairs would reemerge from the building rolling a handtruck carrying bags or boxes. The agents watched him push the truck around the corner, past the Diamond City store, and up the long, busy block of 47th Street, through the Hasidim and the hawkers and the armed men load-ing and unloading shipments from armored vehicles. Never crossing a street, he would roll the handtruck and its cargo all the way up the block, almost to Fifth Avenue, and turn left just before reaching the corner into 1 West 47th Street. The agent watching on the street would then see the same man come out of the building with an empty hand-truck.

The drug agents and prosecutors meeting in Atlanta on February 23 had no idea that New York DEA agents were beginning to learn about La Mina and Chepe and an account numbered "Mina 30." Nor did they realize that DEA in Los Angeles was investigating a possible drug money laundry operating out of the jewelry district there.

And if the people meeting in Atlanta, who were mostly from DEA, had no knowledge of what their own agents were doing in Los Angeles and New York, they certainly didn't know that their counterparts at the Fed-eral Bureau of Investigation were beginning to learn about La Mina, too.

One month before the Atlanta meeting, an employee of an armored-car service, Loomis Armored, Inc., reported to the FBI something odd that had happened in December. It concerned a shipment from a regu-lar customer in the New York jewelry district, a company called Oro-simo, which had an office in a large building at Fifth Avenue and 47th Street, where Loomis also had an office. Loomis employees would pick up boxes reported to contain gold scrap and jewelry from Orosimo's one-room office and bring it to Loomis's office to ship to Los Angeles. Loomis would load the boxes into its trucks, take them out to Kennedy Airport to a secure cargo space, and load them onto planes to Los Angeles. There, Loomis would take Orosimo's goods to their destina-tion: a company in the L.A. jewelry district called Ropex.

One day in mid-December, a Loomis employee noticed that one of the boxes had developed a tear or a puncture hole. The opening was large enough to offer a view inside, and the Loomis employee took a look. Inside, he saw no gold scrap, no jewelry. Inside the box he saw only money.

Loomis policy required inspection of damaged parcels, so the employee took a closer look. Opening the box, he saw stacks and stacks of currency. The sender had claimed the contents were worth $800,000. The Loomis employee apparently was staring at $800,000 worth of cash.

A Loomis manager called Ropex to ask why a parcel that supposedly contained gold scrap in fact contained money. Interest rates are better at Ropex's bank in Los Angeles, American International Bank, than at New York banks, the Loomis manager was told. The explanation made no sense. It was unlikely the interest rates in L.A. would be different from New York. But even if Ropex had an unusually high interest-bearing account in Los Angeles, why not deposit the money in New York and wire-transfer the sum? Surely that would be safer, cheaper, and simpler than physically flying currency from one coast to another.

And even if the explanation made sense otherwise, why was Loomis taking Orosimo's money to a business—Ropex—instead of a bank?

Loomis reported its suspicions to the FBI in New York, where a report was dutifully written and filed. But even though the shipment was marked for delivery in L.A., no one from New York contacted the FBI in Los Angeles, where a money-laundering investigation had been triggered by the tip from the Wells Fargo banker.

Meanwhile, on Thursday, February 25—the same week as the DEA meeting in Atlanta and Devlin's debriefings of the informants in New York—the FBI in Los Angeles learned something interesting from the Federal Deposit Insurance Corporation. An FDIC audit of American International Bank's main branch in L.A. had shown that a company in the L.A. jewelry district was depositing hundreds of thousands of dollars in small denominations every day. The company's name was Ropex.

The bank was then wiring the sums to the New York bank account of a company called Ronel Refining Corporation. Based in Florida, Ronel refines gold.

Within a week after learning that, the FBI in Los Angeles was back at Loomis Armored, Inc., interviewing a source whose job it was to oversee the company's western operations. That manager told the FBI that for a year and a half, Ropex had been hiring Loomis to pick up boxes and bags of currency from its L.A. office and take them to Loomis's sealed vault, which was located in the same building as Ropex. There, Loomis employees would count the money, notify American International Bank, and then load the currency into Loomis trucks and take it to the Federal Reserve Bank. The money would be deposited and credited to Ropex's account at American International.

According to the Loomis source, the deposits generally fell somewhere between $500,000 and $1 million.

*I*f all of these agents had put their information together, they would
have known:

Cocaine distributors working for a major Colombian trafficker were
taking the proceeds from drug sales to 1200 Sixth Avenue—the corner
of 47th Street and Sixth, in New York's jewelry district—to a place called
ABI. From there, the money would go up the block to a building at
1 West 47th Street.

That building housed a business called Orosimo, which was using
Loomis to ship boxes of cash to a company in Los Angeles called Ropex,
which was depositing it at American International Bank in L.A. From
there, comparable sums were being wire-transferred to New York
banks, to the account of a gold refinery.

At the same time, another jewelry business based in L.A., Andonian
Brothers Inc. (ABI), was depositing huge sums of money in banks, too.

Atlanta, and now New York, had the name of the money laundry, La
Mina, and knew that one of La Mina's customer accounts went by the
code "Mina 30." Atlanta agents knew Martínez used that account; New
York agents knew a man nicknamed "Chepe" used it.

Atlanta DEA agents were washing money for a Chepe, too. They knew
one of Chepe's employees was called Chucho, because that was the
name of the man who answered the phone when Ramón was looking
for Serrano.

And if they had put it together, they would have seen that the telephone number Ramón dialed to reach Serrano during that interrogation
matched one of the numbers the three Colombians in New York called
whenever they dropped off Chepe's money at 1200 Sixth Avenue.

And though he hadn't mentioned it, Francisco Serrano knew whose
office that telephone number reached. From the degree on the wall, he
figured he was in the office of Geraldo Moncada.

Like a giant jigsaw puzzle that had been scattered everywhere, pieces of
La Mina suddenly were turning up all over the place. But they were
landing in the hands of different agencies in different cities and none of
the holders of the clues knew about each other. All of them figured they
were onto a drug money laundry of considerable size. But what were
its dimensions, and how did it work? Who ran it, and who were they
servicing? Where, exactly, did this piece fit, and where was the next one?
And how could the agents put together the jigsaw pieces to see the big
picture?

11: Back to Aruba

Eduardo Martínez still wanted to meet Jimmy Brown, and the DEA wanted to get Martínez on videotape. In a series of telephone calls between Atlanta and Medellín, Martínez told Cesar they should pick some place Mr. Brown would like to visit. Caracas, Buenos Aires, Santo Domingo?

"Wherever he wants to go, he can name the place," Martínez said.

"What he likes a lot," Cesar told him, "is the Caribbean islands."

Martínez suggested San Andrés, a quiet island near Nicaragua. But Cesar rejected that because San Andrés was part of Colombia.

They finally settled on Aruba.

This time, there was no question that John Featherly had to be there. He was the whole reason for meeting. Featherly would come down from Washington to play Jimmy Brown, while Cesar would make another appearance as Alex Carrera. Ramón would come, too, but Serrano decided to forgo this meeting. Maybe being held hostage in Panama had shaken him; maybe he was weary of the middleman role and decided to let them deal with each other directly.

As case agent, Skip would go, too, to work backstage with a "tech man" from DEA who would wire the hotel room where the agents hoped to hold the main meeting.

To impress Martínez with Brown's stature, the Americans stayed at one of the more expensive resorts on the island, the Golden Tulip, several steps up from the Concorde where Ramón had stayed a year and a half earlier when he had first met John Featherly, Skip Latson, and Buddy Parker.

The idea of returning to Aruba did not thrill Ramón. He had sworn when he left the island that last, miserable time he would never return. And while he wasn't on the cusp of a life-changing decision this time, he still didn't like the place. Too barren and at the same time too glitzy.

On Tuesday morning, March 8, Ramón and Cesar trekked up the road through Aruba's constant wind to a nearby hotel to meet Martínez and his associate, Ivan Ospina, Martínez's brother-in-law and brother of the unpleasant man who had accompanied Martínez to Panama two months earlier. The four chatted in the lobby for twenty or thirty minutes, then decided to meet in Jimmy Brown's suite at the Golden Tulip before lunch.

Despite the importance of this meeting—the future of Jimmy Brown's laundry depended on it—the atmosphere was more relaxed than in Panama. This time, the drug agents were in friendly territory, a resort, in fact. They all dressed accordingly.

If Eduardo Martínez harbored anger or distrust, he didn't show it when he walked into Jimmy Brown's fifth-floor suite with his brother-in-law. Relaxed and ebullient, Martínez entered the room full of charm and friendliness. Ramón offered Cokes and beer, and Cesar talked about having yet another terrible cold.

Ramón directed Martínez to the two-seat sofa, next to Cesar's spot, while the other three took seats on the longer sofa to their right. A square glass coffee table sat in the middle, a large round vase in its center.

The small talk was virtually all in Spanish, leaving Featherly out.

"Doesn't Jim speak any Spanish at all?" Martínez asked.

"No, none," said Ramón.

Cesar and Ramón would be acting as interpreters.

As they chitchatted about Aruba and the incredibly expensive Golden Tulip, the talk turned to gambling, which was one of Featherly's passions and one of Aruba's main attractions.

"I don't understand gambling," Ospina said. "From the moment one goes into a casino, one starts to lose."

Yet Ospina and Martínez were gambling that moment in a high-risk game where, unbeknown to them, the odds were stacked. Dressed in fashionable resort whites and exuding an easy charm, the handsome Martínez hardly looked like a loser through the lens of a hidden DEA camera directly across from him. Skip Latson and the DEA technical expert were watching him live on a television monitor in another hotel room: Martínez sank back into the sofa with one arm across the back and an ankle resting on his other knee, beer in hand, with not the slightest idea that a DEA camera was recording his every move.

If Martínez had walked over to the balcony and looked across the swimming pool to the squat building that housed the less expensive rooms, he could have almost spotted the *"Do Not Disturb"* sign hanging from the door of one. Behind that door, the two DEA agents sat at a bank of electronic equipment.

The technician had earphones to monitor the sound level, and every now and then he would hand them to Skip so he could hear what was happening. All five men in the Golden Tulip room were audible and visible—which is not always true with undercover tapes. The technical part of the meeting seemed to be going very well. The question was whether Martínez would say anything worth recording.

Martínez stood to take a telephone call in the next room, one of several he would take during their meeting. He was monitoring a volatile banking situation in Panama, where Noriega had shut down the local banks to avoid a run. Panama's economic and financial instability had sent a shudder through the international banking community, but so far, the banks doing international business were still open and operating. Martínez had been talking daily to Clara García at Banco de Occidente in Panama City.

Martínez returned and apologized for the interruption.

"Panama," he told them, "is not a pleasant city to do business in." So far, bank accounts belonging to Americans were safe, but they should plan for the worst and find an alternative place for their banking.

Martínez suggested Uruguay, which has American banks and does business with Panamanian banks. He knew about Uruguay through "the other people I work with." In an apparent reference to La Mina, he said, "Their money leaves Uruguay in metal and comes back to Uruguay in dollars." The bank in Uruguay sends the money to Panama for him, he said. Cesar translated.

With the right bank, Martínez said, they would not have to go to Uruguay to do their banking, but could work through a branch in Panama. He tried to remember the name of a particular bank with offices in both countries. "I think the bank's name is—I don't remember if it's the BCC—"

"Oh yes," said Ramón. "The BCC, yes, Bank of—"

"of Credit and Commerce," Martínez said, remembering.

(The first of several U.S. indictments charging BCCI and its representatives with money laundering and other crimes had yet to be issued. Among law enforcement agencies and, later, the U.S. public, BCCI would become known as the Bank of Criminals and Crooks International.)

Martínez said he had opened an account at BCCI "because the bank was a friend." He had filled out forms in Panama to open an account in Miami. "The manager sent the documents via the bank mail to Miami, they authorized the account, they gave me my number and I started operating from Colombia."

He added, "Without going to Uruguay, you guys can do the same."

Featherly asked through Cesar whether Martínez had contacts in Uruguay they could use.

Yes, he had contacts, but using them would be difficult, he replied. He knew them through Jimmy Brown's competitor, La Mina, Martínez explained.

That organization, he went on, uses "a real system" to move the money. "You understand? It's gold. Gold. They export gold. They have mines in Uruguay. They export gold to the United States.

"And from the United States they make wire transfers to pay for the gold exports that were made from Uruguay," he continued. The group receives the gold in the United States, he said, and pays for it in dollars, which are moved to Uruguay. He had learned about banking in Uruguay through La Mina.

Martínez was dangling La Mina before them, again. The agents badly wanted to grab a piece of it.

Featherly volunteered to talk to the contacts in Uruguay himself. He would have loved for Martínez to put him directly in touch with somebody—anybody—connected with La Mina.

Martínez said he could deal with the Uruguayan bankers. He could persuade them to set up new corporate accounts for him. They didn't have to know he would be using the accounts to throw business to their competitors.

They talked about other countries as possible way stations for the wire transfers—Aruba, the Caymans. Martínez said the Caymans would be good because Occidente had a branch there.

"The idea is to work with the Banco de Occidente . . . because the Banco de Occidente is going to make it easy for us," Martínez said. Occidente would open an account in its name at the Atlanta bank.

Once the money went into Occidente's account in Atlanta, it would be safe. "They can't take the money away from the Banco de Occidente. It's a bank," said Martínez, apparently referring to the possibility of government seizure.

"Exacto," said Ramón. The CI explained to Featherly why this would work better. The way things are now, with the money going through so many banks, Jimmy Brown's organization assumes the risk during that time. But once the money gets to Occidente, Occidente assumes it. So the sooner it gets to an Occidente account, the better, said Ramón.

"In other words," said Martínez, "it's safe for you guys and also for me."

Martínez told Featherly he could depend on the two bankers Cesar had met in Panama City, Clara García and William Guarin. "They know what we do, and we've had ties for more than ten years," he said.

But are the bankers high enough up in management "so that they can do this with no problem?" Featherly asked. The drug agent's real question was: How high does the apparent corruption go?

"There's no problem whatsoever," Martínez responded. "The bank understands that, and that is its function, and that's what it was opened for." It helps that he gives them such high-volume business, he added.

As for the way their business operates, Martínez said he understood the Brown organization kept his money safe, but he wanted the money moving faster.

Featherly in turn said he understood the importance of speed, but he didn't want to move so quickly that the system became unsafe. Gesturing with his hands, he said he had people helping him in some but not all of the banks he was using. In some banks, they will not stop all of their business to count his money. In those banks, "I gotta take my turn," he said.

Once the cash is deposited, it moves faster because wire transfers take less time, said Featherly.

Martínez wanted to know exactly how many days it took for the money to get through the U.S. banks. He asked about the risk to those funds while they traveled through the banks. Can the bank seize the funds?

Featherly said the chance of that happening was "small, because I'm a legitimate businessman." With all of his companies, he did a lot of high-volume business at the bank, said Featherly. The bankers would not do anything to lose his business.

"I make some legitimate money. It comes and goes." At the bank, "they'd never figure it out."

What worried him was not the bank, said Featherly. The danger was on the street, at the point where his people picked up the money. That is why he insisted that his people go with Serrano's people to get the money. Leaning forward, Featherly said his people know how to hold on to money, even if stopped by cops. In a case like that, he said, they would not deny ownership. They would claim it as Jimmy Brown's cash, or as money belonging to one of his businesses. He had lots of covers to explain it, he said. He had a contact in Las Vegas who would claim he won it gambling. He had an import business that could overstate sales. With the cash, "they may think I'm trying to steal money from my partner," or to cheat the IRS, but that could be handled.

"There's a lot of good ways to do it where it doesn't become drug money." There. He'd said the words: "drug money."

In translating, Cesar left out some detail, like the specific covers Featherly named, and even his reference to drug money. He did say, however, that with the volume from Brown's legitimate companies, "nothing can be traced."

Martínez asked how much of his business could Featherly handle. Maximum amount in a single pickup? Five hundred, Featherly said, meaning a half million dollars. Maximum number of pickups a day? Four, he said.

The DEA agents in New York and Los Angeles probably would have screamed had they heard Featherly commit them to handling that much money, that frequently.

Ospina expressed concern the money would accumulate, but Featherly assured him that once the money got into the bank, it would be safe.

Ospina wanted to know more about Brown's companies. Were they real businesses, or were they corporations existing on paper only?

Both, Featherly told him. "Most of them are operating small, but on paper they look big. Not Fortune 500," Featherly remarked.

"Up to now," Ramón cracked.

Martínez went into other problems, like too many people having too many telephone numbers and account numbers, making it impossible to trace any problems that occur. They worked out ways to resolve that.

Despite his numerous complaints, Martínez seemed neither angry nor impatient. In fact, he didn't even seem critical. Though he was serious about money and obviously sophisticated, his demeanor was friendly, a man willing to help his partners knead the kinks out of their venture.

"I never felt any hostility or distance," Featherly would say three years later. "We'd been doing business for a long time, even though we hadn't met. It was only a question if we could do business better."

When he opened his pitch for them to lower their fees, Martínez was earnest. "A very tight competition for money processing has developed," he told them. In addition to them and to La Mina, "other men have turned up, and still more men have turned up who also make the rounds" (his term for laundering money). With all that competition, Martínez said, the price is coming down.

At the same time, fluctuations in the exchange rate between U.S. dollars and Colombian pesos had made money processing more expensive for Martínez. Now, the 7 percent commission the U.S. money launderers were taking was worth more Colombian pesos, even though the sum in U.S. dollars was the same. Martínez gave the recent history of the devaluation of the peso against the dollar.

Meanwhile, La Mina was considering reducing its own commission, which was 7 percent, like Brown's. "We're waiting for a reply from La Mina as to what processing costs they're going to quote us," Martínez said.

He also mentioned that his own commission was lower for Brown's laundry than for La Mina, because in the case of the Atlantans, Martínez had to split his 1 percent commission with the man who put them together, Ivan Ospina.

Martínez told them he had been sending all of this money through Brown's laundry while La Mina was closed for the holidays. But since their January meeting in Panama six weeks ago, he had sent $28 million through La Mina.

"It's a big volume," Martínez said. "If we can't do it all with you guys . . . we'd split it in two."

Having reminded the Americans that he had another, highly efficient laundry considering a fee cut, that he had other potential competitors waiting for a chance, and that he personally made less money by using Brown's group, Martínez said that they, too, needed to "adjust the costs."

It's like the car business, he said. If the United States imposes a higher tariff on Japanese cars, the company has to eat some of that additional cost to stay in the market.

Ramón got that message loud and clear. He told Featherly in English that because Martínez had to split his fee with his brother-in-law, "by using us, he's making a half percent less. That's all. That's the bottom line. And he can drop the bullshit."

Martínez, apparently not understanding Ramón's remark, continued. "At most, we're moving downward between one and one-half percent," he said. La Mina would be charging somewhere between 6 percent and 6.2 percent, down from 7. The new people were offering to process the money for 6.2 percent, he added.

At the same time, La Mina had become more efficient. Getting money through La Mina used to take five days; now it took one. "I deliver to La Mina today, and tomorrow, first thing in the morning, I have the money deposited in Panama." Martínez told them he sent his own money through La Mina, not through their laundry, because it was faster.

Does La Mina guarantee the money's safety? Featherly asked.

Yes, with insurance, Martínez said. With a knowing smile to Ramón, he added, "Ramón knows what it means. With insurance." Martínez picked up the briefcase sitting next to him and put it down again in a nervous gesture.

Cesar laughed uncomfortably, remembering the meeting in Panama where Martínez explained what happens when money gets lost. That was the part Cesar had found threatening. "You already explained that insurance to me," he said now.

"The person answers with his word," Martínez said. He said it was just like when he took Serrano to be questioned by the owner of the $1 million that had been seized. "I took Rubén to the office. Rubén faced up to it," Martínez said, using Serrano's pseudonym.

Getting back to his money squeeze, Martínez had the clear impression he was not getting through. He picked up a hotel information sheet and turned it over on the coffee table, leaning forward to write on it. He said to Cesar, "I'll explain it to you on a piece of paper so that you will understand how it works."

Using initials to indicate people's first names, he said,"There are people who have money in the United States. A product of what? We all know what from."

Cesar translated to Featherly, pointing to the paper, "These are people who have money, the product of you know what."

"Aha," Featherly said.

Martínez explained that these people had dollars he bought from them. He launched into a complicated discussion of dollars and pesos and commissions and how the relative value of one affects the other. This was hard to follow, especially since the Atlantans had no idea Martínez was buying and selling currency. They saw him as a money mover for traffickers and hadn't thought much about the need to convert dollars into a currency more useful to the Colombian traffickers.

"You understand?" Martínez asked Cesar.

"Yes," said Cesar. When he started to translate to Featherly, he said, "He's just explaining—"

"The exchange, they're losing," Featherly responded, apparently picking up the gist of Martínez's scribbling. "He sold it on the black market," said Featherly, who knew that Colombians use black market money exchanges to evade government restrictions on foreign currency.

So the peso's devaluation meant higher costs for him, Martínez continued, because the 7 percent commission he paid cost him more in pesos. At the same time, Brown's competition was getting stiffer.

A new group had emerged that will charge only 6 percent, he said. And Martínez's partner—the owner of some of the money passing through—had told him to stop doing business with La Mina until it lowers its commission.

Ramón asked about the new competitors.

They are Panamanian Jews in the diamond business, Martínez told him. And they are very wealthy.

"What's he saying?" Featherly asked. "Make six percent?"

Ospina said to Martínez, "Talk to him about the official price."

Featherly was still asking for an explanation, pointing to Martínez's drawing. "Is this the exchange to pesos?"

Ramón tried to explain, but made no sense.

Featherly said he had heard on the news that the value of the dollar went up today.

"But that's against European currencies," said Martínez.

Martínez said he wanted them to understand that he was still making money with them—he was not losing—even though he had to give away half his fee to Ospina.

Cesar translated, prompting Featherly to respond, "I know he's not losing. He's here."

Martínez said the reason he had stopped sending money through the Atlantans was to give them time to streamline their operation.

As for lowering the commission, Featherly said he needed time to consider that.

With that, the business seemed to be over, and the men started discussing lunch possibilities. As each of them rose and headed for the door, they disappeared from the television monitor Skip and the DEA tech man were watching. The pair could hear the voices but saw only vacant sofas.

Then, as the voices died down, Ramón appeared on screen again. He reached down to where Martínez had left his drawing, picked it up, and stuffed it into his pocket before walking off camera.

Moments later, Martínez reappeared. But he wasn't looking for the drawing. He had left behind his briefcase, which he picked up before vanishing from view.

At first, Skip didn't know exactly what they had. He hadn't listened to the whole thing because the technician was using the single set of earphones most of the time, and much of the meeting was in Spanish. Nonetheless, he could tell that "we had a good recording, and everything was going well. And I knew Martínez was doing a heck of a lot of talking."

For its content and its technical clarity, this was a tape a jury could love. Not to mention the bosses back home at DEA.

It was a remarkable piece of evidence.

After a late lunch at a mediocre Chinese restaurant, the five men split up, agreeing to meet that evening in the same hotel room for drinks before dinner.

Featherly went to see Skip to talk about what had transpired, to tell him the plans for the evening, and simply to relax with a friend.

All Cesar wanted to do was nap, rest up from the exhausting meeting and give his body the rest it needed to get rid of his awful cold.

He hadn't rested for long when the telephone rang. It was John Featherly, and he was not a happy man. He was angry at Cesar for his performance that morning. Cesar—as Alex Carrera—was supposed to be Jimmy Brown's sidekick, not the man in charge. But Cesar had not deferred sufficiently to Featherly in the meeting, Featherly told him. Jimmy Brown was supposed to do the talking, not Alex Carrera.

In fact, Cesar and Martínez had acted downright chummy, in part because they spoke the same language, and in part because they had met each other before and had spoken on the phone several times. Featherly had never met Martínez and had established no rapport before that day. And he was forced to rely on Cesar and Ramón to tell him what was being said.

Get into your role, Featherly said on the phone. Let me do the talking. With a flash of Irish temper, Featherly put Cesar in his place. You don't make the decisions, you're the translator. If there's a question to be answered or a decision to be made, you ask me.

Daytime resort wear had given way to sports jackets and darker slacks when the five men met again in Jimmy Brown's suite, camera running.

Martínez said he would talk to Clara García at Banco de Occidente about setting up an account in Atlanta.

"It may be good if Clara comes to visit me, in person," Featherly said. That way she, too, could get on DEA videotape, he didn't add.

"Oh yes, sure. Clara can go," Martínez said. "I'll tell her and she'll go." He said she could explain to him in person about Occidente's branch in the Caymans and take him the necessary paperwork. He said he would call her as soon as he returned.

"Does Clara speak English?" Featherly asked.

"Yes. Perfectly," came the answer.

Featherly brought up another matter that had concerned Martínez: the $1 million seized in California. He did not know whether he could retrieve it, said Featherly, but "whatever can be done, will be done."

Martínez said his partner was "ready to pay whatever is necessary" to recover the funds.

Ramón said to Martínez, "Can someone explain to Jimmy who the money belonged to? That it wasn't yours?"

Martínez said that was what he had been trying to do at their morning meeting. The way it works is this, he said. Someone such as Ivan Ospina has money to be picked up in the United States that he wants to sell to Martínez for pesos. Martínez and Ospina agree on a price, and Ospina notifies his employee in the United States to deliver the money to who-ever Martínez has hired, someone such as Serrano. Once Serrano gets the money in the United States, Martínez releases the pesos to Ospina, who then pays the money's true owner.

At every pause in Martínez's explanation, Cesar translated what he had said, faithfully and humbly.

The man Martínez called his partner receives money from "many Ivans and many Rubéns in the United States," he said. "They pay him for their deals. Five hundred, a million, two million."

In the case of the seized $1 million, Martínez said, his partner understands that his money is lost. "But if there's a possibility to recover it, well, that would be great. And he'll pay whatever he has to pay."

That money, Ramón asked, "was not yours?"

"It was Chepe's," said Martínez.

"Chepe's?"

"The partner," said Martínez.

Martínez resumed his explanation. He said sometimes he does not convert dollars to pesos. Sometimes his partner wants his money in dollars. That is when Martínez passes along the money after taking out 1 percent for "making the round."

His partner is not holding Martínez responsible for the $1 million, but Martínez has told him he will try to help.

His partner is most eager to recover that loss. "Rubén was with me over there, at the partner's office, face to face with him," said Martínez. So the man who interrogated Serrano was Chepe, apparently a significant drug trafficker.

Martínez described that meeting, "We were all together like now, talking and discussing what had happened." The whole process sounded much less threatening than it had sounded when Martínez described it in Panama. And it certainly sounded friendlier than it had felt to Serrano.

Martínez told them the brother of the guy who was stopped tried to blame Serrano's people because it had happened in their rental car. But Martínez had defended Serrano. The man at the wheel of the car might have already been targeted for investigation, he said.

As a result of those discussions, "we reached the conclusion that my partner accepts losing the money, but the responsibility lay with . . . those who lent the rental car to him—right?—as well as with him for having received a rental car."

Rental cars should not be used, he said, because no one knows who had the car before, or whether it had attracted the attention of law enforcement for some unrelated reason.

Martínez gave a detailed and accurate account of the event, down to the fact that it was a "small-town cop" who made the stop.

Featherly said, "It sounds to me like it was a uniformed traffic man who just got lucky."

"Maybe if it had been a federal cop, he wouldn't have let him go," said Martínez.

"I don't think so," said Ramón.

"No, afraid not," said Featherly. "He'd be in jail."

Martínez said cops in the Los Angeles area were picking up people on bogus traffic charges. That came as no surprise, of course. But Martínez elaborated. The cops use a remote-control device to burn out a car's lights, and then pull over the driver for having a broken light, he told them.

Featherly laughed. "Really? I didn't hear that." Not in all his years in law enforcement had he heard of such a device.

"Hmmm," said Ramón. "Strange."

Later in the conversation, as the men again discussed possible changes in their banking, Martínez said he would ask Chepe, who had "the largest volume of money," whether he wanted some of it sent to Europe. Martínez mentioned his partner's bank there, Deutsch-Südamerika-nische Bank. An offhand remark, that information would turn out to be remarkably useful later.

Martínez said he could not move "money for purchases" to Luxembourg because it would take so much time.

He explained that Chepe's money travels from Panama to one of three places: to Santa Cruz, Bolivia, for purchases; to the United States to buy planes; or to Luxembourg as savings. Martínez did not say what Chepe bought in Bolivia, but the country's chief product is coca leaf and paste, from which cocaine is made.

Martínez said his own business was really just a money exchange. "Dollars against pesos, every day, dollars against pesos." He saw himself as little more than a money exchanger.

"You know what," Ramón interjected, "how about going down and having a drink?"

"Ready," Martínez said.

Ramón said they had an early morning flight to catch the next day. "Is there anything else to discuss?"

As they considered the list of topics they had covered, looking for loose ends, Martínez went off on a discussion of the relative cost of the dollar against the peso in various U.S. cities, with Miami the most expensive. As a result, Martínez said, "we pay three percent for the process in Miami," where he least liked to do business. The dollar is cheaper in New York, he said. It's cheapest in Los Angeles.

Martínez said that for Jimmy Brown's work, "costs really have to be reduced." The fee for Los Angeles should be 6.5 percent, he said. For New York money pickups, 6 percent. With those rates, "we would start processing."

If they agreed to that, Martínez said, they could set up an account in the Caymans as an alternative to Panama and he would send his business to them instead of to La Mina.

"We're not doing rounds with La Mina, because I haven't had a reply from them" on the proposed cut in fees, he explained. Martínez told them La Mina's answer was slow because it had to be decided in a meeting of La Mina's five partners, who were Uruguayan, Chilean, American, Argentinian, and Colombian.

Martínez motioned to Cesar to get him a piece of paper at the end of the table.

"Let me explain to you how it works," said Martínez. "La Mina is a gold multinational that exists as an entity throughout the world." It has gold mines in Chile, Uruguay, Peru, and possibly Venezuela, he said.

Cesar translated: "They own, they actually own, gold mines."

"I never heard of them," Featherly said. He moved to the edge of the sofa for a better look at the paper. Cesar and Ramón moved closer, too.

"Is that their commercial name?" Featherly asked.

No, no, said Martínez. It's a nickname, like Pacho or Rubén.

Writing, Martínez said La Mina invests in gold mines in South America and has gold refineries and jewelry stores in Los Angeles, Miami, Houston, and New York.

"Retail stores?" Featherly asked.

"Yes, where they sell jewelry," Cesar told him.

"So in this country they are gold exporters—right?—where the gold mines are," said Martínez. "And in the United States, they're gold-importing corporations."

"Gold for jewelry?" Featherly asked.

"Physical gold."

"For jewelry? Not gold bullion?" Featherly asked again, sitting back deeper into the sofa.

"Yes, solid," said Martínez.

"But then it's melted down," Ramón said to Featherly.

La Mina exports, say, 100 kilograms of bar gold from Uruguay, Martínez explained. But only 10 kilograms are actually gold. The rest is an alloy, such as lead.

"I understand," said Featherly. He was amazed at how much intelligence Martínez was volunteering about La Mina. "He was talking so much," Featherly would say later. "I just told myself just to sit there and listen. It's coming right out of him."

La Mina pays insurance and taxes on the metal bar as if it were all gold, Martínez went on, creating paperwork to explain the large sums of cash La Mina receives. If the cops look into La Mina, they see documents showing the sale of large amounts of gold.

Martínez said that on four or five occasions, cops had arrested people they had seen leave La Mina's U.S. stores. "They don't nab them right away, but follow them for fifteen, twenty days, a month, until one day they stop them, and then they grab them," said Martínez.

But the charges never stick, because there is never any evidence of a crime. The paperwork from the gold sales covers the crime.

"Who's following?" Featherly asked.

"The police."

Ramón asked, "The feds, I suppose, right?"

"It's a federal crime," said Martínez.

"They're watching these people?" asked Featherly, wondering which agency already had La Mina in its sights.

"And the IRS," said Martínez. "La Mina has survived IRS audits—everyone has tried to get them. But it's been around for fifteen years. . . ."

Ospina said of the cops trying to pin a crime on La Mina, "They imagine it, but . . . they can't prove it against them."

"The IRS descends on them and audits their accounting books, and they're perfect," added Martínez.

Featherly said he was surprised that Martínez didn't mind doing business with a group so closely watched by law enforcement. "That's fine for them. Me, I like nobody to know I'm here," he said with a laugh.

Martínez agreed that it's better to be invisible.

Martínez talked a little more about La Mina's organization. But with that subject exhausted, Featherly said, "Why don't we go eat now?"

"Yeah, good idea," Ramón said. "Shall we eat?" he asked Martínez and Ospina.

"Sure," said Martínez. He picked up the paper he had been writing on, ripped it up, and threw it in a trash can on the way out.

This time, Cesar returned to retrieve the paper.

Coming out of the meeting, "everybody felt great," says Cesar. The five men dined at the hotel restaurant, one of the finer places on the island, savoring drinks and a leisurely, two-hour dinner. They tried to think of any business not covered, but mostly it was a relaxed, social occasion. Martínez handed around cigars he said were the same kind he had given Noriega.

Martínez was up for a night of fun, even a game of chance. He and Ospina invited the gringos to join them at the casinos, especially Featherly, the only real gambler in the group. Featherly declined, blaming the early morning flight. In fact, he knew he didn't have the money to gamble as Jimmy Brown would.

"They would have expected me to be blowing hundreds and thousands . . . instead of my couple dollar bets," says Featherly.

After dinner, Cesar and Ramón sat at the hotel pool for an hour or so, while Featherly met with Skip, who had been hanging around the restaurant unobtrusively to get a better look at Martínez and Ospina.

The Americans didn't really have an early morning flight. Instead, they waited until they were sure Martínez and Ospina had left, and then Featherly and Cesar went to help Skip and the tech man pack and remove the equipment.

Everything had gone so well it was hard to believe. "I couldn't have asked for anything better," says Featherly. They had Martínez and Ospina on tape discussing money laundering and showing remarkable expertise. These Colombians not only inculpated themselves, they also implicated Banco de Occidente and the two individual bankers. Not only that, Martínez had given them more on La Mina and was considering connecting Featherly to La Mina's bankers in Uruguay.

As he checked out of the hotel, Featherly handed the cashier Jimmy Brown's MasterCard, which Skip had gotten for him. But the cashier came back with distressing news. Jimmy Brown, big-shot money mover for the mob and now for the Medellín drug cartel, had a ceiling of only $2,500 on his credit card.

Beyond discrediting the big-shot image, the MasterCard ceiling posed a very real problem. Featherly had charged all the expensive rooms at the Golden Tulip, the drinks, the dinners, the plane ticket—everything. The total crashed through the $2,500 limit.

Featherly was more than peeved. If Martínez had witnessed their checkout, it would have been disastrous, possibly fatal. And even though Martínez wasn't there, none of the agents wanted to use cards with their real names on them.

"We really didn't have a way to pay the bill at that point," says Skip. Other than the $2,500 MasterCard, "we didn't have any undercover credit cards."

Somebody had to do something to get them out of Aruba. Ramón stepped up to the desk and offered his credit card.

Ramón Costello, former drug trafficker and now an informant for the DEA, had plenty of room on his card to pay for the trip. His credit was better than Jimmy Brown's.

*T*he Atlanta group took little time to decide whether to lower the commission charged Martínez.

At five thirty in the afternoon after returning to Atlanta, Cesar put in a call to Martínez in Medellín, tape recorder running.

In his undercover role, Cesar told Martínez that he, Jimmy Brown, Ramón, and Rubén had been talking all afternoon. "Jimmy . . . told me to tell you that the cut would be a half percent."

"Six and a half percent?" Martínez asked.

"Yes. You know," said Cesar, "cut a half from what we were doing before."

The guys in Atlanta wanted badly to resume their business with Martínez. They hadn't bothered to discuss the issue with Ed Guillen, the DEA agent controlling the Fis-Con accounts in New York. To their way of thinking, it was no concern of his.

If they had asked, they would have heard that Guillen had a problem with lowering the commission. If the Atlanta laundry became too competitive, it would not only draw customers from real laundries like La Mina, but would also attract customers away from other government undercover laundries, such as the other Fis-Con cases he was running. That would really screw things up for Guillen and the other DEA agents working money cases.

And it wasn't just DEA, either. By lowering the commission, Jimmy Brown's group would be undercutting FBI laundries and IRS laundries and Customs laundries, everybody's laundries. If DEA started stealing suspects—and therefore cases—an interagency war would surely ensue.

That's what happens when you let agents inexperienced in money matters run the undercover operation, says Guillen. A more knowledgeable agent, like himself, could probably have kept Martínez's business without giving away the store, he says.

Atlanta's first mistake, according to Guillen, was having Featherly pose as the head of the organization instead of a go-between. "They forced themselves in a position, where . . . Martínez could always feel like he could negotiate with them, for lower charges, commission rates, whatever. If they had not done that, and always alluded to another boss in New York or wherever . . . it could have put an immediate end to those types of negotiations," says Guillen.

But it could have put an end to the case, too, since Martínez insisted on meeting the men at the top of the money services he used, and since he didn't want to pay standard rate for a substandard service.

12: Linking the Dots

Virtually obscured by the clash of egos at the February meeting in Atlanta was a quiet DEA investigator from headquarters who listened and silently took notes. While the others argued, this detective absorbed the information flying about the room, no matter how incongruous it seemed to others.

Such was the job of the intelligence analyst, and such the style of Gail Shelby, a mild-mannered woman in her late thirties. The Atlanta group had asked headquarters for analytical support for the Serrano-Martínez case, and headquarters had deemed the case potentially significant enough to send her.

Drawn to the agency at the dawn of the war on drugs in the early 1970s, Shelby had aspired to detective work since childhood, when she had read every Nancy Drew book she could find. When asked, she would say she wanted to be Nancy Drew when she grew up.

That's what attracted her to law enforcement, even though she started out in DEA as a secretary. Always reaching for more intellectually challenging tasks, Shelby worked her way into investigations, albeit as a detective whose clues were all on paper.

As a DEA intelligence analyst, Shelby carried no gun and kicked down no doors. Leaving the flashy work to others, she spent her days poring over reports and interviewing agents, running computer searches and looking for links among evidence others had gathered. She was supposed to draw the lines between the dots the agents provided to see what picture emerged. The trick was locating the dots and then deciding which ones belonged in the picture. At that, Shelby was diligent, always hunting for another piece of information and trying to understand its significance. As an analyst specializing in financial intelligence, she had connected significant dots for the Pisces investigation, which made her a good choice for the Atlanta money-laundering case.

Her introduction to the case came at that February meeting in Atlanta, where agents from New York and Los Angeles were openly skeptical of the information she was supposed to pursue. This did not matter to Shelby. Atlanta had clues, and her job was to follow them.

When she returned to Washington, Shelby hit the DEA computer data base. The Narcotics and Dangerous Drugs Intelligence System (NADDIS) keeps names and information from each DEA-6, which is the report an agent files whenever a case opens and whenever a development occurs. Shelby punched in "Mina and "La Mina." She tried "Mine" and "Gold Mine" and "Gold," hunting for anything that might connect.

As she worked, Shelby recalled something one of the New Yorkers at the Atlanta meeting had mentioned—something about a mining company that washed drug money through jewelry stores in L.A. and New York. She punched in the name of the company, SA Mines/Cal Colombia Mines, NY, and found an address at 580 Fifth Avenue. She called DEA–New York for more information and was told of another new money-laundering investigation being worked by Phil Devlin and Kevin Mancini. She reached Mancini.

Yeah, three Colombians had walked in off the street, talking about cocaine and money, Mancini confirmed. They claimed to have been dropping off drug money at a penthouse office in the jewelry district. He told her the coke they distributed and the money they collected belonged to a Colombian they called "Chepe," who also went by a nickname Mancini pronounced "KEE-ko." In Spanish, that would be "Kiko," but Mancini and Devlin spelled it "Quico" in their reports.

The names hit; the jewelry connection hit. Shelby says Mancini didn't mention La Mina, and the New York CIs hadn't mentioned gold or jewelry stores. But the office receiving the drug money was right there in the jewelry district of New York.

It struck Shelby as too much of a coincidence. The two laundries had to be the same. The longer Mancini talked, the more certain she became. She told him she believed his case and the Atlanta one were related and suggested he call Skip Latson.

Until recently, Mancini had been helping the Atlanta group with the Fis-Con money pickups in New York. But that work slowed, and after the money stopped coming in January, he moved to another enforcement group and was soon working with Devlin on the information Larry, Curly, and Moe had given them.

Mancini already knew about Martínez, and he knew Martínez had stopped sending money through the Atlanta laundry. In fact, as a New York agent assigned to help the Atlanta Fis-Con case, Mancini had attended the December 10, 1987, meeting in Atlanta where Ramón's first meeting with Martínez was mentioned. He was there when the Atlanta agents talked about the ledgers for an L.A.-based laundry called La Mina.

Mancini says he called Skip, but Skip remembers being the one who initiated contact.* He says he recalls it vividly because they clashed immediately. To a large degree, it was a culture clash between a friendly southerner and a wary New Yorker.

"I started out by saying from what I heard they had a really good, potential case . . . and I was impressed," says Skip. "And his immediate reaction was, like, 'Don't stroke me! What the hell do you want?'

"And I was really taken aback, because I was impressed. But you know, it's just the way of New York. If somebody comes on and compliments you, something's wrong."

Whoever initiated it, Mancini remembers the call, too. But the only part that stuck with him was the fact that Martínez preferred La Mina to the Atlanta laundry because La Mina was so much quicker. He didn't see that this information could help his new investigation in New York.

Skip says he learned of several similarities between the Chepe the New York CIs had described and the one Martínez described. Skip believed they could be the same man.

By this time, Mancini and Devlin had written and circulated reports on the informants' story and the new investigation it prompted, according to Elaine Harris, who supervised Mancini and Devlin's group. The reports from New York named Chepe, La Mina, and La Mina 30, and listed key addresses, phone numbers, and other information, Harris says her records show.

Whatever the New York agents reported, Shelby and the Atlanta agents say they didn't see it for months. Harris vehemently denies her agents withheld information, though they would not have been the first agents in history to have done so. "New York was known for that," says Cesar. Still, Devlin says he and Mancini filed everything as they were supposed to. Shelby speculates the reports could have become stuck in DEA's bureaucratic pipeline. Even when processing works smoothly

* Mancini's recollection of the call comes from testimony he gave in a 1990 hearing in Los Angeles. He was not interviewed for this book because the Special Agent in Charge of the New York office declined to allow an interview.

DEA-6s sometimes take weeks to get from the agent's desk into the computer system where other DEA personnel can check them.

Part of the reason why neither Shelby nor Atlanta knew the details of New York's investigation could lie in the New Yorkers' belief that their case was separate from Atlanta's, so they had no reason to direct their DEA-6s to Atlanta. The New Yorkers believed their Chepe was different from Atlanta's, and the broad term "La Mina" could apply to any money-laundering operation using gold or jewels. Besides, Atlanta had its own undercover laundry. How could that be connected to the real laundry the New Yorkers were investigating?

By early April, Shelby had flown to Los Angeles to learn what she could about the L.A. part of the Serrano case, the Fis-Con case. She read reports, sifted through the evidence, talked to agents.

As she made her way through the Fis-Con case file in L.A., one piece of evidence stopped her cold. It was a ledger confiscated a year earlier in the bust made after the toys-in-the-car-trunk incident. Cops had found the "pay and owe," as they called it, while raiding a house that surveillance targets had led them to. The confiscated ledger was kept in a secure evidence room, while a photocopy—which is what Shelby found —reposed in the case file.

Shelby read through the columns of names and numbers, trying to discern their meaning. At the top of one of the pages, her eyes stopped: "Mina #30."

She knew from Atlanta's agents that Martínez's account with La Mina was coded "Mina 30."

She ran down the page. There it was again, "Mina #30." And again.

The find thrilled Shelby. "That gave me a good clue," she says, "that there was some kind of a connection out in Los Angeles with the whole La Mina thing."

The three entries in the ledger showed that $2.5 million had traveled through the Mina 30 account in the space of ten days in December 1986. At each of the rows bearing the name La Mina and the numbers, another name appeared: "Raul." Who was Raul? At this point, Shelby just tucked it away in her notes and her memory.

Shelby learned the ledger had been seized in a spinoff from Fis-Con a year earlier, when the cops found toys in the trunk of Serrano's abandoned rental car. Agents following Serrano in Los Angeles also surveilled the men with whom Serrano had met that day and followed them and their contacts to two suburban houses, which the agents raided. They found an apparent stash house for cocaine at one of the addresses, while the house on Llano Street in Woodland Hills apparently served as an office for a lucrative business, judging from the numbers in the ledger found there.

But who kept this ledger, and how were they related to Martínez? Shelby didn't delve into it then. But the Mina 30 connection was enough of a link to report. As soon as she spotted it, she told the Fis-Con case agent in Los Angeles, Dan Ortega.

He understood the significance immediately. In meetings he had attended in Atlanta, it had troubled him that no one outside Atlanta seemed to believe in La Mina. Now, with the entries in this ledger, maybe Atlanta's information would be taken more seriously.

Ortega called Cesar Diaz. And on April 7, 1988, Cesar wrote a DEA-6 to report the black and white corroboration of Martínez's fantastic story.

Shelby learned something else in Los Angeles, too. She picked up scuttlebutt about another money-laundering investigation under way and decided to check it out. Just in case. She asked one of the co-case agents for a rundown. He told her a Wells Fargo banker had alerted DEA-L.A. to a possible money laundry operating out of the jewelry district. It looked like many millions of dollars were being run through a company called Andonian Brothers Inc. (ABI), which was owned and run by an Armenian family.

By this time, bank records were showing that ABI had moved more than $25 million through its corporate account between November and January. This was a gigantic operation—nearly as large as the one Martínez had described. He gave her the few case reports that had been filed at that point, but there was nothing to connect the investigation directly to La Mina. And while Martínez had mentioned a lot of nationalities, he had never said Armenians were running La Mina.

Still, Shelby tucked away that information, too; it might fit into something she would later learn.

*I*n the months since the Wells Fargo banker first reported her suspicions to the DEA in Los Angeles, agent Dave Barkett had become increasingly convinced of the significance of the find and increasingly frustrated at DEA's unwillingness to commit the resources needed to uncover and prosecute these money launderers. He had done the usual background checks into the businesses and the people the banker had led him to, but it would take teams of surveillance agents watching locations and following people even to begin to understand what was going on inside those offices.

"I kept asking for manpower, I kept asking for a group to support this case, but I didn't get it," says Barkett. The upper-level management in L.A. at that time was "too small and too cautious."

Group 6 with its money-laundering expertise was the natural home for the case. But supervisor Tony Ricevuto says his group was too busy with the Atlanta investigation and the prosecution of Pisces defendants to take on a new probe.

So Barkett did something considered heretical within DEA: He called the FBI. In fact, Barkett didn't just call the FBI. He called the IRS. He called Customs. He called the State Bureau of Narcotic Enforcement, and he called the L.A. Police Department. Acting on his own, agent Dave Barkett turned the L.A. investigation into a multi-agency affair.

FBI personnel say that the banker, Drusilla Leightner—not Barkett—made the case a multi-agency matter when she tipped off so many agencies at the beginning.

Regardless, the joining of the FBI and DEA into a single investigation meant that significantly more ground could be covered and the special skills of the two groups could be tapped. But it also guaranteed that spats over turf and clashes over investigative cultures would dog the probe. An L.A.-based DEA agent defines the difference: "I like to think of the Bureau as corporate law enforcement. And DEA is just full of cowboys." DEA investigations are "much more independent and spontaneous."

The people at FBI like to say they go for the long-term approach to an investigation, whereas a "buy-bust" mentality permeates DEA, where the typical case involves an undercover agent buying a kilogram or two of cocaine and arresting the seller.

More important, according to the widespread attitude at DEA, the Bureau never merely participates in an investigation; it runs it. Call in the FBI and you might as well give up your own investigation. With five times the agents of DEA, the Bureau has the resources to overwhelm.

But Barkett knew the FBI was already on the case. In addition to the banker, the FBI had sources within the Loomis armored-car company, and appeared to be far ahead of DEA. Unless DEA committed a lot more agents, it might as well forget doing anything. There was no way DEA could run the investigation at this point, and it was better to be part of a group effort than to trudge along in the dust kicked up by the hordes running ahead, Barkett figured.

Within DEA, Barkett set out to get the case assigned to a group supervisor who would take it seriously. He started lobbying a supervisor new to L.A., Vince Furtado, who had been brought in from Boston.

Furtado, a balding man in his forties, speaks with the accent of a lifelong working-class Bostonian. He remembers Barkett telling him that "the management in the division was not giving him the support he needed . . . the FBI was off and running at full strides, and so was the IRS, and this was clearly a DEA case and if he didn't get somebody to help him, it was gone."

Furtado could see a case like this would be long and tedious, and it was questionable whether DEA could ever catch up with the other agencies. But he told his boss he wanted to take it on because "it needed to be done, and . . . if we didn't get involved pretty quick, the case was a goner." Furtado's boss gave him the case to supervise.

By March, FBI agents from Los Angeles had met with the Loomis regional security director at company headquarters in Oakland, and the report made to FBI–New York of the broken box containing $800,000 eventually found its way to FBI–Los Angeles. At the meeting the agents learned that during the previous summer, Orosimo Corporation in New York had hired Loomis to take boxes of gold scrap and jewelry from its office at Fifth Avenue and West 47th Street and to ship it to the Ropex Corporation in Los Angeles. Ropex's address was 550 South Hill Street, a contemporary medium-rise some called the Jewelry Mart Building, located on the edge of Los Angeles' jewelry district.

Loomis sources told the agents they believed that Ropex and Orosimo were owned, at least in part, by members of the same family. The family were ethnic Armenians, and their last name was Koyomejian, sometimes spelled Kouyoumjian.

In addition to sending Loomis their own business, the Koyomejians had also referred another family of Armenian businessmen, the Andonians. Like Ropex, the Andonians had hired Loomis to move boxes from New York to Los Angeles, boxes weighing from 40 to 100 pounds and valued at around $1 million. Loomis knew a box of jewels or gold that heavy is generally considerably smaller than what they were transporting for Ropex and the Andonian Brothers. In fact, Loomis would turn out to be a treasure trove of information for the agents.

But some of the most valuable evidence came as trash. Agents had started rummaging through refuse left by these businesses, finding envelopes with names and addresses, and scraps of papers bearing numbers. They could see from the discarded labels and boxes that the company was getting shipments from other cities, not just New York.

"Soon we were getting things from Miami, Houston, San Jose . . . I think Detroit was involved. I mean every time we turned around there was a new city sending money to Ropex and Andonian-L.A.," says Barkett. If these were cocaine profits, as DEA believed, they were profits from cocaine sold all over the United States.

One Thursday in April, a discarded box containing more trash—and clues—turned up in Ropex's garbage. The box was addressed to Ropex-L.A. and had been shipped from Ropex in Houston. The label said it had contained $740,000 worth of jewelry, but now it contained only rubber bands and a few torn corners of twenty-dollar bills. It looked like the real contents of the box had not been jewelry but money, apparently bundled with rubber bands and totaling $740,000.

But the best discards were not boxes or bands but paper. An FBI agent sorting through Ropex's trash one day found what appeared to be a ledger covering late 1986 and all of 1987. Bound between black, leather-like covers, this was Ropex's business ledger, and, if the numbers in it could be believed, Ropex was handling millions each week.

"It was rather shocking," says agent Carl Knudson of the Los Angeles office of the IRS, which was analyzing the financial records in the case. The ledger contained not only sums but customers' first names, too. The Koyomejians simply had tossed out this incredibly valuable information.

The most remarkable thing the ledger showed was the trading in gold. An unbelievable volume of gold trading. "They were showing millions and millions of dollars of gold being purchased and sold," says Knudson.

"We were astounded," he says—astounded at the size of the operation, astounded that Ropex would simply toss out its ledger, astounded that the ledger dated back to 1986.

"We were just surprised they kept this operation going so long."

Back in Washington, Gail Shelby and her immediate boss, Mike Orndorff, set about hunting for more pieces to the puzzle that might be lying about the country unnoticed. When they heard about the Ropex ledger, they wanted to check it out.

Orndorff, a slightly disheveled-looking guy in his thirties, got on the phone to Los Angeles. DEA-L.A. didn't have a copy of the FBI's find, but the IRS did.

Orndorff put in a call to the IRS and reached Knudson. The IRS agent brought out a copy of the newly discovered ledger and started reading it aloud to Orndorff, who was looking at Shelby's copy of the ledger from the Llano Street raid a year earlier.

The Ropex ledger contained lots of first names and apparent code names for the customers buying gold, but the one that came up most often, and the one that made the largest gold purchases, was "Raoul." In January 1987, for example, he showed up every few days buying 70, 85, 100 kilograms of gold at a time, paying $1 million to $2 million for it, according to the ledger.

Knudson told Orndorff about Raoul, and Orndorff spotted a similar name, "Raul," among the names in the Llano Street ledger. Knudson in Los Angeles and Orndorff in Washington flipped to the ledgers' December 1987 entries. In both ledgers, Raoul/Raul had three entries, with the dates and the dollar amounts almost the same. In both, the three sums came to roughly $2.5 million over ten days. A possible hit.

"At that point we thought, Oh boy, this looks real interesting here," says Shelby, especially since the Llano Street ledger listed Mina 30 on the same line as Raul. Shelby had already tentatively linked New York to

Atlanta's information. "So, bingo, it looks to me like New York, Atlanta, and Los Angeles are tied together in the case."

The two were amazed at their find. After Orndorff got off the phone, Shelby says, they sat there and looked at each other. "And he said something to me, you know, he mentioned . . . the word 'Orosimo' when we were talking." Knudson had spoken of Orosimo, the company sending boxes to Ropex in Los Angeles.

"I said, 'My God, Mike! . . . I have heard the name of the company before! I think Orosimo has come up in the New York case.' And we both looked at each other and we said, 'Oh boy. And I went running into my office and I started sifting through my documents," recalls Shelby. Sure enough, the DEA agents in New York had told Shelby about Orosimo.

"At that point," Shelby says, "we realized that it looked like we really had something. . . . It looked like a large, international—very large, international money-laundering organization." And they knew from Martínez that it was washing money for the Medellín cartel.

Orndorff went to tell his supervisor the news. He and Shelby now had an outline of something big they needed to fill in. His boss agreed. Orndorff's supervisor called a meeting in Los Angeles to bring together all DEA personnel holding pieces of what seemed like the same puzzle. He set it for the following week.

Because of the huge sums of money Martínez had said La Mina was laundering, "we felt that time was of the essence," says Shelby, "and that we really needed to get everybody together as soon as possible and have them lay their cards on the table, lay their cases on the table, which in fact they did the following week."

By that time, Shelby had prepared a DEA-6 laying out all the connections between the Atlanta, New York, and Los Angeles cases.

*I*n a two-day meeting in the middle of May, a score or more DEA agents from Los Angeles, New York, Houston, and Atlanta met in a DEA conference room in Los Angeles—along with a couple of prosecutors and cooperating IRS agents—to tell each other what they had. Skip Latson related Martínez's description of La Mina and passed on new information that an Argentinian named Raúl helped run it; Dave Barkett talked about the money and the boxes arriving at Ropex and Andonian Brothers in L.A., and the huge cash deposits that followed them. The agents from New York talked about Chepe's cocaine operations and the money laundry he used, La Mina.

La Mina at work was what the agents from New York, Los Angeles, and, more recently, Houston, were watching. None of La Mina was happening in Atlanta; it was just that the Atlanta agents had access to at least one of La Mina's customers. Atlanta offered the overview, as seen through the eyes of Eduardo Martínez.

Shelby pulled it all together, explaining the matching ledgers and the other links between individual probes. The money flowed from New York, Houston, and elsewhere to Los Angeles, via Loomis. In Los Angeles, it was deposited into accounts at several banks. From there, wire transfers sent money to a company called A-Mark, a large West Coast precious-metals wholesaler that had been transferring the sums to a Syrian-owned bank in London and to Banco de Occidente in Panama. Beginning in March, when banking turmoil was reaching high pitch in Panama, A-Mark stopped sending money to Occidente and instead began wiring funds to two banks in Montevideo, Uruguay. March was also the month of the Atlantans' Aruba meeting with Martínez, when he had urged Featherly to use Uruguay or the Caymans instead of Panama for banking.

Shelby's presentation showed the money laundry called La Mina stretching the width of the United States and reaching beyond to other continents. Just as the drug traffickers and money launderers crossed state lines and nations' borders, so must the investigators look beyond their own turfs and link up with each other. A plan was set up for each office to exchange their DEA-6s and otherwise keep each other informed.

The mind-boggling scope of the thing meant that L.A., in particular, needed to commit more agents. Vince Furtado threw all of his group's ten agents into the case, and his bosses gave him five more agents, too.

This was the first acknowledgment by anyone other than the Atlanta team that Martínez's tale was probably true. There really was a money laundry called La Mina based in L.A. that was washing multiple millions of dollars each week for major drug traffickers. No one had corroborated the gold mine part of the story, but investigators knew at this point that La Mina's storefronts claimed to be jewelry and gold companies, and they tended to locate in the jewelry districts of New York and Los Angeles.

L.A.'s Barkett realized Atlanta's intelligence related to the case he was working. At roughly the same time as this meeting, the DEA agent in L.A. who had been in charge of helping Atlanta make the Fis-Con money pickups, Dan Ortega, alerted Barkett to the meeting Martínez had had in Aruba. He told him Atlanta had a videotape Barkett should see. Barkett did, and he knew Martínez was talking about his case when he talked about La Mina.

Still, not everyone at that May 1988 meeting in L.A. was convinced that the similarities in their cases meant they all had pieces of the same criminal enterprise. New York's Kevin Mancini, for example, remained dubious that Atlanta's intelligence related to anything he had going.

The idea of linking hands across the continent would not appeal to an independent, strong-willed drug agent like Mancini. The bureaucratic mess of sending reports all over the place drags the pace. And once different cases connect, an agent cannot make any significant move without checking with everyone else. The New York contingent was not enthusiastic.

But headquarters wanted to coordinate, not only among the many DEA field offices, but also among the various agencies that had already been drawn into this thing. Two days after the meeting of DEA personnel, another meeting convened in Los Angeles, again drawing together authorities from Atlanta, New York, Los Angeles, and Houston. This time the agents and supervisors came not only from DEA but also from the FBI, the IRS, Customs, and the California Bureau of Narcotic Enforcement.

With the day-and-a-half-long meeting, a gigantic mix of federal agencies from far-flung corners of the country came together. Not every piece of information was shared, but at least they all saw each other face to face, learned generally who was doing what, and how they could contact each other. Whether this loose and, in many cases, reluctant body of snoops and cops could form the juggernaut necessary to find its elusive target remained to be seen.

13: Peering Down the Mine

While scores of federal agents began the task of piecing together evidence they were gathering, Ramón traveled back to Colombia to gather more. He and Serrano had something of a reputation among Colombian drug traffickers at this point, as both money movers and cocaine movers.

In his rounds, Ramón kept hearing that the man Martínez called his partner, Chepe, trafficked in cocaine in levels comparable to those of Pablo Escobar himself. Unlike the very public Escobar and Jorge Ochoa, however, Chepe kept a low profile, so low he had barely shown up on DEA's screen until now. Even his name was a mystery. Ramón had heard him called many names, which he passed along to DEA-Atlanta. But he had not heard the name Serrano believed he had read on the engineering degree in Chepe's office: Geraldo Moncada. Serrano had not mentioned Moncada's name to Ramón or to their partners in Atlanta.

"This was a very big guy," Ramón says. But within U.S. law enforcement circles, "they didn't know he existed."

So when Martínez suggested to Ramón that he meet with Chepe, Ramón happily agreed.

For all his rumored success, neither Chepe nor his office impressed Ramón. Martínez took Ramón to a low, glass-plated office building in downtown Medellín, not to the construction office Serrano had visited. Inside, cheap, bare paneling covered the walls in Chepe's office.

Chepe himself had no particular presence or charisma, unlike Escobar or even Martínez. A short man of slight build, Chepe had fine features and wispy brown hair. So this was the man who had interrogated Serrano in January about the $1 million seizure. He hardly seemed intimidating now.

Chepe wanted to do business with Ramón and his contacts—cocaine business, not money business. The $1 million loss had shaken Chepe's confidence in Jimmy Brown's laundry. But he was always looking for new cocaine routes, and Martínez had told him Ramón could help bring in a load. Chepe said he had 700 kilograms of cocaine he wanted to move to New York, and he wanted Ramón's Atlanta contacts to help him do it. He told Ramón that although he had aircraft of his own, he wanted Ramón's people to supply their own plane for the maiden voyage.

The CI was happy to conspire in another criminal enterprise with Chepe. He said he would check with his people on the availability of a plane and get back to him.

This dual investigation was working in unplanned ways, even though not a single drug importation scheme had panned out. Here was a major suspect no longer willing to send money, but still willing to plan a cocaine venture with the confidential informant. It was a way to keep Chepe on the line and to link dope directly to the money Chepe had been sending Jimmy Brown's laundry.

Despite all the good news, the bad news was that the $1 million seizure had scared Jimmy Brown's only remaining customers, Chepe and Martínez. The laundry's agonizing slowness hadn't inspired confidence, either. The agents had tried everything to keep their business: lowering the charge, offering to change the money route, answering any question Martínez posed. But nothing could overcome the uneasiness caused by the $1 million seizure and the sluggish pace. For all their efforts to please, the agents had no more money customers at the moment, though several potential clients were at the door.

Martínez was sending his business to La Mina. Despite what he said in Aruba to the contrary, he was still sending money to La Mina, he told Ramón now.

If the DEA wanted to know more about Martínez's money laundering, it would have to look into La Mina.

As on West 47th in New York, shops in the jewelry district of Los Angeles glow with gold, batches of golden chains hanging on suspended hooks, rings, bracelets, and earrings shining from display cases. Here, too, arcades teem with a seemingly endless number of small businesses displaying all kinds of jewelry in cramped booths. And as on 47th Street, window-shoppers attract salesmen who cajole them to come inside for a closer look at the diamond rings.

Less compressed and claustrophobic than West 47th, the West Coast version sprawls through several blocks of downtown L.A., intermingling jewelry shops with stores selling cheap electronic goods, cut-rate athletic shoes, or discount clothing. There are juice stands and there are money exchanges. Multi-colored lights flash and rock music blares from one electronics store. The district draws immigrants from all over, and the salespeople, the shopkeepers, and the multi-racial pedestrian traffic reflect the international flavor. Everywhere the signs in shop windows say, *Joyería* (Jewelry) and *Mayoreo* (Wholesale). A Mexican restaurant stands next to an Italian jewelry store, both boarded up.

Aging buildings, some with once-grand marble foyers, open onto busy sidewalks. Inside, security guards monitor walk-in traffic and keep an eye on banks of closed-circuit television screens. Couriers scurry past, carrying small but obviously heavy packages. Armored-car guards haul bags and boxes in and out.

Upstairs, on any floor, a visitor's every move is captured on camera, from stepping off the elevator to strolling down the dingy hallway. Not only does building security maintain cameras, so do most of the businesses. A visitor can be seen by any number of people who are themselves unseen behind solid doors or doors with glass panels painted or papered over, or covered with blinds hung from the inside. Almost every door bears a security company's sticker, and almost all are locked and equipped with buzzers. Behind these ugly doors, gems and precious metals are in various stages of becoming someone else's jewelry. Only people with specific business to conduct are allowed inside. The creepy secrecy that permeates these hallways is broken only by an occasional showroom, with plate-glass windows that offer the passer-by a view of radiant merchandise.

Three floors up from the busy street, at 220 West Fifth Street, Andonian Brothers offered just such a showroom, with cases full of golden jewelry. Down the hall and around the corner, behind doors that blocked the view, Andonian Brothers and their related businesses had more space, some of which connected to the showroom. In fact, Andonian Brothers and associated businesses occupied a good share of the space on the third floor of the Jewelry Trades Building, a deep but narrow old structure near Broadway and Fifth Street.

Not all of the office buildings are ancient and worn. At the western edge of the district, across a small park from the glorious Biltmore Hotel, the seventeen-story International Jewelry Center houses hundreds of businesses behind its glass and white concrete exterior. Located at 550 South Hill Street and also known as the Jewelry Mart Building, the structure features a sparkling granite lobby, where low, silver planters hold colorful plants. Elevators play Muzak as they carry passengers upstairs to carpeted hallways. As in the older buildings, cameras hang from ceilings, and an occasional glass-windowed showroom breaks up a sea of visually impenetrable doors.

Despite its glossy appearance, "the Jewelry Mart is filthy in terms of under-the-table and illegal activity going through that building," says DEA agent Barkett.

Plenty of cops and agents had tried to make cases against tenants of the Jewelry Mart Building. Now, in the late spring and early summer of 1988, the FBI, the DEA, the IRS, and Customs, assisted by local and state officers, all had agents watching a particular business on the ninth floor. That business was Ropex, and it was receiving shipments of purported gold scrap and jewelry from New York almost daily.

The feds believed the boxes contained nothing of the sort. By this time, agents rummaging through Ropex's trash had found tally sheets, money bands, bank currency bags tagged to contain hundreds of thousands of dollars, and torn pieces of one-, five-, and twenty-dollar bills. Notes retrieved from the trash seemed to back up their suspicions. One piece of paper dated April 25 listed the sums 649,500 and 900,000 as "in," for a total of more than 1.5 million. Next to those numbers was the word "out," showing the entry "AIB-300,000." Supplementing these clues were Loomis records, which showed that on April 26 an armored car picked up $300,000 in cash from Ropex and took it to the Federal Reserve for credit to Ropex's account at American International Bank, or AIB.

With all that evidence of cash on the premises, the trash was also yielding more signs that Ropex was selling gold. On April 27, the FBI found eight invoices, typed on company stationery, reporting that Ropex had sold $990,000 worth of gold to eight people on April 25 and April 26. All of the sales were conducted in cash, according to the invoices, which listed the name of each buyer and his or her country, Mexico or Canada. The invoices could, of course, explain the cash Ropex was handling. And certainly the ledger showed a huge volume of gold trading.

But a straight jeweler whom the feds used as an information source told agents that nobody in the jewelry business handles anywhere near $1 million in cash transactions over a two-day period...nobody engaged in a legitimate business, that is.

The legitimate business these companies claimed to conduct was described in Dun & Bradstreet reports, business license information, and incorporation documents. Agents pored over that information, filling in blanks with utility company and driver's license records. From those early record checks, the feds learned that Ropex claimed to be in the business of making and selling gold jewelry, wholesaling fine gold, and importing Italian gold jewelry. In 1987, the company projected $20 million in sales. First incorporated in California in 1980, Ropex was wholly owned by its president, an ethnic Armenian named Wanis Koyomejian, who also owned an affiliated company, JSK Bullion Corp., located in the suite with Ropex in the Jewelry Mart. JSK Bullion claimed to be a wholesaler dealing in gold bullion, silver, and coins. Like Ropex, JSK projected 1987 sales at $20 million.

Koyomejian, forty-six, had arrived in the United States from Syria in about 1979, and was living with his wife, a twenty-one-year-old son, and a younger daughter, in the middle-class suburb of Northridge northwest of Los Angeles. An older son of twenty-three lived in another Northridge home, which he owned with his parents, and which was valued for tax purposes at $226,000.

The records provided names and addresses of other family members or others associated with the businesses, and their titles. From the trash, the agents could even learn who was salaried and what they were paid.

The same family that owned Ropex also owned Orosimo, the New York company that had been shipping boxes (including the box containing $800,000) to the Los Angeles companies. Dun & Bradstreet described Orosimo as a wholesale jewelry company owned by Simon Kouyoumjian, the twenty-three-year-old son of Ropex's owner, although they spelled their last names differently. The young owner had told Dun & Bradstreet all of Orosimo's sales were in cash, but he had declined to give sales figures.

Preliminary checks into Andonian Brothers showed it to be owned by brothers Nazareth, thirty-two, and Vahe Andonian, thirty-five. Like the Koyomejians, the Andonians were ethnic Armenians who had come to the United States from the Middle East—in their case, Lebanon. They seemed to be doing quite well in America. Their company reported $44 million in sales for 1987, a significant jump from its impressive 1986 figure of $14 million.

The Andonians too lived in a comfortable suburb. The brothers and their families had hillside homes around the corner from each other in La Crescenta, an area off the Foothill Freeway, wedged between mountain ranges on the northern edge of L.A.'s sprawl.

The feds were learning not only who these people were and where they lived, but also who they telephoned and with whom they corresponded. A device they installed on telephone lines listed every phone number called from the companies under surveillance. A few New York telephone numbers showed up with great frequency. And with a mail cover, the feds were getting from the Postal Service the return addresses on mail sent to these businesses, as well as the addresses of whomever the suspects were writing.

At the same time, Loomis and bank records were showing astounding sums moving from New York to Los Angeles. Loomis not only delivered boxes to Andonian Brothers and Ropex; the company also picked up what was admittedly cash from the two companies and took it to various area banks or to the Federal Reserve for credit to a Ropex bank account. As for the cash hand-carried into banks by Andonian couriers, the couriers would tell bank employees that the Andonian Brothers acted as a gold brokerage, collecting cash from smaller jewelry companies to buy them gold from a wholesaler. In fact, bank records showed the Andonians were using the receipts to buy gold from A-Mark, the precious-metals dealer.

None of that fit the normal practice, as an industry source told the IRS. There was no reason for small businesses to use a broker such as Andonian Brothers, because small jewelers could buy gold directly from A-Mark, too. And when jewelers did buy gold, they paid with checks or letters of credit, not cash. Why would anyone take the extra risk and extra cost of giving cash to a middleman?

Even with all this information, the agents needed more. They needed to see and hear what was going on at Ropex and Andonian Brothers. They couldn't tap phone lines or hide microphones or cameras inside the businesses without court permission. And they couldn't get court permission without stronger evidence that crimes were being committed, and without first trying less invasive measures.

But there was nothing to stop them from installing hallway cameras. No one could possibly expect privacy in a public hallway where cameras hung from the ceiling every few feet. In went more cameras on the ninth floor of the Jewelry Mart Building to monitor Ropex.

The FBI rented office space in the Jewelry Mart and set up a surveillance post. On television monitors, they could see who went in and out of Ropex's offices. A Loomis guard usually came between 9:00 and 10:00 A.M. with a handtruck loaded with four or five boxes. He would ring the office buzzer, someone would take him into Room 975, the JSK Bullion office, and he would roll in the boxes. A few minutes later, the deliveryman would leave with his empty handtruck.

Agents noted it all: number of boxes, date, and time of delivery. Loomis records would later tell the agents the claimed values of the packages the agents had seen being rolled into Room 975, that is, how much money the boxes contained.

As agents watched on television monitors, Ropex principals or employees would leave the office later in the morning or in the afternoon, carrying satchels, briefcases, suitcases, or jewelry display cases.

To follow these people to their destinations, crews from four federal
agencies as well as local and state officers were on hand. But even with
all that manpower, keeping up with them after they left the ninth floor
was tricky at best. The lobby had front, rear, and side exits, and there
was no guarantee the courier would even come down to the lobby. Six
elevators ran between seventeen stories, plus the underground garage.
An agent staking out the lobby wouldn't know if the target went instead
to one of the four underground parking levels, or to another business
within the Jewelry Mart.

"It was enormously difficult . . . to mount a surveillance that could
cover all of these possible exits," FBI agent Bruce Stephens would later
testify.

The private security cameras and building guards also made it impossible to keep agents posted in the hallways, the lobby, or the garages.
Security guards or L.A. police officers acting on complaints from building tenants sometimes rousted surveillance agents from their posts.

"We could not put people standing around hallways all day," Stephens
would later recount. "We couldn't put people in front of garage doors
with armed guards, who were waiting for the arrival or armored cars.
We couldn't surround the building from the outside without being obvious."

And even when they could follow a courier from the ninth floor to
the street, keeping up with him in the heavy pedestrian traffic was
another matter. Cars didn't help, because so many of the streets in the
district are one-way.

But from the middle of April on into the summer, surveillance crews
organized by the FBI would follow couriers carrying cases and satchels,
sometimes a duffel bag, from Ropex's offices through the crowded sidewalks and rundown buildings of the jewelry district. Time and time
again, the courier would wind up at a bank—Independence Bank at
Sixth and Olive streets, American International Bank on Wilshire Boulevard, Mitsui Manufacturer's Bank, City National Bank—these people
seemed to have accounts everywhere.

Later, the feds would match their observations with Currency Transaction Reports (CTRs), which the government requires for any cash deposit of $10,000 or more. From these reports, which the IRS was
retrieving from its data center in Detroit, the agents learned that on the
same days they saw couriers going into banks, the banks were reporting
cash deposits into those businesses' accounts of sums ranging from
$50,000 to $640,000 at a time. IRS employees in Detroit had not noticed
these astonishing cash sums before.

In L.A. the numbers fit with what the Wells Fargo banker had told the
agents about Andonian Brothers, too.

With Ropex, not all the money left the offices that way, however. Loomis would also arrive regularly for afternoon pickups to haul away boxes or bags and deliver them to the Federal Reserve, which would credit Ropex's bank account at American International Bank.

Later in the summer, as if to dispel all doubt as to the contents of those boxes and cases going in and coming out of Ropex and JSK Bullion, the closed-circuit television cameras once captured a man going from one office to the other carrying a large stack of cash. On another day, someone was seen taking a money-counting machine into Room 975.

These businesses seemed to be bursting with cash, but not with customers. But how could the feds prove the money was dirty? And could they show the jewelers knew the money was dirty?

They needed an informant to infiltrate these groups; but these were family operations, and the Armenian community was too close knit for a stranger to be trusted. Maybe they would just have to keep watching, from the outside, until they had a strong enough case to take cameras and microphones inside.

At DEA in Los Angeles, the group supervisor assigned to this case, Furtado, had been irked that Barkett had brought the FBI into it. The FBI began with fifteen agents on the case, with plans to bring in another thirty or more if necessary. DEA could never match those numbers. Management could assign up to fifteen agents—a huge commitment for DEA. Furtado hated being so far behind the FBI already, so he called his counterpart at the Bureau.

"I needed to get some control over what he was doing," says Furtado. The two men started breakfasting together at least once a week.

The investigation focused on Ropex and was going full blast under the FBI's leadership when Barkett was transferred to Washington. To replace him, Furtado picked an aggressive, twenty-nine-year-old agent who had just returned from assignment in Bolivia, Mike Orton.

Orton was happy to be back in the States from the jungles of South America, where he had worked on Operation Snowcap, in which DEA agents stationed in Andean countries helped local authorities locate and raid hidden cocaine labs and airstrips. "After living in a puddle for two months in Bolivia," Orton says, "all I wanted to do was ride down a smooth road and eat a pizza."

One of Orton's first acts as case agent was to stop sending agents to help the FBI surveillance of Ropex. The probe was turning up great evidence, but Orton says he decided DEA should focus on the Andonians, who were getting comparatively little attention at that point.

Orton took some heat, he says, but it would have been worse if he had had a different supervisor. Furtado had to keep his agents in line with Washington's policy of interagency cooperation, but he didn't care to service the FBI, either. His weekly meetings with the FBI weren't going well, and he believed the Bureau was still cutting his agents out of the probe. "Every time we were trying to get something done," Furtado says, "they were giving me an excuse as to why it couldn't happen."

Furtado says at about his third meeting with his FBI counterpart, Ralph Lumpkin, "I said to him, 'Look, this can't go on the way it's going on.' I said, 'We're going to be in a real power struggle here if we don't have a meeting of the minds.' "

Furtado says the FBI was insisting on controlling Ropex and Andonian, but he would not hear of it. "I said, 'Time out . . . You have Ropex; I have Andonian.' I said, 'I have all the manpower I need, and we have total control of Andonian.' "

Lumpkin says he recalls nothing like that happening, and he denies he was trying to limit the DEA's role. "He may've been doing that to me. I wasn't doing it. He may have thought I was, but I wasn't."

Lumpkin says Furtado never told him he didn't want to follow in the FBI's dust. But the FBI supervisor adds: "Vinnie was under tremendous pressure from his own people . . . to make [DEA] the lead agency" in the overall investigation. "They were very proud people and worked very hard—as we all did."

Lumpkin insists there was a natural split between the two groups of apparent money launderers, and the supervising investigators agreed among themselves that it made sense to divide themselves up accordingly, with one agency taking charge at Ropex and the other getting Andonian.

The way FBI agent Fred Wong puts it, "To peacefully co-exist, the case was split in half." The FBI took the lead in the Ropex probe, while DEA took the Andonians.

Orton set up a watch post in the second story of an abandoned Crocker National Bank building across the street from the building that housed the Andonian Brothers. Next, he rented an office on the seventh floor of the Jewelry Trades Building and dubbed the fake business Pacific Basin Investments.

The DEA wanted to install hallway cameras on the third floor, where the Andonians were, but needed after-hours access to do it. So Orton checked out an LAPD cop working security at the building, decided he could trust him, told him the DEA was investigating the Andonians, and asked him to take a long walk one night in June. On that night, Orton brought in an electronics expert, who took cameras too small to be seen and installed them into broken acoustical ceiling tiles. A coaxial cable run through an air shaft in the building would feed images from the third-floor cameras up four floors to monitors installed in Pacific Basin Investments.

That office served as a staging ground for the surveillance. There, agents monitored and logged the comings and goings of Andonian Brothers. When they saw someone emerging with a suitcase or a bag, one of the agents would rush to the elevator and try to beat the target to the ground floor.

This was difficult, given that they were four floors above. Sometimes on the way down from the seventh floor, the elevator would stop on the third floor and the target would step in. "You just ended up standing a few feet from him," says one of the surveillance agents, Selby Smith. When that happened, he would "just kinda smile and look like nothing's going on."

Sometimes the people would take the suitcase or bag to a bank, sometimes to Ropex or another business. Sometimes, they would take it to a car, which allowed the agents to get a license number, a name, an address, a driver's license, and, eventually, a photograph. Still, matching a name to a person who popped up on cameras was tricky at best.

To try to keep people straight, the agents started putting together a player book listing each target and what was known about him or her. Slowly, the profiles started filling out. Likewise, Orton says they started compiling a vehicle list, a list of houses, and fact sheets on business entities. Everything had to be cross-filed.

"This is not macho kind of work like kicking a door in," says Orton. "It is tedious work."

But sometimes, evidence just happened.

That's how it was for Selby Smith, age twenty-four, who had just come out of DEA training when he was assigned to watch Andonian Brothers. During his first week as a DEA agent, Smith reported for work at the Jewelry Trades Building one morning and noticed a Loomis truck at the curb. He knew little about the case at that point and didn't think much of it when he stepped into an elevator with a Loomis guard.

Middle-aged and overweight, the guard was sweating in the June heat, stomach protruding over his belt. His gun stuck out to the side of his holster, where he had been leaning on it. Next to him a large yellow canvas bag pulled shut rested on a handtruck. The doors closed, and the elevator started upward.

"We're standing there and he says, 'Hey, wanna see some money?'" Smith recalls.

"And I said, 'Um, yeah. Sure.' And he opens up the bag and it is just pure cash." Bills bundled with rubber bands fattened the bag to about two feet wide and filled it to a height of four feet. Peering inside, Smith was looking at more money than he had ever seen in his life.

"I just said, 'Man that's a lot of money. How much is in there?' And the guy says, 'Half a million dollars.'"

At that point, the elevator stopped on the third floor. The guard drew the drawstring shut, rolled the handtruck out of the elevator, and started down the hall toward Andonian Brothers. The elevator doors closed.

Smith continued up to the seventh floor, where Orton was already stationed at the surveillance room. "I walk in and I go to Mike, I say, 'Mike, you wouldn't believe what just happened to me...'"

Smith had become the first agent to see cash going into Andonian Brothers—or going toward it. The camera did the rest. When the videotape of the Andonian Brothers from that morning was played back, Smith recognized the guard caught on camera rolling a large bag into the Andonian Brothers' back office.

DEA agents were watching the homes of the two Andonian brothers, too, and stealing their garbage to look for information. This was impossible without risking being spotted by a neighbor, so Orton worked out a special arrangement with a sanitation worker who worked that block. The garbage collector would keep the Andonians' refuse separate from the rest and drive it down the street where Orton waited. The agent would give the sanitation worker coffee to drink and doughnuts to eat while Orton went rummaging through papers, the remains of Armenian food, and used disposable diapers.

At the Jewelry Trades Building, agents had worked out a system for grabbing the trash there, too. After hours, an agent would take the trash left outside the Andonians' office and replace it with the trash the Andonians had left the previous day, which the agents had already checked.

The other agencies—the FBI, the IRS, and Customs—were assisting the DEA in the Andonian investigation, just as DEA was supposed to be helping out at Ropex. At weekly meetings, the agencies would exchange reports and surveillance logs. In fact, a lot of information, but not all, circulated among the agencies. Despite the cooperation, jealousies and distrust intensified.

Orton insists the FBI gave him plenty of reason to be suspicious. One day late in summer, Orton was watching the closed-circuit television monitors when who should appear to remove the Andonians' trash but two FBI agents. That is a preposterous allegation, according to the FBI agents who ran the probe, who say all of their people knew about the cameras and knew they couldn't trespass without creating a major interagency incident.

But Orton says it's exactly what happened, and that he complained that the FBI agents were overstepping their bounds. According to Orton, they complained in turn that DEA wasn't doing its job.

He acknowledges slacking off; that was part of his plan. His larger goal was winning court approval to install cameras, mikes, and phone taps inside these businesses. Both investigations at this stage aimed at getting just enough evidence that illegal activities probably were occurring, but not enough to make a prosecutable case without hidden electronic devices. If the judge believed the government could get what it needed without such an invasion of privacy, the request would fail.

"What it boils down to is that intrusion is necessary because you have tried all investigative methods, and you've failed," says Orton. "Well, oftentimes I would go out on surveillance or on trash pickups with the intention of failing. I used to call them 'negative surveillances.' Just one more day of documenting to the court what a loser I am."

In reality, the information they could get merely by watching and digging through trash was inconclusive. "If I do trash, what's it gonna show me?" asks Orton. "He's got an adding machine tape that's three feet long, and it has seven-digit figures all over it." But what did that mean? Nothing, given the Andonians' ostensible line of work.

"Is it gonna show me that he's got receipts indicating the transshipment of twenty or thirty kilos of gold buillon? He's a gold broker, that's what the man does," says Orton.

Still, the picture was filling out. By June, the mysterious "Raul"—whose name had appeared next to Mina 30 accounts on two different ledgers —had a putative last name. DEA in Los Angeles had identified one of the principals in the Andonian operation as Raúl Vivas, an Argentinian who owned a gold refinery in Montevideo. He appeared to be a major player in La Mina, and kept an expensive new Spanish-style house in the suburb of Sylmar, on the northern edge of the greater L.A. area.

The feds knew enough about Vivas to start looking into his bank accounts.

The IRS subpoenaed Vivas's bank, Republic International, and the prosecutor asked the bank not to disclose the subpoena to Vivas.

The bank turned over Vivas's records, but it also sent a copy of the subpoena to Vivas. Suddenly, trashed records at the jewelry store were turning up shredded. And all the surveillance possible could never catch Vivas at his home in Sylmar: spooked by the IRS subpoena, Raúl Vivas had fled to Argentina, taking his family with him.

News that La Mina was under IRS scrutiny traveled through the network of South American money launderers from Argentina to Colombia. It reached Francisco Serrano, who passed it along to his partner in

Atlanta, Cesar Diaz. While meeting with Cesar in Atlanta in mid-July to discuss potential new customers for Jimmy Brown's laundry, Serrano told Cesar La Mina was being investigated by the IRS in Los Angeles. This was news to Cesar, who was barely aware that IRS was part of the L.A. probe.

The Colombian drug traffickers were getting nervous about using La Mina, Serrano told Cesar. Serrano figured they might be ready to come back to Jimmy Brown.

14: Pulling Together, Pushing Apart

The huge, loose mass of federal agents now assigned to La Mina sometimes rolled, sometimes faltered. As it went, it dredged up information about La Mina.

At DEA headquarters, Gail Shelby compared reports from Los Angeles, New York, Atlanta, and now Houston, looking for more connections, more leads. She'd call up one agent, pump him for information, find a link to another city, then call an agent in that city to tell him about it. And she kept putting her findings into cables and memos and DEA-6s to remind everyone they were all working on one huge case.

Each verbal nugget about La Mina that Martínez had given Cesar and Featherly was turning up in New York and Los Angeles as real. Money in Los Angeles was being wire-transferred to a bank in Montevideo where Martínez had said La Mina had bankers. He had given agents the name "Raul," which showed up on two ledgers in L.A., as well as in the Andonian investigation, as Raúl Vivas. The CIs in New York had reported they dropped off drug money for credit to an account known as "Mina 30," the same account Martínez had said he used. And the major Colombian in the New York case was a man known as "Chepe," or "Quico," just like Martínez's partner.

Now, Shelby was trying to match up phone numbers. She had been poring over the DEA-6s Skip Latson had given her pertaining to Chepe and found the telephone number in Medellín that Ramón had used to reach Francisco Serrano in January when Serrano was being interrogated about the seized $1 million. The number was 32-44-67.

She remembered the CIs in the New York case had given the agents telephone numbers for their contacts in Medellín. So she put in a call to New York. Yes, the CIs gave eight telephone numbers, one of the agents told her. He found the list and started reading them to her.

No hit on the first one, or the second. But soon he said: 32-44-67.

It was one of the numbers the CI was supposed to call after he had sold the cocaine, received payment, and took the cash to Andonian Brothers Inc. in New York's jewelry district to be credited to the Mina 30 account.

And the man whose cocaine he was selling, the man who would eventually get paid through the Mina 30 account, was a man in Medellín known as Chepe.

Bingo.

Shelby wrote another report and sent it throughout the growing universe of DEA offices working the case. "I wanted to keep showing these links between the cases," she explains. "I felt it was crucial to do that so that everybody really—I don't know—believed in what they were doing."

She reported the matching phone number, and she reported other, new links. She concluded, "There is a strong likelihood" that the organization under investigation in New York and Los Angeles was the same La Mina that Martínez had described.

And, she added, "according to Martínez, La Mina is the largest money-laundering organization used by Colombian traffickers in the United States."

But out in the field, memos are only words on paper. In a drug agent's day, they don't command the attention that real live gumshoeing does. Shelby's cables simply weren't getting much notice in Los Angeles or New York. In Atlanta, however, whose agents had sought her help in the first place, these links were prized. Buddy Parker remembers when she connected the telephone number: "It's like, 'There's the same frigging number! My God!' "

Shelby's boss, meanwhile, was going up the bureaucratic line, pitching the significance of the investigation and the need to pull it together. At the same time, Ron Caffrey in Atlanta was making the same spiel to higher-ups in Washington. They both wanted to push this case above the clamor of the hundreds of other cases so that the men at the top would see it as an enormous money laundry in need of an enormous, unified investigation.

Otherwise, agents would be stumbling over each other, duplicating each other's efforts . . . and worse. The big danger was that one office or agency would make a move that would impede or endanger another office's investigation or agent.

Politically, within DEA, the time was right. The agency was warming to the idea of money-laundering probes, and this was clearly its biggest yet. And there was a lot of pressure to cooperate with other agencies, since Congress was complaining that interagency jealousies wasted government resources and benefited criminals.

But who would run the investigation?

David Westrate, the Assistant Administrator for Operations and the number-three administrator in the agency, called a meeting at headquarters in Washington, D.C., of key DEA personnel from his own department as well as Atlanta, New York, Los Angeles, and Houston. The fact that the DEA administrator in charge of all investigations had called the meeting automatically confirmed its importance. DEA was beginning to put a lot of stock into this investigation.

At 2:00 P.M. on July 14, 1988, some two dozen men, plus Gail Shelby, jammed into an eleventh-floor conference room at DEA headquarters in downtown Washington off McPherson Square.

The reason for gathering these far-flung DEA agents and managers quickly became clear to Furtado from Los Angeles. "The rest of the country was concerned that we were going to take control...of the whole thing, and they wanted a piece of the action." His agents had just written a lengthy proposal to turn the case into a Special Enforcement Operation, with DEA-L.A. in charge, and Furtado figured the DEA offices in the other cities weren't pleased.

"Every office there had begun a struggle, a power struggle within DEA as to who would run the case. So, not only was I fighting a war out in Los Angeles, I'm fighting a war now in Washington," says Furtado.

John Featherly, now stationed in Washington on the cocaine desk, attended the meeting and remembers it differently: "I think the deal was, let's find out what we have here and then we go from there. Everybody was putting out on the table what they found out from their investigations."

Through surveillance and records checks, the Los Angeles contingent had amassed an impressive body of evidence at this point. Through Loomis records, the feds had so far counted $92 million traveling through Andonian Brothers and Ropex, and could project an eventual, annual total of $400 million. And that did not include money that Brinks and other armored-car services were hauling for them.

From Atlanta, Caffrey volunteered that his team was considering trying to send money through La Mina. But he didn't want anything done from Atlanta to jeopardize anyone else's investigation.

The New York office, which was just now installing cameras in the hallways, had little more than the evidence the informant had supplied. But no other office had an informant actually inside La Mina. Working a case without an inside source is working it blindfolded; it's still possible to discern what's going on, but doing so is slower and vastly more difficult. New York reported its main CI had patched things up with Chepe during a recent trip to Colombia. In fact that very afternoon, agents in New York were debriefing the CI about his meeting with Chepe.

In Houston, the DEA had fended off an FBI charge for control of the case, so that investigation was just now starting up, reported the head of the Houston office.

Featherly and Caffrey argued for a coordinated investigation, saying the various teams were all looking at pieces of the same huge criminal enterprise, the one Martínez had described to Atlanta's agents and CI. "I'm not saying the case in Atlanta made direct probes into these other two cases undercover," says Featherly, "but the overall investigation and the evidence indicated that they were one." He met resistance.

As the discussion wore on, Featherly realized agents in the other cities still didn't believe they were all investigating the same entity or that they should be contributing to a single, nationwide investigation. "They really wanted to cut it up," he says. The New York and Los Angeles contingents seemed to want to keep working their cases independently.

At a break in the meeting, Featherly says he urged Shelby to discuss her latest findings, which she already had distributed by DEA cable. She suggested Featherly do it himself. Back in the meeting, he went down the list of links among the cases. They had to be the same laundry, Featherly argued. That New York's Chepe and Atlanta's Chepe had the same telephone number would surely erase any doubts.

And now, a new report from Customs backed up a Martínez statement that had been ridiculed at earlier meetings. Martínez kept telling the Atlanta agents that La Mina exported gold from Uruguay to the United States, despite the fact that no gold mines exist in Uruguay. But now Caffrey and Shelby had copies of a Customs report tracking U.S. gold importation from January 1986 through August 1987. True, the latest figures were a year old. But the findings were nonetheless relevant: Of the forty-four countries shipping gold to the United States, the second largest gold exporter was Uruguay.

To be sure, Uruguay only accounted for 5 percent of the total gold shipments over that time. Another report confirmed that Uruguay had no gold of its own, but somebody there was getting gold from somewhere, and they were shipping it out to the United States.

Half of the gold shipments from Uruguay were going to a company called Prosegur. Located on the sixteenth floor of the Jewelry Mart Building, seven stories up from Ropex, Prosegur was an armored-car company. Agents had watched couriers from Ropex and Andonian Brothers carrying packages into Prosegur's offices.

For nearly three hours, agents and DEA managers had been painting a picture of the largest money laundry U.S. law enforcement had ever uncovered. Says Westrate, "We were really into what appeared to be . . . the real heart and soul of the financial aspects of these Colombian cocaine cartels."

Mostly, Westrate had been listening until then. But it was getting late in the afternoon, and as the DEA administrator in charge of all investigations it was time for him to speak. He told the group this sounded like an excellent case with the potential to spin off related probes for years to come. Westrate said he'd like to use the case to get DEA's two most wanted men, Pablo Escobar and Jorge Ochoa.

Westrate was impressed, all right. The way Furtado remembers it, Westrate said, "I think we have finally found where all the money from the [Medellín] cartel is being laundered."

Furtado says, "And everybody is sitting there looking at him, like, 'Yeah, David, it kind of looks like that's what it is.' "

Westrate told the group he needed five minutes, took one of his guys with him, and left the room to talk to the top man at DEA, Administrator Jack Lawn.

When Westrate returned, he had marching orders.

Each of the different DEA offices needed to coordinate to avoid duplication of effort, and to prevent an action taken in one city from ruining the investigation in another. To accomplish that, the investigation would be run out of headquarters, specifically out of DEA's new Financial Intelligence Unit in Washington. This was the section where Shelby worked, and it was headed by the gregarious and street-wise Doug Ross. Ross, who had already had his people privately present their findings to Westrate, would oversee the effort, with input from HQ's heroin (Los Angeles had found a possible link to heroin sales) and cocaine desks. The representative from the cocaine desk would be John Featherly.

Atlanta would continue its investigation but would maintain a track parallel to the New York–Los Angeles probe, so that if one investigation faltered, the other would remain intact.

Westrate said DEA should not only coordinate internally, but the agency should also work with other agencies, as well as the Department of Justice and local prosecutors. It would become an international Special Enforcement Operation, with DEA as the catalyst.

"We had to get together with everybody else, to coordinate these cases," says Westrate. He asked Ross to set up an interagency meeting.

Westrate was the boss, so what he said went. But it didn't go over well
with the agents and supervisors, who thought they had been doing just
fine on their own.

Meanwhile, the agents in New York were pushing their case forward.
Their main CI had just returned from Colombia and was pouring out
everything he could remember about his meeting with his chief cocaine
supplier, Chepe. Perhaps the most important thing the informant could
do was confirm Chepe's real name.

The agents had already come up with a tentative identification: Luis
Hernando Garces-Restrepo. They did so shortly after the CIs appeared
at DEA in February by sifting through reports from prior investigations
involving someone nicknamed "Chepe." There were lots of Chepes in
DEA's files, but Garces-Restrepo's profile seemed closest to the man
described by their CI. He had been implicated in a major cocaine load
coming into New York a year earlier. The New York agents started using
Garces-Restrepo's name for the La Mina Chepe at the beginning of the
case. But the profiles did not match perfectly. They could use some sort
of confirmation.

The DEA agents checked various government offices for a photograph
of Garces-Restrepo, and found one at Immigration, according to their
supervisor, Elaine Harris. Unfortunately, the picture had been taken in
1969—twenty-one years earlier—but it was the best they could do. The
agents showed the photo to the CI.

Yes, this is the man I know as Chepe, the CI said with certainty. At
least, this is what he would have looked like twenty years ago, he said,
according to the New York agents' supervisor.

Until now, Atlanta agents had not been certain of Chepe's identity.
They had come up with a string of nicknames: "Chepe," the more re-
spectful "Don Chepe," "Kiko," "Kiki." Through Ramón and Serrano, they
had heard the name "Moncada," but Serrano had still not mentioned to
anyone the engineering degree he had seen on the wall in the warehouse where he had been interrogated. Besides, Ramón had heard several last names believed to be Chepe's. He used a lot of names.

So the Atlanta group at first went along with the name New York
provided. But the more information about Chepe surfaced, the less
comfortable the Atlanta agents became with it. DEA had a description of
Luis Garces-Restrepo from the earlier case, and it did not match Ramón's
description of Chepe. It didn't even match the Chepe description that
New York's CI had given. Garces-Restrepo weighed around 200 pounds,
whereas the Chepe Ramón and Serrano met was a slight man, no more
than 150 pounds. DEA had Garces-Restrepo as an architect in Bogotá,
but the New York CI said he was an engineer in Medellín.

In a luxury hotel room in Aruba while a hidden DEA camera rolled, Colombian money launderer Eduardo Martínez explains his trade to men who had been washing millions of dirty dollars for him, though not doing a very good job of it. From left, Martínez's associate, Ivan Ospina; DEA group supervisor John Featherly; informant Ramón Costello (only his white pants leg is visible); special agent Cesar Diaz; Martínez. (U.S. Attorney's Office, Atlanta)

In Aruba to decide whether to become a DEA informant, cocaine trafficker Ramón Costello photographed the men who had come from Atlanta to convert him: Assistant U.S. Attorney Buddy Parker (left), DEA group supervisor John Featherly, and DEA special agent Skip Latson—all dressed as vacationers.

DEA special agent Cesar Diaz, from Atlanta, at Banco de Occidente in Panama. His mettle and his nerves were tested during an earlier trip there, when the then-green agent posed as a drug money mover and met with high-level Colombian money launderer Eduardo Martínez. (Courtesy Cesar Diaz)

The mysterious "Don Chepe," whom DEA-Atlanta identified as Gerardo Moncada, provided New York City with tons of cocaine monthly in the late 1980s. Moncada, considered Pablo Escobar's near-equal, used a number of groups to wash his drug proceeds, including DEA-Atlanta's money laundry, BCCI, and "La Mina" or the Mine, based in the jewelry districts of New York and Los Angeles. (U.S. Attorney's Office, Atlanta)

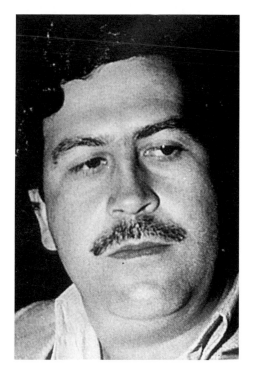

DEA-Atlanta jumped into the major league when its informant said he met with drug boss Pablo Escobar (left) to arrange a smuggling venture. Outside Atlanta, some drug agents dismissed the informant's account of the Escobar meeting as a snitch's self-serving lie. (DEA)

*In the Los Angeles sub-
urbs, a surveillance crew
photographed money
courier José Britto ar-
ranging another cash
pickup, his last before
arrest. Britto helped
Francisco Serrano
gather proceeds from
drug distributors and
deliver the money to the
Atlanta laundry. (DEA)*

*One load of dirty
money spinning
through the Atlanta-
based DEA laundry:
$1.2 million in drug
proceeds picked up
March 1, 1989, in Los
Angeles for Eduardo
Martínez. Drug agents
secretly photographed
this load, deposited it
in undercover DEA ac-
counts in Los Angeles,
and wired it to banks
in Atlanta, New York,
and Panama. (DEA)*

Now unboxed, the $1.2 million intercepted on March 1, 1989, is pictured with some of the agents who helped the Atlanta investigation: Special Agent Orlando Lopez of the California Bureau of Narcotic Enforcement (face obscured); Detective Joseph Rengel, Torrance, California, Police Department; Sgt. Ian Grimes, Torrance Police Department; DEA Special Agent Daniel Ortega (face obscured). (California BNE)

Working out of Atlanta, Assistant U.S. Attorney Wilmer "Buddy" Parker III, formerly a small-town Alabama party boy, landed a case whose dimensions constantly amazed him.
(Fulton County Daily Report)

Parker's boss and friend, Craig Gillen, told lawyers for Banco de Occidente that he was locked in an underwater battle with them and that he could hold his breath longer than they could. (Fulton County Daily Report)

Then Assistant U.S. Attorney Russell Hayman, a brash and bright prosecutor in Los Angeles, oversaw the multiagency Los Angeles investigation into the gold mine, La Mina.
(© 1986, Los Angeles Times)

Then DEA group supervisor Vince Furtado of Los Angeles, who hated to follow in the FBI's dust, headed the DEA group that investigated the Andonian Brothers' operation. (Courtesy Vince Furtado)

In New York, armored cars constantly line 47th Street between Fifth and Sixth Avenues—the heart of New York's jewelry district, where legal activity and illegal activity look alike. Here, the massive dirty-money group called La Mina hired armored transport services to pick up millions of dollars in drug proceeds, which were then boxed up, labeled as jewelry and gold, and flown to Los Angeles.

Couriers with millions of dollars from the sale of cocaine took the money to an office in this building on Sixth Avenue in New York, around the corner from 47th Street. Through a doorway squeezed between Diamond City and the Home Savings bank, they dropped off money and then called Colombia to report that they had. At that point, the money was in the hands of La Mina's money launderers.

The International Jewelry Center at 550 South Hill Street in Los Angeles's jewelry district was home to Ropex, a small jewelry store that took in more cash in the average month than Tiffany's did in a year. FBI Special Agent Bruce Stephens (left) and Group Supervisor Ralph Lumpkin, along with unpictured FBI agent Fred Wong, ran the Ropex investigation. (FBI)

Wanis Koyomejian, an ethnic Armenian who settled in Los Angeles, owned Ropex, which took in boxes and boxes of cash each week. The jewelers claimed the money came from selling gold, not cocaine. (FBI)

On this, the first day the FBI's hidden camera was operating inside Ropex's inner office, agents watched in awe as workers unboxed and unbundled stacks and stacks of cash, ran it through money counters on the desk, and stacked it on a credenza. When agents raided Ropex months later, they found a line of green smudge on the wall behind the credenza.

(U.S. Attorney's Office)

Working through the night, the FBI installed a hidden camera for the DEA in the back room of Andonian Brothers jewelry company—upside down, as shown by the date and time imprinted on the tape. DEA agents turned their monitor bottom up to watch Nazareth Andonian, foreground, and one of his employees (later acquitted) count millions of dollars. (DEA)

Money counting wasn't all that happened in the secure rear room at Andonian Brothers jewelry store, as DEA agents monitoring the view quickly discovered. Nazareth Andonian's affair with an employee, often conducted on the money counting table as they took a break from counting, posed a dilemma to agents taping the scenes. (DEA)

Fear that cops were literally at his door (they weren't) caused Sergio Hochman to flee his New York apartment and return to Montevideo—abandoning $3 million in drug money he had been counting. When Hochman finally returned to the U.S., his voice on a tapped telephone line sent hundreds of federal agents and prosecutors across the country into "takedown" mode. (FBI)

Raúl Vivas ran the giant money laundry La Mina from Uruguay. The name "Raul" showed up as a big customer in ledgers seized in a drug and money raid in a Los Angeles suburb, as well as in a ledger that turned up in Ropex's trash in a seemingly unrelated investigation. (FBI)

DEA Special Agent Michael Orton, in rear, helps collar a grim-looking Nazareth Andonian, whom the DEA had been watching for a year as hundreds of millions of drug dollars passed through his hands. Insisting on his innocence, Andonian would later be sentenced to 505 years in prison—without parole. To the right, Ralph Lochridge of DEA–Los Angeles. (DEA)

U.S. marshals and local police in Los Angeles took control of this jewelry business as part of the takedown. In all, federal agents seized a score of jewelry businesses in Los Angeles and New York that day, as well as homes, cars, and, later, large chunks of commercial property owned by the money washers. (© 1989, **Los Angeles Times***)*

U.S. Attorney General Richard Thornburgh (left) credited multiagency, nationwide cooperation when he announced the largest drug-money-laundering case in U.S. history. But the press conference inflamed jealousies because DEA Administrator Jack Lawn (center) gave DEA-Atlanta the bulk of the credit, and FBI Director William Sessions kept quiet. (Department of Justice)

While CNN carried the Thornburgh press conference live internationally, DEA agent Cesar Diaz, in his undercover role, was still trying to arrest Eduardo Martínez, who was hiding out in this bank in Panama.

For DEA-Atlanta, Colombian money launderer Eduardo Martínez was the elusive prize. (Wide World Photos)

The photo ID had to be bad, the Atlanta agents would later figure. Sometimes it happens. After all, they had used an old picture and hadn't even given the CI a lineup of photos from which to choose, which would have made the identification more credible.

The New York office stood firm on Chepe's identity. "I sat down with the CI many times, and Restrepo is he. He is our Chepe," says Harris.

If Atlanta had some other identity for their Chepe, fine, the New Yorkers responded. Maybe there were two Chepes. The New York office hadn't entirely bought the idea that the two investigations were related, anyway.

The Atlanta agents were virtually certain that these two Chepes were one person, regardless of his name. Almost everything the New York CI said about Chepe fit the man Ramón had met, the man who was Martínez's partner:

—Chepe told Ramón he owned several airplanes; the New York Chepe owned an airline called Aviel.

—Both Chepes had a top lieutenant who went by the name "Chucho."

—Atlanta's Chepe also used the nickname "Kiko" ("Keko" by the Atlanta agents and "Quico" by the New Yorkers).

—Both Chepes trafficked in huge amounts of cocaine, and both were associates of Escobar's.

—Both Chepes used bank accounts at Banco de Occidente in Panama.

—Both used a money laundry called La Mina, which used jewelry- or gold-related businesses to cover drug proceeds.

—The New York Chepe's drug profits went to an account code-named Mina 30; that was the name of the account used by Eduardo Martínez and his partner, Chepe.

—Both Chepes could be reached at the same Medellín phone number: 32-44-67.

Given all that, who could doubt that the two Chepes were one?

"It would be real easy if our CI had not identified the picture," says Harris. But "he looked at a photo of Restrepo and said, 'That is our Chepe.' " All DEA reports from New York pertaining to this investigation would be filed under the name Luis Hernando Garces-Restrepo.

Unconvinced, DEA-Atlanta nonetheless continued using that name for Atlanta's reports on Chepe, too. Says Buddy, "I took the attitude that, hell, I don't know whether it's really Moncada or whether it's really Luis Garces-Restrepo, but this human being is the same human being."

But Harris in New York insists, "No matter what anybody wants to say . . . they cannot be made into one."

Thus began the "two Chepes" debate, which would rage for years.

That same week in July 1988, FBI agents in Miami set up surveillance at the Tamiami airport to watch one of their informants meet and fly off with suspected cocaine smugglers in a different case. The informant, who went by the name Alvaro, was helping the FBI make a case against a Colombian trafficker looking for a way to bring thousands of pounds of cocaine up from Mexico into the United States.

Alvaro was acting as the trafficker's representative in the States, and on this day he was meeting with three men who had said they could get the cocaine into the States with their own pilots, their own plane, and their own landing strip. At Tamiami, Alvaro met the trio and their two pilots and climbed into their twin-engine plane. The plane was to fly over the airstrip, which was located in South Georgia, and to land in Atlanta, the hometown of the transportation expert.

The three new FBI suspects looked good. As Alvaro had told his handlers at the Bureau, their names were Allen Weston, the transportation man, and his two brokers, Ramón Costello and Francisco Serrano. The FBI already had Ramón and Serrano on tape.

To Skip Latson—whom Alvaro knew as Weston—things seemed to be going well. Serrano had brought him a possible smuggling venture, which looked promising. After all the failed deals, it looked like this one might really happen. The plane, the pilots, the strip all met with Alvaro's approval.

Still, there was this one odd thing that Skip noted after they landed in Atlanta. Not only were DEA agents posted about the airport doing surveillance, Skip recognized a couple of Georgia Bureau of Investigation agents, too.

From the suburban airport, Skip drove Ramón, Serrano, and Alvaro to a nearby Applebee's restaurant for lunch. No sooner had he sat down than his beeper started sounding. He turned it off, but it beeped again. And again.

Skip went to use the phone. Cesar was desperately trying to reach him. While Skip had been laying his spiel on Alvaro on the trip from Miami to Atlanta, the FBI had been checking out the twin-engine plane. By the time the plane landed in Atlanta, the Bureau had tracked the plane to DEA-Atlanta.

Alvaro, Cesar told Skip, was an FBI informant. Of the six men on that plane—four ostensible smugglers and two apparent drug pilots—only one was for real: Francisco Serrano. The DEA already had more than enough evidence against him. Skip had walked into an ongoing FBI investigation—as a suspect.

Skip made it a quick lunch and dropped Alvaro and Serrano off at their downtown hotel.

. . .

Nothing much had happened in the Atlanta case since the meeting in Aruba in March, but by late July 1988, it looked as though the money-laundering part of their operation was poised to take off again. Serrano had been negotiating with high-level members of the other large cocaine cartel, the one based in Cali, Colombia. These new customers, who included some of the DEA's most wanted men, needed Jimmy Brown's people to pick up money in Miami, New York, Los Angeles, and Chicago at a rate of $750,000 to $1 million a week—in each city.

Through the laundry, Serrano was pulling in a whole new set of very important traffickers. The investigation, now a year and a half old, was taking off in yet another, exciting direction.

The prospect of drawing in the Cali cartel's top guns—José Santacruz Londoño and José Rodríguez Gacha—traveled up the DEA bureaucracy. A memo to Westrate spelled out the plan, and headquarters became hot for this to work.

Serrano needed to work out the details with Jimmy Brown, so Featherly traveled to Los Angeles to meet with him and Ramón. As usual, Jimmy Brown traveled in style.

No place would do for dinner but Bernard's, the elegant—and pricey —dining room of the Biltmore Hotel. Featherly loved fine food and drink, and Jimmy Brown allowed him to enjoy them as part of his cover. The tab would be paid from the commission Jimmy Brown's laundry had already earned. So on this particular Wednesday night in July, he strolled through downtown L.A. with his business partners, Serrano and Ramón, from the Sheraton Grande where he was staying, to the Biltmore for dinner at Bernard's some six blocks away.

In this rarefied setting, with countless waiters bringing them whatever they wished, the three men mulled over the millions of dirty dollars the world's top cocaine traffickers would be sending them soon.

Serrano explained that he had known José Santacruz Londoño for three or four years, and that he was twice as big in the drug business as Pablo Escobar and Jorge Ochoa put together. This man generated something like $200 million in drug proceeds a month, Serrano claimed.

That was hard to believe. But Featherly, stationed at the cocaine desk at headquarters, knew the name, and he knew he was one of the Cali cartel's top traffickers. Serrano said Santacruz was working with another well-known trafficker, José Rodríguez Gacha, another giant in the Colombian cocaine trade. Featherly was amazed and thrilled by Serrano's new connections.

They talked about setting up bank accounts and working more smoothly and more quickly than before. A collection of phony corporate accounts spread among several banks in each of the cities would provide cover. Serrano's plan involved setting up an office in Atlanta: there the banking transactions would be tracked and reported to Medellín, where Serrano's wife could write checks to their customers as soon as she was notified that money had been deposited. They could start out small and then grow to meet the enormous demand their new clients promised.

By meal's end, it was time for a fine cognac. The three men dining at a nearby table, undercover surveillance agents, marveled at the alcohol the threesome was putting away.

At about 10:00 P.M., Featherly picked up the check and charged the meal to Jimmy Brown's undercover credit card. The tab topped $500 for the three of them.

But Serrano was in a superb mood. The rotund man had downed a lot of scotch, a lot of cognac. As he and his two American friends left the opulence of the Biltmore, Serrano gazed through the small park in front of them and recognized, just beyond it, a familiar-looking office building.

That's the building that houses our competitor, Serrano said to Featherly and Ramón. He pointed to the seventeen-story medium-rise at 550 South Hill and said, That's where La Mina is.

Where? they asked.

There, he said, indicating a floor where the lights were still on.

Featherly wanted badly for Serrano to lead him into La Mina, but Serrano had demurred months earlier when Featherly suggested sending a batch of dirty money through La Mina to see how they'd move it. Looking at the lights across the park, Featherly decided to make another run at it now.

They have a real business, right? Featherly asked.

Right, said Serrano. They have jewelry.

If I wanted to get my girlfriend a piece of jewelry—say, a two- to three-thousand-dollar bracelet—I could get it cheap here, right?

Yeah, you could get a good price, Serrano said.

Will you bring me here? Featherly figured once he got in the door and sat down with these people, he could work his way into their underlying business.

Serrano laughed. Finally he said, I'll get Raúl to take you there.

Raúl who? Featherly asked.

Raúl Vivas, said Serrano. He's an important player in La Mina.

A fine meal. A fine night. And all capped off with a ticket to La Mina.

Francisco Serrano had connections, all right, and he used them at every opportunity, according to his partners in Atlanta. It was almost a reflex. He couldn't let even the hint of a possible deal go by without trying to make it happen. Thirty-, 50-, 100-kilogram deals, small considering Serrano's potential. "He was just out hustling and scrapping to make money any way he could, now that the money laundering was down," says Skip.

Sometimes Serrano involved his friends from Atlanta, the agents say. Sometimes he didn't.* When he did—and the deal actually went through —they'd set up a seizure in a way that would free them of suspicion, get the coke off the street, and help justify the continued investigation.

All the while, Serrano was becoming ubiquitous in the world of L.A. cocaine traffickers. By mid-August, one of his longtime friends and associates, Carlos "Junior" Guarin, was trying to move 1,300 pounds of cocaine stockpiled in Mexico into the Los Angeles area, bit by bit.

Serrano had unwittingly introduced Guarin to the DEA a year earlier, and they were still talking about moving cocaine from L.A. to New York together. Serrano's main watchman in L.A. for the DEA, agent Dan Ortega, figured the time would come to pop Guarin, and had promised the bust would go to an LAPD officer who had been helping surveil Serrano. He says he told the officer, Gene Stephens, "This guy's a good crook. Junior's living at this address. You guys might want to take a look at him."

The cops surveilled the house at 9763 Yolanda Avenue, a quiet, middle-class street in the suburb of Northridge, and began building their case. They punched the address into the Narcotic Information Network (NIN), a data base for local, state, and federal law enforcers in the L.A. area. When a cop or agent working the Los Angeles area comes across a drug suspect, he or she is supposed to check with NIN to see whether any other agency is already working the case.

Arresting Junior Guarin was simply a matter of timing at this point. They needed to catch him with as much dope as possible, but they needed to do it when Serrano was out of the picture. Serrano was too good a bird dog in too big a DEA hunt to take him out. Dan Ortega had set that condition when he spun off the Guarin case for the LAPD's Gene Stephens.

But on Monday, August 15, the arrangement between the police department and the DEA started coming unglued. The L.A. Sheriff's Department had gotten wind that something like 50 to 90 kilograms of cocaine were going to be moved out of the Yolanda address, and a detective named Joe Nunez wanted to move on it. Nunez had run the address through NIN and found Serrano's and Guarin's names, as well as the fact that the LAPD already was working the case. He called Stephens, who had known nothing about the cocaine, but who tried to persuade Nunez to delay the bust to save Serrano from arrest. Stephens tried to

---

* Serrano denies doing drug deals without Ramón, but agents and officers in Atlanta and Los Angeles say otherwise.

tell the deputy of Serrano's importance to the DEA, but he wasn't sure he had prevailed. Stephens also called Ortega to tell him about the sudden appearance of the Sheriff's Department and Nunez's eagerness to make this bust. Stephens was steamed, and so was Ortega.

This couldn't be happening. Ortega called Nunez, who clearly wanted to move on the coke. "I said, 'Wait a minute, wait a minute. Let me fill you in a little bit as to who you're dealing with here. One of them is Francisco Serrano,' and I told him about who he is, gave him some pretty hard background, but, you know, obviously you can't tell it all in one telephone conversation," Ortega says.

"And I told him, 'Please hook up with the LAPD people, you know, Gene Stephens. Talk about it so you'll get a clear idea of who Francisco Serrano is and why it's very important.

" 'Because if you're going to take this house down, please, one consideration is Francisco Serrano cannot go down. . . . He doesn't go down,' " Ortega says he told Nunez. "I said, 'This guy is much bigger than a fifty-kilo case.' " He pleaded with Nunez to simply wait until Serrano was out of the way before arresting Guarin. Ortega figured Serrano would probably be spooked by Guarin's arrest, even if he wasn't caught himself. But he also figured Serrano would keep working, at least on moving money, if not cocaine.

"That was the best I could do," says Ortega. "I couldn't say, Just let the fifty kilos go." So he told Nunez, "Take down Junior Guarin, he's a good crook, and get the fifty kilos off the street. But Francisco [Serrano] we need to let go."

Nunez agreed to meet with Stephens before the bust. He planned a meeting for the following morning to coordinate with LAPD and to plot how to take down Guarin without touching Serrano.

But in the meantime, Nunez took five other deputies out to Northridge to have a look.

Before the 1994 earthquake, Northridge was like most of the suburbs in the flat floor of the San Fernando Valley. Northridge was cut into square blocks; no streets winding around rolling hills here. Comfortable, one-story homes built in the 1950s occupied modest lots with well-tended gardens.

Such was Yolanda Avenue, where at 7:30 P.M. on August 15, just before sunset, an unmarked van quietly drove up, passed 9763 Yolanda, and parked, Nunez would later report. The deputies were positioned about 100 feet beyond the house, a cream-colored brick ranch-style. From the van's rear window, Nunez peered out at the house and into the two-car garage at the front.

The garage door didn't face the street directly but ran at a right angle to the front of the house. From where he sat, Nunez had a nearly full view of the open garage, where he could see the back of a 1985 Mercury station wagon, tailgate down, he would later testify.

Inside the car, a large blue bag bulged with packages. Protruding from the bag, the plastic-wrapped parcels were all the same size, the same shape. They looked like kilogram packages of cocaine to Nunez.

Inside the garage, a screen door leading to the house stood ajar. As the deputies watched, a man appeared at the door, looked out, emerged with more packages, and walked over to the station wagon, where he placed the packages in the bag in the back of the wagon. The man, who was in his late thirties and of slight build, disappeared into the house. It was Junior Guarin.

Given what Nunez already knew and what he just saw, it looked to him like the man was loading up his station wagon with cocaine to take it some place else, he would later testify.

Apparently, this was more than Nunez could stand. That bag was overflowing with packages of cocaine. The sheriff's deputies decided to move now, DEA or no DEA.

They changed into raid jackets identifying them as deputies, and just as some of them were walking up the driveway, Guarin reappeared in the garage. When he saw the officers, Guarin ran back into the house, according to Nunez.

Nunez walked through the open door, where a sign read: *"Pintura Fresco"* (Fresh Paint). Inside, he saw another man and two women seated at the kitchen table, playing cards. One woman was Guarin's wife, the other their housekeeper. The man was Guarin's houseguest. His name was Francisco Serrano.

Nunez asked for permission to search the house, but Guarin and his wife, who said they lived there, refused. Nunez went off to get a search warrant, leaving other officers behind to secure the residence.

An hour later, Nunez returned, this time with a warrant. Sure enough, the substance Guarin had been loading into the car appeared to be cocaine—nearly 200 pounds of it. The deputies found no loose cocaine in the house. But on top of the washing machine in the laundry room off the garage, they found a 9 mm Intratech pistol, loaded.

The deputies arrested Guarin, his wife, and Serrano. The second woman, whom a defense lawyer would later accuse of working as Nunez's informant, became ill and was taken to the hospital.

Serrano would later insist that deputies could not have seen the rear of the station wagon from the street, because Guarin would never have left the garage door open while loading cocaine. He and agent Ortega say the deputies moved on the basis of information from the woman inside the house. Serrano also denies knowledge that Guarin had cocaine in his car.

However it happened, Francisco Serrano, the eloquent lawyer and consummate dealmaker, the man who had been leading DEA-Atlanta agents into the highest levels of the drug and dirty money trade, was hauled off to the Los Angeles County Jail.

Gone was DEA-Atlanta's ticket to the Cali cartel, to the Medellín cartel, and to the immense money laundry called La Mina.

15: Operation Polar Cap

Ortega could not believe what had happened. The Narcotic Information Network's whole reason for being was to prevent this kind of thing from happening, to keep some sheriff's deputy from blowing a major investigation.

"Here we went through all this, through all this notification, and they still went out and made the arrest," Ortega says. Even if Nunez couldn't bear to watch that much cocaine being loaded up and taken away, at least he could have waited for Guarin to drive the stuff away from the house.

But no. He had to move that very minute. And now Atlanta's investigation looked dead. Gone. Without Francisco Serrano, the Colombians surely would stop talking to his gringo partners.

"I will tell you I was very unhappy about it because I had to let everybody in Atlanta know that our major unwitting informant, the guy who was leading us to all these couriers and getting us all this good information, was now somebody that we couldn't track in the case," Ortega would later say.

Ortega called Cesar in Atlanta, who did not take the news well. Angry and stunned at this sudden turn of events, Cesar says, "I just thought that was dumb. California should have never done it."

Cesar put Skip on the line for a three-way conversation so Ortega could give them the shocking details. Skip and Cesar in turn rang up

Buddy. You won't believe this, they said. Buddy could hardly contain himself. "I was furious!" But he wasn't angry at the sheriff's office, not at first. Buddy's fury was directed at Francisco Serrano.

"Here is this guy who is working for us, but just doesn't know it, and he's really fucked things up. I mean, how can you do this to us?" Buddy wondered. That Serrano was doing cocaine deals was hardly shocking. But he had violated the understanding between him, Ramón, and the others by doing it behind their backs.

"I mean, how can he treat his fellow crooks like this?" Buddy asks. He was taking it rather personally considering Francisco Serrano had never met or even heard of Buddy Parker. But Buddy had been following Serrano's activities, watching him on videotape and listening to him on audiotape. To some degree, Buddy helped direct Serrano's activities, through the advice he was giving DEA. In fact, Buddy had been Serrano's protector of sorts, as Serrano kept wandering into the sights of other federal cops from Miami to San Francisco. But this time, neither Buddy nor the DEA agents who were working Serrano could protect him.

The more Buddy found out about how the arrest had happened, the angrier he got at the officers who had pulled it off. But at least the arrest had not thrown suspicion on Serrano's friends in Atlanta. For whatever it was worth, Cesar and Ramón could continue talking to Serrano under-cover.

This was scant comfort. Not only was the linchpin in Operation Fis-Con gone, but he had been taken down at the precise moment he was poised to move the investigation into an important new phase. Skip had just written his higher-ups a memo outlining Serrano's new plan for a massive money laundry to serve the Cali cartel. And with Serrano's promise to get Featherly into La Mina, he could have given the Atlanta group an insider's view of the largest money laundry the feds had ever uncovered.

The Atlanta group had been preparing to reveal these plans to a massive gathering of prosecutors and agents from all the agencies and all the cities involved in the La Mina probe, as well as high-level bureaucrats from Washington. Set for August 24–25, the conference would take place in Marina del Rey, a yuppie enclave and resort town near the Los Angeles airport.

Given the high ranks of the Washington attendees and the fact that they were coming from Justice, DEA, FBI, Customs, and IRS, Buddy figured "that was going to be about as significant a meeting there's ever been on any one case."

Until now, the guys in Atlanta had eagerly anticipated the meeting, scrambling to put together as impressive a presentation as they could. After all, they had been the first to hear about La Mina and had met with skepticism and ridicule. Now, people finally believed their intelligence —high-level people. Now, DEA headquarters was hot on La Mina and agents all over the country were feverishly digging into La Mina. The guys in Atlanta didn't exactly expect a round of you-told-us-so's at Marina del Rey, but they had hoped to show off their evidence. Mostly, they wanted to be part of the investigation they had helped initiate.

Now, with Serrano's arrest, the man who had brought them La Mina was off the street, and their way into the organization was shut. The man who had promised Featherly he could get them inside was sitting behind bars.

At Marina del Rey, Buddy predicted, "We're going to say our piece and make our point, then say, 'By the way, we don't know what we can do undercover any more.' . . . It was a very depressing way to begin this trip."

Spindly masts of sailboats tethered to docks fill the artificially rectangular waterways of Marina del Rey. A town dedicated to pleasure boating, Marina del Rey draws high-paid young professionals to live and play. For L.A.-based federal law enforcers who were hosting this meeting, Marina del Rey was a handy place to get away to. On August 24, 1988, close to a hundred federal agents, prosecutors, and bureaucrats descended on the Marina Beach Hotel, a contemporary nine-story building on Admiralty Way—the boulevard forming a crescent around the marina. For this conference, the meeting room on the lower level was swept for electronic bugs.

When the room filled with agents and the long table on the dais filled with bureaucrats, it was immediately clear who was hosting the gathering. The man in charge of the FBI's Los Angeles office made the welcoming remarks, followed by an FBI official from Washington, who introduced the other men at the front table, all high-level administrators from the various agencies in Washington—"suits," as field agents call the bureaucrats from Washington. Most of the suits had joined a consortium aimed at coordinating the far-flung investigation. These emissaries from Washington called themselves the "working group," a name that caused hilarity among agents in the field.

The IRS man called for unity; the Customs man warned against unilateral action. From DEA: Congress was tired of interagency turf battles, this investigation would pull everyone together. The Bureau spokesman bemoaned the widespread misconception that agencies couldn't work together. Chuck Saphos of the Justice Department said this was the first truly multi-agency, international investigation. And they all stressed the importance of the case, and the unprecedented opportunity and need for cooperation. This investigation was top priority at all of the agencies, they said.

They also unveiled the name of the probe: "Operation Polar Cap." First used by the Los Angeles DEA, the name had no particular meaning. In fact, it was picked for its meaninglessness. The DEA in Los Angeles had dubbed the case "Polar Cap" to throw attention away from the sunny, snow-free climate of Southern California. Pure coincidence connected "Polar" to snow, and snow to cocaine. Now, all the agents and all the prosecutors in the room were part of Operation Polar Cap.

Regular teletypes and conference calls, a shared computerized data base, and biweekly meetings in Washington would keep everyone connected and informed of the latest developments. As for a lead agency, there would be no such designation nationally. If it made sense to name a lead agency locally, that would be fine.

Out in the audience, the call for unity wasn't going over well. "I'm sitting there listening, and I'm saying, 'What a bunch of bull,' " says Furtado, DEA supervisor from Los Angeles. He knew firsthand about the interagency squabbles in L.A. But they were minor compared to the situation in New York, where all-out war had broken out between DEA and FBI agents.

DEA agent Phil Devlin from New York, for example, who first met the three CIs who had walked in off the street, heard the message of unity but saw something else. "The FBI more or less organized the thing at Marina del Rey," he notes. "They rented the space, took care of security measures. . . . They'd manipulated themselves into the driver's seat." He found this ironic, at best, because the FBI in New York had seemed so steadfast in its refusal to cooperate with the DEA.

From the Los Angeles delegation, DEA agent Orton was feeling the FBI's breath down his neck, as the two agencies raced to petition a court for electronic surveillance. And Orton's problems weren't merely across agency lines. By this time, he and one of his DEA–New York counterparts, Kevin Mancini, had had so many disagreements that Mancini was telling people he intended to "kick my ass," says Orton. So at a break in the Marina del Rey conference, Orton confronted Mancini with this rumored threat and informed him that if he was planning to fight him —and win—he should "bring his lunchbox because it's going to be an all-day affair."

On a less emotional level, the idea of seeking nationwide permission before taking a significant step didn't sit well with Russ Hayman, the prosecutor in Los Angeles overseeing the effort there. Situations arise when quick action is necessary. Calling around the country from agency to agency simply would not work, he argued.

At least talk it out on the local level, he was told.

Still, as a high-level IRS man noted, the agencies shouldn't choke each other, or hold each other back from what needed to be done. Most of the investigation was covert, anyway, reducing the likelihood that one agent's actions would jeopardize another agent's case. But when it comes to conducting an overt interview or issuing a subpoena, he said, the agencies must talk to each other. Otherwise, like a line of dominos, a premature revelation that ruins one part of Polar Cap could topple the whole investigation.

As the roomful of feds worked out ways to share information, the warning from the front of the room was clear. The last word before the lunch break came from the FBI emcee of the show. He repeated that the headquarters of each of the agencies would simply not tolerate a unilateral action out in the field. Neither would they tolerate withholding of information.

For the rest of the afternoon, and into the next day, the delegations from each of the Polar Cap cities would parade up to the dais and describe the state of the local investigation, often with blown-up graphics or stacks of handout summaries to help everyone follow along.

First up: Los Angeles, with Assistant U.S. Attorney Russell Hayman acting as master of ceremonies for the agents' presentations. Hayman told the gathered feds that law enforcement in L.A. first noticed an apparent money laundry in the jewelry district long before now. Hayman dated interest in La Mina back to the spring of 1987—more than a year ago—and said it was first noticed by agents working Operation Pisces. He told the story of the man who unwittingly led agents into the Jewelry Mart, spotted the tail, dropped a suitcase containing $500,000, and fled.

This was the first time anyone in the Atlanta delegation had heard Hayman describe this abandoned suitcase. At least he finally was weaving the Atlanta group's contribution into the fabric of the case history. He pointed out that the Atlanta Fis-Con investigation had uncovered information about a group called La Mina, which used bogus gold shipments and which operated in the Jewelry Mart.

But it was not until January 1988, when a Wells Fargo banker tipped off authorities, that specific information about a specific business gave the agents something to work with. Hayman outlined the investigation that sprang from that, and called on a host of agents to fill in the details.

For most of the afternoon, agents from the IRS, DEA, FBI, and Customs in Los Angeles painted a picture of an organization awash in cash. The IRS, which had been piecing together bank, Loomis, and government records, tracked hundreds of millions of dollars a year from the La Mina companies in New York and Houston to Los Angeles, and then to bank accounts in Latin America. Agents said the L.A. companies would deposit the cash in their bank accounts, then wire-transfer funds to precious-metals dealers or a gold refinery to buy gold. Most of the gold was coming from a refinery in Florida called Ronel, which was wiring the money to New York bank accounts controlled by companies in Uruguay, and then to foreign bank accounts.

The volume of business was straining the firms with which the La Mina companies were doing business, an IRS agent told the assembly. Metal Banc, a precious-metals dealer with offices in L.A., Miami, and New York, couldn't meet the demand for gold, so the La Mina companies spread their business around. For a while they used an L.A. company called A-Mark, but that didn't last. A-Mark officials became suspicious when a call from Ropex for a certain amount of gold would be quickly followed by a call from Ronel, the Florida refinery, offering to sell A-Mark the same amount of gold that Ropex had just requested. Sensing that it was an unwitting accomplice in a shadowy scheme, A-Mark dropped out of the loop, leaving the La Mina companies in Los Angeles to deal directly with Ronel, which they did. They began wiring funds to Ronel, which then wired the sums on to Uruguay and Panama, the IRS reported.

The elaborate money route and the sums involved were staggering. The IRS had tracked $285 million moving from Andonian Brothers and Ropex to the refinery, Ronel, in 1987, for example. And Ropex's biggest customer, to whom it sold $171 million worth of gold in 1987, was Raúl Vivas.

With the IRS presentation, "everybody was astounded that these two organizations were moving as much money as they were moving," says Mike Orndorff, Gail Shelby's immediate supervisor at DEA.

"I think we scared everybody else," says IRS agent Carl Knudson.

The FBI came next, identifying all the Ropex businesses and key individuals and revealing the fruits of their trash searches and surveillances, with the DEA following with the Andonian side of the investigation. But one thing the FBI had that no one else did was a source in Montevideo—a man who had come to the attention of FBI agents there because of a phony gold scheme. He was also connected to a Uruguayan company receiving proceeds from La Mina. The company, a money exchange house, went by the name Cambio Italia or, sometimes, Letra.

Two FBI agents had flown to Uruguay just a couple weeks earlier to interview this source, who turned out to have been in on the beginnings of La Mina in 1985. The source told the FBI that at a wedding in Argentina in 1985, an acquaintance of his, Sergio Hochman, had introduced him to a man named Raúl Vivas. The three men soon began discussing ways of making money, and, more specifically, ways to earn it by laundering it. The informant made contacts among drug traffickers in South America and in Los Angeles and helped Vivas and Hochman get the operation moving. The informant told the FBI that Vivas, who was living in Los Angeles, headed the organization and set it up with Hochman, who had been living in New York until recently.

He explained to the FBI how it worked:

The drug trafficker would give his money and his account number to the Hochman-Vivas organization, which was charging anywhere from 7 to 12 percent. When the launderers received the funds in the United States, they would call Cambio Italia in Uruguay and ask for an amount of gold equal to the money delivered, minus their commission. Cambio Italia would see to it that gold-coated lead bars were sent to certain refineries or jewelry companies in New York, Miami, and Los Angeles. When the "gold" arrived in the United States, it would be certified as real, valued at the agreed-upon price, and payment would be wired through a New York bank to accounts in Uruguay held by Cambio Italia/ Letra to pay for the ostensible gold purchases. Then, the money would travel by wire to New York, and then on to Panama or Uruguay.

The Atlanta agents knew they had been on the right track, and the FBI presentation proved it. This was exactly the way Eduardo Martínez had described La Mina. Every single thing that Martínez and Francisco Serrano said about La Mina was checking out.

Informative as the briefings were, much of the business of the conference was taking place over drinks after the meetings, at dinner, and in informal caucuses in the hallways and hospitality rooms. Like others, the gregarious Buddy was glad-handing and schmoozing, making drinking pals of newly met agents and prosecutors while gathering more potentially useful information.

At the same time, the delegations from New York and Los Angeles— the two cities with the biggest chunks of La Mina—had each assumed they would play the lead roles in Polar Cap. Each believed they had the most significant piece of the case, and each began positioning to claim the eventual prosecution.

As was clear from the presentation, L.A.-based agents had pulled together an amazingly detailed portrait of La Mina, from its formation to its money flow. And in Hayman, the L.A. delegation had an aggressive and articulate, sometimes abrasive, advocate. Agents who chafed under Hayman's tight grip nonetheless concede Hayman's willingness to go for the big one, and his ability to hold onto it once he got it.

But if the Los Angeles group was planning to make Operation Polar Cap its own, it would have to contend with arguably the toughest district in the country, New York. Whether it's mobs or drugs or complicated financial crimes, historically New York has been the premier place for criminals and law enforcers alike. The high crimes it hosts, along with the city's size, sophistication, and position as a major port and business center, make for a formidable set of federal agencies, whose ranks are filled with some of the most competitive and ambitious agents anywhere. The U.S. Attorney's Office for the Southern District of New York —Manhattan—attracts some of the sharpest legal talent in the country. In agency after agency, when it comes to federal law enforcement, the New York office typically sees itself as the big gorilla in a land of lesser beings.

The New Yorkers opened the conference's second day with Assistant U.S. Attorney Jonathan Liebman taking command of the presentation away from the warring agencies. Playing to the strength of the New York evidence—the confidential informant—he pitched the need for a clear connection between drugs and dollars. Liebman said jurors and sentencing judges would need to see clearly that these clean-seeming money movers were faciliating the very dirty cocaine business.

Professionally produced drawings and graphic displays behind him, Liebman laid out La Mina as the CI had laid it out to the DEA. He talked about Luis Garces-Restrepo as Chepe, high-level trafficker and La Mina customer. He told them about the storefronts in the diamond district, and the names of suspects garnered through utility records, mail covers, sources, and Loomis records.

Liebman pointed to blown-up charts showing men carrying suitcases down 47th Street, and Loomis and Brinks taking boxes of money to Los Angeles. In the audience, agents and prosecutors followed along with the handouts that matched the graphics.

The New Yorkers clearly had inside information, not only from their CI but also from a couple of Loomis sources, one of whom was becoming friendly with the Koyomejians, the family that ran Orosimo and its successor storefronts in New York* and Ropex in Los Angeles.

But what really impressed the others was that the New Yorkers already had court approval for wiretaps. The petition had been filed and granted the day before the conference, and Liebman said he hoped the agents would be listening to telephone conversations at the targeted businesses within a week.

This "threw everybody for a loop," says L.A.'s Furtado, "because we clearly could have been up [tapping phone lines] before everybody." He says New York should have coordinated with Los Angeles on the timing, because a wiretap in one city could jeopardize court approval of another one elsewhere.

---

* Orosimo closed down in May 1988, but the Koyomejians opened other businesses to receive and send cash.

Though concerned, Furtado was impressed New York was that far along. And from what Liebman was saying, La Mina was popping up all over the place. A search warrant issued in a seemingly unrelated money-laundering case in New York had turned up a piece of paper with the notation: "Paolo, La Mina, 139 Fulton St." The government already knew the name "Paolo," because the DEA's CI said that was the name of one of the men at 1200 Sixth Avenue. And Andonian Brothers' downtown location was an office at 139 Fulton, near the World Trade Center and Wall Street.

In yet another initially unrelated investigation, undercover Customs agents in New York had received dirty money boxed up and marked "La Mina."

Closing out, Liebman repeated that once this investigation concluded, he wanted to see drug dealers and money launderers sitting at the same defense table. He also urged speed, given the enormous sums of money and amounts of drugs involved.

For all the evidence New York had offered, and despite the unified front Liebman presented, the real business of the New York delegation was beginning to unfold upstairs. During the lunch break, New York DEA agents and prosecutors took to the privacy of an agent's hotel room to hash out how to handle the FBI.

They invited Furtado from L.A., who had plenty of experience handling the "feebs" as he supervised the Polar Cap investigation on the West Coast. "There was real fighting going on in New York," says Furtado. In fact, the way the agents in New York had been bad-mouthing each other to agents and prosecutors from elsewhere, the fight had become common knowledge at the conference.

The way the New York DEA agents saw it, they had done all the work, had run the surveillances, had milked the CIs, had gotten the case to the point of wiretaps; and all the FBI had done was send in an agent every now and then to photocopy DEA reports. Customs and IRS were helping out a lot, and so were local authorities, but the FBI had contributed nothing—had even turned down DEA's invitation to participate as a team member. Now, just as the wiretaps were about to go up and the investigation was on the verge of taking off, the Bureau was angry the DEA had not consulted it before submitting the wiretap petition.

Furtado told them he'd do what he could to help deflect FBI interference. As far as he was concerned, the DEA was the lead agency in the war on drugs, the lead agency in drug enforcement, and the lead agency on Polar Cap, at least in New York and probably everywhere else, too. He says he told them "it was incumbent upon us, that no matter what went on anywhere, that we took care of business. That was my main concern. Because if we didn't take care of business, it would not have been done. We had the expertise, and we were the people that knew what really needed to be done."

From the prosecutors, who seemed allied with the DEA agents, came the plea to quit fighting. Unless all this squabbling ended, one of them said, New York would lose the case.

Furtado was getting the distinct impression this group believed New York to be the lead Polar Cap city. He had no problem supporting DEA–New York in a power struggle with FBI–New York. But he could not go along with New York taking the leading role in the case over Los Angeles.

To be sure, New York served as a major collection point for La Mina, where many millions of dollars in drug proceeds were being fed into the laundry. But the money laundering was being done from Los Angeles. "We were the ones who had the biggest piece of the pie," says Furtado. "We had the whole pie as far as I was concerned. . . .

"I tried to explain to them it was something that had to be done both nationally and internationally, and the only way it was going to get done is if we all were in unison doing the right thing."

But New York was hot for a wiretap, though it could hurt L.A.'s chances for electronic surveillance. One factor a judge considers is whether anyone else is already monitoring calls. If so, a new intercept may not be necessary.

"I told them, 'Look, my concern is that you guys are up [on the wires] way in advance of us; we're not going to be able to coordinate what we're doing with what you're doing," says Furtado. Los Angeles had a lot more telephone lines to monitor than New York did, and therefore a lot more investigative work was necessary to build the case for wiretaps.

All that talk of unity when the conference opened was sounding emptier by the hour.

The next delegation up was Atlanta, and Buddy Parker was ready. For weeks he had been pumping his contacts at Justice to get a feel for what would transpire at the meeting. Skip Latson and Cesar Diaz had been organizing their evidence and information into presentable form. A ten-page handout started with the case that had brought Ramón under their wing, listed and described the principal defendants in Operation Fis-Con as well as the drug loads planned, the money and cocaine seized, the suspects arrested.

But the centerpiece was Skip's list of twenty-one characteristics of La Mina, as told by Martínez and Serrano. The list, which he had first prepared for the meeting in May in Los Angeles, matched the revelations offered by the New York and L.A. presentations.

Buddy began by telling the agents about Ramón and how he had met with Pablo Escobar and Jorge Ochoa in Medellín as part of the investigation of this case. Ramón also had been doing business with money movers in Medellín, men who told him about his chief competitor, La Mina. Through this connection, the government could in fact link the drugs to money as New York prosecutor Liebman had urged. Atlanta could provide that nexus, Buddy said, through Martínez and Chepe. For hard evidence, there was a videotape of drug money launderer Eduardo Martínez discussing La Mina.

Buddy then walked his audience through the history of the Atlanta probe and what it had accomplished. He introduced them to Francisco Serrano and to Eduardo Martínez, and he discussed the $1 million seizure that had brought Serrano face to face with the money's owner, Chepe. He talked about the interrogation, and how it gave the Atlanta DEA one of Chepe's phone numbers.

That telephone number, Buddy told the agents and prosecutors, matched a number for the Chepe the New York informant knew, Garces-Restrepo.

Then Buddy turned the presentation over to Cesar, who gave a more detailed rendition of what they knew about La Mina and how they knew it, from the ledgers Martínez showed Ramón back in October, through the meeting at Banco de Occidente in Panama and the one on Aruba, up through the moment just four weeks earlier when a boozy Francisco Serrano had pointed to the 550 South Hill Street building as the Los Angeles home of La Mina. Cesar also informed the group that Serrano had found out La Mina was under IRS investigation in Los Angeles.

But now, he had to add, Serrano was off the streets. He had recently been arrested in Los Angeles and was being held on a $2 million bond.

Then it was Buddy's presentation again, and he wanted to drive home his belief that all of them were onto the same money laundry. He ticked off each piece of Atlanta evidence that matched the other La Mina probes. With those links—and with the drug evidence the Atlanta case had turned up—the government could show that the money being laundered was, in fact, drug money, Buddy said.

As for Atlanta, Buddy said the piece of the case he wanted to prosecute was the indictment of Banco de Occidente and the targets who had only appeared in the Atlanta case, such as Martínez. It was the first open pitch for venue, but was noncontroversial. No one could dispute Atlanta's claim to the bank, although it had shown up as one of the banks in La Mina's shell game. It's doubtful anyone else had even thought about going after Banco de Occidente at that point, anyway. And Buddy was making no move on the part of the investigation that would obviously fall to either New York or Los Angeles, the actual operation of La Mina. The only role he sought for that part of the probe was to offer evidence to whichever jurisdiction wanted it.

Buddy figured he had made a convincing argument. Not everyone agreed.

"Whatever he said, I basically discounted it," Carl Knudson of IRS–Los Angeles says of Buddy's presentation. "He was just promoting himself." As for Atlanta's evidence, "it's nice to know. It's good intelligence, but . . . for use in court, it's worthless. . . ."

Likewise, Hayman says, "We had already scrubbed the Atlanta information, and there wasn't actionable information in there. . . . There were no names, there were no addresses, there were no locations." All Atlanta offered was a generalized view of La Mina from the Colombian viewpoint. And "we didn't need Eduardo Martínez to tell us that we were on to the right target," says Hayman.

Some of the participants believed the Atlanta group was merely trying to talk its way into a case that did not naturally belong to it. The only thing that brought Atlanta into Operation Polar Cap was Buddy Parker's strong personality and willingness to follow evidence as far as it would take him, Furtado from Los Angeles believes.

This view of the Atlantans was not universal. "Anyone who's in this business, who knows how difficult it is, had to admire what they had accomplished," says a New York Customs agent, Arthur Donelan. He says he respected Buddy for piecing every scrap of information together until it added up to something. "A lot of prosecutors think too much like defense lawyers. But Buddy Parker is an agent's prosecutor," says Donelan.

FBI agent Bruce Stephens from Los Angeles said the Atlanta presentation made him realize that, at the very least, a "loose linkage" could exist between all the cases. But how strong was it? Dirty money brokers interact with each other all the time, but whether these people were all working in one organization was another matter. "None of us were convinced at that point," says FBI supervisor Lumpkin of Los Angeles. Buddy had shown "the likelihood that people they were looking at [from Atlanta] might have something to do with the people that we were looking at" in Los Angeles, Stephens would later testify.

At Marina del Rey, Stephens says he and others began sensing "that perhaps what everybody was working on, these five different agencies all over the place, that maybe there was some connection."

As for that part of Buddy's presentation where he called for a unified investigation, several key people apparently missed that. Furtado had been listening to the Atlanta group when, by his account, one of the guys from Washington "came to me and said, 'Vinnie, there's a fight going on downstairs. You better get down there and straighten that thing out.'"

Furtado went to the room that ironically would later be used as the hospitality suite, where he found DEA and FBI agents from New York yelling at each other. He tried to calm everyone down, arguing that the only people who benefited from these interagency wars were the crooks and drug traffickers. "I really tried to make it clear to everybody that the case was more important than everybody else," says Furtado. The overriding impression the conference at Marina del Rey left on Furtado was that everywhere he turned, there was some sort of power struggle going on. Usually a loud one.

In the back rooms, the agents who were actually conducting the investigation—as distinct from the bureaucrats—were busy carving one another up. They accused each other of lying and cheating and holding back information critical to the case. The suits can say whatever they want, they can put a good face on things, and they can demand cooperation. But if the agents don't want to cooperate, they don't.

The gulf between the rhetoric on the main stage and what was happening everywhere else struck Furtado as ironic.

By 5:15 P.M. of the second day, the conference concluded with more high-minded talk of a coordinated investigation. The FBI offered its data base to collect and collate all Polar Cap information. And Buddy made a pitch for winding up the case as soon as possible, given the sums of money representing tons of cocaine. He suggested January 1989—five months away—and a general consensus seemed to form.

With that, it was time to drink and dine, and to nurse the gaping wounds the fights had inflicted.

For all the rancor in the other delegations, the Atlanta group felt good. Buddy and his wife, Rebecca, who had flown out the previous day so they could vacation together in California after the conference, hooked up with a group of agents and prosecutors to hit the night spots. At the restaurants and bars they went that night, other conference goers would recognize Buddy and congratulate him on his presentation and on the Atlanta case. He believed his presentation had helped make believers out of skeptics and that he had made it clear Atlanta had something to offer.

True, it would have been better if he could have offered Serrano as a way into La Mina. But he was pleased that the whole thing had been pulled together into a giant investigation, with a structure set up for information sharing. He was well aware of the power struggles around the country, but he was getting along great with these guys. Buddy now had new contacts all over the country, people with whom he could trade information.

With New York and Los Angeles competing, with the obvious dishar-mony within the delegations, Atlanta was like a haven of peace and sanity. No one viewed Atlanta as a threat, which allowed Buddy and the others to move among the Polar Cap agents and prosecutors without arousing suspicion or enmity.

But most important, Buddy had staked his claim on Banco de Occi-dente, which was no small thing. Prosecuting a bank for drug money laundering had never been done before.

16: A Man in Between

A few miles from Marina del Rey, Francisco Serrano sat gloomily in the L.A. County Jail. Through Francisco's lawyer, Ramón sent word to his old friend and partner that he could take messages of reassurance to Francisco's wife in Medellín, if Francisco wanted. And he told the lawyer to tell Francisco that he would have a visitor soon. "Alex" —Cesar Diaz—would be in Los Angeles and would stop by to see him.

Cesar, of course, had come to town for the Marina del Rey conference to tell a roomful of feds all about Francisco's exploits. When the conference was over, he took a ride down to the jail, an imposing structure at downtown's edge, in a railroad gulch near L.A.'s Spanish-style train station.

Cesar wanted to show up as Alex, Francisco's business partner and sympathetic friend, to keep the undercover scenario going. He wanted Francisco to confide in him, to tell him his suspicions as to how he got caught and to say what, if anything, he was telling people back in Colombia. Cesar wanted to preserve whatever chance remained that Martínez and their other customers would still do business with Ramón and the agents, even with their go-between locked up.

In addition, this was the logical thing for Alex to be doing. If Francisco felt abandoned by Alex and Ramón, he just might tell the authorities about their criminal business together.

Alex was Francisco's first jailhouse visitor. "He was happier than hell to see me," says Cesar.

Francisco told him what had happened the night of his arrest, but that it was nothing to worry about. The arrest had nothing to do with money laundering, nothing to do with Alex or Ramón or Jimmy Brown. In fact, Francisco was eager to get out so they could get the business going again. Cesar told him he'd like to continue the business, too.

Francisco needed money, he told Cesar. Could he leave $200 or $300 for his jail account? Cesar assured Francisco he would take care of him. Francisco told Cesar not to worry, either, that he had said nothing to the police about the money laundry.

One of the many things Cesar did not tell Francisco was that, through Buddy Parker, he and Skip were doing all they could to keep Francisco behind bars. Buddy, who had tried for a year and a half to keep Francisco out of jail, had now urged the deputy district attorney in Los Angeles to seek a high bail. He outlined for the local prosecutor Francisco's importance to a major federal investigation, and he said if let out on bond, Francisco might skip to Colombia and never come back. It was partly at Buddy's insistence that bail was set at $2 million each for Francisco and for his friend, Junior Guarin.

At that point, the case against Francisco was turning to mush. The Sheriff's Department's informant, the woman inside the house, was refusing to come forward as a witness. And while 89 kilograms of cocaine was plenty of evidence to convict Guarin, the government had nothing to connect Francisco to the drugs. The prosecution couldn't show that Francisco knew what was in Guarin's station wagon. The state crime lab checked the packaging and found only Guarin's fingerprints.

The sheriff's deputy had screwed up in arresting Francisco in a way that would stick. He had been so eager to bust Guarin—putting at risk the eighteen-month federal investigation of Francisco—and now Francisco was going to walk.

Buddy, Cesar, and Skip tried to predict what Francisco would do if released. Cesar figured that no matter what happened, he would maintain contact with his partners in Atlanta. He did not believe Francisco would drop out of sight. "His relationship with the CI [Ramón] was too tight, and now his relationship with us was too tight. And he was making money with us," said Cesar.

"Even if he had gone back to Colombia, he still would have been our best spokesman down there," Cesar maintained. It would not necessarily blow the case and might help it if Francisco were freed to return to Colombia.

But Buddy feared that once Francisco went south, he would never return, even if he did maintain contact with the guys in Atlanta. Buddy figured Francisco had been so spooked by the arrest that they would forever lose the chance to make him face the charges they had spent the last year and a half building.

Buddy wanted to keep him behind bars, but the local L.A. case was not the way to do it. He couldn't seek an indictment on the money-laundering case or an indictment on the drug conspiracies Skip had been working. If he did, the case against Martínez and the other probable defendants would be disclosed before the feds could arrest them. And there was no way to indict Ramón on the Fis-Con conspiracies without surfacing the Aruba tape and other evidence that would show the feds were onto La Mina.

But Buddy had something else on Francisco, something he could pull out now. Long before Ramón had become a confidential informant, he had brokered some cocaine loads with Francisco. In fact, Francisco had helped arrange the loads that had put Ramón under indictment and turned him into a CI. Francisco had never been indicted for that. There was no time like the present.

Buddy appeared before a federal grand jury in Atlanta, took in witnesses, and came out with a sealed indictment charging Francisco Serrano with conspiring to smuggle cocaine into the United States in 1982.

On the morning of October 18, 1988, a cheerful Francisco Serrano was brought to municipal court in downtown Los Angeles. He knew the local prosecutor would be recommending a dismissal of charges against him, so he figured he would soon be free.

"He was a happy guy," recalls Daniel Ortega, who had been Atlanta's chief L.A. contact for the Fis-Con case. Present in the courtroom that day with three other plainclothed federal agents, Ortega soon would dramatically alter Francisco's mood.

In the first case of the day, Deputy District Attorney Carole Chizever stood to plead "in the interest of justice that this case be dismissed against him [Francisco]." But any elation Francisco may have felt was deflated by her next words:

"However, there are four drug enforcement agents in the audience, and I have an order for the court to sign. . . . I just found out late yesterday that Mr. Serrano has been indicted in Atlanta, Georgia, on federal charges of cocaine smuggling and conspiracy and a few other charges."

Chizever told the judge that DEA agent Daniel Ortega had brought copies of the indictment to show Francisco and the judge. She asked to have Francisco released to the custody of the four DEA agents.

Francisco would be let free from state custody only to be booked into federal custody. "We didn't want to give him any opportunity whatsoever to hit the street," says Ortega.

An interpreter was translating this turn of events for Francisco. Still, says agent Ortega, "he was very, very confused as to what could be going on."

Francisco's lawyer, John Taussig, stood. "I just wonder, lest Mr. Serrano be whisked right off, if I could be given five minutes just to talk to him briefly?" he asked.

"He is to be taken right now, I take it?" Judge Elva Soper asked the prosecutor.

"As soon as the court wishes," said Chizever. She told the defense lawyer she could give him the name and number of the federal prosecutor in Atlanta—Buddy Parker—handling Francisco's case.

Judge Soper looked at the indictment and an order the prosecutor presented to her, then said, "The court has signed the order for Mr. Serrano to be released to the DEA."

Again, from the defense attorney: "May I get an order that I be given about five minutes to talk to him and explain that?"

"Yes," the judge said.

Taussig explained to Francisco what had just transpired. But there was no way Francisco could have understood why he was being led into another nightmare—a longer and scarier one—just as he was waking up from one bad dream.

Then Ortega and the three other agents approached. "I've got an arrest warrant to execute here," Ortega says he told Francisco as he handed him the documents.

"He was asking, 'What's this all about?' " says Ortega.

". . . And I said, 'I don't know. I'm just serving something for the Atlanta office.' "

That night Junior Guarin's lawyer called Cesar and told him Francisco had been rearrested and would need a lawyer in Atlanta. Cesar feigned shock and said he'd try to help. In truth, he could do nothing. For a drug agent and eventual witness against a defendant to line up a defense lawyer would be asking for trouble.

These days it seemed as if there was not much Cesar and Skip could do about anything in this case. Cesar had just come back from Panama, where he and Ramón had returned to Banco de Occidente in an attempt to get Clara García to incriminate herself. Cesar had tried a couple of approaches. He had asked her help in setting up an account, and he had broached the subject of the recent money-laundering indictment of the Bank of Credit and Commerce International (BCCI), whose Panama branch was known as Noriega's bank. This was the bank Martínez had mentioned would be friendly to them. Indicted along with the bank and its principals was the shadowy figure identified only as "Chepe" or "Kiko." Perhaps in talking about BCCI, García would reveal information only someone involved in money laundering would know.

The BCCI angle flopped. Sure, she wanted to know more about the indictment and eagerly read the newspaper clipping Cesar had brought. So what? As a banker in Panama, of course she would be interested in the story. Who was Chepe, she wanted to know. Did Martínez have any accounts at BCCI? She had a lot of questions, but she didn't seem to have much information about BCCI.

And no, she couldn't help with setting up accounts. Tensions between the U.S. government and Noriega had escalated, and domestically Panama was in chaos, she explained. The government was freezing bank accounts. No bank could guarantee the safety of a deposit. At Banco de Occidente, management was monitoring and restricting the movement of money into and out of the bank.

But even though she offered no solid proof she knew she was handling drug proceeds, García made it clear that some of the bank's customers were people to be feared. In trying to recover funds frozen by the government, threats had been made against bank directors by certain customers who wanted their money. García did not name these people, but she said it would have been very difficult for her if her customer Martínez had had a large sum of money at Occidente when the freeze set in. If that had happened, she said, the owners of that money would have pressured Martínez for it, and he would have pressured her. She did not want to get into a situation like that. What she did at the bank was only a job, after all, and not worth that kind of trouble.

This was not the sort of remark one would make about a customer whose business was coffee exporting or emerald excavation, Cesar figured. It was *exactly* the sort of thing one would say about drug traffickers, however. Clara García should have known the source of Martínez's money.*

While Ramón, Cesar, and Skip were trying to tie down the case against the bank, Ramón kept trying to get business going with Martínez again. Martínez was friendly enough on the telephone. But since Serrano's arrest—in fact, since the January meeting in Panama—Martínez had not sent Jimmy Brown's laundry business. Neither were the smuggling ventures panning out.

As for Francisco Serrano, Atlanta was in no hurry to receive him. Even

---

* Attempts to interview Clara García for this book were unsuccessful. Her Miami lawyer, Edward Carhart, says García did not know the source of the funds.

if he turned informant, he couldn't do the agents much good, because he had already told Cesar and Ramón virtually everything he knew. But he could do them harm. If they revealed their identities to Francisco, he could get word to Colombia and spoil any chance of nabbing Martínez. Neither did they want to risk his blowing the whole Polar Cap investigation.

For these reasons, no one was eager for Francisco to cross over and snitch for the government. But while the Atlanta group decided against pushing Francisco, they made sure he had a way to flip if he wanted to. After rearresting him, DEA agent Ortega broached the subject with Francisco, who showed little interest. He expected to be shed of the Atlanta indictment soon because "they have nothing on me," Ortega remembers Francisco saying.

When the feds moved Francisco to Atlanta in mid-November, they put him in one of the suburban county jails the federal government uses as a holding facility to supplement the crowded, aging Atlanta Federal Penitentiary. He had been in this Georgia jail for two weeks when Cesar dropped by the Wednesday after Thanksgiving.

Peeved that Cesar had waited so long to see him, Francisco said he had just about given up on him. Depressed over his plight, Francisco told Cesar he was hurt that Ramón had kept his distance, too. No call, no visit, nothing.

Ramón couldn't come forward, Cesar explained, because he had been a middleman who brokered the smuggling venture described in Francisco's new indictment. Ramón was very nervous about this situation.

That's no excuse, Francisco said. Anyway, he was glad to see Cesar.

Francisco said he needed money to hire a lawyer; meanwhile he was using a public defender. This well-educated, articulate dealmaker, a man who months earlier was moving millions of dollars through the international banking system, was too poor to hire his own lawyer. His wife and son needed money, too, and Francisco was helpless to support them. All his other friends had deserted him. Cesar had to help him.

Francisco said he realized Cesar and the Jimmy Brown organization owed him nothing, but couldn't they lend him some money for a lawyer? He was trying to collect on some debts people in California owed him, but he didn't know if that money would come through in time.

Cesar told him that everyone Francisco had been involved with had been nervous since his arrest, hinting that they feared he might inform on them.

Francisco was insulted. If they had only talked to him instead of hiding from him, they would know he was a man of honor. He would not rat on his friends and partners.

What Francisco did not say was that he had just initiated his first knowing contact with a DEA agent the day before. He had called Ortega, although he hadn't committed to flipping. Still, Francisco was beginning to consider the notion. He didn't tell Cesar, but of course Cesar knew all about it. To Ortega in L.A., Francisco sounded like a man considering crossing the line, but he also sounded very nervous about it. Francisco told Ortega he would only speak to him, not to any other government agent.

So Ortega came to Atlanta with a suburban L.A. police detective who had worked on the Serrano case, and at 11:00 A.M. on Thursday, December 8, went to Buddy Parker's office. There, in his cluttered corner room, Buddy introduced Ortega and the detective to a Spanish interpreter and an Atlanta lawyer who said he was considering representing Francisco. As for Francisco, he had been brought to the Russell Building and was waiting in a holding facility in the U.S. Marshal's office.

Buddy told the lawyer a little about the indictment against Francisco, admitting the cocaine venture already was six years old and therefore would be tricky to prove. But Francisco had more troubles than this indictment, Buddy said. The FBI in Miami had taped him discussing cocaine smuggling with Blas Canedo—the trafficker whom FBI informant Alvaro represented when he flew with Francisco, Ramón, and "Allen Weston" to Atlanta after DEA-Atlanta and FBI-Miami walked into each other's investigations. Canedo was under indictment in Miami, and more people probably would be charged, Buddy told the defense lawyer. Francisco could be one of them.

Buddy said this to the lawyer to give a credible reason for the interest federal law enforcement was showing in Francisco, because a six-year-old cocaine venture wouldn't fully explain it. Yet he still did not want to reveal the real source of Francisco's troubles in Atlanta. Neither Skip nor Cesar would be showing up to meet the lawyer or to see the still unsuspecting Francisco. If he decided to cooperate, it would be worth seeing whether he fingered Cesar, Skip, and the rest of the cast of fake money launderers and smugglers.

Buddy wrote out the standard immunity statement for the interpreter and the lawyer to take to him. When they returned, it was still unclear whether Francisco was ready to cooperate. Nor was it clear who would represent him. The private attorney said he would, but only if Francisco found funds to hire him, and only if Francisco went to trial, not if he pleaded guilty and flipped.

Buddy then tried to reach the public defender handling Francisco's case. She was nowhere to be found. Somebody had to advise Francisco of his rights.

So Buddy took Ortega upstairs to the magistrate assigned to the case. Buddy told the magistrate he had a defendant apparently willing to flip, and he had this L.A.-based agent in town to talk to him. But someone first needed to explain to Francisco what was happening, and offer him the chance to talk to the drug agent without his lawyer being present, if that was what he desired. The government was willing to offer Francisco protection and to move his wife and son from Colombia to the United States for their safety if Francisco agreed to cooperate. The magistrate said he would explain everything to Francisco.

In the middle of all this, Cesar, who was working out of his cubbyhole at the DEA office in the Russell Building, received a message on his undercover phone to call the same private attorney who had been meeting with Buddy as soon as possible. The lawyer had apparently left the federal building to return to his office, because the number he left was his law firm.

Because the call came in on Cesar's undercover phone, the lawyer obviously believed he was contacting a friend of Francisco's, not a drug agent. He must have gotten Cesar's number from Francisco, or the L.A. attorney. Cesar knew the Atlanta lawyer by reputation, but he couldn't remember whether they had seen each other in court. He didn't think the lawyer would recognize his voice. The main risk in Cesar's returning the call, in Buddy's opinion, would be getting the prosecution into the middle of an attorney-client relationship, even though Francisco had not actually hired the lawyer at this point. Cesar returned the call, tape recorder running.

The lawyer said he was calling on behalf of Francisco Serrano. He wanted to know whether Cesar would pay Francisco's legal fees.

No, said Cesar, he would not.

You might want to think about that a little longer, the lawyer said. He hinted at what Buddy had told him that morning about the Blas Canedo case, that more people could be implicated along with Francisco. The message was clear: If Cesar didn't help Francisco, Francisco could hurt Cesar.

Of course, even in his undercover role, Cesar had had nothing to do with cocaine smuggling, just money laundering. But while the lawyer may have been off target, it felt like an awkward attempt at a shakedown to Cesar.

Think about it, the lawyer said. He'd call back later.

Cesar and his supervisor went upstairs to tell Buddy what had happened, and found him with Ortega and the detective waiting in the office of Buddy's boss and friend, Craig Gillen, head of the Drug Task Force. Cesar had barely arrived when the magistrate called to report he had met with Francisco, explained his rights, and offered him the chance to meet with Ortega. Francisco had said he wanted to consider the possibility but did not want to do so now. He would initiate contact, he said.

What next?

Maybe Francisco would call Los Angeles trying to reach Ortega, they figured, so Ortega called his office about 2:00 P.M. to leave instructions as to how Francisco could reach him in Atlanta. As it turned out, Francisco had already called the night before, at about 8:00 P.M. Atlanta time. He left a message with a detective on duty saying it was imperative for Ortega to call him as soon as possible. Francisco's detailed and frightened message said someone he believed to be connected to the drug trade had contacted him and warned him not to cooperate with the government. The organization would find out if he did, Francisco was told. He was told who his lawyer would be, and he was told to use no other attorney, either private or public.

If Ortega could not reach Francisco before the scheduled meeting in Atlanta, Ortega should understand why Francisco would not talk to him in the lawyer's presence, the message went on. He feared for the safety of his wife and child, who were still in Colombia, and he feared for his own life, too.

No wonder Francisco had been so noncommittal. And here Buddy had already told the lawyer that Francisco was considering flipping. On the other hand, it was hard to know whether Francisco's fears were well founded. Buddy and Craig had no reason to believe the lawyer's ties to drug traffickers were anything beyond the normal attorney-client relationship. As for pressuring Cesar for legal fees, the call that day had been unseemly but not illegal.

Buddy and Craig decided they must try again to have Ortega meet with Francisco that day to offer the government's protection to him and his family. Still unable to reach the public defender assigned to Francisco, Buddy contacted another public defender who agreed to come over. They enlisted the help of yet another magistrate (the first one had left the courthouse), who met with Francisco and, speaking through an interpreter, again explained his rights—including the right to meet with Ortega without the lawyer present.

At 4:45 P.M., Francisco and Ortega finally met, with the interpreter and the public defender present. Ortega explained he had just received Francisco's message from the night before, and told him what the government could do to protect him and his family. Francisco said he believed his family was safe for now, because he had not told the government anything. He made that point clear to the public defender: he had not passed along any information to the government. He understood that he would be meeting with the prosecutor the following week, and that was fine with him. Ortega gave Francisco the number for DEA-Atlanta to use as a contact point. In fifteen minutes, the meeting that had taken all day to arrange was over. And still, Francisco Serrano was no informant.

17: Breaking the Gold Code

While Atlanta's Fis-Con investigation sputtered, La Mina investigators in Los Angeles were picking up momentum, spurred on by competition. The FBI beat the DEA to win court approval for electronic surveillance, and on September 19, 1988, the feds had their first black and white view of the inside of the Ropex offices they had been watching for months from the outside. Now they could peer into the little rooms that were the receiving point for millions of dollars a week. Now, with the government's view extended beyond the front door, the agents could see what happened after the Brinks and Loomis guards dropped off their cargo.

The scene inside these boring rooms astounded the agents and prosecutors who viewed it. They saw people nonchalantly breaking open boxes, unloading cash, sending it through money counters, then re-bundling and stacking it. For all the excitement in the room, they could have been counting paperclips.

As dulled as the Ropex employees seemed to be, the activity generated awe in the people watching through the hidden lens.

"I couldn't fathom one little group of people so nondescript handling so much money," says Lumpkin of the FBI. "They would sit down in this room for six or seven hours and not say ten words to each other and count all day long."

These were not flashy people, nor did they look like sophisticated financiers. Yet there they were, methodically processing millions of dollars for the Colombian drug lords. Says an amazed Lumpkin, "They were people you would never connect to cocaine."

"It's a powerful image to see all this money coming in," says Assistant U.S. Attorney Jean Kawahara, who was helping Russ Hayman. For nearly every bill that whirred through the money counter, someone had bought a vial of crack or a gram of powder. All those drugs. All that money.

"It's one thing to hear about it, to have some awareness of it," says Kawahara. "It's another thing to see it going on."

The DEA agents, whose wiretap affidavit had gone through several revisions before it was submitted and granted in early November, installed bugs on the Andonian Brothers' business phones, down to the fax lines.

The technical part was easy. The hard part was finding interpreters fluent in two distinct Armenian dialects (Turkish-Armenian and Syrian-Armenian), Farsi, Vietnamese, Spanish, and French. Armenia's geography and political history, plus these particular Armenians' dealings with Colombians and other nationalities, vastly complicated the job of understanding what was heard through electronic eavesdropping. This was a virtual United Nations, and a whole bank of foreign-language speakers was needed to interpret what was coming in over the wires.

Finding, polygraphing, and hiring competent people was only part of the chore. Setting up a system where the right interpreter would listen to the right conversation, and simultaneously translate and log it, was no easy task either. But the DEA was determined to get such translations and to prevent untranslated conversations from accumulating.

And so in a small room at DEA-L.A. headquarters several blocks up from the jewelry district, six translators and fourteen agents assembled around six tables (one for each line being monitored) with earphones, paper, and pen, ready to listen in and translate conversations. The calls would be recorded electronically, as well as logged by hand.

At the same time, the agents would make quick assessments as to whether a call might yield evidence. If a conversation bore no relation to suspected illegal activity—such as a call to order a pizza or ask for a date—the monitor had to hang up immediately. "Minimization," as it is called, attempts to avoid unnecessary invasions of privacy. If it is not done conscientiously, a judge might later refuse to admit incriminating conversations as evidence. However, erring by overminimization could lose a potentially key piece of evidence.

The payoff was immediate. On the first day, they heard conversations about pickups and deliveries. In one call, a woman from Andonian

Brothers reached the First Los Angeles Bank to check on the company's balance. She was told Andonian Brothers had $3.9 million in the bank.

But the best conversation they picked up that day was a call from one of the Andonian brothers to a man named Richard Ferris, the president of Ronel Refinery in Hollywood, Florida, where La Mina had an account.

Ferris told Nazareth Andonian he had received the fax.

I never lie to you, Andonian said. I will always do a great job.

After some chatter about a problem Andonian was having with one of the banks, the talk turned to a man with whom Andonian apparently was competing, the man whose companies were being investigated by the FBI, Wanis Koyomejian.

How is his business doing? Andonian asked Ferris.

"He's hardly doing anything," Ferris replied. Wanis had been having a hard time lately.

"You're doing almost everything," Ferris told Andonian. "He's getting very frustrated."

If Wanis Koyomejian's lack of business frustrated him, the FBI must be frustrated, too. The Koyomejian/Ropex part of La Mina had been FBI territory. If the Koyomejians had lost their share of the business to the Andonians, it meant the FBI had lost at least some part of the case to the DEA.

At the end of the business day, the men and women in the wire room went about assessing what had come over the wires and relating it to other information. A pattern soon emerged: a call would come in from New York or Houston cryptically reporting the number of boxes that had been sent that day, with some mention of kilograms and grams. The caller would ask about the previous day's shipment, and Nazareth Andonian would confirm that it had come and everything was fine. Through the hallway cameras, agents saw Loomis or Brinks workers roll into Andonian Brothers the boxes that Andonian had been told on the telephone to expect.

In addition, Furtado says, "Andonian was calling gold supply houses . . . the biggest ones in the world . . . and getting them to sell him gold. And he would lock that gold in at a price on the second London fix," that is, the price as set in London at the close of the trading day. But the agents did not understand what these gold trades were about, or how they fit into the picture.

In one conversation they monitored, Nazareth Andonian explained to one of his Los Angeles associates how the thing worked: "They come, give the money, place it on your table. You count it, put it in the bank. If there is anything wrong, they will tell you. The next day, you release the gold."

Andonian added, "But this is very dangerous work because your percentage is very small, and the risk is very big."

On the morning of December 7, 1988, Mike Orton was manning the surveillance post when a room bug at Andonian Brothers picked up the agitated voice of one of the regulars, a man named Ruben Saini. Orton heard Saini tell Nazareth Andonian that someone that morning had followed his brother-in-law, Juan Carlos Seresi, as he was taking his children to school.

As it happened, Seresi not only had his children with him, he also had $600,000 in the trunk of his car. He wrote down the license plate number of the car following him and tried to shake it as he went over to Saini's house to drop off the cash. He told Saini what had happened, and Saini brought the money to the Andonians downtown while Seresi led his trackers on a bizarre route through the San Fernando Valley, spotting more surveillance cars and writing down those license plate numbers, too.

Saini and Seresi were key targets of the Andonian investigation. Operating out of a storefront called J.C. Jewelers, they collected money from Colombians for Raúl Vivas, then passed it along to the Andonians.

Orton was almost as surprised at the surveillance as Saini and Seresi. He hadn't assigned anyone to watch them. He asked Furtado whether he had put a tail on Seresi. He hadn't.

What the hell is going on? Orton wondered.

He called an emergency meeting in the wire room at the DEA-L.A. office, where agents from federal and state agencies were also helping staff the phone taps and record the conversations.

Did anyone have a tail on Saini? Orton asked. That would be a violation of the cooperative arrangement between DEA and the other agencies.

No, the Customs agent said it wasn't his agency. Ditto from IRS. No one knew who could possibly be following Seresi. Orton and the DEA agent in charge of the L.A. wire room, Tony Coulson, called the FBI and the other agencies looking for an answer, but found none.

By this time, Andonian, Saini, and Seresi were on full alert. Having finally lost the tail, Seresi called in to Andonian Brothers to talk to Saini and check out the "material" (the $600,000) which Saini assured him was being "weighed." The sounds of money-counting machines could be heard over one of the room bugs.

Seresi told Saini to gather the "little papers" and "burn everything," and to tell Saini's wife to do the same. This sounded like an instruction to destroy incriminating documents. Saini called his wife at home and told her to burn "everything you have there concerning the bills and all that." Whatever it was, it was not the sort of thing a legitimate business-man would be saying upon learning that a partner of his had been followed, the eavesdropping agents believed.

To Orton and Coulson, the reaction to this mysterious tail was turning up good stuff on the wires. Someone—who?—had put the whole investigation at risk but hadn't killed it. The Andonians kept doing what they had always done, except that now the feds had recorded conversations showing obvious fear of discovery.

Eventually, DEA learned who was behind the tail. Customs had been trying to get enough evidence to write a wiretap affidavit for J.C. Jewelers —Saini and Seresi's operation. The Customs agent assigned to the DEA wire room in L.A. had been secretly reporting to Customs the intelligence that was coming in over the wires. Every day at about 10:30 or 11:00 A.M. he would get up from the table, ostensibly for a stretch and a trip to the bathroom. In fact, he was using a pay telephone downstairs to call in the latest information from the wire.

Interagency jealousy notwithstanding, the agents were collecting good information from the wires and the hallway cameras. Still, it was not good enough.

Says Furtado, "We had to get inside and actually get a video of what they were doing. We knew what they were doing . . . we *had* to get the evidence."

The court order permitted hidden cameras as well as phone bugs, but installing video was considerably trickier. DEA had tried to link into the Andonians' own internal cameras, splicing into the coaxial cable that led to the lenses they had inside their offices. But the Andonians' cameras were pointed at areas the DEA didn't care about—showing, for example, jewelry-manufacturing equipment but not the back-room activities of the Andonians and their employees.

The agents would have to break into the offices and deal with the building's very sophisticated security system. The Polar Cap "working group" in Washington had combined FBI and DEA technical experts for situations like this, and headquarters told Furtado to use a couple of FBI security experts along with a couple of DEA technicians.

Furtado's agents had meanwhile checked out another LAPD officer moonlighting as a security officer at the Jewelry Trades Building, and had decided they could trust him to help. They picked a night he would be on duty and waited for the building to empty out. Not convinced the technical team could disarm the alarm system—and fearful they could set off a silent alarm to the Andonians' homes—Furtado also sent surveillance teams to watch their houses. Finally, the time arrived.

"So," as Furtado tells it, "we go in. The FBI [technicians] take care of all the perimeter alarms, pick all the doors so we can get in, and then they say, 'Okay, we think we're ready to go.'

"So, I said, 'Okay. This is it.'

"They break in. They open the doors," and the security system that was supposed to have been disabled went into a high state of alarm.

"Everything lights up like a Christmas tree," Furtado goes on. "It was incredible. All the lights go on, all the alarms go off. . . .

"So, the FBI guys and my guys scramble in there to the master box to try and shut all of the alarms off. . . . The guy at the security box downstairs . . . calls me upstairs and he says, 'What is going on up there? The whole board is lit up! I've never seen this before!' "

The feds could handle the security guard, but what about the Andonians? Had they been alerted?

"We immediately contact our guys in the field to see if anybody's moving. And they say, 'No. Nobody has moved from any of the locations.'

"The guys upstairs scramble and they finally get the alarms all quieted down. . . . But the guy downstairs from security gets a call from the [central] office and they ask him, 'What's going on over there? You got a break? . . . The alarm's coming in here.'

"And he tells them, '. . . Something seems to be wrong with one of the doors . . . and the alarms are going off. It seems to be a shortage.'

"So, he has some kind of a code that they expect him to come back with, which he has, and he gives them the code, so they know everything is legit. He is able to keep them at bay. . . .

"So for the next two or three hours we proceed to put cameras in and we've got all the phone lines blocked off so the signals don't keep going out on the alarms," Furtado continues. "We get our cameras in where we want them, and we put the bugs in where we want them. We put a couple of bugs over the internal rooms that we never knew what was being said in them. We put a couple cameras in those rooms. We put a camera in the fan in the money-counting room—it was the only place we could put it. . . .

"After we get the cameras in . . . we got everything all locked up and we've got like twenty minutes before we've got to get out of the building. People are going to start reporting to work. We say to the guys, 'Is everything all set now? Is the alarm going to be set and everything.'

" 'Oh yeah. Everything is okay. . . .' They close all the doors. We take all of our things off the phone lines . . . [and] it all lights up again. I mean, it's just like gangbusters." Furtado is exasperated.

"So, there's nothing we can do at this point. We decide we're out of there. We get downstairs. We go out and tell the guy, 'You're going to have to call that company in and have them fix it.' "

When the security company came in, Furtado and his group worried whether the phones would ever work right again, and whether their work would be discovered. All that day, over the phone taps, they heard the Andonians calling the security company, screaming that the alarm system kept going off.

Eventually, the security company got the systems working without discovering the cause of the disruption.

When DEA agent Manny Figlia arrived at the surveillance post that morning, he saw a new television monitor added to the ones he had been using for weeks to watch the hallway outside Andonian Brothers. He squinted to make out the image on the screen, but it was hard to figure out what was what. Soon, a hallway monitor showed a delivery-man rolling boxes into Andonian Brothers. And soon after that, there was movement on the new monitor, only it didn't make sense. A man's head had moved into view, but it was upside down. The FBI had installed the camera bottom up!

Figlia crooked his neck. Once he realized what was wrong, he could make out the objects in the tiny room—a table, a pillar, a calendar. And as he watched, the upside-down man began talking to someone unseen. He bent over the table and reached for something out of cameraview. Suddenly, the object came into full view: it was a stack of cash. The man removed two rubber bands and put the stack back down. He reached for another stack, took off the bands, flipped through the stack to inspect it, and put it down. Then he reached for another stack.

This is it, Figlia thought to himself. He was finally seeing the contents of the boxes he had been watching deliverymen drop off day after day.

The man was inspecting and arranging the stacks on the table, announcing numbers from time to time to his partner. Then came the whirring of an off-screen money counter. Soon, the man was wrapping paper money bands around the newly counted stacks of cash.

Excited but very uncomfortable, Figlia wondered how long he could stand the contortions necessary to watch the upside-down monitor. "I got tired of the blood rushing to my head," he says.

Suddenly, a solution occurred to him. Figlia walked over to the TV set, picked it up, and turned it upside down.

The picture looked just fine.

"I'll be honest with you," says DEA supervisor Furtado. "We were relieved" finally to see these people doing what the agents had believed they were doing. Even so, "it was astonishing. Every single box that they opened was chock full of bills. And they would just dump it on the table. It was like a manufacturing operation."

People would come into the room and stand there, hour after hour, counting money. They'd count it, bundle it, stack it, and slide the stacks into long, flat, plastic bags, which they would then label and seal. Count, bundle, stack, bag. All day long, very matter-of-fact. Count, bundle, stack, bag.

While that was happening in the counting room, the phones were ringing in the office—and in the DEA wire room.

On December 20, interpreters and agents in the L.A. wire room recorded a conversation between Nazareth Andonian and an associate in New York he called Tío. Andonian complained to Tío that business was slow.

Tío told him not to worry. Business would pick up shortly. He knew this, Tío said, because he had been told that Mina 30 would be coming soon. He added, "Mina 30, that comes big, you know."

One day not long after the counting-room camera was installed, an agent was watching when Nazareth Andonian and a female employee stopped counting money and disappeared from view. They huddled in the camera's blindspot for a few minutes, and when they emerged, the woman was no longer wearing a blouse.

A startled scream from the agent awoke Figlia, who had laid out on the floor of the surveillance room for his usual afternoon nap. Figlia remembers his partner's urgent voice pulling him out of sleep. When he saw the images of the two suspects fondling each other, one of them half-naked, he understood. The couple was engaged in an increasingly steamy sex scene, which was being captured on hidden camera and recorded for posterity, thanks to the federal government.

Figlia called the wire room at DEA headquarters across downtown. Mike Orton answered. We need instruction, Figlia said. The money counting had stopped, Nazareth was all over his employee, and this private moment was being recorded by the DEA.

What do we do? This was just the sort of thing that could get the agency in deep trouble in court. Should they turn off the recorder?

What's going on in the room right now? Orton asked.

"What do you want me to tell you? They're going at each other!" Figlia says he retorted, irate that Orton wanted details when a speedy decision was needed. By this time, the woman was sitting on the counting table facing Andonian. The couple was obviously having sex.

"Look Mike, do something," Figlia urged.

Orton asked whether money was still visible. It was.

As long as there's money on the table, Orton told him, you keep that camera going.

And so, with federal law enforcement watching and a hidden lens recording every move, the couple continued what agents would soon realize was a regular afternoon habit. If no money was present or if the encounter became particularly explicit, the agents would turn the camera off, wait a few minutes, then tune back in.

But on this particular day, hundreds of thousands of dollars were strewn about like some sort of aphrodisiac for the couple and a lure for the feds. Passion ran its course while a government camera rolled.

By now, scores of Polar Cap agents and cops from city to city were mining La Mina for information, occasionally distracted by a turf skirmish but usually moving forward. At the same time, the men and women they secretly watched kept receiving, counting, and moving boxes and boxes of cash. The wires kept humming with voices talking in many tongues. They talked about "kilograms" and "grams," but none of it made sense. The drug agents naturally first suspected these people must be discussing cocaine, but that didn't add up. No, they must be talking money and gold.

The Andonians talked frequently with Ronel Refinery, usually with Richard Ferris, the president. Calls from and about Cargill Metals, a gold broker supplying some of the gold the Andonians were buying, showed Cargill employees suspicious of the whole thing, and the Andonians and Ferris worried.

But what did it all mean? In Los Angeles, the agents tried to follow the money in both directions: backward to link it to drugs, and forward to decipher the gold trades and the ultimate means of washing obviously dirty money. But each attempt to follow the money back to where it had bought cocaine failed. True, other Polar Cap cities claimed to have the drug nexus, DEA–New York with its CI and DEA-Atlanta with the launderer Martínez. But none of that had been corroborated in the Andonian investigation. In addition, Orton suspected some of the money he watched being counted and bagged had come from local drug sales.

The DEA agents knew how the drug world worked, but international gold trades were another matter altogether. Nothing in their professional training or experience had taught them about that.

"We knew they were committing a crime. I mean, that was obvious, because there was just too much money coming in," says DEA agent Selby Smith. "But *how* they were laundering the money . . . was the killer."

Smith, the green agent who had peered into a Loomis guard's money-filled duffel bag back in June, by December was helping out in the L.A. wire room. Overseeing that operation was an agent, Tony Coulson, who decided it was finally time to discover the meaning of all these calls. So one morning a few days before Christmas, he and Smith sat down with all the telephone transcripts, the Currency Transaction Reports (CTRs), and the Loomis records. Coulson was determined to make sense of them.

He picked a date: December 13. In the first noteworthy conversation, Nazareth Andonian took a call from one of the La Mina entities in New York, Z&G Gold Exchange. The man who went by the nickname "Tío" (Spanish for "Uncle") was calling.

"The correct thing is two kilos, 554, one-half," Tío said.

Coulson and Smith pulled out the Loomis records and saw that on the previous day, December 12, Loomis moved $2,554,500 from Z&G Gold in New York to Andonian Brothers in L.A.

Tío obviously was using the word "kilo" to mean million, to say that $2,554,500 had been sent.

The next seemingly relevant conversation that day had been logged in at 2:00 P.M., when Nazareth Andonian called a jewelry retailer, Jesico, Inc. Andonian discussed the London fix—the price of gold in London —which was $428.30 an ounce. A cryptic conversation followed, which Coulson and Smith believed involved the purchase of 8 or 10 kilograms of gold.

Coulson sat down with a calculator, analyzing the price of gold, the number of ounces in a kilogram, and the key words in the phone conversations. He was certain that in this conversation "kilogram" meant kilogram, not million. But nothing seemed to add up.

He called a gold broker he trusted who said gold is measured in troy ounces, which are slightly larger than ounces used in other weights. There are 32.15 troy ounces to a kilogram. So a kilogram of gold as priced in London at closing would be $13,370.

But it still would take a lot more than 10 kilograms of gold to account for more than $2.5 million. The agents looked for further clues.

In the afternoon of December 13, Nazareth Andonian called Republic Bank in New York. He ordered 177 kilograms of gold to be credited the following day to an account held by Ronel at a London brokerage house.

At the price quoted in the earlier conversation, 177 kilograms would cost $2,437,262, coming closer to the sum that had been shipped. The other piece of information in the conversation was that Andonian was passing the gold along to Ronel.

Moving back to the Loomis records, the agents saw that just after 6:00 P.M. on December 13, $2,568,000 was picked up from Andonian Brothers for deposit at First Los Angeles Bank. That had to be the previous day's shipment from Z&G in New York, plus a little more.

The next morning, December 14, a telephone call from Andonian Brothers to the bank indicated what happened next to the money. The bank confirmed that $2,568,000 had been deposited, and that, as Andonian Brothers had instructed, $2,491,000 had been wired to Republic

Bank in New York. The difference between the sum deposited and the amount wired out probably represented the 3 percent commission the Andonian Brothers would keep for the transaction: $77,000.

The difference between the cost of the gold and the amount wire-transferred to Republic would cover the bank's fees for handling the transaction.

The agents found that later on the morning of December 14, Richard Ferris at Ronel in Florida had called Nazareth Andonian.

"Did you get the 177?" he asked.

"Republic again," Nazareth answered.

Piecing those telephone conversations together with Loomis records, CTRs, and advice from a friendly broker, the agents were beginning to make sense out of the puzzle. They reasoned that it worked like this:

One of the New York companies would ship money to Andonian Brothers in L.A. after calling in the count, substituting the word "kilogram" for "million," and "gram" for "thousand." Andonian Brothers would take out a commission and use the rest to buy gold, in this case from a bank. The bank credited the gold to Ronel Refinery, where, obviously, a co-conspirator worked. From Ronel, the gold could then travel to others in the conspiracy, or it would be sold back to Andonian or to gold brokers, who would resell it to Andonian.

"We were elated when we figured it out," says Smith, and it hadn't been nearly as hard as they'd assumed it would be.

They picked another day: November 2. They culled through the transcripts, pulled the ones that seemed relevant and, again, it seemed to work. When a kilogram was mentioned in calls between L.A. and New York, that clearly meant $1 million. When a kilogram was mentioned in calls to gold brokers, that meant gold. The money was traveling the same way it did on December 13, and so was the gold.

They went through another day's calls, and another. Yes, it all fit. They had cracked the gold code!

Smith typed up the explanation, applying it to certain telephone calls. Furtado posted the paper in the wire room, where work was tedious, the space cramped, the noise level high, and morale badly in need of a boost. Above the explanation Furtado tacked up a big sign he had made: "THIS IS THE RESULT OF YOUR GREAT WORK."

18: Shutting Down the Mine

By the beginning of 1989, the Los Angeles agents believed they had about all they were going to get.

Says prosecutor Russ Hayman, "We had been able to sketch the octopus. We knew basically where it was, who it was. We had taken it down as low as we could on the street" by following the couriers. "We had taken it as high as we could, back to Montevideo"—to La Mina managers.

Meanwhile, the agents were watching the Andonian Brothers wash $5 to $10 million a week, representing 400 to 800 kilograms of cocaine. Over a year's time, they would spin hundreds of millions of drug dollars into gold. That had to stop, and soon, Hayman believed. "The longer we waited, the more money the traffickers would run through this organization and get into their . . . bank accounts."

At a mid-January 1989 meeting of key L.A. personnel, Hayman urged case supervisors to agree on a date to stop investigating and start arresting. Takedown in Los Angeles would have to be coordinated with the other Polar Cap cities, and Hayman wanted the L.A. agents to propose a date. He wanted to shut down La Mina as quickly as possible, he told them. "Every week's delay had to be justified by . . . obtainment of some additional law enforcement objective," says Hayman.

DEA–Los Angeles was more than eager to wind up the case. The tedium of the wire room was burning people out. The DEA was hoping to seize drugs or money to help make the case and bleed the organization a little. Furtado had authorized his agents to take any opportunity they found without disrupting the larger investigation. The FBI's cooperating cops had followed a Ropex courier to 641 pounds of cocaine and seized it, but so far the DEA had no strong drug connection to the Andonians.

Cooperating local and state cops resumed surveillance, hoping to follow the couriers to a drug connection. But the targets kept giving them the slip. Nothing was working, and morale in the wire room kept deteriorating. "We were ready to take care of business and get the thing taken down," says Furtado.

Not so at the FBI. "We just didn't know enough about what was going on," says Ralph Lumpkin, the FBI's Polar Cap supervisor in Los Angeles. He wanted the case to draw the big picture of the drug and money cycle, but "we hadn't really gotten behind the dope angle like we had wanted to." Moreover, the probe was about to expand in Florida, and Lumpkin thought it would be worth waiting for that.

FBI agent Bruce Stephens puts it this way, "We didn't want it to go on forever, [but] the Bureau's always interested in the long term. We're not an instant gratification agency."

But there was another reason, too. FBI agents were up to their necks in telephone conversations taped but not yet translated. "We had tons of tapes we were behind on," says agent Fred Wong. "If you make an arrest . . . you gotta be ready to go to court." The agents had been working off rough summaries of conversations the interpreters gave as the calls came in, but those summaries were hardly court-worthy. So, while the DEA was ready to move, "we wanted to catch up with our evidence," says Wong.

You'll never catch up, Furtado countered when the FBI asked for more time. You're way too far behind, and getting further behind every day. The DEA could be ready in two weeks. He suggested January 30 for a takedown date.

The FBI supervisor said he needed six months.

Hayman, in the words of one of the men there, "blew a gasket." He would not keep the investigation going that long. He would not let federal agents stand by and watch money launderers send cocaine profits back to the drug barons so they could get richer. At some point, Hayman told the others, law enforcers become responsible for criminal activity they know about but do not stop.

Finally they settled on a takedown at the end of February. That gave them about six weeks. It seemed like an eternity to the DEA agents, but to the FBI it was not time enough. In any case, that was the date they would take to the multi-agency, multi-district meeting scheduled by the Washington working group for Marina del Rey the following week.

· · ·

*T*his time even more agents, supervisors, and bureaucrats converged on Marina del Rey from New York, Los Angeles, Washington, Atlanta, Miami, Houston, San Jose, and elsewhere. By now, the matter of which jurisdiction would get which piece of the case to prosecute had been worked out among the prosecutors and Chuck Saphos, chief of the Justice Department's Narcotic and Dangerous Drug Section in Washington, D.C.

Los Angeles was the center of the organization, with spokes to New York, Houston, and Miami. Los Angeles was where the cash was pumped into the banking system and converted to gold and wire transfers, where the money was washed, and where the key players lived. The other cities acted as gathering points for cocaine proceeds to be fed to Los Angeles. L.A. was La Mina's U.S. hub.

"Ultimately," says Jonathan Liebman, one of the New York prosecutors, "there was absolutely no question but that the case—the main case —had to be brought in a district where the wrongdoers resided, and where they were primarily active." And that was Los Angeles, he says.

This view infuriated agents who had been working the case in New York. They figured they had a great case with all that money being dropped off and moved, and with the confidential informant linking the money to drugs. Some of these agents thought the main thing New York lacked was an aggressive prosecutor.

"I really do not believe that the [U.S. Attorney's Office for the] Southern District of New York was up to the task of this case," says Elaine Harris of DEA–New York, who supervised the Polar Cap group. "The case was so complex . . . I do not think the Southern District wanted to tackle" it.

Liebman calls that charge ridiculous, given the aggressive, competitive prosecutors who worked in Manhattan. "You know, the Southern District of New York is not known for giving away cases. And the Southern District of New York did not give away a case here."

Liebman insists the facts of the case dictated who would prosecute. But others say there were holes in the New York investigation, too. The La Mina storefronts changed name and location so frequently that it felt like each time the agents put together pieces of the puzzle, someone would come along and scatter them. Electronic surveillance became virtually impossible, because every time the crooks moved, the feds would have to find them and seek court approval to tap the new phones. By the time the government had petitioned the court, won approval, and set up the wire, the business had changed locations again. Eventually, the prosecutors decided it wasn't worth it.

The animosity between the FBI and other agencies in New York had hurt their case. But the worst problem in New York was disagreement among prosecutors and DEA agents on the use of the confidential informant who had put them onto La Mina in the first place. The U.S. Attorney's Office insisted the government bring charges against the informant for his admitted crimes. Mary Lee Warren, chief of the narcotics unit for the U.S. Attorney's Office, kept telling the DEA group this would make his testimony more palatable to juries. How could the government trot out a drug trafficker as significant as this CI without charging him with some sort of narcotics crime? Unless he pleaded quilty to a crime, there was a real question whether she would even allow him to testify.

That suggestion, in the opinion of New York DEA agent Phil Devlin, was "absolutely outside normal practice. It was heretical." How could you charge a man when the only evidence of previous crimes was what he himself had offered? All he had to do was plead not guilty and invoke the Fifth Amendment. The DEA agents could testify to what the CI had told them, but they were not about to do that to him or to the two other men who had accompanied him to the DEA in the middle of that February night.

"I would have told the guy to plead not guilty," responds Harris. There was "no way any of us would have testified against those CIs" who had brought them the case.

Without a conviction to show a jury, prosecutors were wary of using the informant as a witness, not only in New York but in Los Angeles, where Hayman also believed he should be charged. And without the informant to testify, the core of the New York case would be missing. Although the agents had evidence corroborating most of the informant's story, the CI's absence created a void.

"You don't build a case on a nontestifying informant," says Liebman.

Along with protecting their CI from prosecution, the DEA agents were shielding him from Polar Cap agents in other cities, too. Agents elsewhere asked to interview him, but the DEA in New York wouldn't allow it.

"We didn't want people manipulating this informant . . . into a poorly thought-out situation, and getting him burned," says Devlin. "We didn't hold back information." Devlin says they would have honored any "legitimate request" to interview the CI, but there were none.

"They had the witness, the best witness in the case, probably," says Skip. But they weren't using him. By keeping him to themselves, they were barring themselves from any significant role in the national case.

When the time came at Marina del Rey to decide once and for all how the Polar Cap case would be prosecuted, the New York prosecutors made no pitch for a piece of it. Nor did they disagree when Hayman recommended that Los Angeles handle nearly all of it.

Hayman wanted to indict the Andonians and the Koyomejians, as well as the South Americans he believed directed the money their way, Sergio Hochman and Raúl Vivas. He also wanted any Ronel Refinery employees in Miami who were in on it. In fact, he wanted just about everybody except the money couriers in the other cities, or anyone connected with the Atlanta undercover operation. The DEA, FBI, and other agencies in Los Angeles had amassed an impressive body of evidence. Hayman told the group drugs had been connected to the case established in December when the Ropex courier was followed to a cocaine source and to 641 pounds of cocaine.

It would be a complicated case to handle, but Hayman wanted all of it—and no one else did. Says Buddy Parker, "It just got so complex, a lot of people didn't want to be involved in trying to structure a cohesive theory." Managing the information alone would be a formidable task. With developments happening daily from coast to coast, "you can never, ever effectively have a working knowledge of the facts . . . because it is so voluminous."

So in control of the case did Los Angeles seem—and so domineering was Russ Hayman—that the man at the Justice Department coordinating the case, Saphos, reminded those gathered that Los Angeles was not in charge of the national case. Just because L.A. wanted things a certain way did not necessarily mean things would happen that way, Saphos said.

That said, Los Angeles got most of what Los Angeles wanted.

Says Liebman, "Would I have liked this case to have developed in such a way that it would have been intelligently prosecuted in New York? Absolutely. Did I hope that on Day One? Absolutely. But I agreed with Russ that the focus of activity was in California."

The Atlanta contingent had no bid on the La Mina operatives, of course. Buddy and the agents would happily seek indictments of the people with whom Ramón and the agents had done business. This would include Pablo Escobar, Jorge Ochoa, and Gustavo Gaviria, the men with whom Ramón and Francisco Serrano had negotiated a cocaine shipment that never happened.

As for money laundering, in addition to Serrano, Atlanta would prosecute Eduardo Martínez, Chepe, the two bankers at Banco de Occidente in Panama, and the bank itself—both the Panama branch and the main bank in Cali, Colombia.

The Atlanta indictments would fill out the picture sketched by the Los Angeles indictments. Martínez used La Mina to launder money belonging to Chepe and to the drug kingpins, the Atlanta group believed. So while L.A. would focus on La Mina as it operated in the United States and Uruguay, the Atlanta prosecution could tie it back to Colombia.

Buddy was pleased that he would be able to spell out such a significant money laundry and drug scheme in an indictment.

But what would that accomplish, other than public disclosure? None of the defendants would be easy to bring to a courtroom in Atlanta, except for Francisco Serrano, already in jail. Positioning Colombian and Panamanian suspects for arrest and extradition would be near impossible, given that Ramón and the agents had no ongoing business with them.

As for the bank, how do you bring a foreign corporation to a U.S. courtroom for punishment?

"This was a prosecution that made no sense unless you just wanted to put into the public record" the money-laundering accusations, says Buddy. Disclosure alone would do nothing to stop the defendants from doing what they were doing, and it wouldn't punish them for it, either.

That was where the forfeiture law came in—the law that allows the government to seize the fruits of illegal activity, be it ill-gotten money or property bought with ill-gotten money. Craig Gillen and Buddy Parker had aggressively pursued criminal forfeitures in the past, as Craig encouraged the attorneys in the Southeastern Drug Task Force in Atlanta to use the weapons Congress kept giving them to fight the drug war. Other prosecutors might wait for case law to develop around new statutes, but Craig wanted his office to create the case law.

Using the forfeiture law against Banco de Occidente would be unprecedented. The bank had no U.S. operations, and the drug money had already passed through the bank anyway. What could they seize? And where?

Craig and Buddy saw an opportunity to use a new feature of forfeiture law: the substitute-asset provision. With that, it didn't matter that the drug money was beyond their grasp. They could go after other assets as a substitute. Occidente had laundered more than $400 million, they calculated from evidence gathered nationally. So all they had to do was find up to $400 million in Occidente assets and seize that.

Occidente had no U.S. offices, but it did have bank accounts in the States—several correspondent accounts to serve as conduits for money its customers were wiring to and from the United States.

An American company buying Colombian coffee, for example, might pay for it through Occidente's correspondent account at Citibank. That way, Citibank could send the money quickly to Occidente in Colombia to pay the coffee exporter. That same Banco de Occidente account at Citibank would also channel the funds of other Occidente customers. Or Banco de Occidente might move a chunk of money from various depositers to its Citibank account to take advantage of favorable interest rates.

Before this case began, Buddy Parker and Craig Gillen had only rudimentary knowledge of correspondent banking relationships. But Eduardo Martínez and Clara García—through the undercover agents and Ramón—had educated them in international banking. Now the Atlantans would use this newfound knowledge to the government's advantage. Gillen and Parker looked at a list of U.S. banks where Occidente held correspondent accounts and reasoned they had located seizable substitute assets.

By using the law creatively, "we could achieve some enforcement goal," says Buddy. They could hurt the bank they believed was laundering money.

At the Marina del Rey conference in mid-January 1989, Buddy laid all that out. To some in the audience, he sounded like a wild man. To others, particularly those agents chafing under prosecutors they believed to be too cautious or too overbearing, this gangly southerner with the booming voice seemed like a hero.

The prospect of pulling this off as part of the larger La Mina takedown thrilled Buddy. It all fit so neatly! And it would be presented to the American public in one big press conference. After the arrests, the nation would know that all of these agents and prosecutors in all of these cities, including Atlanta, had brought down the largest drug money laundry ever before uncovered.

With no intercity debate about dividing up the case, and despite internal strife in New York and Los Angeles, the national picture looked smooth. "Every single presentation in the room," says L.A.'s Furtado, concluded by saying "they would support L.A."

The main message of the conference was that this was a huge, multi-tentacled creature that had to be captured all at once. Only extensive coordination and cooperation could accomplish that. Cables, telephone conferences, meetings. It would be coordinated out of Washington, but everybody had to pull together.

And no one—no one—could make a significant move alone. A stray seizure or arrest—a nip at one of the tentacles—could send an alarm throughout La Mina, scattering the suspects and shutting down the laundry before the feds could move. Act alone, the agents were told, and you could send the whole huge investigation crumbling down.

The FBI won more time. Takedown date was finally set for March 8, 1989. Within the restless DEA group in Los Angeles, there was resentment at having to wait that long.

A week after the Marina del Rey conference, on Tuesday, January 24, the DEA was listening when Nazareth Andonian received a call from New York about 10:20 A.M. from a man nicknamed "Lito." The call came from Z&G Gold Exchange, the business on West 48th Street that the feds had connected to La Mina. It was 1:20 P.M. in New York.

"I am going to send you a few boxes tomorrow," Lito said in Spanish. In the DEA–L.A. wire room, an interpreter alerted the agents. "Hey, we got boxes coming in from New York," agent Coulson recalls.

The men on the phone talked about business picking up after the holiday lull. And then Lito gave Andonian astounding numbers: he said he was sending thirty boxes.

Andonian Brothers and its related companies had been taking in two, three, at the most four or five boxes per shipment from New York. But the shipments had slowed around Christmastime. Apparently the drug proceeds had been stacking up during the holidays.

Lito said he would send fourteen of the boxes to one of their related companies in L.A., and sixteen to another.

Then he gave Andonian another number, a number that seemed to indicate the content of the boxes. He said, "4-8-6-9."

To make sure Andonian had gotten the number correctly, Lito repeated it." Okay, so you have 4-8-6-9," he said.

"Four kilos, eight sixty-nine," Nazareth confirmed.

Coulson knew exactly what the numbers meant, having broken the code the previous month. Lito was shipping thirty boxes containing $4,869,000.

"We said, 'This is it!' " Coulson contacted Orton and showed him the transcripts. Orton saw the numbers and said to Coulson, "This conspiracy comes to an end today."

The way Orton tells it, he called up Kevin Mancini at DEA in New York. They had spoken frequently enough that they knew each other's voices.

"Kevin, consider this an anonymous call," Orton says he began. Then he said that if Mancini were to head to the Loomis office and locate boxes marked for delivery to certain jewelry stores in Los Angeles, he would find nearly $5 million inside.

Orton didn't want to take the money in L.A. because the people he was watching would grow suspicious. It could "heat up my wiretap." But if DEA in New York knocked it off, the feds would get the drug money, and the crooks in L.A. would suspect someone on the East Coast screwed up. And if things went the way Orton expected them to go, the wiretaps would be full of interesting conversations the next day.

Orton had consulted no one before acting. He didn't tell his boss, and he certainly didn't tell any of the other agencies working the case.

In New York, his call led to a hastily arranged meeting of DEA, Customs, and IRS agents and supervisors working Polar Cap. Everyone wanted to take the money, but how? They contacted the U.S. Attorney's

Office, but prosecutors refused to seek a search warrant. A unilateral action like that could give away the whole investigation.

But that wasn't the last word. The agents had learned that Loomis had taken the boxes to the cargo space it used at John F. Kennedy Airport. This was just perfect. Customs routinely sent a drug-sniffing dog through the area because it served as a transshipment point for international cargo. Customs could take a dog there, perhaps on an ostensible training exercise or perhaps to make an apparently routine check. If the boxes contained money as they suspected, and if the money had been used to buy cocaine, it would probably contain enough residue to pique the interest of the dog.

At a West L.A. restaurant, a beep on FBI supervisor Ralph Lumpkin's pager interrupted his lunch. It was Russ Hayman, with news that Customs and DEA in New York wanted to seize nearly $5 million that was en route to the Andonians. What did Lumpkin think about it? Lumpkin said it was a terrible idea. A seizure that size would send the crooks packing and ruin the chance of nabbing anyone of any importance in the organization. Hayman agreed.

The way Furtado of DEA–Los Angeles tells it, Lumpkin was furious. What the hell is going on? Lumpkin shouted when he called Furtado. None of the Polar Cap agencies was supposed to act before meeting with everyone else. Hadn't that been made clear at Marina del Rey? He told Furtado he could not believe the DEA would even consider doing something as serious as seizing millions of dollars without first consulting the FBI.

The truth was, Furtado was annoyed, too, because Orton had acted without consulting *him*. But to the FBI, Furtado stood up for his agent. These things happen quickly. When an opportunity like this presents itself, you can't book a hotel conference room and gather the hundreds of agents who might be interested, Furtado told Lumpkin.

Hayman, too, called Furtado demanding an explanation and making threats. If that seizure takes place, the evidence will never be admitted in court, Hayman said, according to Furtado. Call New York immediately and call off the whole thing, the prosecutor insisted, according to Furtado.

Hayman says he does not recall opposing the action, although "I may well have expressed some concerns about the evidentiary basis of the seizure."

But Furtado remembers it well. "We had several conversations where we had less than a meeting of the minds." The FBI and Hayman kept telling him to call off the dog. Literally.

That's not all they wanted. "They wanted to know which one of my agents made the decision unilaterally," Furtado says. ". . . And I said that my agents don't do things unilaterally, that they do things after we've discussed them and that they knew what their marching orders were. Their marching orders were that if they could take something, to do it. And that they wouldn't be second-guessed about it."

Orton remembers Hayman's fury and his threat never to use the evidence in court. "I said, 'Russell, I am gonna seize it anyway. You do what you want with it. That's a prosecutor's decision. I made an investigative decision.'"

The debate reached the Justice Department in Washington, where, at quickly arranged meetings in Chuck Saphos's office, the FBI vented outrage at the turn of events and fear that Operation Polar Cap would come crashing down if the money was taken.

"There was concern," says Saphos, "that evidence might be destroyed or . . . the bad guys would just stop doing business and split. That would be the worst of all cases. And we'd be left with millions of hours of videotape and audiotapes of money laundering—and no defendants."

He stepped in, and by late afternoon Eastern time it was decided that the New York agents would let the money go through. There would be no seizure, everyone agreed.

Furtado called DEA in New York to stop the operation. But he was told that everyone was out at Kennedy, and no one had reported back to say what they had found.

According to Furtado, "I said, 'Well, I got some real problems out here with some organizations that don't want this thing to happen.'" He was told it might be too late to stop it. Furtado said, "Try and find out for me and get back to me."

By that time, seven or eight federal agents and their supervisors had arrived at Kennedy and met the Customs dog handler and his charge. Sure enough, thirty boxes waiting for shipment sat in the Loomis space, each of them completely wrapped in silver duct tape like so many of the boxes the agents had seen.

One of the boxes had a hole in it, though, about an inch in diameter. Through it, a stack of paper was visible. The agents could see it was currency. The handler led the dog to the boxes.

At the one with the hole, the dog went berserk: He scratched. He jumped around. He acted as if he was trying to dig his way into the box. The dog had alerted, as they say. And the agents had the probable cause they needed to seize the boxes and everything in them. They started packing them up to take downtown.

When DEA—New York called Furtado back, it was to say that the seizure had already happened.

Furtado called Hayman and the FBI. "I told them that the green light had been given, that I supported my guys a hundred percent, and that it looked like it might be a little too late.

"They were really pissed off."

Orton, on the other hand, felt great. The Andonians had never heard of Mike Orton, and they surely didn't know he was listening to them, watching them, and growing more frustrated every day. Now, he had set events into motion that would upset the Andonians greatly. Orton told himself, "Now the crooks are going to start responding to *me.*"

So, "At the end of the day I walked up to the wire room and said, 'Gang, be here bright and early tomorrow and we will have an interesting day.'"

Nazareth Andonian arrived early at work, too, that Wednesday morning, apparently eager to receive the huge shipment and start counting it. Just after 8:00 A.M. he called his contact at Loomis. When will my shipment from New York be delivered? he asked.

The man at Loomis didn't know anything about a shipment from New York. But he assured Andonian he would check into it and have it delivered as soon as he found it.

Forty-five minutes later, Loomis called back and told Andonian there were no packages for him from New York.

Andonian immediately hit the phones. He called Buenos Aires, looking for a man named "Avo," who couldn't be located. He called one of his partners in L.A., asking if Avo had called. He called Argentina again to leave a message for Avo to call him. It was a "very important matter."

The DEA was recording and logging all of the calls. The pen register showed each telephone number he dialed, and when his nervousness caused him to punch a wrong number, hang up, and redial, Orton laughed as he saw the partial numbers come over the register.

At 9:10 A.M., Andonian called New York. In a series of conversations, he learned that Customs agents had visited one of the La Mina businesses in New York to ask about the boxes. The agents were told the boxes contained polishing powder. When the agents said the boxes did not contain that at all, they were told to contact Andonian in Los Angeles.

At noon, Nazareth Andonian placed a local call to his sister, who had also spoken to New York. She told her brother she had heard the "money did not come and that the atmosphere is very hot."

Yes, Andonian said. That is true.

In the basement of a building in the New York World Trade Center, Customs employees worked for nearly five days, photographing, unboxing, counting, tallying, and repackaging the contents of those thirty boxes.

Using tables covered with brown wrapping paper to catch cocaine residue, and wearing plastic gloves to protect from the irritating dust, a half dozen or more Customs cashiers and agents toiled over this task in a room-sized vault called the sales and seizure room. They put four money counters to work whirring through the stacks of cash. It was slow going. Handling so much money can be surprisingly tedious.

In the end, the tally came to $4,866,141.

As for the whitish dust that flaked off the bills, a DEA chemist arrived to analyze it while the agents counted. It was cocaine.

Finally, a year after the tip from the Wells Fargo banker and eleven months after the confidential informant walked into DEA's New York office, the feds had something to show for their efforts: nearly $5 million in drug proceeds.

This was very good evidence. They had actual cash—cash covered with cocaine residue—being shipped from one set of suspects in New York to another set in Los Angeles. From the wires, they had worried telephone calls. They had calls to La Mina's bosses in South America, and as the suspects tried to figure out what had happened and to assess damage, the wires turned up more incriminating calls, and more suspects.

"When we seized that money, all the lights went on," says Furtado. "We got the best phone calls we ever got."

FBI agents say the seizure in fact scared off a couple of the lesser New York targets, who scattered, never to be seen again.

But Furtado insists the seizure was worthwhile. "That's what made the case."

It also reinvigorated the Atlanta case.

Suddenly, Eduardo Martínez was calling again.

"Partner!" Cesar Diaz exclaimed into the telephone, genuinely happy to hear Martínez's voice.

"Happy New Year, partner!" Martínez responded.

Two weeks after the seizure in New York, Martínez was calling Cesar for the first time in months. Ramón had tried to resume business but it had never gotten off the ground. In fact, the Atlantans hadn't handled any of Martínez's money for a year, not since the trip to Panama. Maybe the $5 million La Mina seizure had shaken Eduardo Martínez's faith in his favorite money laundry.

For whatever reason, he was back on the phone to Cesar, and he wanted to do business.

"When could we start?"

"We are ready, brother," said Cesar. "We are ready."

No one had expected Eduardo Martínez to reappear so suddenly. The feds had thought that the La Mina gang would react in New York or Los Angeles; they had not anticipated a new development in Atlanta. So while the Atlanta group cranked up Jimmy Brown's laundry, Polar Cap agents in Los Angeles and New York watched their targets anxiously, figuring they might run or get rid of evidence. If they shut down all of La Mina, the agents would have to be ready to move. The feds didn't know what the jewelers would do, when the roller-coaster ride would take off or where it would go. But something was bound to happen. A $5 million loss could not be ignored, even by an organization used to moving hundreds of millions a year.

Yet, none of the La Mina operatives seemed to be going anywhere. The money had stopped coming from New York, and Nazareth Andonian was telling callers his business was down. But for weeks there was no action the feds could discern.

In fact, the group seemed to doubt that cops had taken the money. Wanis Koyomejian told Nazareth Andonian in a monitored conversation that he didn't believe the government could simply take and hold $5 million. In fact, Koyomejian said he didn't believe the government had done it at all. He and Andonian sounded as if they suspected their business associates in New York of ripping off the money.

From Buenos Aires, Avo—the man Andonian had tried to reach the morning after the seizure—told Nazareth Andonian things were very hot down south. Avo offered to bail Andonian out, telling him he would give him "five" from his own pocket.

But the conversation that would turn the investigation upside down was not one the DEA picked up. It came on February 21 over a Ropex telephone line monitored by the FBI: Hello, a male caller said to Wanis Koyomejian. This is Sergio.

Sergio Hochman, believed to be a major power behind La Mina and possibly *the* major power, had suddenly popped up in the investigation for the first time in months. He had been out of the country and living in Montevideo since the previous May, when a knock on the door of his New York apartment spooked him into fleeing the country. With $3 million in cash lying on his table, a nervous Hochman saw through a closed-circuit monitor two men in suits at his door and feared they were law enforcement. Hochman, who didn't answer the door, was so shaken that he walked out of the apartment that day, the money still on the table.

Now he was back in the country, and he was telling Koyomejian he'd be over to visit that day. The feds believed panic over the $5 million loss had brought Hochman to the United States to find the problem and fix it. In reality, the seizure had nothing to do with his return. Hochman had been out of the business for months and had no stake in the $5 million: he had come back to try to set up his own money laundry. Whatever his role had been in La Mina, he had no role in it now.

But federal investigators knew none of that at the time. They were also wrong about Hochman's importance to La Mina in the first place. That was because when they were listening over the telephone wires and room bugs, they kept mistaking the name "Celio" for "Sergio," so they had been attributing the activities of money launderer Celio Merkin to Sergio Hochman. Merkin, who had helped establish the operation in Los Angeles, occupied a considerably more important position in the organization than Hochman. The FBI learned of Merkin's existence belatedly, and even then had trouble distinguishing between the two first names.

By February 1989, the feds had realized their mistake, but they still weren't sure how much of Merkin's work they had confused with Hochman's. Still, they figured they had a big fish on the line when they heard Hochman talking to Koyomejian. "Hochman, we thought, was *the* prize," says FBI supervisor Lumpkin.

When Wong heard the name over the wiretap, "I called out the troops." But had the man said "Sergio" or "Celio"? Wong says he really couldn't tell, but he had another reason to think it was Hochman. In the four weeks since the seizure at Kennedy, Wong had been checking the Customs computer system more frequently, which contained the names of foreigners entering the United States for whom a law enforcement agency had placed a lookout. Wong had figured the seizure could draw La Mina's South American bosses into the country to find the weakness in their operation, so he kept looking for their names. Sure enough, on February 19, Sergio Hochman's name had turned up on the computer as having entered the country through New York, with plans to travel to Los Angeles on the twentieth. Manifests of nonstop flights between New York and Los Angeles on the twentieth showed he had, in fact, come to Los Angeles with a ticket to return to New York on the twenty-first.

The feds needed to find him, but "we didn't know what he looked like; we didn't know whether he was old, young, whatever," explains Wong. He told the agents monitoring the Ropex cameras and the room microphones to look for a man they had never seen before and listen for the name "Sergio."

So when two strangers showed up at Ropex that morning, the feds took note. And when they left, they left with a surveillance team in tow. They followed them to the Bonaventure Hotel, where the staff said yes, a Sergio Hochman had been staying there, but he was checking out that day.

The Polar Cap agents didn't know who the other man was, but with

Hochman, they believed they had a rare opportunity to get their hands on a major money launderer. They also believed that opportunity would pass quickly if they didn't act on it. Hochman would be returning to New York that evening, and he had a ticket back to South America after that.

Suddenly, one of the chief targets had put himself within striking range. This could be the best chance the feds would ever get to take him. But they would have to act quickly, and they would have to take down all of La Mina at once, because surely his arrest—especially coming right after the $5 million seizure—would send all other targets running.

The feds had been preparing for a March 8 takedown, still two and a half weeks away. They would have scores of people to arrest, homes and businesses to search in Los Angeles, New York, Miami, and other La Mina cities. Could they pull together all those search warrants, all those affidavits, and organize all those search and arrest teams in time? Was Hochman worth it?

A surveillance team followed Hochman and the other man to an oceanside restaurant along the Pacific Coast Highway and watched them eat a seafood lunch. Wong peeled off for a meeting in prosecutor Hayman's office, where Furtado, Lumpkin, and other Polar Cap agents debated the possibilities. Hayman alerted the Polar Cap lawyers on the East Coast.

When the call came, Buddy Parker was in the kitchen of his home in one of Atlanta's graceful older neighborhoods. Chuck Saphos was on the line from Washington, along with his appointed Polar Cap coordinator, Peter Djinis. So were Hayman in Los Angeles and Jonathan Liebman in New York.

Hochman was in the United States, and they wanted to arrest him, but that would mean shutting down all of La Mina. How could they pull that off? And where should Hochman be taken?

Hayman said he wanted to get Hochman while he was in Los Angeles. The FBI was already onto him, and if he left town, the feds might lose him.

But if he went to New York, he would lead them to more suspects, Liebman countered. They thought he had planned high-level meetings to get the organization working right, and Liebman argued the feds would make a bigger hit if they let Hochman lead them in New York. He wanted DEA to take Hochman there.

The problem with New York was surveillance, Hayman said. It was too easy for a target to give agents the slip in midtown Manhattan, with its crowded sidewalks and streets, and with taxis, buses, and subway entrances offering endless possibilities for escape. DEA had had a terrible job following suspects during the course of this case, and this was no time to risk another failed surveillance.

The lawyers reached consensus that Hochman would be taken in Los Angeles. But how could they coordinate such a massive takedown in so little time? The Polar Cap teams in New York and Los Angeles would work around the clock for the next two days and get it done, Hayman and Liebman said. What about Atlanta? Could Buddy shut down his case simultaneously with the takedown in L.A. and New York?

The other lawyers didn't care much whether Atlanta was in or out. La Mina didn't reach to Atlanta, anyway, so the agents there were not investigating its ongoing operation. "They really weren't a consideration," says Hayman. "We were keeping plugged in with Buddy for what insights he could lend as a result of information gleaned through Martínez. But in an operational sense, they weren't involved in the investigation."

But Buddy wanted badly to be in on the big event, to be part of the case Attorney General Richard Thornburgh would be boasting about.

Except for the latest developments with Martínez, Buddy had already presented all his evidence to a grand jury. But he hadn't asked for an indictment so far in advance of the takedown. In fact, he didn't even have a bill of indictment written at this point; he was still drafting it. Perhaps he could wrap that up and begin notifying grand jurors immediately to come for an emergency session.

More problematic was Craig and Buddy's big plan to seize Banco de Occidente's bank accounts. While writing the indictment and putting the grand jury onto full alert, Buddy would have to draw up warrants and motions for the money freezes, win court approval for this highly unusual action, have the warrants certified, and somehow get them served on the various banks around the country that had Occidente accounts.

That would take time. The lawyers talked about arresting Hochman and holding him incommunicado for up to twenty-four hours so the feds could get their act together without his alerting the rest of the La Mina organization. But even that wouldn't give Buddy the time he needed for the indictment and the bank warrants. He would have to forget his bold move on Occidente if Atlanta was to be ready.

And he also could forget Martínez. The new contact with him had pumped up hope that Cesar could lure Martínez to Panama for an arrest. But there was no way to set that up on such short notice.

It all gave him a sickening feeling. He could have had everything ready, if only he had known.

But now, to pull this thing off, "I'd have been up all night long, bleary-eyed, trying to draft this complex indictment." It would be too easy to make some stupid mistake, and he certainly didn't want his biggest case ever disclosed in a sloppy, perhaps fatally flawed indictment, not with the Attorney General of the United States watching and announcing it to the world.

Getting in on the big media splash wasn't worth giving up the possibility of catching Martínez, losing the chance to freeze millions of Occidente's dollars, or risking a mistake in the indictment that would ruin all the hard work he and the drug agents had done.

While La Mina went down, Cesar would stay undercover with Martínez, and Buddy and Skip would get cracking on the paperwork. They still would aim for March 8, while everyone else in Polar Cap from New York to Los Angeles would take down their cases and win all the accolades. When Polar Cap and La Mina were revealed to the nation, no one would know that a group of guys in Atlanta, Georgia, had had anything at all to do with it.

When Sergio Hochman showed up at a gate of the Los Angeles airport for his trip to New York on Tuesday evening, February 21, he had with him the man agents still could not identify. Silently, ten or so agents formed a perimeter around the two men, while quickly, almost surgically, Wong and two other agents walked up to the pair, identified themselves and their purpose, and whisked them away.

The stranger was assigned to two agents, who would drive him around while the Bureau determined whether he was a Polar Cap target. Meanwhile, Wong took Hochman to FBI headquarters in the federal building west of downtown, where Hochman talked to Wong for hours before being locked up in the Culver City jail. Sergio Hochman already was cooperating with the investigation. But he didn't tell anyone that the man he was with at the airport that evening had helped him launder money in New York.

All night long, Polar Cap agents, cops, and prosecutors worked to get ready for takedown the next morning. The copying machines in the U.S. Attorney's Office in Los Angeles were burning up from overload, and the agents were working without benefit of sleep. In all the chaos, Hochman's mysterious traveling companion was forgotten. The same two agents had driven the man around the city for some eight hours when Lumpkin finally remembered and authorized them to let him go.

And sometime in the early morning hours, agents and prosecutors awoke a federal judge at his home, where the groggy, bathrobed judge scanned hastily finished affidavits and signed warrants to search and warrants to arrest.

On Wednesday morning, February 22, they began bursting through doors. Guns out, they rounded up the men and women they had been watching and listening to for months, whose garbage they had searched, whose lovemaking they had taped, whose bank accounts they had scoured, whose every move they had noted.

Orton led a team of federal agents and marshals to the Andonian Brothers offices in the Jewelry Trades Building, where they rounded up Nazareth and Vahe and a dozen other employees. Stacks of records, ledgers, and other papers were seized, along with the money counters.

The same thing was going on at the Ropex offices, also in the Jewelry Trades Building, where the FBI took Wanis Koyomejian, other key Ropex players, and anything that looked like evidence. Some of it proved embarrassing to law enforcement. At Ropex, the raiding agents found a stack of completed IRS 8300 forms reporting—falsely—that Ropex customers had paid cash for many millions of dollars' worth of gold. Apparently the fact that astronomical sums of currency were being spent on gold at a single small business had piqued no suspicion among IRS bureaucrats not involved in Polar Cap; they had returned the forms to Ropex on a technicality—no one had signed them.

But on this day, all of that was coming to an end. Sixteen businesses in L.A.'s jewelry district and three in New York's were hit, while agents in Miami moved in on the Ronel Refinery. Luxury cars were seized and buildings the money launderers owned were declared federal property. In the suburbs flung out from L.A.—in Northridge and North Hollywood, in the hills of La Crescenta and way up to Sylmar at the northern edge of L.A.'s sprawl—agents and marshals banged open doors, handcuffed suspects, and searched the expensive and not-so-expensive homes of the people who had been mining for gold.

The case got big news treatment in the La Mina cities, and the national press reported it, too. But the announcement from Washington took place on paper only; Thornburgh decided to wait until the last piece of the puzzle was in place in Atlanta before holding a press conference. Instead, he issued a written statement disclosing Polar Cap and declaring it "the largest drug money laundering investigation ever conducted by United States law enforcement agencies." He said the probe had broken open an organization that had washed at least $1 billion in drug proceeds in two years' time. He reported that federal agents were executing thirty-seven arrest warrants in Los Angeles, New York, and Miami, and eighty-five search and seizure warrants.

Thornburgh named and congratulated each of the agencies and most of the cities. Of course, he did not mention Atlanta. But he did say he expected "further announcements within the next several days."

19: Cranking Up the Old Laundry

The day La Mina was shut down, Eduardo Martínez learned the news from his contacts in New York. By nine thirty the following morning, he was on the phone to Cesar, telling him he was ready for business and warning him to be careful.

"I don't want this to bring us problems," Martínez said.

In the two weeks since Martínez had renewed contact with Cesar, the Atlanta DEA had been dusting off the laundry's machinery to handle the work Martínez was promising. Now, it was ready to go—and none too soon for Martínez. He was ready, too, but the La Mina takedown had upset him. He asked Cesar whether Jimmy Brown's laundry had anything to do with jewelry stores. Cesar assured him it did not.

Martínez told Cesar to caution his people in New York and Los Angeles "not to make a mistake, not even with a cent. Do you understand?"

"Yes, yes, yes," Cesar said.

"That, if they perceive risk, not to do anything," Martínez said.

"Yes," said Cesar.

"Call them and ask them to be very careful of everything," Martínez repeated.

The operation would work much as it had before, only this time they would not be using Banco de Occidente. Cesar had heard from one of the Ospina brothers that Occidente had stopped doing that sort of business.

That's true, Martínez confirmed.

"What happened with those people?" Cesar asked.

"Ah, the owner of the bank does not want to do international transactions of any kind because," Martínez paused, "they made a big fuss, you know?" Apparently some of Banco de Occidente's customers were drawing unwanted attention.

Martínez assured Cesar the bank had not gotten into trouble. But bank management nonetheless decided to eliminate foreign transactions "just for the image."

"Some said it was a 'washer' bank," Martínez explained.

Of course, Banco de Occidente was not the only bank in Panama that could handle this kind of work. Martínez said the money should be wired to his accounts at a Panama branch of another Colombian bank headquartered in Medellín.

On Monday, February 27, undercover drug agents in Los Angeles posing as Cesar's co-workers picked up nearly $900,000 from a courier working for one of Martínez's customers. The next day, in midtown Manhattan, a Colombian named Julian opened his car trunk to a pair of undercover agents and handed them two suitcases containing more than $500,000 in cash. Jimmy Brown's laundry was in business again after a thirteen-month hiatus.

Every working day that week, drug dollars poured into the hands and bank accounts of New York– and Los Angeles–based agents helping the Atlanta group. Cesar and Martínez were constantly on the telephone to each other, reporting sums of money and bank accounts, and tracking the faxes they were shooting back and forth. At week's end, more than $4.3 million in cash had been pumped into the Atlanta undercover laundry.

Nothing had come out. By the beginning of the second week, Martínez was starting to worry. "We need to speed up the payments, brother, so that I can continue," he told Cesar Monday morning, March 6. "You understand?"

That afternoon, a grand jury would vote to indict Eduardo Martínez on charges of contributing to cocaine trafficking by laundering millions of dollars in drug proceeds for the Medellín, Colombia, drug cartel. He would be indicted alongside some of the biggest drug lords in the world.

By this time, Buddy had taken Cesar, Skip, Ramón, and a host of cops and agents from Los Angeles and New York into a federal grand jury to lay out the evidence they had gathered in the two and a half years since the original meeting with Ramón on Aruba. They had hours of undercover tapes, beginning with that first meeting between Serrano, Ramón, Featherly, and Jaime Parra at the Ritz-Carlton in Atlanta, and ending with Martínez's recent telephone calls to Cesar. But Buddy didn't stop with the Fis-Con evidence. He also introduced the jurors to La Mina and showed that Martínez—as Mina 30—was a big customer in that criminal enterprise, too. And with the links Gail Shelby had found between the New York and Atlanta investigations, Buddy showed the jurors that the same Chepe who met Ramón and Francisco Serrano—the man who worked with Martínez and who had been the source of the $1 million seized in L.A.—also used La Mina to launder the proceeds of his considerable cocaine business in New York. He backed that up with ledgers seized during the takedown in February.

By now, Francisco had reluctantly agreed to cooperate, so he, too, had testified. Francisco had been wavering for months when Buddy decided to give him a nudge. After the Marina del Rey meeting and the Hochman arrest, Buddy knew the Atlanta takedown was coming soon, and he needed to pull together everything he had.

Buddy brought Francisco and his public defender to the conference room near his office and told them he wanted to introduce Francisco to some people. He told Francisco that once he saw these people, he would understand the breadth of the evidence against him. Until then, Francisco had not mentioned the money laundry to Buddy, and Buddy had said nothing about it. Francisco had not known the feds knew about Jimmy Brown's laundry or the cocaine loads he had tried to arrange through Skip, as Allen Weston.

But that day in the conference room, Francisco quickly understood the feds knew more about him than he had suspected. In walked Jimmy Brown and a grinning Alex Carrera.

Francisco was speechless. Buddy suddenly realized he had arranged a very cruel trick and feared Francisco might have a heart attack from the shock. He had thought of these two men, especially Cesar, as his friends and partners for two years.

You work for the DEA? Francisco asked. They assured him they did.

It was on that day that Francisco Serrano decided to roll. However reluctant, he became a government witness.

Even then, he gave the feds almost nothing they did not already know. But one thing he did give them was Chepe's name. Asked to recount everything he knew about Chepe, he recalled the day more than a year earlier when he was called into Chepe's warehouse office and questioned about the $1 million seizure in Los Angeles. He remembered the engineering degree on the wall, and he thought he remembered the name on it: Geraldo Moncada.*

That was the name under which Chepe would be indicted.

---

* This was the name Francisco remembered; eventually the Atlanta DEA learned that Moncada's first name was Gerardo.

The resumption of business with Eduardo Martínez brought more urgency to the need to indict. A March 15 takedown was planned, and on Monday, March 6, even as Martínez was continuing to send money through Jimmy Brown's laundry, the grand jury in Atlanta secretly returned a seventy-five-page indictment, half of it copies of computer printouts showing bank transactions. At Buddy's request, a judge immediately put the document under seal.

The list of defendants began with Pablo Escobar and ended with Banco de Occidente. The indictment named Jorge Ochoa, as well as Escobar's cousin and partner, Gustavo Gaviria, whom Ramón and Serrano had met at the compound. Just below Gaviria was Geraldo Moncada, listed with his string of aliases, including the name New York was still using, Luis Garces-Restrepo. Moncada, the indictment said, organized and supervised the U.S. distribution of cocaine and the laundering of the resulting proceeds for the Medellín cartel, with New York named as his chief territory. Moncada not only used the Atlanta undercover money laundry, he also laundered more than $1 billion in drug proceeds through La Mina, the indictment charged.

Next came Eduardo Martínez, along with his cousin-in-law and partner, Juan Carlos Ospina. The indictment said Martínez acted as a broker for drug traffickers seeking money-laundering services. Specifically, it stated Martínez had sent more than $15.2 million through the undercover laundry from late 1987 through March 3, 1989—more, counting the sums he sent through with his cousin-in-law, Ospina. He also used La Mina, the indictment said, without listing specific sums.

The indictment named Jaime Parra—the man who vanished in Las Vegas and was still a Pisces fugitive—as well as one of the traffickers implicated in the smuggling part of the Atlanta operation. The names of the two bankers in Panama who had been helpful to Martínez and Cesar were also there, Clara García and William Guarin. As for Francisco, he was indicted separately, along with the other two Ospinas and the cast of people who had brought him money and helped him get it to Jimmy Brown's organization. A third indictment named more people who had conspired to send cocaine through Allen Weston.

The main indictment—naming Escobar, Moncada, and Martínez—told the story of the two-year investigation. It charged the defendants with conspiring to distribute "multiple tons of cocaine and marijuana" in the United States. To facilitate that crime, the indictment said, the defendants caused the drug proceeds to be delivered to money-laundering operations in the United States, where the funds would be deposited into banks and then wired to accounts in Panama, Uruguay, and Europe.

The government spelled out the role that moving and cleaning money play in the crime of drug trafficking: "The removal from the United States of the proceeds of the Cartel's drug trafficking was integral to the perpetuation of the defendants' conspiracy. The Cartel used its drug moneys to pay for such drug expenses as the acquisition of aircraft, boats, cars, stash houses, laboratories and the purchase of raw materials." In addition, money laundering allowed cartel members to become very wealthy.

The last overt act mentioned had happened on March 3—the Friday before the Monday grand jury action—when Martínez moved another $490,000 into Jimmy Brown's laundry. In fact, on the day of the indictment and all through that week, the laundry was still taking in cash for him, nearly $2 million more.

In New York, Ed Guillen's group kept surveilling and going undercover for the pickups, and a team in Los Angeles did the same.

In Atlanta, plans were being made to lure Martínez into a meeting so he could be arrested, while bosses in Washington planned a major public announcement to coincide with it. Attorney General Thornburgh was planning a major press conference to describe Operation Polar Cap, including the Atlanta probe as well as the La Mina investigation.

The U.S. Attorney in Atlanta, Robert L. Barr, Jr., Buddy's boss, wrote Washington to ask that the press conference be held in Atlanta since, after all, the Atlanta agents discovered La Mina first, and the Atlanta indictment laid out the whole picture from start to finish. Moreover, his office's prosecution of a Colombian bank and its Panamanian branch was unprecedented.

Memos and cables flew from city to city, agency to agency. They listed couriers to be arrested, bank records to be subpoenaed, property to be seized.

While tracking that activity, Craig Gillen and Buddy Parker busily prepared to mount an unprecedented action against a foreign bank and its customers. Assembling agents' affidavits, statutes, and whatever case law they had, they got ready to apply their substitute-asset theory against Banco de Occidente.

The government could prove, the prosecutors believed, that the bank had laundered hundreds of millions of dollars in drug proceeds that had traveled through La Mina or the Atlanta laundry. While that money was gone, Buddy and Craig believed they had found a way to seize something from the bank, if not actual drug proceeds. Under the substitute-asset theory, the prosecutors wanted to freeze all money coming to Banco de Occidente's U.S. bank accounts. Beginning on takedown day, no money would leave those accounts. Upon an adjudication of guilt, the government could seize the funds. If the bank were found not guilty, the funds would be released.

What made this idea so unusual—and so incredibly unfair, some would later say—was that the money to be frozen did not actually belong to the bank, but rather to its customers. Each of Banco de Occidente's correspondent accounts in U.S. banks was nothing more than a pipeline through which the funds of several international customers flowed.

But under federal law, the funds represented bank assets, not money belonging to innocent individuals or companies, because the account was opened in the name of Banco de Occidente. Under U.S. property law, Craig and Buddy contended, what matters is the account holder, not the source of the funds traveling through the account.

And because they were Occidente assets, the funds in Occidente's accounts could be frozen in lieu of the millions of dollars in drug proceeds that had already passed through those accounts, they would argue in court.

Through Martínez and the business DEA-Atlanta had conducted with him, agents learned that the Panamanian banks he was using kept correspondent accounts in New York, Miami, and San Francisco. These were added to the undercover bank accounts at Citizens & Southern in Atlanta, Chemical Bank in New York, and elsewhere, to bring to sixteen the number of U.S. banks with accounts Buddy wanted to freeze. He drew up an order that would do just that, and prepared to ask a judge to sign it.

The problem was setting a date for all this coordinated action. Takedown had to be tied to the most important suspect able to be caught: Eduardo Martínez.

Martínez and Cesar had been talking for weeks about getting together with Jimmy Brown and Ramón, either on Aruba or in Panama. Martínez was amenable but elusive. He'd agree to a time and place, unwittingly sending the gigantic U.S. law enforcement apparatus into overdrive, only to change his mind and reschedule.

Apparently he was less concerned about arranging a rendezvous than he was about dragging his money out of this incredibly slow laundry.

"I need your help with the payments, brother, because I am completely cleaned out," Martínez told Cesar on Wednesday, March 8, two days after his secret indictment.

He was still directing payments through the Atlanta organization, but his customers were getting worried. "I need your help to be able to show my face again, brother."

Cesar said he'd try. But still the money didn't come. By the end of the second week of Martínez's resurgent business with Cesar, $6.2 million in cash had gone into Jimmy Brown's laundry. Still, nothing was coming out.

Cesar gave Martínez all sorts of excuses, but the real problem was with Eddie Guillen, the DEA–New York agent in charge of Fis-Con's bank accounts. Guillen had decided to slow down the laundry to an even more sluggish pace than before. Knowing DEA-Atlanta was laying plans to arrest Martínez, Guillen wanted to keep as much money in the pipeline as possible so it could be seized at the time of arrest. The way he saw it, the more money seized, the more damage done to the drug traffickers. The less money laundered, the less help the government gave the bad guys.

Too bad if Martínez didn't like it, Guillen told them. A good under-cover agent can come up with an inexhaustible list of excuses to placate a crook.

Skip and Cesar tried hard to keep Martínez happy, and for two very good reasons, to their way of thinking. First, Cesar needed to maintain access so they could arrest him. Second, Martínez had said he'd throw a lot more business their way if they could show they could handle it. Skip envisioned cramming $10, $15, maybe $20 million in the pipeline for the government to seize at takedown. He saw no reason to limit the size of the pickups, as Guillen wanted, or to dole out the money in piddling amounts to Martínez.

No, we are not going to do it that way, Skip told Guillen.

Yes you are, Guillen said, because I won't release any more money than I see fit.

The argument went on up the line, until Caffrey intervened and worked out an agreement with one of Guillen's superiors in New York.

Still, every release of funds required another series of phone calls to New York, another tug of war, and three or four days lost while Martínez complained ever more bitterly. It got to the point where Guillen would rarely return phone calls to Atlanta. Meanwhile, Martínez was calling Cesar every day, several times a day. Cesar dreaded these calls. He was running out of excuses.

"Why is it so slow this time?" Martínez would say.

"It's—listen," Cesar replied. "What they told me is (pause), the guy up there (pause), I mean, it's going in as much as possible so as not to attract any attention."

Martínez wasn't satisfied. His customers were driving him crazy, he said. He needed to know where the money was.

Cesar said he'd call Jimmy Brown to find out and then call Martínez back to tell him what Jimmy said. He hung up and put in a call to New York.

An hour later, Cesar still was waiting for a call back from Guillen when his undercover phone rang. It was Martínez.

"Did you talk to the boss?" he asked.

"Yes. I already called, and they're checking on everything for me. I'm waiting for them to call me back. I'm sitting here like an idiot, waiting for them to call." Genuine irritation showed through.

"I'm waiting, too," said Martínez. "I need them to help me on this, buddy. We're so poor here. . . .

"You've got to tell him to help us," Martínez went on. "And if he wants more numbers, we'll give him more numbers."

Eventually, Guillen let a little bit of money go, but Martínez wasn't satisfied. At this rate, it would take months for him to receive the money already delivered to Brown's laundry.

"Listen, I think we have to talk," he finally told Cesar.

At last Martínez was showing a little enthusiasm for the face-to-face meeting they had been trying for weeks to arrange.

"Yes, yes!" Cesar said. "That's why I wanted you and I to meet with Jimmy . . ."

Still, plans to meet kept evaporating, while pressure built for the Atlanta team to take down the case. Martínez's patience dissolved, replaced by fury and a degree of fear. Some very serious men were squeezing him for their money, and he was squeezing Cesar.

"Why don't you pay the account?" Martínez demanded. "As a measure of caution or prevention, fifteen or twenty days is okay. "But we're already over a month!" His customers were climbing all over him, he said.

Cesar told Martínez he was absolutely right. Jimmy Brown had been upset about the poor service, too, and wants to bring Martínez the money personally.

"That way," said Cesar, "you'll have it right away." They could meet in Panama within the next few days. Would that be all right?

Of course, said Martínez. "If . . . we could clear up everything that's outstanding this week, there wouldn't be a problem."

He didn't care whether he got his money through bank wire transfers or in cash. "I can get the paper, or it can be in a bag," he told Cesar. He would be happy to meet in Panama, if that's what they wanted, if that would speed things up.

"But it can't keep going the way it has been," warned Martínez. "That's impossible. You understand?"

Time and place were set for 9:00 A.M., Wednesday, March 29, at the Marriott in Panama City. John Featherly couldn't come, but Cesar would be carrying cash. Five million dollars, to be exact.

Martínez's agreement had sent the Atlanta DEA office and Buddy Parker into high gear, churning out the papers necessary for an international arrest, making arrangements, winning approvals in Washington. Cesar would go with two other Atlanta-based agents.

He bought three round-trip air tickets, plus a one-way, open ticket from Panama to Atlanta in the name of Eduardo Martínez.

On Tuesday, March 28, as scores of federal agents began fanning out around the country for their various assignments, Buddy walked into the chambers of U.S. District Judge Marvin H. Shoob. Opinionated, somewhat liberal, and wary of the government's power, Shoob nonetheless signed a set of remarkable restraining orders giving the prosecutor everything he wanted. It meant that no matter how much of Martínez's money remained in the undercover laundry, the government could get many millions of dollars more.

The orders plugged up the accounts of the Panamanian banks Martínez was using around the United States, allowing money to come in but nothing to go out, collecting like bathwater under an open faucet. From the time the orders were served, the U.S. banks were to refuse to honor any demand for those funds. At the same time, the U.S. banks were prohibited from notifying Occidente officials about the order.

The orders also instructed the banks to inform the agents as to each account's balance at the time of the freeze, and to report the balance again forty-eight hours later.

So while federal law enforcers were organizing agents to arrest couriers and to seize cars and real estate owned by defendants, they were also setting up teams of agents, mostly two-person pairings from DEA and IRS, to serve orders on sixteen banks from coast to coast. The idea was to hit all of them as close to 9:00 A.M. Eastern time as possible, when Cesar would be meeting Martínez in Panama. Buddy called each of the agencies in every city to see that they understood the order and to ensure that teams were organized to serve them.

For his task on takedown day, Skip would go to a bank Clara García had implicated as being friendly, Continental Illinois Bank International in New York. Skip would take not only the restraining order, but also a search warrant for the offices in the bank's Latin American section. To execute the search and serve the restraining order, he would bring with him the Atlanta-based IRS agent who had been analyzing the bank accounts, Jack Fishman, as well as New York Customs agent Art Donelan, who had been working Polar Cap, and five more IRS agents.

Buddy was feeling the pressure. This was a very big deal, what with so many agencies and agents carrying out his plan, with Cesar attempting to collar a major Colombian suspect in Noriega's Panama, with some of the most violent criminals in the world indicted over his signature.

Nearly three years earlier in Aruba, Buddy had hoped that Ramón, whom he saw as an odd, nervous man, would bring him his biggest case yet. But this was far bigger and more complex than anything Buddy had imagined.

Buddy saw to it that copies of the indictment, the court orders, and the affidavits went to Washington. Word came back that Thornburgh would hold a live press conference in Washington at 10:00 A.M. to announce the case. DEA and IRS in Atlanta were getting charts made, briefing papers typed and copied. Buddy was taking calls and questions from Thornburgh's press secretary, who was checking the facts of the case.

With the Attorney General of the United States watching and the national and international press about to be alerted, Buddy just hoped nothing would go wrong.

20: Return to Panama

Cesar and his two backups flew into Panama the evening before the arrest and went straight to the bayside condominium of Rene De La Cova, who at that time was DEA's acting attaché in Panama. Cuban-born De La Cova, a tall, outgoing man in his mid-thirties, would be Cesar's guide to Panama this time. In a strategy session that evening, they decided to wait until morning to alert their Panamanian counterparts to their plans.

To make an arrest in Panama, U.S. officers had to work through the Panamanian Defense Forces (PDF), Noriega's police force. This was still true in March 1989, despite the mounting tension between Noriega and the United States, and the growing evidence of corruption within the PDF. Under normal circumstances, the DEA would have given the PDF more time to organize for an arrest. This time, there would be only an hour's notice for fear the PDF would tip off Martínez.

De La Cova accompanied Cesar and the other two Atlanta agents into one of Panama City's worst neighborhoods, El Chorrillo, at about 8:00 A.M. on takedown day, Wednesday, March 29, an hour before Cesar was to meet Martínez across town. There a small, one-story building housed PDF, about a block from Noriega's headquarters. In this crowded neighborhood, washing hangs from the balconies, and bright colors painted onto concrete buildings belie the poverty within.

At first, the agents literally could not get in the door of the PDF. An iron gate blocked the entry. For ten minutes or more, they tried to get the attention of someone inside.

Now running late, De La Cova located Captain Luis Quiel, the man designated as PDF liaison to DEA. A solidly built man in his late thirties, Quiel had risen from inspector to captain and was the only PDF officer De La Cova knew who could bypass the chain of command and all of Noriega's majors and colonels: Quiel could pick up the telephone and reach General Manuel Noriega directly. De La Cova suspected Quiel was not entirely straight in his anti-drug efforts.*

Nonetheless, the DEA was still getting help from the PDF in 1989. In fact, in Noriega's campaign against U.S. accusations of complicity in the drug trade, he was making a big show of his anti-drug efforts. Anyone the DEA wanted arrested, the PDF arrested.

Quiel and De La Cova, who had worked many cases together, seemed to get along. The normally gregarious De La Cova was friendly, while his Panamanian counterpart, dressed in business attire, was professional and matter-of-fact. De La Cova introduced Quiel to the Atlanta agents and explained why they were there.

Cesar pulled out the documents Buddy had given him: an arrest warrant and a DEA affidavit saying why Martínez should be detained. To Cesar, who felt every second tick by, Quiel seemed to be moving in molasses.

Quiel made a telephone call, which eventually brought a lower-ranking officer to his desk, a huge, sleazy-looking man named Evaristo Gómez. Quiel explained what was happening, and they summoned three more PDF officers. The trio, all in plainclothes, were introduced to the DEA agents as the guys who would make the arrest.

De La Cova said he would go to his office at the U.S. Embassy and monitor the situation from there, while Cesar, the other two DEA agents, and the three PDF officers headed to the Marriott, where Cesar was to meet Martínez in the lobby. Cesar would be carrying his briefcase, which was clearly too small to contain $5 million in cash. But he would tell Martínez the money was in his car outside. When he and Martínez shook hands, this would identify Martínez to the PDF cops, who would move in to arrest him.

By the time this all got settled and everyone was in their cars headed to their respective posts, it was well past nine. Cesar was late for his meeting.

---

* De La Cova was not alone in his suspicions. A major drug trafficker and a former PDF officer later testified at Noriega's trial in Miami that Quiel used his position to protect the Medellín drug chiefs. But then, later events showed that De La Cova himself was not entirely straight, either. In 1994 he pleaded guilty to stealing $700,000 in an unrelated money-laundering case in Florida.

The PDF crew took one car, with the DEA agents following in a second. The Panamanians led the way through the winding streets of the poor neighborhood until they reached the Avenida Balboa, a broad boulevard running alongside the dark water of the Bay of Panama. They drove by the U.S. Embassy, with its white stucco exterior, red tile roofs, and massive palm trees painted white at the base. It was way past nine now. Cesar was definitely late.

They followed the curve of the bay around to near the cluster of high-rises where De La Cova lived, then drove on, passing Paitilla Airport, where small planes ferry vacationers to island resorts, and drugs and money in and out of Panama.

Finally, they pulled into the familiar driveway of the Marriott, where Cesar had first met Eduardo Martínez fourteen months earlier and where Martínez had warned Cesar to be careful because the DEA was everywhere.

Cesar walked into the lobby and looked around. No Martínez. Carrying his briefcase, he strolled past the Spanish fountain to the registration desk, where all the clocks told him he was late. The one for Panama City said 9:20. So did the one for New York. In forty minutes, the Attorney General of the United States would reveal the case Cesar was still trying to conclude.

Cesar asked the woman behind the desk for Eduardo Martínez.

Mr. Martínez is not here, she told Cesar. He had been in the lobby at 9:00 A.M. but had left. However, he had told her someone would be coming for him, and had left a message for Cesar. She handed over a piece of paper.

Martínez's note said he had had to leave the Marriott, but he gave a telephone number where Cesar should call him.

Damn! Cesar went to a pay telephone in the lobby and dialed the number. It was busy. He dialed it again. Busy.

By this time, Cesar was edgy, to say the least. He gave it a rest. Paced around. Tried it again. Still busy.

Ten minutes crept by. He tried the number again.

"Banco Ganadero," said a female voice. This was the bank where Martínez's accounts were receiving money from Jimmy Brown's laundry.

Cesar asked for Eduardo Martínez. He was told to hold for a moment. The moment dragged on. Finally, Martínez's voice came on the line.

Cesar greeted Martínez and apologized for being late for their meeting, blaming it on the late arrival of his plane. He made it sound like he had flown in on a private plane.

Martínez said he had waited for him at the hotel as long as he could.

Cesar said he was at the hotel now, and had "the baggage" with him. Why don't you come over? he asked.

No, Martínez did not want to go back to the hotel. Cesar should come to Banco Ganadero, he said.

Cesar didn't like the idea. He knew the lay of the Marriott, and he knew Martínez had friends at Banco Ganadero. At Banco de Occidente Martínez had been treated like royalty, and it was probably the same at the Ganadero bank. An arrest would be much easier in the hotel.

Why don't you come over here? Cesar said again. He didn't want to carry his luggage around town, he added.

But Martínez was insistent. He had business to conduct at the bank, he said, including the business between him and Cesar. Obviously, Martínez was planning to make the deposit there.

Cesar just wanted to get in the same room with Martínez. He agreed to go to Banco Ganadero.

The three PDF officers and the two DEA backups had been hanging around the lobby, so Cesar pulled one of the PDF men aside and discreetly told him what was happening.

Once they returned to their cars, they were ready to leave when a door in the first car opened. One of the Panamanians climbed out. He had to make a call, he said to Cesar.

An increasingly anxious Cesar waited outside while the PDF officer went back into the hotel.

The clock was ticking toward 10:00 A.M. when the guy finally emerged and the two-car caravan pulled out of the Marriott parking lot. Thornburgh would be holding his press conference soon—a press conference that would be televised live on CNN.

On the way to the bank, Cesar used the mobile phone De La Cova had given him to call and report what had happened. They drove back past the airport and into a neighborhood lush with banyan trees and palms, where Spanish colonial homes had been converted into banks or torn down to make room for two- or three-story modern office buildings. Wedged between some of the city's major thoroughfares, this neighborhood housed many of the Panamanian branches of the smaller international banks, standing in the shadow of high-rises bearing names like Bank of America.

The two cars drove past Banco Ganadero, which was on a small, treeless lot. The lobby was glassed in on the two sides closest to the street, so people inside could look out and passers-by could see in. The plan was this: The PDF officers would wait outside nearby, watching through the lobby windows. Cesar would go in and ask for Martínez. When Martínez came out and shook Cesar's hand—unwittingly identifying himself to the watching PDF—the Panamanian officers would come in and arrest him.

Cesar walked into the glass-walled lobby, briefcase in hand, stepped down into the sunken reception area, and walked up to the receptionist.

He greeted her and told her he wanted to see Eduardo Martínez.

One moment, she said. She made a telephone call and then told Cesar to wait. Mr. Martínez would be down soon.

Cesar walked around the lobby. He noticed two men sitting side by side on one of the sofas. Dressed in business attire, one was tall, thin, and graying, and appeared to be in his middle to late forties. The other one was a younger man, not so tall.

Though small, the reception area felt larger than it was because of the glass windows and high ceiling. Along one side of the lobby, tellers worked behind a typical bank counter. Off the other side, a staircase led to split-level office space with open corridors visible from the reception area. Some of the offices had doors and windows with views into the lobby. A window curtain in one of the upstairs offices cracked open. Someone was peering down.

Cesar looked out toward the street and saw the three PDF officers. They were coming into the bank. How odd, he thought. That wasn't part of the plan. They were supposed to wait until they spotted Martínez.

They didn't go to the receptionist. They didn't approach a teller. They didn't seem to have any business at all to conduct. They just walked in and stood near the door. Anybody watching would have figured the three men were there with Cesar or with the two men on the sofa, except that they didn't acknowledge any of them.

This made Cesar very uncomfortable. In cop vernacular, these guys were stinking up the place. Cesar waited for another couple of minutes, but became too uneasy to stay in the same room with those PDF guys.

He told the receptionist he would wait outside, walked out front, and waited for another five minutes or so. Still no Martínez.

Cesar went back into the bank to check with the receptionist, who had gotten up from her desk and was heading toward him as he came in through the front door.

She said she had been coming to tell Cesar that Mr. Martínez had left the building, but he had told her to advise Cesar to wait for him. He would be back soon, she said.

Martínez hadn't left through the front door, or Cesar would have seen him. And why would a man who expected to receive $5 million in cash keep the guy who had brought it waiting for so long, and then leave? Something had gone wrong.

Cesar noticed that the older of the two men who had been sitting on the sofa was now upstairs in an open hallway with another man, and both of them were looking down over the railing.

"I just had a real bad feeling," says Cesar.

He went back outside to wait. Five minutes passed. Then ten. It was close to eleven o'clock—two hours after he was supposed to have met with Martínez and an hour after the press conference was supposed to start. Martínez should have been in custody by now. Where was he?

The three PDF officers headed back out toward the parking lot. Cesar followed.

He told the PDF contingent and the two DEA agents what the receptionist had told him. From the way she acted, the way the whole scene had unfolded, the men decided Martínez probably was still in the bank. They figured he'd never left, though he was obviously avoiding Cesar. Something had tipped him off, and he was just playing it out.

Cesar had expected the PDF officers to watch the rear doors of the bank in case Martínez tried to leave. Anyone who has taken Cop 101—or simply watched a little television—knows to do that. But no, they just stood around their car, and Cesar didn't think it was his place to tell them how to do their job. This was their territory, and it was their job to figure out how to arrest the guy.

Finally, Cesar got into his car, picked up the mobile phone, and called the DEA office at the embassy. He told De La Cova what had happened, and he said he needed a PDF officer with more rank or authority to take command of the situation.

While this debacle was unfolding in Panama, reporters from major U.S. news organizations had gathered for the press conference in Washington, where Attorney General Thornburgh had brought in DEA Administrator Jack Lawn, FBI Director William Sessions, and Assistant Treasury Secretary Salvatore Martoche, who oversaw law enforcement at Treasury, which includes the U.S. Customs Service and the Internal Revenue Service.

Live on CNN Thornburgh unveiled Operation Polar Cap, "the largest money-laundering crackdown" ever mounted by any U.S. agency, "a unique and closely coordinated effort carried out across the nation and across international boundaries." Beginning a month earlier with the first takedown, Polar Cap, he said, had broken up a "billion dollar money laundering ring [with] direct links to the Colombian Medellín drug cartel."

He announced that 127 people had been charged—most of whom had been rounded up in February—more than half a ton of cocaine had been confiscated, and more than $45 million in cash, jewelry, and real estate had been seized, with more to be seized with the Atlanta indictments.

Whatever reluctance law enforcement had shown toward money-laundering cases, Thornburgh showed none. "One of the most effective weapons in our war on drugs is to take the profit out of illegal drugs," he said.

Thornburgh praised the cooperative effort of the various agencies, districts, and state and local authorities, and credited the "private citizens [who] aided the undercover operation that was carried out to bring this to fruition."

Then he stepped over to an easel, where a blown-up map of the Western Hemisphere was labeled "MONEY FLOW." "The proceeds moved across the country," Thornburgh said, tracing arrows that arched from New York, Houston, and Miami to Los Angeles. "The laundered money moved north and south," he added, indicating lines that dropped down from New York into Panama, Colombia, and Uruguay.

The map showed Jimmy Brown's laundry as a set of thinner lines connecting Atlanta to New York and L.A. Thornburgh explained Atlanta's presence in the case by saying the billion-dollar money laundry "was discovered by the undercover operation out of Atlanta, which provided an entry into this highly sophisticated, highly complicated operation."

Tell us more about the undercover operation, a reporter at the press conference asked Thornburgh.

The Attorney General said these were "fascinating and intriguing stories," and he called on the agency heads to tell them.

Sessions of the FBI made a comment about the significance of the four agencies being able to trace the money. Then he deferred to Lawn of the DEA.

Lawn had been thoroughly prepped. "This particular operation began with our undercover personnel in Atlanta," where an undercover money laundry had been set up, he told reporters. "A major figure in this investigation told us in Atlanta that we were not processing funds quickly enough, that there was an organization in Los Angeles to which he referred, an organization called La, La, La Miña. The mine." (He mispronounced it "MEEN-ya.")

Without mentioning Martínez by name, Lawn nonetheless described precisely what he had said to Ramón and Cesar. "He said you should learn from that organization. This is the way they launder money. They can launder money within forty-eight hours. He outlined for us how the money was laundered. We then met with our counterparts in Los Angeles, each of whom had received information from cooperative citizens about large quantities of money being laundered through banks. . . ."

Acting on that information, DEA joined forces with other federal agencies, Lawn said. "This is how Polar Cap began."

Nothing about the wiretaps, the trash searches, the surveillance, or the incredibly tedious work in Los Angeles. As for New York's DEA office, it wasn't mentioned at all. And the FBI? Where was the FBI in this? Lawn's rendition of Polar Cap finally gave DEA-Atlanta the credit Atlanta believed it deserved. But it shortchanged the scores of other Polar Cap investigators around the country, most of whom believed Atlanta to be barely connected to the Polar Cap probe. The press conference would further inflame jealousies. Out in Los Angeles, for example, "There were some hard feelings," says FBI supervisor Ralph Lumpkin. "Some real hard feelings."

As if to mollify the egos he sensed were being bruised, Thornburgh stepped up to the mike as Lawn wound up. "I just want to add one thing in particular," said Thornburgh. "We often hear an awful lot about turf wars and jurisdictional disputes in federal law enforcement. . . . This is an example of how, in an effort carried out by four, highly specialized, competent agencies . . . the whole can truly be greater than the sum of the parts."

By the time the other agencies' roles were mentioned again, CNN had switched back to its Washington bureau. Little, if any, of that would make it into news accounts.

The press conference continued. Lawn announced that the PDF had arrested a major figure in the case in Panama that morning, only to correct himself minutes later when an off-camera aide advised him the arrest had not yet been confirmed. Although De La Cova in Panama was communicating with the DEA in Washington, no one realized at that point that the arrest had not gone down as planned. Reporters questioned Thornburgh and Lawn on why the PDF helped in the expected arrest, given General Manuel Noriega's U.S. indictment for aiding and abetting the Colombian drug cartels.

"My understanding is, there has been a continuing law enforcement relationship with the PDF that has provided substantial aid to our federal law enforcement agencies," Thornburgh said stiffly.

Cesar's call to De La Cova brought out a higher-ranking PDF officer, the sleazy-looking Gómez, and a couple more backups. Gómez told Cesar they would search the bank for Martínez. Cesar and the other DEA agents waited in the parking lot, figuring the situation was too dangerous for Cesar to go into the bank.

Frustrated and angry, Cesar brooded over the many things that had gone wrong that morning. What was it that tipped off Martínez? Whatever it was, it must have happened after Cesar talked to him by phone from the Marriott.

De La Cova was still getting calls from Washington for updates. He passed along what Captain Quiel had told him, that Martínez was in the bank, and that the bank was surrounded by the PDF. Of course, the PDF had not actually surrounded the bank, and it wasn't at all clear that Martínez was inside.

By this time the press conference was over, but Quiel's version of things was passed along to Washington reporters, who followed the story throughout the day.

In Atlanta, U.S. Attorney Robert L. Barr, Jr., waited till noon to call his own press conference, because Washington had insisted that the Attorney General go first. Alongside him were Buddy Parker and Ron Caffrey, both tense; Craig Gillen; and regional representatives of Customs and the IRS. Barr's staff handed out statements, copies of the indictment, and a bulky affidavit signed by Skip Latson that outlined the whole case. Barr introduced the people with him and read his statement. But the normally talkative U.S. Attorney refused to take questions, citing the Medellín cartel's reputation for violence and revenge, "as well as the complexity of this case and the ongoing prosecutions. . . ."

Craig and Buddy had persuaded Barr to limit his remarks, not only because of the uncertain situation in Panama, but also because they believed him to be too talkative.

Meanwhile the PDF officers were now inside Banco Ganadero, but Cesar wasn't at all sure what they were doing. They had told him they would conduct an office-to-office search, checking IDs and questioning everyone. Cesar could see cars coming and going from the bank's rear parking lot. Whatever the Panamanian cops were doing, they weren't keeping people from leaving while they searched. This was the loosest operation Cesar had ever seen. Too bad it was the most important case of his career.

Around twelve-thirty or so, Cesar spotted a familiar-looking man walking down the sidewalk. It was one of the men he had noticed in the lobby earlier, the same guy he had later seen upstairs looking down at him over the railing. He had seemed suspicious to Cesar, but the PDF had let him walk out the door. At that point Cesar knew they would never get Martínez this way.

"I said, Hey, this thing is over," Cesar says.

Cesar returned to the DEA office at the U.S. Embassy frustrated, furious, and embarrassed. Everybody had had their task to do to take down this very important case, and he had drawn the longest straw. He has supposed to bring home the biggest prize in a case significant enough to warrant a nationally televised press conference by the Attorney General of the United States. For two and a half years he had been working toward that moment when he would collar a major money launderer for the Medellín cartel. Well, the moment had come, and Cesar was empty-handed.

He didn't blame himself. He believed he had been at the mercy of those PDF goons, who were incompetent at best and probably corrupt.

Cesar nonetheless felt he had let the boss down when he called Ron Caffrey at DEA in Atlanta to tell him the whole sad story. Even as he did, news stories were still reporting that the PDF had surrounded a Panamanian bank where a major suspect in this case had been cornered.

The news coverage apparently persuaded the PDF to take the case more seriously. By day's end, the cops had located the plane that had brought Martínez to Panama, and had arrested the two men Cesar had seen in the bank. One of them was the pilot who had flown him to Panama and the other was a close associate of Martínez.

La Estrella de Panamá carried an Associated Press account of the story on the front page the following day, complete with a photo of Thornburgh in front of his "MONEY FLOW" map. The second paragraph said Banco de Occidente of Panama had been indicted for allegedly washing more than $1 billion in drug funds. The sole mention of the abortive attempt to arrest Martínez came in the story's last paragraph, carried on an inside page. It said only that DEA chief "Lawn said that authorities also hoped to realize an arrest yesterday in Panama with the help of the Defense Forces of this nation. Thornburgh said that federal authorities were continuing cooperation" with the PDF.

On Friday, two days after the failed arrest attempt, Panamanian officials issued arrest warrants for the two Occidente bankers under indictment in Atlanta. Officers went to the bank and arrested Clara García that morning. William Guarin was picked up on the street outside his home as he prepared to go to work. Whatever press coverage they had seen of Polar Cap and the indictment of Occidente in Panama, they apparently had no idea they had been implicated and would be sought. Using information Cesar provided, Panamanian authorities brought their own charges against the pair—charges that would be adjudicated in Panama.

Cesar had returned to Atlanta with an unused plane ticket bearing Eduardo Martínez's name and a stack of documents from Banco de Occidente. Taken by the PDF from some banker's briefcase during the arrests—improperly, apparently—the papers meant nothing to Cesar at the time. But they would later turn out to be a valuable consolation prize.

21: The Big Freeze

By the time takedown happened, Ramón was well out of the way, relocated by the feds to a place in the United States where he would be safe. He could not help but be concerned about all the commotion his becoming a snitch had caused. On the one hand, the bigger the case the better his chances of serving no time. That, after all, had been the point of the exercise. But it was also true that a case like this exposed him to a lot more danger than a minor one would have.

It was clear from the indictment who the snitch had been. He was the only one not named—anywhere. From Overt Act Number 1 through Overt Act Number 89, Ramón's name did not appear. Not his real name nor any of his aliases. Francisco Serrano was there. The traffickers and money launderers were there. The agents were at least mentioned. It would be clear to anyone who had attended any of the meetings that Francisco's gringo sidekick had to be the snitch.

None of the Colombians knew Ramón's real name except for Francisco, who had more right to hate him than anyone. Francisco had trusted Ramón completely, had loved him as a brother. Ramón believed Francisco's trust in him was what had put him behind bars. He wouldn't blame Francisco for blowing his brains out, given the chance.

Buddy and the agents blame Francisco Serrano for his troubles, not Ramón. Had he not been so eager to get rich off the drug trade, Francisco would never have fallen in with Ramón.

Naturally, neither Ramón nor the agents wanted Ramón's indicted business associates to be able to locate him. The only way the money handlers and drug traffickers could reach Ramón was by telephone. The DEA had moved him out of his Atlanta undercover apartment but Ramón kept the same telephone number and calls were patched into his new home. A month or so after the takedown, he started getting odd calls on that phone. Suddenly, strangers wanted to know where he lived.

In early May 1989, a young woman claimed his number was on her telephone bill, apparently because houseguests had called it while staying with her. To verify which of her guests had called him, she wanted to know his name and where he lived. Ramón asked for her name, but she would not give it. He asked for her phone number; she declined. Ramón hung up.

A couple weeks later, another young woman called and reached Ramón's housekeeper. The caller said she was with UPS and had a package to deliver to Sandy Baxter, the name under which Ramón's number was listed. She said she needed Baxter's new address to deliver the package. The maid, on Ramón's instruction, hung up.

A few days later, the housekeeper again answered Ramón's phone to find a female caller on the line. Speaking first in English and then in Spanish, the woman wanted to know the address where the phone was located. Again, the maid hung up.

A couple weeks after that, Ramón told Skip about the calls, and the phone number was changed. The calls ended.

For Ramón, the case and its consequences were winding down. Without any defendants to testify against, all that was left was his sentencing.

*T*he feds now concentrated on Banco de Occidente. On the day of the takedown, while U.S. Attorney General Dick Thornburgh was drawing attention to the bungled arrest attempt in Panama, DEA and IRS agents had fanned out to sixteen banks around the United States, serving orders to plug up Banco de Occidente and Banco Ganadero accounts. These were extraordinary orders, and not all the bankers complied without protest. From the moment the agents started hitting the banks after 9:00 A.M. Eastern time on March 29, 1989, Buddy Parker's telephone rang steadily with calls from bank executives and lawyers questioning the order. But within forty-eight hours, $22 million had collected in these accounts. Most of that ($17.5 million) was in the form of demand deposits at Continental Illinois Bank International in New York.

The frozen funds represented almost double the amount the Atlanta undercover laundry had sent through Banco de Occidente. Yet it was far below the ceiling the feds believed they were entitled to reach. Between La Mina and Jimmy Brown's laundry, they figured $412 million in drug funds had been flushed through Banco de Occidente during the previous two years, so the U.S. government was entitled to $412 million in bank assets.

Of course, the $412 million had long since passed through these accounts. The only drug proceeds the feds froze that day was the money Martínez recently had directed into Jimmy Brown's laundry, $4 million that Martínez's customers were expecting. Given the grilling adminis-tered to Francisco after the $1 million seizure the previous year, it's reasonable to assume Martínez eluded the DEA only to face angry Co-lombian customers.

Within twenty-four hours of the Thornburgh press conference, Miami lawyers representing Banco de Occidente were calling the U.S. Attor-ney's Office asking what was happening. Incredulous that the federal government would move on money belonging to the bank's customers without so much as a hearing, the lawyers said they wanted a meeting with the prosecutors, and soon.

That Friday, two Miami lawyers and an Atlanta lawyer serving as local counsel, Jerome Froelich, rode up to the eighteenth floor of the federal building in Atlanta to meet the men responsible for this remarkable development. From Miami came Kirk Munroe, a forty-year-old former federal prosecutor and now a partner in a firm specializing in commer-cial litigation and white-collar crime. Munroe and his partner, Bill Richey, who was unable to attend this first meeting, would lead the defense of the bank. Tall, bearded, and blond, Munroe is a friendly, down-to-earth man, normally of good humor. But as he walked into the office of the U.S. Attorney for the Northern District of Georgia, Munroe was in no joking mood.

The Atlanta-based co-counsel introduced the pair of Miami lawyers to the prosecutors who had gathered: Buddy Parker, Craig Gillen, two assistant U.S. attorneys in the asset forfeiture unit, and U.S. Attorney Robert Barr. Barr's corner office with its plate-glass windows offered a view of downtown Atlanta.

The lawyers settled down on either side of the conference table and the discussion began.

Banco de Occidente is a good bank, a legitimate bank, not a drug bank, its lawyers told the prosecutors. This incredible show of govern-ment might was way out of line. Banco de Occidente didn't deserve it, and its customers clearly didn't. What in the world was going on?

Buddy explained the case against Banco de Occidente and the basis for the freeze order.

Munroe told the prosecutors they had no authority to freeze these accounts. He demanded the release of the funds.

The prosecutors said they would do no such thing. They had clear authority for what they had done, and their position had been supported by a U.S. district judge. If the bank believed the government to be wrong, then it should go to court and litigate the issue, but understand that the government will be fully prepared to argue its position in court.

The bank most certainly would challenge the government on this, Munroe responded. The government can't simply swoop down out of the blue, with no warning, offering no chance to rebut allegations, and plug up the accounts of a perfectly clean bank.

The prosecutors insisted they could do precisely that, given the law Congress had granted them to fight the war on drugs.

What kind of evidence did the government have against the bank, the bank lawyers wanted to know.

The prosecutors handed over copies of the indictment and affidavits.

For twenty to thirty minutes, the lawyers sparred. They sized up each other and the situation at hand. The tone was somber and serious, but without angry outbursts or fist pounding. Still, the lawyers on either side made it unmistakably clear they were dead set on proving their position, and that they expected to prevail in court.

As the meeting broke up and the visiting lawyers made their way down the corridor, Craig told Munroe he was prepared to litigate this until the end, only he put it more vividly than that.

Munroe says Craig told him, "Your client is on the bottom of the swimming pool. We've got our foot on your client's neck."

Craig remembers it differently. He believes he made the swimming-pool comment later in the litigation than Munroe recalls. And he says he told Munroe, "We're like two people who have death grips on each other on the bottom of the swimming pool, and I think I can hold my breath longer than you can.

"If you . . . think you can hold your breath longer than I can, litigate."

In Craig's version, the fight is more fair and the government less malevolent. But in telling the story, Craig pauses. "I did say the deep end of the pool," he adds.

Cesar came back from Panama that weekend with Banco de Occidente records showing bank assets around the world. The way the feds read them, the records showed that on March 29, the day Martínez gave Cesar the slip and Thornburgh announced the case, Banco de Occidente moved $63 million in assets to accounts in Germany, Switzerland, and Canada. The bank's lawyers would later say the bank shifted the money for reasons unrelated to the prosecution. Given the tension between Noriega and the U.S. government, the Panamanian bankers merely wanted to move funds away from both of them, they say. Still, the transfers included $8.6 million from U.S. accounts that was supposed to have been frozen by court order, prosecutors believed. At least two U.S. banks reported to authorities that they had received calls that day from Occidente bankers directing them to transfer funds to Europe.

When Buddy looked at the papers Cesar had brought back from Panama, he saw the potential for more seizures. Why not freeze those accounts, too, he asked Craig.

Why not, indeed.

Buddy and Craig pulled out a decision from the 11th U.S. Circuit Court of Appeals in Atlanta involving the Bank of Nova Scotia. The court said a foreign company—specifically, a bank—with a U.S. outlet was subject to U.S. law. The decision had been affirmed by the U.S. Supreme Court. What else did they need? It was true that, unlike the Bank of Nova Scotia, Occidente had no U.S. outlet. But the European and Canadian banks holding Occidente accounts each maintained U.S. offices. Those should do just fine.

It would be bold. It would be unprecedented. But these two lawyers believed in marshaling every weapon they could find to use against the adversary.

As for the murky way they got the documents, that didn't matter. Perhaps suppressible as evidence in a criminal trial, the documents were only being used for a temporary restraining order at this point. Buddy began drafting his argument and the order he would persuade a federal judge to sign.

On Tuesday, April 5, Judge Shoob ordered two Swiss banks and a German bank to refrain from disbursing the Occidente assets they held in Switzerland, Germany, and Canada.

Agents served Shoob's orders at the U.S. offices of the three foreign banks holding those accounts: Union Bank of Switzerland in New York; Deutsch-Südamerikanische Bank in Miami; and Swiss Bank Corporation in downtown Atlanta, just a few blocks from the federal building.

Cesar and Skip, who were in Miami, took a call from the Royal Canadian Mounted Police and a prosecutor in Toronto who wanted to know more about the case before getting a seizure order.

The prosecutors predicted the phone lines to the U.S. Attorney's Office in Atlanta would soon be buzzing with more angry bank lawyers.

While the prosecutors were plotting their next move, the bank and its lawyers were trying to react to the first round of freezes.

After the meeting in Atlanta, Kirk Munroe, his partner Bill Richey, and two more of the bank's lawyers from Miami flew to Colombia to try to explain to the bank president and the senior management how the U.S. government could possibly be doing what it was doing. Richey, an intense yet lively fellow, says he tried to explain what was happening, but the bank's top officers were incredulous over what they were hearing. In Latin America, only individuals can act criminally, not corporations. The bankers simply did not believe the Miami lawyers when they told them corporations could be held responsible for the acts of middle-level managers. The concept did not click. When the bankers finally understood what they were saying, it seemed so bizarre that they doubted their attorneys' grasp of the law.

On top of that, to understand that their depositors' money could be taken in lieu of alleged drug funds that had passed through Occidente long ago was too much.

Besides, no one had brought suitcases of cash into Banco de Occidente. These funds were transferred by wire from very respectable U.S. banks—Citibank, Chase Manhattan, Morgan Guaranty Trust, and Chemical Bank of New York. If indeed cash from drug sales was involved, it was deposited in the United States, not Panama. Where were the U.S. banks named on this indictment? Under Panamanian law, only cash could be "laundered." By the time the money arrived as a wire transfer from another bank, it was already clean, to their way of thinking. The bankers and lawyers decided to fight it out.

The $22 million hit hurt badly, but the bank could manage by pooling its resources. Occidente would prepare for war, but its lawyers also advised them to prepare quietly for surrender. After all, the Attorney General of the United States had announced this case to the nation and the world, and was not likely to go soft. It was a politically popular prosecution in the States, where anti-drug sentiment was running high, and where a Panamanian bank headquartered in Colombia would be viewed as automatically suspect. The United States meant to make an example of Occidente, the lawyers told the bankers. And $412 million in drug funds was hard to ignore.

That said, the lawyers started arming for war. Munroe would go to Panama to see what he could learn at the scene of the alleged crime, and to meet Occidente's Panama lawyer, Antonio Dudley.

Dudley, a striking and eloquent lawyer well known and well connected within the banking community, had already explained to Panama's National Banking Commission what was happening, insisted on the bank's innocence, and assured the commission the bank could meet its obligations.

"We were rolling up our sleeves," says Dudley. The lawyers were planning motions, plotting strategy, and analyzing the documents the prosecutors had given them. They were convinced that once a judge understood that the substitute assets belonged to innocent people with no link to drug trafficking, the orders would surely be overturned.

The frozen funds included, for example, a $2 million payment Bogotá's government-owned electric company had tried to make to the World Bank through Occidente. The World Bank had financed further development of electrical service in Bogotá, a commendable project having nothing to do with drugs, Munroe said as he pleaded with the Atlanta prosecutors by phone. At least thaw out that $2 million so the electric company won't default, he implored, so the World Bank will have that money for some other worthy development project.

No way. Assets are assets, came the reply. The prosecutors believed Banco de Occidente had laundered $412 million in drug funds—an astounding sum—and the U.S. government had every right to hold on to bank assets up to that amount, no matter the source.

"The United States is expected . . . to seek out crime and, in this case, to aggressively seek out funds that are products of drug dealing and money laundering," comments Craig. "And we did that."

At midday on Wednesday, April 5, a week after the first freeze orders, Munroe was working in his room at the Marriott in Panama City, where Cesar had expected to arrest Martínez a week earlier. As Munroe was preparing for an appointment, he got news that changed everything. He no longer remembers whether it was a CNN broadcast or a call from an Occidente officer, but he remembers well what was said: The U.S. government had ordered a European bank to freeze Occidente's account.

Still reeling over the U.S. accounts, the bankers now were stunned. The U.S. prosecutors had reached beyond Panama, into Europe and Canada, for deposits that belonged to the main branch in Cali, Colombia. It was true that the main bank was under indictment along with the Panama branch, but none of the documents from Atlanta revealed evidence against the main bank. A major part of its assets were in Europe, mostly in the form of time deposits. The first round of freezes hurt, but this hit could mortally wound the bank.

Munroe in Panama and Richey in Miami began calling around the world to learn the dimensions of the new freeze. "It was clear they got everything real fast," says Munroe.

Twenty million dollars in Germany, frozen. Next came word from Switzerland: $28 million frozen. In Canada, $12 million. Added to the $22 million in the United States, the bank had $82 million in untouchable deposits. This represented 90 percent of the bank's liquid assets, now iced. For a bank the size of Occidente, with total assets of roughly $150 million, it was a disaster.

Dudley returned to the Panamanian National Banking Commission. Having just told the commissioners the bank could handle the U.S. freeze, now Dudley had to say the bank was badly hurt.

Dudley asked the commission to intervene, and on April 7 the commission voted to insulate Occidente from its customers' legal claims until the resolution of the case, and to appoint an intervenor to manage the bank. The commission explained to the bank's customers that the situation was temporary. They had not lost their money—just the use of it. But for all practical purposes, the bank was shut down.

At the same time, the Banking Association of Panama, a trade group to which all banks in Panama belong, took up the matter of Occidente. Not wanting the case to further sully the already muddy reputation of Panamanian banks, and unconvinced that these two bankers could move that much money without knowing its source and without senior management knowing it, too, the group's ethics committee launched a move to expel Occidente from the association.

Its reputation in ruins, its customers unable to retrieve their funds, its assets tied up around the world, Banco de Occidente could not go on in this condition. As eager as the executives had been to fight early in the week, by week's end survival had superseded the issue of fairness. Litigation would take time and money, neither of which the bank had any more.

As predicted, Craig was fielding telephone calls from lawyers for the growing number of U.S. and foreign banks restrained by the Atlanta orders. He emphatically stated the basis for the court orders, faxing lengthy indictments and affidavits overseas as quickly as government equipment could move. He told them the U.S. government had clear authority to do exactly that under the Bank of Nova Scotia case.

"We think we're right, and if you disagree with us, then that's why they have a clerk's office. You can file what you want to," Craig says he told them. Seek an emergency stay, if you like; just tell us when to show up for the hearing. But in the meantime, Craig advised, you better tell your client bank to keep handy the millions of dollars we are seeking, because you are going to lose.

Posturing aside, nobody wanted to go to court over this. What the foreign banks needed was cover, something to protect them while they carried out the U.S. court order. What they needed were court orders from the countries where the accounts were located, the lawyers told Craig.

The Atlantans, Justice Department officials in Washington, and DEA representatives abroad already had been talking to their counterparts in Switzerland, Germany, and Canada. To seek a local court order required them to open cases in each of those places. But how could they prosecute a case based on evidence they had not seen, from agents and prosecutors they had not met, using legal theories they had never before heard? It was no small thing to prosecute a bank and freeze its assets, especially in Switzerland, the proverbial bankers' paradise.

At the same time, Occidente was demanding release of its funds. A request for a wire transfer from Deutsch-Südamerikanische Bank in Hamburg had come in, and the bank was fearful of liability if it did not honor the request. German law required the bank to honor legitimate demands for deposits. The banks were leaning on their governments for guidance, and for a local court order to cover them.

Unless the U.S. government could send someone to explain in person this strange case and the Americans' incredible requests, the freeze might thaw.

In Texas to give a lecture, Buddy received a call from the DEA attaché to the U.S. Consulate in Frankfurt.

The German prosecutor is willing to help, the attaché said, but he wants to meet the U.S. prosecutor and discuss the case in person. And he wants to do it immediately. By Saturday evening Buddy was on his way to Germany with Skip.

In Wiesbaden, near Frankfurt, at the headquarters of the federal police, or Bundeskriminalamt (BKA), the lengthy documents Skip had sent by overnight mail to arrive Friday had been translated into German in time for the Monday morning meeting. Not only that, the BKA officer and the prosecutor had read the papers, assimilated the information, opened a case, and posted a wall map showing the involved locations. They had a clear take-charge attitude, and felt certain they could get a court order.

Buddy and Skip moved on to Bern, where a U.S. Embassy representative lectured Buddy about the history of Swiss bank secrecy laws and the purposes they served. The laws had helped oppressed people hide money from their oppressors, as Jews did from Nazis. Nonetheless, the Swiss authorities proved amenable to pursuing the matter.

That night, a DEA agent stationed in Bern took Buddy and Skip for a few beers and out to dinner. Buddy had been told to call Washington and Atlanta daily to report his progress and to track developments there. After dinner, at about nine o'clock, as he rode through the beautiful old section of Bern from the restaurant to the U.S. Embassy, Buddy used the car phone to call his Justice Department contact in Washington, Peter Djinis.

Djinis, who had helped coordinate the Polar Cap case, told him the government of Colombia had now weighed in on the side of Banco de Occidente. Colombia's minister of finance had been to the State Department and the Justice Department that day to find out how the U.S. government could be doing this. Moreover, Colombian President Virgilio Barco, an anti-drug president, was coming to Washington for an official visit and would speak to President George Bush about the matter if it wasn't settled first.

Buddy was relieved to hear the U.S. State Department was already on board and cooperating with the prosecution, because it looked like Occidente would be bringing a lot of pressure to bear. It was clear, says Buddy, that they had to do everything correctly, "because within our government the next thing that happens is somebody in the State Department will perceive this as jeopardizing something else that they find in our country's interest. . . ."

It had happened in the Noriega case, and it could happen here. All he needed was for someone in State to start pressuring the U.S. Attorney's Office in Atlanta.

The hours that Bill Richey and Kirk Munroe were not spending on airplanes or in meetings were spent in telephone calls. With key lawyers and bankers stretched across several time zones, and with the bank in desperate straits, they were billing twelve- to eighteen-hour days and running up gigantic telephone and travel accounts. They had hired top-flight lawyers in Switzerland, Germany, and Canada, and lawyers in Panama for the two arrested bankers. They explored what it would take to defend Occidente on all fronts: Atlanta, Panama, Toronto, Germany, Switzerland.

The lawyers believed they could prevail on the freeze orders, but it would take at least a couple of years in court. The bank could not last for a couple of years under the management of a Panamanian intervenor, with its depositors unable to use their money.

The attitude at the bank was, "You can litigate this, and you can win, and the bank will be dead," says Richey. It was already technically insolvent.

By telephone, the lawyers asked the prosecutors why they wanted to destroy a perfectly good bank, a bank that helped Colombian coffee exporters and other businesses build Colombia's legitimate economy. Tearing down legitimate institutions could only hurt the anti-drug effort.

But by Monday, April 17, less than three weeks after the first round of freezes and two weeks after the foreign action, Munroe and Richey were back in Atlanta to explore the possibility of settlement.

It was hardly a friendly meeting. "These two, they didn't understand banking," Richey says of the prosecutors who had brought the bank to its knees. Just because Occidente has $82 million in foreign deposits doesn't mean the bank has that money to use for itself, they explained. That money belongs to depositors. Innocent depositors, not Pablo Escobar. That money is clean money.

The prosecutors stood firm. Banco de Occidente was named as the account holder on those accounts. Under U.S. law, the money was Occidente's. And Occidente stood accused of washing $412 million in drug funds, period.

The lawyers begged the prosecutors to check out the bank's reputation. This is not a dirty bank, they insisted. Buddy acknowledged the government did nothing to check out Occidente. In fact, he had no direct evidence against top management in Colombia. All he had was a cryptic statement from Clara García and the belief that this much money laundering couldn't happen without higher-ups knowing.

The bank lawyers told the prosecutors the Panama branch had $7 million in capital, at most. Why not release all but $7 million? That way, the depositors get their money while the two sides try to work out a settlement.

No, no, no, came the answer.

Craig, especially, was intransigent. After nearly every telephone call with him, Richey would ask Munroe, "What do you think of this madman?"

The following week they went at it again. The bank's lawyers returned to Atlanta for meetings Tuesday, flew to Bogotá, and returned to Atlanta on Friday for another try. They were trying to come up with a fine substantial enough to indicate the seriousness of the crime but not so big as to kill the bank. Buddy says he opened with $20 million, although Munroe says it was $25 million.

"That took everybody's breath away," says Munroe.

"They laughed," recalls Buddy.

There was no way Occidente could pay that. Look at the audit, the lawyers told the prosecutors. This bank doesn't have that kind of money.

The bank's first offer was closer to $1 million—which the prosecutors considered ridiculously low. The prosecutors pulled their number down, but it was still way too high, the lawyers insisted. You're asking the bank to commit suicide; we might as well go to trial.

Richey returned to Miami to prepare for an unrelated trial, while Munroe stayed in Atlanta. On Saturday morning, April 29, the lawyers— including the bank's Atlanta attorney, Jerome Froelich—met outside the federal building. Some brought coffee, others brought doughnuts, and everyone wore shorts and sport shirts and spread out on the play equipment of a day care center for government workers. Finally, the wall between the two sides began to give.

The lawyers on both sides agreed to basic principles: the bank's lawyers would prove to the prosecutors how large a fine the bank could survive; and the prosecutors would try to harness the effort it had set loose around the world, so that a settlement in Atlanta would free up frozen funds everywhere. The Atlanta prosecutors had sicced the rest of the world onto Occidente; they would have to call off the dogs.

As for the bank, the Panama branch would have to plead guilty. There could not be a "no contest" plea to this one. But the government would drop the charges against the main bank in Colombia. There was no clear evidence against it or its management.

The prosecutors checked with Washington and the bank lawyers checked with Occidente. With those approvals, negotiations began in earnest.

Meanwhile in Germany, bank lawyers had managed to dissuade the government from taking up the case that Buddy had presented. The government lifted the freeze on the $20 million deposit in Hamburg on the ground that these funds were not drug proceeds. Occidente had its first victory. But the bank still could not use the money, because moving it could subject it to a freeze.

As plea negotiations continued, the size of the proposed fine kept shrinking. The bank's certified audit from a Big Eight accounting firm showed the Panama bank with $6.7 million in capital.

Buddy recognized it would do no good to fine the bank more money than it was worth. He had to accept the audit, "unless we were prepared to say that this auditing and the whole financial condition of the bank as found by this outside auditor was premised on fraud," he says. He had no reason to doubt the audit, which had been prepared before the bank's indictment.

"All the institution was worth, bottom line, was seven million."

In June, the prosecutors made their final offer: The government would recommend a $5 million fine. Buddy insisted that was as low as he could go. Take it or go to trial.

The bank lawyers protested that was still too high. It would leave the Panama bank with less than $2 million in capital. The branch might as well close its doors. But when they traveled to Colombia to present the offer, to their surprise the bank president and top management said Occidente might be able to do that, if the feds could let the bank pay it out over time.

They could; negotiations continued.

For the prosecutors, it proved more than embarrassing to return to the same Swiss and Canadian officials and ask for money to be released that they had insisted be frozen. The Atlantans had fully convinced these people the bank should not get this money because it represented drug funds. The Swiss and the Canadians had taken this unusual step and were now completely on the side of the prosecutors. How could they now ask that it be released? Switzerland didn't even have a legal mechanism to do what the U.S. government now wanted it to do.

"Buddy stood on his head to get the money," says Richey.

U.S. government lawyers kept chipping away at the barriers. In Panama, Antonio Dudley portrayed the U.S. turnabout as a vindication of sorts. But he feared a guilty plea would be tantamount to ruin. He had been telling the banking commission as well as the trade association that Occidente was innocent of the charges and was being unfairly attacked by a U.S. government trying to smear the Panamanian banking community. He told the bank's managers in no uncertain terms that a guilty plea would undermine the bank in Panama.

"It's going to be a futile exercise if you save the bank's money in the U.S. . . . if the bank's license is revoked," Dudley pointed out. What good is it to win the war if everybody's dead?

But the prosecutors insisted on a guilty plea or a trial, and the bank could not afford the latter. No one had predicted how complicated it would be to reach a plea agreement. There were so many issues to be settled, involving several governments, various banks, and an array of new legal principles. Just when the lawyers succeeded in nailing one thing down, another would pop up.

Finally, in August 1989, it all came together.

The government would drop the case against Banco de Occidente's main branch, but Banco de Occidente of Panama would plead guilty to drug conspiracy and conspiring to defeat U.S. tax-collection efforts on the La Mina money.

The government would recommend that Occidente-Panama forfeit $5 million, to be paid out over four years. This would be a forfeiture rather than a fine, for two reasons. First, the Swiss and the Canadians wanted to share the money they helped wring out of Occidente, and U.S. law permitted sharing a forfeiture, but not a fine. Second, the U.S. portion of the forfeiture would go to a special fund set up for crime fighting, courts, and prisons, instead of the general treasury where a fine would go.

The United States would get $3 million; Canada and Switzerland would each get $1 million. The bank would pay the first installment at sentencing.

The two indicted bankers, Clara García and William Guarin, would lose their jobs.

Lastly, the government would ask the judge to lift all remaining freeze orders.

"**C**all the matter of *United States of America* vs. *Banco de Occidente, Panama*," the courtroom clerk called out at 1:30 P.M. on August 14, 1989, reading off the case number to U.S. District Judge William C. O'Kelley in the federal building in Atlanta.

Craig sat with Buddy at the prosecution table, along with U.S. Attorney Barr, who had seen to it that the event would draw as many reporters as possible. Across the aisle at the defense table sat Bill Richey and the bank's local counsel, Jerome Froelich.

"Good afternoon, your honor," Buddy opened. "If I may proceed. Through a negotiated plea agreement, the government of the United States has entered into plea agreements with the defendant corporation, Banco de Occidente, Panama, S.A., in criminal case number 89-086A."

The plea document had already been signed by the new general manager at Banco de Occidente in Panama. The bank admitted to the two counts, which carried a maximum penalty of $10.5 million, plus the forfeiture of any drug proceeds.

Buddy led Richey through a series of questions aimed at determining the bank's awareness of the charges and the implications of pleading guilty to them. He then launched into a discussion of the facts of the investigation, beginning at the start of 1987: the money pickups; the meeting with Pablo Escobar; Eduardo Martínez's revelations about La Mina; the meeting in Panama City at Banco de Occidente, where the money launderer, "Mr. Martínez," was treated "with the utmost and highest respect," Buddy told the judge.

He laid out all the evidence that implicated the bankers Clara García and William Guarin. And he talked about the meeting in Aruba and the investigation of La Mina.

"It was through these efforts that the government documented that approximately $1.2 billion was laundered by the La Mina organization, and of that amount of money, approximately $412 million had been moved through the Panamanian accounts of Banco de Occidente, Panama, S.A."

"Mr. Richey," the judge asked. "Do you have any quarrel with that statement of facts or what they could prove?"

"No, your honor," Richey replied. However, "I will have some comments upon the significance of some of those facts."

Judge O'Kelley then asked a standard but critically important question: "Is the plea a free and voluntary plea?"

"Yes, your honor," Richey said. "Banco de Occidente, Panama, is pleading guilty knowingly and understands what they're doing, and is guilty."

But from that point on, Richey qualified the degree of the bank's guilt to the point where Occidente almost sounded innocent. At Occidente, "the board of directors and the higher management and the ownership of this bank had no idea whatsoever what was going on," he said. That fact had been "absolutely shown" by the government's investigation.

But at the Panama branch, "These employees were corrupted by the narcotics people . . . and these [money-laundering] acts did occur as the government described on the premises and using the facilities of the defendant Banco de Occidente, Panama." At least that's what the government says, Richey added.

Because of that, and because U.S. law makes the corporation responsible for the actions of its employees, the bank was guilty, Richey explained.

That wasn't the only reason for the guilty plea, of course. When the judge asked whether the defendant had been threatened or coerced into pleading guilty, Richey answered in the affirmative.

"There has been the heaviest economic coercion that I've seen in a lawsuit of this type, your honor," Richey said. "Yes, there's substantial coercion."

With nudging from the judge, Richey gave the figures on the bank's financial status and the effect the freeze had on it.

"The net result," he said, "was that the bank was placed into receivership at its own request . . . because it was insolvent."

Richey explained that the bank would have continued to litigate the matter, except that it would not have been able to stay alive long enough to see the litigation to its end.

Judge O'Kelley, who had already heard all of this in chambers the week before, prodded Richey further. "Now, as I understand it, the bank's contentions are that the monies that were seized were not all necessarily the proceeds of drug operations but were other independent, innocent depositors' funds."

"It's our position, as strongly as we can make it," Richey replied, "that not a penny of those monies were drug proceeds." That was why Germany freed up the funds, he added.

The same thing that happened to Occidente, he said, could happen "to any large, honestly run banking institution in the world dealing with substantial international transfers through wire." All it takes is a crooked employee or two, he said.

"The bank is deeply concerned," he went on, "as to whether it is humanly possible to prevent this type of operation occurring in any of numerous banks in the world, given the ability to corrupt people which the narcotics people have, and given the huge volume of wire transfer traffic that occurs in banks around the world as a normal part of daily business."

Now Richey had painted Occidente as a victim not only of the U.S. government, of the corrupt employees, but also of the drug traffickers themselves.

As for the mention of Pablo Escobar during the proceedings, Richey said, "I want to emphasize as strongly as I can . . . that this bank and its board of directors and its owners have absolutely nothing to do with Mr. Escobar," or any of the other accused drug traffickers.

At the bank's highest levels, he added, "these are honest and honorable people.... They're trying to run a good bank."

It was starting to sound as if the defendant, not the prosecution, was fighting the war on drugs. Richey talked about the importance of preserving good Colombian banks like Occidente to promote legitimate trade so that Colombia's economy and people were financially strong enough to resist the temptations of the drug trade.

Richey ended by saying the plea agreement allowed the bank to survive, which was good for Colombia and good for the anti-drug effort.

The prosecutors let him have his say, without rebuttal. The government had its guilty plea and would be getting a hefty payment from the bank as part of the penalty. Buddy detailed the plea agreement to Judge O'Kelley.

This was the first time the United States had shared its reward for fighting crime with another nation. And while it meant that the U.S. government would only get $3 million from this major case, it also meant international cooperation would be easier in the future.

Near the end of the proceedings, Buddy acknowledged that the bank had suffered greatly from the government's actions. He urged the judge to accept the plea agreement as is because "it is vital to the existence of the bank....

"Otherwise, this bank, having had to hire attorneys around the globe in multiple countries, having lost interest, having suffered as any bank would suffer for these several months under the indictment and the allegations of having been involved in narcotics ... faces a heavy burden and we respectfully request that this court follow the government's recommendation."

Judge O'Kelley noted that the plea agreement had been approved at the highest level at the Justice Department, and said that "the sentence as recommended is within the bounds of propriety and reasonableness."

The judge had become convinced, he said, that "this was not a banking organization established for the purpose of violating the law, but was an existing legitimate banking operation, some of whose employees fell into criminal activity." He, too, had had concerns about the bank's ability to survive, he said.

Judge O'Kelley accepted the guilty plea and the government's complicated recommendations for penalty and pronounced sentence.

With that, Richey offered the bank's first installment payment on its forfeiture: a $2 million check, payable to the U.S. Marshal for the Northern District of Georgia.

"If the appropriate marshal would present himself, I'll give him the check," said Richey.

"Well, I have a memo on my desk that the appropriate United States Marshal is on leave or somewhere at the present time," Judge O'Kelley said.

"Am I required to keep it?" Richey joked.

"Your honor, I'll accept," Buddy volunteered.

Richey gave Buddy the check. Symbolically, he was the more deserving government official, anyway.

In Panama the guilty plea was viewed quite differently.

"In Panama, we had a legal problem, and we had a moral problem," says lawyer Antonio Dudley. "In Panama, if you're guilty, the bank closes down. It's as simple as that."

Dudley tried to explain to the banking commission that Occidente had to make a deal with the United States to survive, and that under U.S. law, the bank took responsibility for its employees. He presented letters from Buddy Parker saying the U.S. government had no evidence against senior bank management, and that the bank would be allowed to continue to do business in the United States.

Dudley finally persuaded the banking commission to let Occidente keep its license to do business in Panama. But he still faced the Banking Association of Panama. The seven-member ethics committee had already voted unanimously to oust this apparently dirty bank. Although the association had no regulatory authority, expelling a member bank would be a serious embarrassment. The only bank previously ousted was already dead when the group had voted.

The guilty plea and the U.S. treatment confused Panamanian bankers. Dudley says the bankers' argument went something like this: "We thought you were a victim, but you declared yourself guilty. Why didn't you tell us you would plead guilty?"

He explained the bank had no other choice, but in Panama that didn't wash. A person who is wronged must fight for his principles, even to the death.

Dudley kept pushing for a copy of the sentencing hearing transcript, but it was taking forever, and the move to oust the bank from the trade association was picking up steam.

He tried to tell the bankers, "This is not guilt like you think of guilt. It's another special, American guilt."

The association and its committees held hearings and questioned key players. Finally, a copy of the sentencing hearing transcript arrived. The bank president wrote a long letter. Buddy sent another. After several tense weeks, the matter came to the Banking Association's full membership.

The impassioned debate raged for three hours, as bankers invoked the honor of the Panamanian banking community, the arrogance of the U.S. government, and the vexing question of the bank's guilt.

Sending $412 million in drug funds through Occidente without the knowledge of the top management would have been impossible, some argued. As one of the bankers would later say, "It's such a small bank, and such a big thing happened. . . . It's difficult to think otherwise."

The trade group could not condone drug money laundering by continuing to associate with a bank admittedly guilty, some argued. Wasn't the reputation of the Panamanian banking community dirty enough already?

For three hours, the bankers debated. About eighty of them were there, and "everyone took a position," says Dudley. "Everyone."

Finally, the vote came. To expel a bank from membership required a two-thirds vote. The tally: a comfortable majority for keeping Occidente in the fold.

"In the end, what cut the ground out from all of that was that Banco de Occidente and the U.S. government agreed to a fine [of] five million," says one Panamanian banker. He adds, "Five million dollars is just walking-around money for these guys."

22: A Prisoner of War

However it was viewed in Panama, the bank's guilty plea satisfied Buddy. Making an international money-laundering case had thrilled him, and he had done it with laws and legal theories rarely, if ever, used before. He had pushed the case and pushed it farther than most would have, and it had worked. Thornburgh issued another press release boasting about the bank's plea and the international sharing of the forfeiture.

It was also true, of course, that Martínez had slipped through the feds' grasp, to the great disappointment of the agents, especially Cesar. Skip had viewed Martínez's arrest as a longshot, anyway. Still, they all had hoped to bring in a major money launderer for the Medellín cartel, and Martínez had been their best bet. They had long since given up on getting Escobar or Ochoa. As for the two bankers, Panama had released them from custody and extradition was unlikely.

On Friday night, August 18, just four days after the bank's sentencing in Atlanta, seven men with submachine guns and other firearms walked up to a platform at an open-air political rally outside Bogotá. Gunfire pierced the air, and the nation's leading presidential candidate, Senator Luis Carlos Galán, fell. Men who had crowded the stage minutes earlier tumbled or jumped off, one of them brandishing a pistol and another still firing a rifle at the platform as he fled.

Galán had advocated a get-tough policy toward the drug traffickers and had campaigned for the resumption of extradition to the United States. For that stand, he had become the latest casualty in Colombia's fight against drugs, a struggle far bloodier than the "war on drugs" U.S. presidents periodically declare. The day before Galán's death, the provincial police commander in Medellín was murdered, and days before that, a Supreme Court justice. The murderous month had begun August 1 when Judge Helena Díaz, who had signed a warrant for the arrest of Pablo Escobar, was gunned down in the street. The warrant was set aside.

That was the way justice worked in Colombia for the drug barons. Since 1981, 220 Colombian judges had been slain. No one knew how many had been bribed. Through intimidation and corruption, drug lords had insulated themselves from the Colombian judicial system. Not so in the United States. This was why traffickers feared extradition so much. For two years, since the Supreme Court lifted Colombia's extradition treaty with the United States, the drug barons had used terrorism to stave off extradition.

But if the drug kingpins believed they could kill the pro-extradition movement by killing Galán, they were wrong. The assassination became a rallying cry for Colombians sickened by the violence and the corruption. It galvanized public sentiment against them, and President Barco declared the country to be in a state of siege. He led the most aggressive charge against the Medellín cartel in years, and an emergency decree gave him the power to extradite Colombians accused of drug trafficking in the United States.

That Friday night, word of Barco's emergency orders—accompanied by a curfew and a ban on alcohol—raced through Bogotá's vibrant nightlife. Bars shut down and roadblocks went up. People ran for cover and cars sped through the streets.

All weekend long, Colombian police raided ranches and homes and any other place drug suspects were believed to be, arresting suspects and seizing property. They took yachts, planes, and hundreds of weapons, palatial homes and rolling estates.

"They were hitting all the *fincas* [ranches], businesses, whatever property that they knew, and everybody knew, belonged to the traffickers," says DEA agent Javier Pena. "They would just go in and take them."

Police were calling anyone who might know the whereabouts of the drug barons, following up on all tips, and scouring Colombia's cities and countryside. By Sunday night, nearly four thousand people had been rounded up. Hundreds were questioned and released, and the raids continued Monday, a national holiday in Colombia.

Still, no kingpins.

At DEA-Atlanta, on Monday afternoon, Ron Caffrey took a call from Washington. Colombian police had arrested someone Caffrey would be interested in: Eduardo Martínez.

Caffrey passed the news to Skip and Cesar, and they called Buddy.

Surprised as the Atlantans were, DEA agents in Colombia were bewildered. They had never heard of Eduardo Martínez before. They had been focusing on helping the Colombians capture the drug bosses.

For whatever reason, Colombian police also were looking for Martínez. According to agent Pena, police had heard Martínez was hiding on a *finca* near the town of Tolú on the Caribbean coast, and that is where they found him.

He was no Escobar, but Martínez's arrest and possible extradition came as big news internationally, because it represented the Colombian government's biggest hit so far in the stepped-up war on the drug trade. Because he was wanted in Atlanta, Martínez became the first test of Colombia's willingness to extradite in the face of an expected onslaught of violence from the drug barons.

There were State Department press conferences and front-page stories. "We are consulting with the government of Colombia on the best way to bring this money launderer for the Medellín cartel to justice in the United States," State Department spokesman Richard Boucher told reporters on Tuesday, August 22.

The networks showed footage of Martínez dressed as he had been when arrested, in a reddish pullover sweater, sports shirt, and tan, corduroy pants. He was posing next to a seal of the Colombian National Police, looking glum.

The State Department told reporters Martínez was "not a major figure," and stressed that the U.S. government was hoping to bring the kingpins to justice in the States. But no kingpins were turning up, so Martínez's significance seemed to grow. Colombian authorities had only Martínez to parade about to sustain the public will for the fight. Much will would be needed, because the traffickers were mounting a bloody counteroffensive, bombing banks and cars and offices, killing innocent bystanders, and threatening more bloodshed if extradition commenced. They declared "total and absolute war" on the Colombian government.

CNN was calling Martínez "the cartel's main treasurer," while a front-page *New York Times* story tagged him a "Major Drug Financier." In Atlanta, he was "Finance Minister" to the Medellín cartel. It was starting to sound as if Martínez had been in charge of the Medellín cartel's finances. That came as news to the men who had built the case against Martínez, whose evidence showed he was a highly significant money mover for the cartel, but not the only one.

In Colombia, Martínez denied it all. The Bogotá daily *El Tiempo* quoted him as saying, "At no time have I had links to the Medellín cartel, and I don't know any of its members."

In Atlanta, Buddy, Skip, and Cesar feverishly prepared paperwork to expedite extradition: affidavits, an extradition request, an official warrant certified by the presiding judicial officer, papers identifying the captured man as the man wanted in Atlanta. Signatures had to be certified. Everything had to be translated and stamped and blue-ribboned, because any deficiency, any error, could give Martínez a way out. Who knew whether he would find a Colombian judge or official friendly to his cause? To make things worse, the requirements kept changing because Colombia's extradition apparatus was so rusty, and there were so many U.S. and Colombian offices involved.

"One minute you were doing something and thinking that something was going to happen, the next minute it was a completely different story, something else was going to happen, and a minute after that it was something else," says Cesar.

If it came off, this would be the first extradition in two years, so no one knew what would happen, says Skip. "They didn't know how much pressure was going to be put on the [Colombian] judges to cut him loose, and what loophole they might look for." So U.S. authorities wanted the Colombians to have every conceivable document as soon as possible, whatever they needed the moment they needed it.

Meanwhile, Colombia's foreign minister and, later, its justice minister, flew to Washington for talks, and Attorney General Thornburgh called for quick action so as not to lose the chance to extradite Martínez.

Pressure built as President Barco delivered a televised plea for help from the American people, whose drug habit, he said, had created "the largest, most vicious criminal enterprise the world has ever known."

Maintaining that "Colombia's survival as the oldest democracy in Latin America is now at risk," the patrician Barco declared that Colombia has lost thousands of martyrs to the traffickers. "Enough is enough," he said.

Washington responded with a $65 million emergency aid package to Colombia, including jets, helicopters, radios, two giant C-130s, and machine guns.

But as for extradition, there were still so many kinks to work out, not only in the extradition itself but also in the handling of Martínez. Who would bring him to the States and how? Where would he be taken, and how could his security and those of his handlers be assured? While the State Department and Justice were hammering out the extradition questions, security and transportation were being hashed out between DEA and the U.S. Marshal Service, in Washington as well as Atlanta.

Skip and Cesar wanted to make sure they were the ones who would bring Martínez in. This had been their case, and now it would be their glory. But more important was the chance to be alone with Martínez on the flight back. Those hours of uninterrupted time with him would be their best chance to persuade him to cooperate with the government. Once he got behind bars, even seeing him would be impossible. When a defense attorney entered the scene, everything would be different. Cesar, who knew Martínez, and Skip, the case agent, were the logical choices for Martínez's escorts, Ron Caffrey insisted to his higher-ups.

One of the suggestions was to get the pair of agents to Bogotá to be on hand when extradition occurred. Caffrey nixed that idea. The situation was too volatile in Colombia to bring more DEA agents to hang around the U.S. Embassy waiting for an event that was bound to further inflame matters. No, Colombian police would fly Martínez from Bogotá to Guantánamo Bay, Cuba, where Cesar and Skip would meet him. They would then escort him on a DEA plane to Atlanta.

But where in Atlanta would the plane land, and how could the marshals protect Martínez and the agents handling him? Where could he be safely housed, and how would he be brought to court? Events leading to this prisoner's arrest and his expected extradition had provoked the most dangerous group of criminals in the world. In Colombia, the "Extraditables" had pledged to kill ten judges for every cartel member extradited. Who knew how far their retaliation would reach?

*F*or Ramón, hidden away from all the commotion, this was a nightmare come true. He watched Martínez on television being paraded about in the Colombian jail, looking more and more grim as the week wore on. Ramón felt bad for Martínez, but he felt worse for himself.

For one thing, when Martínez's arrest seemed impossible, the idea of his getting paid for his work as an informant seemed possible. Paying an informant for work did not usually sit well with juries, but with the guilty pleas from the bank and from Francisco, and with Martínez's escape in Panama, it had seemed there would be no trials in this case. All that changed with Martínez's arrest. Ramón could kiss that money goodbye.

But losing the money wasn't what bothered Ramón most. The risk of being found and killed by avenging drug traffickers weighed much more heavily on him.

*O*n Monday, August 28, a week after Martínez's capture, the U.S. government formally requested his extradition. Pounds of documents were submitted. Extradition would occur any time now, Colombian officials announced.

Skip and Cesar flew to Miami with DEA pilots brought in from Texas. Finally, they would bring their suspect to Atlanta.

On Tuesday, the twenty-ninth, President Barco granted extradition. Another day passed. Proceedings had hit a further snag in Colombia: Martínez was appealing.

Skip and Cesar flew back to Atlanta, and the DEA pilots headed home.

The case seemed to be swirling above the agents and prosecutors who had set off this whole chain of events. From the moment Martínez was captured, it was clear that Washington and Bogotá were running the case now.

But the Atlantans needed to know what was happening, so an unofficial line of communication was opened in tandem with the official one. On the side, Skip was talking to Pena in Bogotá to track developments. Pena would tell Skip unofficially what was happening and what papers would be needed, so Skip could move. Sometimes Pena received documents before his boss did, though without the official seal.

At the same time, the pressure intensified. Buddy had felt the eyes of the world peering over his shoulder on the bank case, but that was nothing compared to this. His case was being explained over network television, and his defendant—the same man he had watched on those undercover videotapes—was showing up on CNN almost hourly, and on the front pages of the nation's leading newspapers. The State Department, the White House, Justice, and, it seemed, the whole federal bureaucracy were busy doing this and that to see to it that his suspect was brought to Atlanta for prosecution.

Finally, two weeks after Martínez's arrest, Skip and Cesar were told to return to Miami. Extradition appeared imminent.

At this point, with anti-drug and anti-trafficker sentiment reaching a pitch in the United States as well as Colombia, President George Bush decided it was time to weigh in. Bush would address the nation in his first Oval Office speech since becoming President nine months earlier. The subject would be drugs.

At 9:00 P.M. on Tuesday night, September 5, with violence raging in Colombia, Bush began his televised speech:

"This is the first time since taking the oath of office that I felt an issue was so important, so threatening, that it warranted talking directly with you, the American people," he said solemnly, calling drugs "the gravest domestic threat facing our nation today."

The President held up a plastic bag containing hard, whitish-looking lumps. "This is crack cocaine seized just a few days ago by drug enforcement agents in a park just across the street from the White House."

(Within days, *The Washington Post* would report that undercover agents had had to manipulate a suspect to meet them at Lafayette Park —the suspect didn't know where it was—to satisfy a White House request for the prop. But for now, Bush was making the point that no place in America was safe from the scourge.)

Bush spoke of the tragedies drugs wreak on children, on families, on America's neighborhoods and the nation's very future. And he laid out his plan to attack the problem, calling it the first comprehensive strategy for fighting drugs: more drug cops, more jails, more judges, more prosecutors, more U.S. money for crime-fighting efforts in Colombia, Peru, and Bolivia. He also called for expanded drug treatment programs and education programs.

He committed the United States to help any government that asks for aid in fighting the drug war, including the use of America's armed forces, when "appropriate."

And the President delivered a message to the drug barons and money launderers. As if he were talking to Martínez himself, Bush said: "We will pursue and enforce international agreements to track drug money to the front men and financiers. And then we will handcuff these money launderers and jail them—just like any street dealer.

"And for the drug kingpins," Bush added, staring into the camera, "the death penalty."

That bravado may have played well with the American public, but it jolted the Colombians and U.S. officials working on Martínez's extradition. Under the new emergency extradition agreement, the United States had promised that no extradited Colombian would receive a U.S. sentence greater than thirty years behind bars. A death sentence was out of the question.

Within the administration, there was fear that the death pledge would upset delicate extradition negotiations. It couldn't have happened at a worse time. Martínez's lawyer was already challenging the legality of the emergency decree from every imaginable angle, and here was the President of the United States promising to break the terms of the extradition agreement. This, at the very moment a commission of high-level Colombian officials was poised to decide Martínez's appeal.

U.S. officials reassured the Colombians that the President's statement represented no backtracking from the thirty-year maximum already agreed to. Martínez would get no more than thirty years.

In Miami, Skip and Cesar and the DEA pilots were ready to take off for Guantánamo Bay. They had arrived over the weekend and waited at their hotel for the go-ahead. Two days into the wait, on Wednesday, September 6, DEA-Atlanta called early in the afternoon. It looks like it will happen today, they were told. Be prepared to get over to the Opa-Locka airport in a hurry.

That same day, in Bogotá, the day after Bush's faux pas, Martínez's appeal was turned down.

Skip and Cesar took a phone call about 4:00 P.M. Extradition would, in fact, occur that day, they were told, but no one knew exactly when. They headed for the airport.

More time passed as they waited there for the final go-ahead. At the same time, Skip kept trying to coordinate the logistics of Martínez's eventual arrival in Atlanta, talking with the U.S. Marshal Service in Atlanta. The marshals had devised an elaborate plan aimed at throwing reporters off the track and keeping Martínez secure. Everyone on the Atlanta end was keyed up, but no one had any idea when it would happen. Frustrated, Skip put in a couple of calls to Bogotá and talked to agent Pena to find out what was happening down there.

Next thing Skip knew, DEA-Atlanta was calling him. Ron Caffrey wanted him to stop calling Bogotá. Apparently, DEA or some other government agency had been monitoring phone traffic in Bogotá, and he had been picked up making unauthorized calls.

At last, at about 8:00 P.M., the word came. Martínez was being flown from Bogotá to Cuba by Colombian authorities. They were to meet him at Guantánamo Bay.

The pilot flew the Marlin 3 around Cuba to avoid Cuban air space, but Cesar was watching for any glimpse of the island as he peered into the darkness. He spotted lights—city lights, lights from the military base?—as they flew into the bay. This was all he could see of his homeland, the island his family had left when he was four. Still, it thrilled him that he would be touching down on his native soil. Skip watched Cesar and was moved, too. For such a young agent, Cesar had helped make an incredibly big case, and part of the reward was a late-night trip to the place of his birth, a place forbidden to him under normal circumstances.

Tropical breezes greeted them as they alighted. "It was a great night," says Cesar. "Man, I loved it."

The agents waited with military personnel while the plane refueled. Within an hour, a couple of lights appeared moving toward them over the bay.

A small plane touched down and the door opened. Out came the pilots, a Colombian police captain, and two DEA agents. Everyone introduced themselves.

Well, where is he? Cesar said.

He's in there, someone nodded to the plane.

Cesar stepped up into the fuselage and glanced down the rows of empty seats. At the rear sat Eduardo Martínez, handcuffed, wearing leg-irons, and belted into his seat.

The two men looked at each other. It had been five months since Martínez had given Cesar the slip in Panama, but now there was no escape. The agent was about to place his primary target under arrest.

Cesar cracked a smile. Martínez smiled back.

Now began what could be the most critical part of the case. After ar-resting Martínez and reading him his rights, the agents would have him to themselves for the five-hour flight. Just because he could remain silent before hiring a lawyer did not mean he would. But once they touched ground, the chances were great he'd obtain counsel who would advise him to keep quiet.

The sooner Skip and Cesar could flip him, persuade him to cooperate, the better. Analysts had been poring over bank records that the cases in L.A., New York, and Atlanta had produced, and it was clear Martínez had accounts all over Panama, Europe, and possibly the United States. The agents figured this was money belonging to Martínez's customers; with his help, the U.S. government could seize millions more in drug pro-ceeds. But they needed to move quickly, because such money moved quickly, particularly when its owners suspected the U.S. government might try to grab it. Not only that, Martínez might have ideas as to where the traffickers were hiding, the agents figured.

This was their chance, facing him in this small, six-seater cabin, as they flew through the humid night over Florida and Georgia. Still, it wasn't quite as cozy as the agents had imagined. They had been forced to take with them the Colombian police captain who had escorted Mar-tínez. The captain was there to symbolize bilateral cooperation, so no one could say the U.S. government had swooped up a Colombian na-tional. A partition divided the small cabin behind the seat where Martí-nez sat facing forward, and the police captain took his place on the other side, his back to Martínez. Still, it wasn't as private as Cesar and Skip had hoped.

Cesar, who had already established rapport with Martínez, took the lead and also served as interpreter when Skip had points to make. Together, they laid out the evidence against Martínez. They told him they had an airtight case, that he was on videotape in Aruba discussing the finer points of drug money laundering and on audiotape advising Cesar how to move the money better. Not only that, Cesar had been with him at the bank in Panama and was prepared to testify to everything Martínez had said and done.

And it wasn't just money, either. He could be convicted of facilitating drug trafficking. To prove that, the government had Martínez talking about moving drugs. They also had large amounts of cocaine that had been seized by cops who had followed Martínez's money couriers.

They had him cold, they said.

Martínez said nothing, but his eyes showed exhaustion and disorientation.

Skip says they told him, "You can do it the hard way—you can fight it, you can plead innocent . . . you can go through your attorney. But that is not going to be in the best interest of you and your family. Because it's going to keep you locked up a long time."

Martínez remained silent; even vacant. He had, after all, spent two weeks in a Colombian prison on an emotional seesaw, with the country in an uproar, while his lawyer tried to stave off the extradition. He had been up all day being moved from here to there. Now, it was well past midnight.

Skip and Cesar had reached the point in their pitch when the suspect normally asks questions and signals his concerns. But Martínez still said nothing. If he had told them he wanted to talk to a lawyer before talking to them, they would have had to stop. But he didn't. He didn't say anything.

The agents explained what they could and could not do for him in the way of sentencing recommendations.

Finally Martínez told them he had nothing to say.

He started dozing, and so did the agents. From time to time they would wake up, think of something else to say to him, get no response, and doze off again. It went on like that for hours.

Martínez was not going to roll. Not now, at least.

"The most we could hope for was that we planted a seed," says Skip.

It was nearly 5:00 A.M. and still dark when the plane neared Atlanta, where fog and low-lying clouds cut visibility to about a mile or two. The pilot, himself exhausted, could see well enough. Still, he knew to be especially careful, given the poor weather, his own fatigue, and the importance of the mission. He had been told to fly into a small airport just west of Atlanta named for a longtime county commissioner, Charlie Brown, where he had flown before for DEA.

He eased the plane down onto the runway and taxied to the main hangar. As the plane rolled in, flashes of light erupted suddenly. Reporters and photographers had learned where the plane would be landing —or at least were manning the obvious possibilities.

This did not seem like the most secure spot. They sat in the plane on the tarmac, awaiting U.S. marshals, who were supposed to take Martínez to a helicopter, then fly him to the federal building, where he would be put into a holding cell to await his first appearance in court. But before that, they had to get him off the plane.

Minutes passed. Finally, a marshal appeared on the tarmac and waved the plane to another hangar, away from the cameras.

There, things began happening very quickly. The plane's engines switched off, the door came down, and a couple of marshals came on board. Cesar took Martínez out of his seat, and the marshals put a bulletproof vest on him. Cesar wondered why they hadn't brought flak jackets for him and Skip, too.

The marshals led Martínez off the plane and over to a U.S. Army helicopter waiting on the tarmac nearby, where Cesar and Skip said goodbye to him. The helicopter chopped the humid air and lifted off.

Finally, Eduardo Martínez was in custody in the United States. Because he had tried and failed to make this happen five months earlier, Cesar, especially, felt a sense of great relief.

23: Truth and Consequences

"It was long before sunrise that federal marshals brought Eduardo Martínez into the federal building," CNN reporter Larry Woods said over footage of a helicopter in a vacant parking lot, its blades still chopping the night, humidity steaming up from the pavement in wisps of light fog.

One man could be seen, and then three more hopping out of the helicopter, one rushing into a kneeling position in front of the chopper, rifle raised, while he looked this way and that. Next a man in the blue jacket of a U.S. marshal jumped out, his body at first hiding from the camera another man, who finally came into view. Eduardo Martínez, wearing a pale flak jacket, was walked briskly across the pavement to the rear door of a waiting black Ford sedan. The sedan drove into the darkness underneath a bridge, headed for the basement entrance of the Richard B. Russell Federal Building.

For Martínez's first appearance in federal court in Atlanta, journalists from all over would pack the courtroom, while photographers and camera crews waited downstairs to capture the lawyers for interviews afterwards.

President Bush got into the act, too. To an American Legion convention in Baltimore, he said, "Yesterday's extradition of a major drug dealer sends a strong signal of the courage and determination of President Barco and the Colombian government to deal with the scourge which drugs are inflicting on all of us."

In fact, the extradition had set off a round of new bombings in Colombia, as well as protests from college students shouting, "Yankee go home!"

In the twenty-four hours after Martínez's arrival in Atlanta, U.S. Attorney Barr was showing up on so many network news shows that Judge O'Kelley called him into his chambers, along with the other lawyers in the case, for a dressing down.

"The last thing I saw on television last night before I turned the lights off and retired was an interview of the United States Attorney on the . . . MacNeil, whatever it is," Judge O'Kelley said, referring to *The MacNeil/ Lehrer NewsHour,* which was re-aired late on public television in Atlanta.

"The first thing I saw this morning was an interview of the United States Attorney on the 'Today Show,'" O'Kelley continued.

The judge wanted that sort of thing stopped immediately. He intended to ensure a fair trial for Martínez, and that meant reining in lawyers from discussing the evidence over the news media ahead of time.

But it wasn't just Barr, complained one of Martínez's attorneys, Edward T. M. Garland of Atlanta. "Last night I caught a brief glimpse of the President of the United States speaking of the defendant in this case as guilty. . . ."

O'Kelley took no position on that, but he told the lawyers to stop feeding the press frenzy.

That was just fine with Buddy and Craig, who listened quietly while their boss was being chastised. They didn't want Barr's taste for publicity ruining their case. Accused of headline seeking in other cases, Barr denied he endangered prosecutions when he told the public what it had a right to know. Nonetheless, throughout Fis-Con and Polar Cap, the prosecutors had purposely held back sensitive information from Barr for fear they would read it in the next morning's *Atlanta Constitution.*

Martínez quickly brought to his side some of the highest-paid and best-known criminal defense lawyers from Atlanta and Miami. The defense team, which seemed to grow at every hearing, soon began attacking almost every aspect of the indictment and extradition in an all-out legal battle.

The seed Skip had hoped he planted with Martínez on that early morning flight showed no signs of sprouting.

At the same time, another seed, planted in Skip's mind by the Colombian police captain on the flight back, was beginning to bear fruit. Skip had asked Captain Oscar Naranjo, chief of intelligence for the Colombian National Police, all about Geraldo Moncada, or Chepe. The captain confirmed the rumors Ramón and Francisco had heard. He said Moncada was on the highest rung of the Medellín cartel. In fact, he put him among the top three. Moncada was deeply involved in money laundering and trafficking with Escobar, but had kept such a low profile through the years that, until recently, it was safe for Moncada to appear in public while the others had gone into hiding.

Skip decided to pull together everything he could find on Moncada, including links to other major cases.

In Tampa, for example, a Colombian fugitive indicted under the name "Don Chepe" or "Kiko" stood accused of sending many millions of drug funds through the Bank of Credit and Commerce International. Buddy and Skip traveled to Florida to compare bank accounts, phone numbers, and other evidence, and concluded that Tampa's Chepe was Moncada.

In Canada, a plane that crash-landed in a bank of snow in early April 1989 was found to contain 500 kilograms of cocaine, which was supposed to have gone to New York on behalf of a Colombian trafficker named "Kiko," said to be a partner of Escobar's. An informant in the Canadian case told the Royal Canadian Mounted Police that Kiko's last name was Moncada.

The more Buddy and Skip looked, the more drug probes involving Moncada turned up. Eventually, they became convinced that Chepe's full name was Gerardo (not Geraldo) Moncada Cuartas, a university-trained electronics engineer in Medellín who owned Colombian real estate, an airline, and a Medellín construction company.

On October 3, 1989, Skip wrote a sixteen-page DEA-6 detailing the scope of Moncada's activities as known so far. In it, he debunked New York DEA's conclusion that the Chepe who turned up in the New York Polar Case case was named Luis Garces-Restrepo. Skip's report concluded convincingly that the New York Chepe had to be the same Chepe DEA-Atlanta had learned about through Martínez, and that his name was Gerardo Moncada, a top-rung trafficker in Medellín. If Moncada was extradited, he would be the most significant drug baron prosecuted so far, and the job of putting him behind bars would most likely fall to the Atlanta team.*

Meanwhile, the war on drugs in Colombia got bloodier. Bombings and terrorism continued as police rounded up more suspects, and as Barco signed more extradition orders. Assassins killed two more presi-

---

* The DEA–New York Polar Cap agents continue to insist that the Chepe named Garces-Restrepo was different from Atlanta's Chepe. "No matter what, it is not one person," Elaine Harris, who supervised that group, said in a 1992 interview.

dential candidates, and drug traffickers were blamed for the downing of a Colombian jet and the deaths of the 107 people on board. Political party offices were bombed, and so was the headquarters of the security police. Rooting out the criminals who had corrupted the judiciary and terrorized the entire nation was costing hundreds of innocent lives and millions of dollars.

The kingpins continued to elude capture, although they cut it close at times. At least twice police arrived at places believed to be Escobar hideouts only to find that Escobar and his entourage had fled moments before. The police were getting good intelligence, but Escobar's was better.

Finally, on December 15, Colombian and U.S. authorities tracked one of Colombia's most dangerous drug barons, José Rodríguez Gacha, to a backcountry hideout. The gun battle that followed left him dead, as well as his son and fourteen bodyguards. The Colombian government had put down forever one of the major narco-terrorists.

The victory was sure to buoy the Colombian government's will to continue the battle. It also served as a reminder that, heavily armed and guarded as the kingpins were, and committed as they were to fighting to the death, the likelihood of arrest and extradition for them was nil. They had pledged to die on Colombian soil rather than spend a day in a U.S. jail. And Gacha's death underscored that pledge.

The question was, what would the drug barons do to avenge his death?

The next day, December 16, in a suburb of Birmingham, Alabama, a judge who served on the Atlanta-based 11th U.S. Circuit Court of Appeals opened a package that had come through the mail. Wrapped in brown paper, it looked like a Christmas gift from a colleague who lived near Atlanta and whose return address was shown in the corner.

Standing there in the kitchen of his home, Judge Robert S. Vance, Jr., opened the box. It exploded in a rain of nails and pipe. Judge Vance, a gregarious man who relished life and laughed big, was killed instantly. His wife, who had been in the kitchen with him, was seriously hurt as she witnessed her husband's murder.

No one knew who had killed Judge Vance or why. But some feared the blood shed in that suburban American kitchen marked a new front in the drug wars. Killing judges was the sort of thing the Colombian traffickers did regularly. Could this be retaliation for Gacha's death?

Buddy didn't think so. It had happened too quickly, for one thing. And why Judge Vance? Federal appeals judges are largely invisible to the average person, and never decide a case alone. Besides, Buddy could think of no recent drug case involving Vance.

Nonetheless, the U.S. Marshal called Buddy, as well as other prosecutors and judges in Atlanta, to warn against opening packages sent through the mail without first having them X-rayed. Christmas 1989 was shaping up as a scary season.

Two days after Vance's murder, authorities intercepted another mail bomb at the 11th Circuit's Atlanta courthouse, a few blocks from the Russell Building. Both buildings were shut down tight for security sweeps.

Who could be trying to blow up Atlanta's federal judiciary? Buddy was worried enough to find someone who could let him into the Russell Building that Monday so he could get his gun, which was tucked away safely in his desk drawer.

And when the building opened again for business, under much tighter security, the offices of several of the prosecutors in the Drug Task Force sprouted signs over their doors that, in morose humor, read: *"I am NOT Buddy Parker."*

The bombs would turn out to be the handiwork of a strange fellow from suburban Atlanta who believed he had been wronged by the 11th Circuit in a long-ago criminal case. Still, the exercise served to remind Buddy and others that Colombia is not the only place where criminals avenge their punishment.

Events in Panama were now reaching a critical point. Noriega had stolen the presidential election in May, leading to more turmoil. A coup attempt by PDF insurgents expecting U.S. help failed in October. And on December 15, Noriega declared Panama to be in a state of war with the United States. In the first hours of December 20, some 22,000 U.S. troops invaded Panama. After hiding out and then taking refuge in the papal nunciature, Noriega finally gave himself up on January 3, 1990.

Riding back on a military plane to Miami, where he would await trial, Noriega was still stunned by events. He told DEA agent Rene De La Cova, sitting alongside him, that he had never imagined the United States would invade Panama.

With Noriega gone from Panama, Buddy Parker saw a chance to push his case further. Suddenly U.S. authorities had access to Panamanian bank records, and Buddy had a lot of questions he thought the records could answer. He wanted to know what had happened to the more than $400 million in drug funds the feds had traced to Banco de Occidente.

Agents and financial analysts traveled to Panama in January 1990 to examine the records, and by spring Buddy thought he had his answer. The analysts had traced $350 million back to hundreds of bank accounts in the United States. These, Buddy reasoned, must be the U.S. operating accounts for the cartel, the accounts from which the traffickers paid for planes and other U.S. expenses.

At the same time, the Atlanta team had been following leads from Polar Cap into other investigations, finding Chepe's tracks in U.S. cases from Florida to Canada. To pull it all together, and to persuade a federal judge to freeze the bank accounts the analysts had identified, Buddy and DEA agent Dave Panek put together a 279-page affidavit. It contained pages of transcripts from Eduardo Martínez's meeting with Cesar Diaz and John Featherly in Aruba, statements given authorities by Sergio Hochman and other defendants in the California La Mina cases, explanations of how La Mina worked, and summaries of other cases Buddy believed related.

Buddy took the affidavit to U.S. District Judge William O'Kelley, who, on April 16, 1990, signed an order plugging up some 700 accounts in 200 banks across the United States and instructing bank officials to turn over the records of those accounts to Buddy. As with the earlier orders, money could come in but none could come out. But this time he used civil forfeiture law, under which assets can be frozen temporarily until the government can prove them to be subject to forfeiture.

This remarkable law enforcement action was trumpeted by the Attorney General in a press release issued the following day: "Our ability to examine these bank records may well be the key to unlocking the totality of the secret financial arrangements of the cartel in the U.S.," Thornburgh said. "This action . . . seeks to lift the veil of secrecy over the financial network of these narco-terrorists, including Pablo Escobar and Jorge Ochoa."

Treasury Secretary Nicholas Brady called it "one of the most significant law enforcement undertakings involving bank account seizures in U.S. history."

Locally, Buddy Parker said that with Escobar and Ochoa already in hiding, squeezing their finances could help dismantle the Medellín cartel.

But even before the nation's press was beginning to report this unprecedented enforcement action, telephone calls began jamming the lines at the Drug Task Force in Atlanta.

A Washington lawyer representing Refco, Inc., one of the world's largest futures brokers, called demanding to know why the billion-dollar trading account that held all of Refco's customers' money was blocked. Did Buddy Parker intend to shut down the Chicago Board of Trade? A silk stocking Miami law firm that never handles criminal work wanted to know why it could not get to its funds. Small companies, too, such as a newsletter publisher in New York, suddenly found they could not withdraw funds from their bank accounts, either.

And it wasn't just private individuals and corporations that found themselves accused of somehow acting as fronts for Colombian drug barons' bank accounts. The government of Taiwan was furious when it learned that millions of dollars belonging to companies doing business in Taiwan were stuck in the Chang Hwa Commercial Bank's correspondent account at Citibank.

Deluged with telephone calls and faxes, Buddy could tell something had gone wrong. As quickly as he could determine that an account was legitimate, he told the bank to unfreeze it. Refco's account was open by trading time in Chicago, for example. Soon, Buddy was before O'Kelley asking him to remove huge chunks of briefly frozen accounts from the April 16 order, a dozen one day, a couple hundred another. By April 28, fewer than 200 accounts remained on ice, while defense lawyers argued at hearings before O'Kelley to thaw out all of them and stop the government from romping through innocent people's bank accounts.

"This boat is way out to sea. It should never have been launched," attorney Edward T. M. Garland, Martínez's attorney, told O'Kelley at one such hearing. "What's being done here is that they have said, 'Once they were drug funds. Now they're in the hands of third parties, and we are going to take them.'"

At some point in the money-laundering cycle, dirty cash in fact becomes clean. Virtually all, if not all, of the 700 accounts belonged to people or companies that had nothing to do with the drug trade. What Buddy now says he did not understand at the time was how U.S. drug dollars were sold for foreign exchange once they hit Panama. Called the parallel market, this was the point where U.S. drug profits were converted into currency the drug traffickers could use at home while the U.S. dollars returned north, coursing through the veins of American business.

Eventually, only a smattering of accounts in Miami were left to argue about. And in July 1992, a federal judge released most of those, too, saying the government lacked probable cause to plug up these accounts in the first place.

A few months after that whole embarrassing episode unfolded, Buddy quietly scored a victory. But no one outside a small circle of people was watching June 22, 1990, when Eduardo Martínez signed a six-page letter agreeing to plead guilty to washing hundreds of millions of dollars for the world's biggest drug traffickers.

Martínez would not only plead guilty, he would also tell government agents whatever they wanted to know about drug trafficking and money laundering, that paper said. Although he had been away from Colombia for nearly a year at this point, he still could be a valuable source. This information fed to the Colombians might enable the government to track down the fugitives it was seeking.

How much help Martínez eventually offered is not clear. But he agreed to cooperate only after getting permission from Colombia to do so—either from Gerardo Moncada or Pablo Escobar, or both. Despite whatever secret communications occurred between Martínez and Colombia, he did not want it widely known he was cooperating. There was no way to hide a guilty plea, but Buddy agreed to help keep it as quiet as possible.

Sentencing was set for August 23, a year to the day from the U.S. request that Colombia extradite him. The hearing would be in open court, but it would be set for 8:00 A.M.—much earlier than normal. And while no one was planning to lie about it if asked, neither would anyone volunteer advance word of the hearing to reporters or anyone else.

For Martínez's first plea, the courtroom had been full of reporters. For his second plea, it was empty of spectators.

At 8:10 A.M., Judge O'Kelley's clerk called the case: *"The United States of America* vs. *Eduardo Martínez."*

The Miami lawyers were gone, no longer necessary for a defendant not going to trial. Martínez was there with his two Atlanta lawyers, Edward Garland and his partner Don Samuel. For the government, Buddy would lead, but was joined at the government's table by the new U.S. Attorney, Joe Whitley.

When it was over, legal documents had been passed around, explained, read to Martínez in Spanish, and signed. Buddy had outlined the case against Martínez. Every step of the way, O'Kelley would ask Martínez whether he understood the plea and its consequences ("Yes, yes. Totally," Martínez would say); whether he understood the charges against him ("Perfectly, yes"); whether he had been coerced or threatened ("No, your honor").

Then Judge O'Kelley asked, "Are you, in fact, guilty of what you're charged with?"

"According to the laws of this country, yes, your honor," Martínez replied.

Not even in this secretly held hearing was the word "cooperation" uttered. The drug war in Colombia was still raging, and it would be foolish to broadcast the fact that Martínez had switched sides. Just twelve days earlier, Colombian police had tracked and gunned down another defendant in the Atlanta case, Gustavo Gaviria, Escobar's cousin and the man Ramón and Francisco had met in the walled compound that day trying to negotiate a cocaine load.

Judge O'Kelley accepted Martínez's guilty plea and put off sentencing until later, to give the defense time to gather what was needed to bolster a plea for as short a prison term as possible.

Francisco Serrano's day in court was coming up, too. The judge handling his case, Robert H. Vining, set it for October 14, 1990. Two years had passed since Francisco had been informed in a California courtroom that federal authorities in Atlanta were seeking his arrest.

For months after his arrest, Francisco had been telling his beautiful young wife in Colombia he was innocent, and she kept urging him to fight the charges. She did not know the nature of her husband's partnership with Ramón, much less that Francisco had cooperated with authorities. That someone has become a snitch is a dangerous piece of information in Colombia, where bloody vengeance is routinely carried out against the informant and, often, members of his family. Buddy kept offering Francisco the protection of the federal government, which could move his wife and son to the United States. The family would be given a new identity, and once Francisco served his time, they could all live together.

But first, his wife, Sol (named for the sun), had to be told the truth. Buddy flew Sol and their son to Atlanta so Francisco could try to persuade them to stay. It was the first time in nearly a year that Francisco had seen his family. Left alone with his wife in a conference room in the Drug Task Force offices, Francisco begged her to stay in the United States with their son where they could be safe. Things were too dangerous for them in Colombia, he implored.

It was all too much for Sol. When Buddy returned to the conference room, she appeared dazed, but steadfastly refused to leave her native land.

After her return home, Sol became increasingly scared for her own safety and that of their son. Over the phone, she told her husband she had been visited by men from the Medellín cartel who warned her against her husband cooperating. The unspoken threat was unmistakable.

Sol became more distraught. "Fear and anxiety ate her alive," says Buddy. Edging toward mental collapse for months, she finally broke under the stress and checked into a mental hospital. On October 13, at the age of twenty-nine, she strung herself up by her bed sheets and choked life from her body.

"Mr. Serrano has suffered more than any one man can in his life," Francisco's lawyer, Jake Waldrop, told Judge Vining at Francisco's sentencing hearing, which was delayed two weeks as a result of the suicide. Francisco had insisted the hearing wait no longer than that.

"No court could punish him as the world has punished him for his conduct," Waldrop said.

Sol's suicide shook Francisco to his soul. He had lost everything—everything except his son, whom he could not see and would not see until he could be free and established enough to send for him.

Buddy, too, asked Vining to be merciful with Francisco.

If the judge imposed the maximum sentence, he would spend the rest of his life in prison. Francisco was hoping the twenty-six months he had already lived behind bars would suffice.

In deciding Francisco's sentence, Vining said that he took into account "what has happened in his life and what I feel like are his future prospects."

He cited Francisco's cooperation and his remorse. No, he wouldn't get life, but he wouldn't get his freedom yet, either.

Vining sentenced Francisco Serrano to four years, nine months' incarceration, to be followed by five years of supervised release. Francisco would get credit for his time served, but that wouldn't even get him halfway through his sentence. He still had thirty-one more months to go.

Crestfallen, Francisco was led away.

Ramón, too, faced sentencing. Not for the money laundering, of course, but for the cocaine smuggling he had pleaded guilty to so long ago, at the beginning of this whole venture.

He would have just as soon avoided his day in court altogether. Although he believed his work as an informant would keep him free, no one could guarantee that. All he knew was that he was free now, and he would like to stay that way as long as possible.

Buddy hadn't pushed for a quick sentencing. He had put it off to get the guilty plea from Martínez first. Next came Francisco's sentencing.

But Ramón had to face judgment for his crimes some day. That day came on January 16, 1991.

As the date approached, Ramón recalled his first trip to Aruba, when his lawyer had told him to expect to spend about seven years behind bars. He didn't believe it, not even then. And he remembered that after the case got started, John Featherly had told him, in an apparent attempt to be encouraging, he could probably work his sentence down to two years, max.

"John, I don't want to do *any* time," Ramón says he responded.

"You'll never walk," Featherly had told him. Forget about even hoping for that.

But that was before Ramón had introduced the Atlanta DEA to Eduardo Martínez. It was before he had ventured into a meeting with Pablo Escobar, risking his life to bring the boys in Atlanta as big a case as possible. It was before they knew about La Mina, and long before the feds shut it down. It was also before Martínez became the first Colombian drug suspect to be extradited to the United States in years—an accomplishment heralded by the President of the United States. And it was before Martínez pleaded guilty, having been convinced that—largely through Ramón's work—there was no way he could avoid conviction.

Ramón was quite certain he deserved to spend not a minute behind bars. In fact, to his way of thinking the charges should be dropped altogether. He had worked too hard, risked and accomplished too much to have a felony on his record.

Through his lawyer, Mark Kadish, Ramón tried to persuade Buddy to drop the indictment against him. Buddy was willing to sing Ramón's praises to the sentencing judge, but he could not recommend a dismissal of charges, he told Kadish. He was adamant that Ramón should have a criminal record for the crimes he had committed. If Kadish wanted to pursue it, he could approach the U.S. Attorney, but Buddy would recommend against a dismissal of charges.

What about a pardon? asked Kadish. If he sought a presidential pardon for Ramón, would Buddy support the request?

Buddy said he knew little about presidential pardons, but he believed they existed as a safeguard for innocent people wrongly convicted. Ramón, said Buddy, is guilty, guilty. No, he would not support that, either.

Without Buddy's help, Ramón had no hope of ridding his record of the charges.

But Buddy would stand up for Ramón at his sentencing. And he did so, effusively.

Ramón's efforts, Buddy told U.S. District Judge Robert H. Hall, "are the primary and sole reason for the Atlanta agents' and attorneys' involvement in what has become the largest national prosecution of drug money laundering in what continues to be the largest, concentrated, coordinated effort on behalf of the federal government's four major agencies, the DEA, the FBI, the IRS and U.S. Customs. . . .

"He unquestionably led to and was directly responsible for Atlanta undercover agents infiltrating Banco de Occidente–Panama," which, as a result, became the first foreign financial institution with no U.S. operations to plead guilty to breaking U.S. laws, Buddy pointed out.

In pleading guilty, he went on, the bank admitted to "aiding and abetting the most notorious criminal organization, the Medellín drug cartel, in the laundering of its drug proceeds. . . ." The resulting $5 million forfeiture from Banco de Occidente set a record as the largest ever in a drug case against a corporate entity.

In ticking off Ramón's accomplishments, Buddy was also outlining the successes he and the Atlanta drug agents had accomplished through Ramón. They had all done it. From that unlikely beginning on Aruba, when Ramón made it clear he would never trust a cop, they had melded into such a team that at one point in the hearing Buddy inadvertently called Ramón an agent.

Buddy called Cesar to the witness stand and brought out the videotape from that second gathering in Aruba, the one with Martínez. Cesar explained to the judge what was transpiring on the tape, like some *Tonight Show* guest setting up a film clip from his latest release.

There was Ramón, asking Martínez to tell him more about La Mina. And there he was, helping the DEA agents negotiate with Martínez over laundering commissions.

Then came Skip's turn to take the stand. Skip, who had overseen Ramón's work for two and a half years, told Judge Hall that in his twenty years as a drug agent he had never known an informant to contribute so much to the drug fight, or subject himself to such danger to do it.

Ramón had gone after the "highest members of the drug cartels, which is what in DEA they ask us to strive for," Skip said.

Then Buddy took up the theme, and expanded it. He referred to the U.S. troops amassed in the Persian Gulf, poised to attack the murderous aggressor, Saddam Hussein. Like them, Ramón had "placed himself in harm's way." And he did it on foreign soil, in Panama and in Colombia, far away from the protection drug agents normally afford informants.

"And the bottom line is, he did a damn good job."

So impressed was the government with Ramón's work, Buddy told the judge, that he had decided to make a sentencing recommendation, despite the plea agreement signed in Aruba, in which he was not obligated to recommend anything.

He asked the judge to assign Ramón a "pro forma sentence, to be suspended," to be followed by five years of unsupervised probation. In short, he recommended a walk.

Ramón's attorney, Kadish, could hardly have done more for Ramón than the prosecution had.

Kadish told the judge that Ramón had done "what you see in the movies, and what you see on TV, and that is to really infiltrate the highest levels of the cartel. . . .

"And when Buddy referred to him as an agent, he really has become an agent," much like the DEA agents with whom he worked, Kadish said. "He is a person that they trust, and he trusts them as well, because they have put their lives in each other's hands. . . ."

Finally, Kadish turned to his client.

"Is there anything you would like to say, or have I said it for you?"

Ramón had planned a little speech, a plea for the judge to drop the charges. But he realized he had lost that fight already, and he was afraid he might embarrass himself.

"I think you've said it for me," he replied.

The judge had said virtually nothing so far. Everyone else had said their piece. Now it was time to pronounce judgment—not only on the crimes Ramón admitted but also on the work he had done since.

Judge Hall didn't waste words. He merely said: "The court sentences you under count one to the custody of the Attorney General for three months, sentence suspended. You are placed on probation for five years of unsupervised release."

Buddy moved to dismiss the remaining five counts.

"Motion granted," the judge said. "That concludes the hearing."

Ramón had avoided prison. When he left the Richard B. Russell Building that day and the prosecutor and agents who had directed his life for three and a half years, he did so knowing he would never have to see them again.

He was once again his own man.

But he wasn't entirely free. Despite everything he had done, Ramón had never come to terms with the fact that he had forever changed the life of a friend, Francisco Serrano.

The way Ramón saw it, Francisco's trust in his friendship had put him in jail and had cost Sol Serrano her life. Ramón believed he deserved at least part of the blame for her suicide, and he hated himself for becoming a weasel, a snitch, a betrayer of a friend's trust. If only Francisco hadn't gotten himself arrested in Los Angeles, Ramón brooded. Ramón told himself he could have figured out a way for Francisco to elude arrest.

Skip insisted to Ramón that Francisco's problems were of his own making. "He's the one who volunteered to be a broker and use his connections and make the money," says Skip. "He was raising his hand to put himself and his family in danger to make a buck.

"And he was doing it freely. No coercion," he adds.

To Ramón, that seemed like rationalization. No matter what anyone said, he would always blame himself.

That would be his punishment.

Epilogue

Here is an update on the status of the main characters of the story as of the end of 1993.

THE DEFENDANTS
Francisco Serrano served his sentence in a minimum security prison and was released in 1992. He is currently living in the United States at an undisclosed location.

Eduardo Martínez was sentenced to six and a half years in prison and five years' probation. After testifying for the government in the Noriega trial as a minor witness in 1992, he went into the government's witness protection program while continuing to serve time. He was released Thanksgiving Day 1993 after four years and two months behind bars, and quickly violated the terms of his probation by returning to Colombia.

Clara García and **William Guarin,** the two bankers, maintained their innocence, and Panama eventually dropped its own charges against them and declined to extradite them to the United States. In 1992, García, self-employed in Panama in the medical-supply business, provided information to U.S. authorities in exchange for dropping the charges against her. The government also dropped the case against Guarin, who in 1991 was working in Panama in a computer software company.

Jorge Ochoa turned himself in in Colombia on January 15, 1991. The authorities had promised no extradition. He quietly began serving a six-year prison sentence.

Pablo Escobar, on June 19, 1991, after the new Colombian president and the legislature officially halted extraditions to stop the violence, turned himself in and began serving time in a luxury prison in his home province, guarded by officers of his own choosing. According to some accounts, Escobar's surrender was the price the "Extraditables" paid to stop extraditions and to stop the government from chasing other traffickers who continued to run Escobar's business. Escobar reportedly collected $100 million a month from these traffickers while in prison.

On July 22, 1992, Escobar escaped from prison as Colombian authorities attempted to move him to a more secure facility. He eluded police and a growing number of other enemies until December 2, 1993, when he was gunned down and killed by police in Colombia.

Gerardo Moncada continued to help run the empire during the thirteen months Escobar was in prison, although Escobar came to believe Moncada and others were cheating him. Moncada's tortured body was found in July 1992, along with the bodies of fourteen others, all of whom were believed to have been murdered at Escobar's order. There were reports Moncada had been tortured inside the prison that held Escobar. These developments prompted the attempt to move Escobar, which led to his escape.

Raúl Vivas, Nazareth and Vahe Andonian, and **Juan Carlos Seresi** were convicted after a six-month trial in U.S. District Court in Los Angeles and sentenced in August 1991 to 505 years each without parole. **Ruben Saini** was convicted at the same trial and received a twenty-seven year sentence, again, without parole. U.S. District Judge William D. Keller said when he sentenced them, "The scale of the laundering operation is without parallel. . . ."

Sergio Hochman and Ronel Refining Corporation's **Richard Ferris** pleaded guilty, cooperated with authorities, and testified against the Andonian defendants. Hochman was sentenced to five years, eight months in prison. Ferris was given eight and a half years.

Of the seventeen people originally indicted in the Andonian case, five were convicted and three pleaded guilty. The other nine were exonerated, either through acquittal or dismissal of charges.

Wanis Koyomejian, his son **Simon Kouyoumjian,** and other Ropex defendants indicted separately from the Andonians were scheduled for trial in 1993, but instead pleaded guilty that September. In December 1993, Koyomejian was sentenced to twenty-three years in prison, to be followed by five years of supervised release. His son was given six years, ten months to serve, to be followed by three years' supervised release.

THE INFORMANTS
Drusilla Leightner, the Wells Fargo banker, was laid off, but the DEA compensated her for her cooperation in Polar Cap. She later took a management job in a suburban branch of another bank.

Ramón Costello's whereabouts cannot be published. That was one of the conditions he set when he agreed to be interviewed.

As for the three informants who showed up at DEA–New York, the DEA eventually lost track of them.

THE PROSECUTORS
Russell Hayman left the U.S. Attorney's Office in Los Angeles after the Andonian trial and became assistant to DEA Administrator Robert Bonner, who had been Hayman's boss as U.S. Attorney in Los Angeles. Bonner left DEA in late 1993, after the change in administrations, to enter private practice in Los Angeles.

Buddy Parker was promoted in 1990 to head of the Drug Task Force in Atlanta, replacing his longtime friend, **Craig Gillen,** who moved to Washington, D.C. Gillen became the number two in command of the Iran-Contra Special Counsel's Office under Lawrence Walsh. He returned to Atlanta in 1993 to enter private practice.

THE AGENTS
Most of the primary DEA agents and supervisors in the Atlanta, Los Angeles, and New York investigations—**Skip Latson, Cesar Diaz, John Featherly, Daniel Ortega, Ed Guillen, Michael Orton, Tony Coulson, Kevin Mancini, Phil Devlin,** and **Elaine Harris**—were still within DEA at the beginning of 1994, although some had moved to other offices. This was also true of analyst **Gail Shelby.**

Ron Caffrey, former head of DEA-Atlanta, moved to Washington, D.C., and, by September 1993, had taken the number-three spot at DEA.

Vincent Furtado, who left Los Angeles to run DEA's Providence, Rhode Island, office, was put on administrative leave in 1993 during an investigation into allegedly inappropriate conduct by one of his agents. The investigation was still ongoing at the time of this writing.

Rene De La Cova, former head of DEA's Panama office, pleaded guilty on January 5, 1994, to stealing $700,000 during a money-laundering investigation in Fort Lauderdale, Florida, where he had been working for DEA after his stint in Panama. At the time of this writing he had resigned from the agency and was awaiting sentencing. Prosecutors said in open court they had no evidence he committed other crimes during his DEA career.

On September 7, 1993, Vice President Al Gore recommended that DEA's, Customs's, and IRS's criminal investigators be merged with the FBI as part of an effort to streamline government and eliminate turf battles among law enforcement agencies. The idea quickly died.

A Note on Sources

To learn the story of Operations Fis-Con and Polar Cap, I interviewed agents, officers, supervisors, and administrators from eight federal, state, and local agencies. I talked to defense lawyers, prosecutors, informants, and private citizens. I gleaned details from agents' affidavits, investigative reports, memos, indictments, transcripts, and government press releases. I viewed videotapes and listened to audiotapes, and scoured newspaper stories, magazine pieces, and televised reports. I read books.

Having done so, I am very much aware of the limitless, conflicting interpretations as to the significance of each person's role in the investigation, and even as to what Operation Polar Cap encompassed and whether it was worthwhile. Many people who spent considerable time talking to me will read portions, perhaps much, of this book as a story different from the one they experienced or the one they had hoped I would tell. But in selecting among the many interpretations of how the investigation unfolded, I chose those I judged to be most heavily corroborated and most credible, based on my research.

Even so, the reader should know this book represents only a slice of the story of this massive investigation. I could not tell every development in the case and produce a book with a coherent storyline told in a readable length. Many events I omitted were fascinating or significant or both.

The most important of these was the Ropex portion of the Los Angeles investigation. The book takes only an occasional glance at this probe, which the FBI headed, while concentrating on the Andonian investigation and the DEA. That choice was dictated by the timing of the prosecutions of the two cases. The Andonian case had been tried by the time I began my research, so the DEA permitted its personnel much freedom in talking to me from the beginning of my research. But in the Ropex case a pretrial legal fight and years of appeals delayed the trial. It also delayed my gaining access to FBI agents, because the Bureau prohibits its people from discussing an investigation while the prosecution is pending. In the interim I relied on court documents for information about that case. Finally, after the Ropex defendants pleaded guilty in 1993, I was allowed access to FBI agents, and the prosecutors in the case felt comfortable discussing it, too. By then, I had written my manuscript, and it was in editing; I could only squeeze the FBI viewpoint and pieces of the Ropex investigation into a near-complete book. I wish I could have reported more especially on what Assistant U.S. Attorneys Steven Clymer and Richard Rathmann in Los Angeles found when they pieced together the complicated story of the Ropex operation.

The reader should know how I reported on people's thoughts and recounted conversations I could not possibly have heard. In almost every case where thoughts are revealed, I based them on what that person told me he or she had been thinking. Often, this was corroborated by someone to whom they expressed their feelings at the time. The rare exception involves people who declined to be interviewed, or could not be located, but who expressed their thoughts at the time to someone who was interviewed. Those instances are noted in the chapter notes that follow.

Conversations containing direct quotes generally come from tapes or transcripts of those conversations, which were recorded by federal agents. In a few instances I use direct quotes in reconstructed conversations if the person I interviewed told me that was what he or she said at the time. Conversations not containing quotation marks were reconstructed based on the recollections of people who were there. Where there were conflicting accounts among the people in the conversation, I either reported the conflicts in the text or resolved them based on the totality of my information. In the latter case, I pointed out the conflicts in the chapter notes.

In two cases, I was granted interviews with informants under the condition that I not use their true names. In the case of DEA-Atlanta's informant, I call him Ramón Costello, the pseudonym he used during the investigation. As for the Wells Fargo banker who triggered the Los Angeles investigation, I took her suggestion and use the names she was given at birth, but which she no longer uses, Drusilla Leightner.

List of Interviews

The following list notes the person's role at the time of the events in the book.

Barkett, Dave: Special Agent, DEA, Los Angeles.
Baudoin, Keith: Special Agent, DEA Financial Intelligence Unit, Washington.
Caffrey, Ron: Special Agent in Charge, DEA, Atlanta.
Carhart, Edward: lawyer representing Clara García.
Chalfant, James: lawyer for Richard Ferris, Los Angeles.
Chizever, Carole: Deputy District Attorney, Los Angeles.
Clymer, Steven: Assistant U.S. Attorney, Los Angeles.
Costello, Ramón (pseudonym): informant for DEA, Atlanta.
Coulson, Tony: Special Agent, DEA, Los Angeles.
De La Cova, Rene: Country Attaché, DEA, Panama; before that, second in command of the Panama office.
Devlin, Phil: Special Agent, DEA, New York.
Diaz, Cesar: Special Agent, DEA, Atlanta.
Donelan, Arthur: Special Agent, Customs, New York.
Dudley, Antonio: lawyer representing Banco de Occidente, Panama City, Panama.
Duncan, Alfredo "Fred": Country Attaché, DEA, Panama.
Featherly, John: Group Supervisor, DEA, Atlanta.
Ferrari, Michael: Detective, West Covina, California, Police Department.
Figlia, Manny: Special Agent, DEA, Los Angeles
Furtado, Vincent: Group Supervisor, DEA, Los Angeles.
Gillen, Craig: Lead Attorney, Southeastern Drug Task Force.
Greenberg, Stanley: lawyer for Nazareth Andonian, Los Angeles.
Gregorie, Dick: Assistant U.S. Attorney, Miami.
Guillen, Ed: Special Agent, DEA, New York.

Hansen, David: Special Agent, DEA, Los Angeles.
Harris, Elaine: Group Supervisor, DEA, New York.
Hayman, Russell: Assistant U.S. Attorney, Los Angeles.
Kawahara, Jean: Assistant U.S. Attorney, Los Angeles.
Knudson, Carl: Special Agent, IRS, Los Angeles.
Ladomirak, Deborah: Special Agent, Customs, New York.
Lasso, Edgardo: President, Banking Association of Panama.
Latson, Albert "Skip": Special Agent, DEA, Atlanta.
Lawn, Jack: Administrator, DEA.
Leightner, Drusilla: Special Agent, Investigations Department, Wells Fargo Bank, Los Angeles.
Liebman, Jonathan: Assistant U.S. Attorney, New York.
Lopez, Orlando: Special Agent, California Bureau of Narcotic Enforcement.
Lumpkin, Ralph: Group Supervisor, FBI, Los Angeles.
McCullough, Kelley: pilot, DEA, San Antonio, Texas.
Munroe, Kirk: lawyer representing Banco de Occidente, Miami.
Noonan, Peter, Jr.: Special Agent, Customs, New York.
Orndorff, Michael: Chief, DEA Financial Intelligence Unit, Washington.
Ortega, Dan: Special Agent, DEA, Los Angeles.
Orton, Mike: Special Agent, DEA, Los Angeles.
Parker, Wilmer "Buddy" III: Assistant U.S. Attorney, Atlanta.
Pena, Javier: Special Agent, DEA, Bogotá, Colombia.
Rathmann, Richard: Assistant U.S. Attorney, Los Angeles.
Ricevuto, Tony: Group Supervisor, DEA, Los Angeles.
Richey, William: lawyer representing Banco de Occidente, Miami.
Romero, Alex: Special Agent, DEA, Los Angeles.
Ross, Doug: Chief of Financial and Special Intelligence Section, DEA, Washington.
Saphos, Charles "Chuck": Chief of Narcotic and Dangerous Drug Section, Department of Justice.
Schnapp, Mark: Assistant U.S. Attorney, Miami.
Serrano, Francisco: money launderer and cocaine broker based in Colombia.
Shelby, Gail: Analyst, DEA, Washington, D.C.
Smith, Selby: Special Agent, DEA, Los Angeles.
Stambler, Errol: lawyer in Los Angeles representing Sergio Hochman.
Stephens, Bruce: Special Agent, FBI, Los Angeles.
Stock, Bruce: Country Attaché, DEA, Colombia.
Vazquez-Bello, Clemente: lawyer representing Banco de Occidente, Miami.
Westrate, David: Assistant Administrator for Operations, DEA, Washington.
Whitley, Joe D.: Assistant Attorney General, Washington; later, U.S. Attorney, Atlanta.
Wong, Fred: Special Agent, FBI, Los Angeles.

Notes

Chapter 1: Crossing Over

13 "Ramón Costello was off..." The section on his walk comes mostly from interviews with Ramón Costello, although Buddy Parker, John Featherly, and Skip Latson confirmed that he left them and later told them he had been on a walk.

15 "Back at the Concorde..." The section about Buddy Parker at the bar comes from interviews with him.

17 "Buddy's and Ramón's family histories..." Interviews with Parker and Costello.

18 "But finally a friend from the old days..." Information about Ramón's past drug dealings comes from interviews with him, Parker, and Latson. In addition, details of the cocaine ventures comes from the report Latson wrote about the meeting on Aruba and a 1989 Latson affidavit filed as a Proffer of Evidence in Support of the Government's Prosecution of Eduardo Martínez in the case of *United States* vs. *Pablo Emilio Escobar-Gaviria, et al.,* Indictment No. 1:89-CR-086-WCO (N.D.Ga.).

20 "While fear of arrest had been following Ramón..." The state of the case and Parker's conversations with Mark Kadish are based on interviews with Parker. Kadish declined to be interviewed for this book.

20 "Twenty years!" Ramón's conversations with Kadish are based on interviews with Costello.

21 "Ramón didn't know it, but the prosecutor he feared..." Interviews with Parker.

21 "DEA agent Enrique 'Kiki' Camarena..." From Elaine Shannon, *Desperados:*

Latin Drug Lords, U.S. Lawmen, and the War America Can't Win (New York: Penguin, 1989), pp. 1, 256, 258.

21 "So when these five men gathered . . ." The account of the meeting is based on interviews with Costello, Parker, Latson, and Featherly.

22 "In fact, the five-page letter . . ." Details of the plea agreement come from that letter.

24 "That was what was on Ramón's mind . . ." Interviews with Costello.

24 "Buddy was happier . . ." Interviews with Parker.

24 "The more the feds tried to put Ramón at ease . . ." Accounts of the CI's state of mind come from interviews with him. Parker, Latson, and Featherly all said he was extremely nervous, and that it was difficult to establish rapport with him. All four discussed the other events in this section.

25 "Charlie's Bar sits . . ." The account of that night comes from interviews with Costello, Parker, and the two drug agents.

26 "Over the next few days . . ." Information in these two paragraphs comes from the four men who were there.

26 "It would be three months . . ." Interviews with Costello, Latson, and Parker.

Chapter 2: Choosing Lures

28 "Ron Caffrey had a plan . . ." Information about Caffrey's plans for a money-laundering case and what he wanted out of it comes from interviews with Caffrey. The description of what kind of boss he was comes from agents who worked under him—Skip Latson, John Featherly, Cesar Diaz, and Ed Guillen.

The fact that the New York DEA office was the largest comes from DEA spokesmen in New York, Washington, Miami, and Los Angeles. That it was the most competitive comes from a number of agents around the country, including some who spent time in New York.

29 "The drug business generated far too much money . . ." The explanation of drug money laundering comes from a variety of interviews (Caffrey, Guillen, Parker, Latson), as well as the following sources: John J. Fialka, "How a Big Drug Cartel Laundered $1.2 Billion with Aid of U.S. Firms," *The Wall Street Journal,* March 1, 1990; Evan Lowell Maxwell, "Gold, Drugs and Clean Cash," *Los Angeles Times Magazine,* February 18, 1990; Peter Ross Range and Gordon Witkin, "The Drug Money Hunt: Narcotic Warriors Target Dealers' Cash as Well as Their Stash," *U.S. News & World Report,* August 21, 1989.

29 "But at DEA, money-laundering probes clashed . . ." Interviews with Featherly, Latson, Michael Orton, and Tony Ricevuto. The story about the badge comes from Parker and Latson.

30 "The Federal Bureau of Investigation had provided . . ." Details on Operation Bancoshares come from an August 4, 1981, FBI press release and the 1981 *Annual Report of The Attorney General of The United States.* The fact that some people believed the FBI helped rather than hurt drug lords in that investigation comes from several DEA and Justice Department sources, including Guillen, Ricevuto, and former Assistant U.S. Attorney Mark Schnapp of Miami.

30 "Only one Atlanta agent spoke Spanish." Interviews with Cesar Diaz and Caffrey.

30 "None of that daunted Caffrey." What Caffrey wanted and did comes from interviews with him, with Featherly and Latson contributing.

30 "Like Caffrey, Skip Latson was looking . . ." The information in this paragraph and the next comes from interviews with Latson.

31 "Featherly did not immediately warm . . ." The information in this paragraph comes mainly from Featherly.

31 "Besides, no one was suggesting . . ." These comments about the dual nature of the Atlanta investigation come from Featherly, Latson, and Caffrey.

31 "In fact, no one was more eager . . ." Costello's views and what he did in Colombia come from the interviews with him.

32 "So one day in the fall of 1986 . . ." Interviews with Featherly, Latson, and Caffrey.

The fact that the case would lead them into "the biggest money laundry ever uncovered" comes from Attorney General Richard Thornburgh's press release of February 22, 1989, and remarks by DEA Administrator Jack Lawn at a March 29, 1989, press conference.

32 "Ramón knew what it would take . . ." This section on Costello and Francisco Serrano comes from interviews with them, with some corroboration from DEA reports.

33 "On Wednesday, October 15, 1986 . . ." The telephone call is based on a DEA transcript, which the DEA translated into English, and the tape itself.

34 "The next day, Skip officially . . ." Latson's case initiation report.

34 "They acquired a particularly useful technique . . ." Information on Operation Pisces comes from then–Assistant U.S. Attorney Russell Hayman of Los Angeles; Pisces DEA case supervisor in L.A., Tony Ricevuto; Parker; Latson; Featherly; DEA agent Alex Romero; and West Covina, California, Detective Michael Ferrari, formerly assigned to help DEA, as well as other local officers and DEA personnel.

34 "This technique dispelled . . ." Interviews with Featherly.

34 "The DEA agents in Los Angeles . . ." The next two paragraphs come from Caffrey, Featherly, and Latson.

34 "Alex Romero, a Pisces agent . . ." The information in these next three paragraphs comes from Romero.

35 "The Atlanta agents weren't keen . . ." Interviews with Featherly, Latson, and Caffrey.

35 "At the same time, the Atlanta agents were roughing out . . ." The information in this paragraph comes primarily from Latson.

36 "For the money launderer . . ." The information in these three paragraphs comes from Costello, Featherly, Latson, and Caffrey.

36 "Featherly's assumed character . . ." Featherly provided the information in these two paragraphs about creating his undercover character. Information about football player Jim Brown comes from David L. Porter, ed., *Biographical Dictionary of American Sports, Football* (New York: 1987).

36 "For Jimmy Brown's sidekick . . ." The information in this paragraph comes from Featherly, Latson, and Diaz.

36 "Skip had no undercover role . . ." The information in these four paragraphs about Latson and Costello comes mostly from Latson, but several agents discussed how relationships with informants should work.

37 "Skip and Ramón were very different . . ." The information about Latson's background in the rest of this section comes from him; Costello's personal history and the thoughts attributed to him come from interviews with him.

38 "In Atlanta, DEA agents were fashioning . . ." Interviews with the Atlanta agents, Costello and Serrano.

38 "Persuading these people to come to Atlanta . . ." Costello talked about the Colombians' reluctance to come to Atlanta; so did Buddy Parker.

An Atlanta Chamber of Commerce spokesman confirmed the use of the phrase "New International City." The information about the Spanish-language radio show comes from Joe Shifalo, a founder and former station manager of WRFG-Radio.

38 "Others might hang back . . ." Serrano said he was eager to get started.

38 "By the end of January 1987 . . ." Information about Jaime Parra comes from Costello, Serrano, and DEA reports.

39 "Regardless, Serrano and his potential customer . . ." This paragraph is based on interviews with Latson and on DEA reports.

39 "The prospect of the first undercover meeting . . ." This comes from Latson and Diaz.

39 "On January 20 . . ." Information about the death of agent Raymond Stastny comes mostly from these newspaper stories, all in *The Atlanta Journal*: Steven W. Ricks and Gail Epstein, "Agent Wounded, Suspect Is Killed in Drug Shoot-out," January 21, 1987; Gail Epstein and Steven W. Ricks, "Man Who Shot Agent Knew He Was Being Watched, DEA Says," January 21, 1987; and Gayle White, "Federal Drug Agent Dies of Wounds from Buckhead Shootout," January 27, 1987.

Chapter 3: Going Under

40 "On a Saturday night in a Holiday Inn . . ." DEA report pertaining to the meeting, and interviews with Skip Latson.

40 "If Serrano was worried . . ." The account of what transpired at the restaurant and the following day comes from interviews with Latson, Costello, and Serrano, as well as a DEA report.

41 "Under the DEA scenario . . ." Described to me by Latson, John Featherly, and Ron Caffrey.

41 "At 6:10 P.M. Monday, February 2 . . ." The details of this meeting come from a DEA report and interviews with Featherly, Costello, and Serrano.

42 "And for that, the DEA rented . . ." The renting of the rooms comes from DEA reports.

42 "Aimed across the bed . . ." The DEA videotape of the meeting provided this information.

42 "When Serrano arrived at 1:00 P.M. . . ." Details about this meeting come from DEA reports, the videotape, and interviews with Featherly, Serrano, and Costello. Dialogue comes from the videotape, transcribed by me. (Citizens & Southern Bank later merged with NationsBank.)

47 "When they showed up at the Ritz-Carlton's restaurant..." Information about what happened over lunch comes from a DEA report and interviews with Featherly.

47 "At his office at DEA..." Details of the call Cesar Diaz made to Alex Romero and those agents' thoughts about that call and the fact Parra had used his American Express card come from interviews with Diaz and Romero.

48 "Less than six hours after..." Jaime Parra's arrival in Los Angeles is described in a DEA report. I also used the interviews with DEA agent David Hansen and Detective Michael Ferrari of the West Covina Police Department for the information that follows.

48 "That agent, Dave Hansen..." That Romero "razzed" Hansen was told to me by agents Hansen and Romero.

48 "Over the next three days..." Details of the Parra surveillance come from Ferrari, Hansen, and a DEA report.

49 "A master at countersurveillance techniques..." Methods criminals in general and Parra in particular used to shake police surveillance were described to me by Ferrari, Hansen, and Romero.

49 "During the three days Parra..." What Hansen thought and some information about the surveillance comes from interviews with Hansen. Again, I used a DEA report for more details of the surveillance.

50 "Tipping off the suspect..." Several law enforcement officers, including Detective Ferrari, agents Hansen and Romero, and DEA supervisor Tony Ricevuto, told me about the risk that a suspect could spot surveillance.

50 "Parra and his passenger traveled..." Parra's route through L.A.-area neighborhoods and on to Las Vegas was described by Hansen and a DEA report. Hansen also described his thoughts at the time, and Parra's driving techniques.

51 "Parra bypassed the registration desk..." Details on the trip to Caesars Palace come from interviews with Hansen.

51 "He drove out of the casino district..." Information about Parra going to the Sheffield Inn and registering comes from a DEA report and was confirmed by Hansen.

51 "The five cops and agents followed suit..." Information about what the officers did at the Sheffield comes from interviews with Hansen.

52 "At 7:30 A.M., one of the cops..." The fact that Parra was gone comes from a DEA report and from the Hansen interviews. So do the officers' actions after that.

52 "They could not be certain..." This comes from Hansen.

52 "If Parra was spooked badly..." The potential for scaring off Parra comes from Romero, and was confirmed by Parra's later conduct, as told by Costello.

52 "Later the cops would learn..." Hansen said this.

52 "Before his sudden jaunt to Las Vegas..." That Parra had been preparing a money pickup for Jimmy Brown's laundry comes from an interview with Hansen.

52 "A couple of days after the Las Vegas fiasco..." Featherly and Diaz told me of flying to Los Angeles, not knowing of Parra's sudden disappearance days earlier.

52 "Serrano passed this along to Ramón . . ." Interviews with Costello and Latson.

52 "Featherly, as Jimmy Brown . . ." The scenario for the Los Angeles meeting comes from interviews with Featherly, Latson, Diaz, and Costello, as well as DEA reports.

52 "The team in L.A. told Featherly . . ." DEA-L.A. supervisor Tony Ricevuto said in interviews he advised Featherly not to come to Los Angeles.

53 "It was after 9:00 P.M. . . ." Details of the meeting at the Tango Bar come from interviews with Featherly, Diaz, and Costello, as well as a DEA report.

54 "Cesar was, in fact, quite eager." Diaz's personal history, his thoughts at the time, and his relationship to Stastny come from interviews with Diaz.

55 "At 7:00 P.M. the next evening . . ." The details about what the surveillance agents saw come from their report. In addition, Costello described in an interview the route he took.

55 "Ramón finally pulled the Cutlass . . ." Costello described what he and Serrano did at the Victory Boulevard apartment complex. DEA reports supplied further detail, such as the apartment number, and the fact that it was the same place Parra's couriers had visited the week before.

56 "They talked about finding the fastest way . . ." Costello told me about this conversation and the incident in the cul-de-sac.

56 "He never even noticed the Mercury." In interviews, Serrano said he never noticed that he was being followed. As for his eagerness to get rich, several undercover agents, as well as Costello, told me Serrano mentioned this to them.

56 "The pair showed up at the Sheraton . . ." Information about Serrano and Costello taking the shoebox to Featherly comes from two DEA reports and interviews with Featherly, Diaz, Costello, and Serrano. Their accounts differed slightly:

A DEA surveillance report said Serrano and Costello first met with undercover agents at the Tango Bar before Serrano returned to the car to retrieve the shoebox to take it to the room upstairs. Another DEA report, which Diaz wrote and Featherly signed, said Serrano brought the box to Featherly at the hotel restaurant, and that Featherly told him to take it to the room upstairs with undercover agent Jack Harvey.

The account Featherly gave in interviews matches Diaz's report, except that Featherly said he chided Serrano for bringing him the shoebox full of money. Diaz's report is silent on that.

Costello also said Serrano took the box to Featherly at the bar, that Featherly refused to accept it and directed him upstairs. But Costello said he did not remember Featherly getting angry at Serrano.

In interviews, Serrano told a story different from anyone else's. Asked about the conflicts, he said he did not remember many details. Where Serrano's story conflicts with others', I have disregarded his account.

56 "Waiting upstairs with Cesar . . ." The account of what unfolded upstairs is based on interviews with Diaz and Orlando Lopez, and Diaz's report.

58 "Serrano told Ramón later . . ." This comes from interviews with Costello; Serrano said he did not remember it.

58 "Next door to the money counting . . ." Diaz's DEA report contains information about the agents next door and their surveillance.

58 "When he returned to the Tango Bar downstairs . . ." Interviews with Costello.

58 "As for the shoebox . . ." In interviews, agents Romero and Ed Guillen described what they did with the money. I also saw DEA reports on it.

58 "But before all that happened . . ." Details about the dinner at the Ravel come from interviews with Featherly, Diaz, Costello, and Serrano.

58 "And when they were finally done . . ." This comes from a DEA surveillance report.

Chapter 4: Testing Ramón

59 "Eight days after that first money pickup . . ." The account of what the surveillance agents saw that day is based on interviews with Detective Michael Ferrari of the West Covina Police Department. The timing comes from Latson.

60 "That evening, Ramón spotted . . ." Interviews with Costello.

60 "The next morning, Ramón called his contact . . ." Costello told me of the call to his contact agent, which fits with what agents Latson and Romero said. Costello and Latson also told me of their conversation.

60 "Ramón didn't know why . . ." This comes from Costello, as do details of what happened at the Days Inn.

61 "On this particular morning . . ." Information about that morning's events comes from interviews with Featherly, Latson, and Costello.

61 "We want to know . . ." Details of the interrogation come from interviews with Featherly, Latson, and Costello, and from a report written at the time that was read to me.

62 "But in Los Angeles . . ." Supervisor Tony Ricevuto in L.A. told me this.

62 "For his part, Ramón was angry . . ." Interviews with Costello gave me this, as well as his attitude toward L.A.'s Group 6.

63 "Once he got back to Colombia . . ." That Parra told Costello he and one of his couriers had spotted the surveillance comes from interviews with Costello and from a DEA report.

63 "U.S. cops weren't all . . ." The same DEA report.

63 "Eventually, word would get to the Los Angeles DEA . . ." Interviews with Hansen and Ricevuto. Hansen and Romero said the agents suspected at the time that their surveillance had been burned.

63 "It pleased Ramón . . ." Interviews with Costello.

63 "Without Parra, the Atlanta money laundry . . ." Costello told of drawing in the Ospinas, which was also reported in DEA reports.

63 "On March 13, Juan Ospina's couriers . . ." Details of the transactions come from DEA reports and from an interview with Romero.

64 "The money represented . . ." This is based on a $14,000 per kilogram wholesale price, which was the going rate at the time, according to a DEA report.

64 "But on the day of the third pickup . . ." The account of Serrano's conversations with Romero comes from an interview with Romero.

64 "The surveillance cops could see..." From interviews with Romero and Detective Michael Ferrari. Serrano denied wiping the steering wheel.

64 "Romero offered to drive..." Serrano says Romero did not offer to help him find his car. Interview with Serrano.

65 "Meanwhile, other surveillance crews had followed..." The account of the parking lot incident and related surveillance leading to the raids on Llano Street and Manning Avenue comes mostly from Ferrari interviews and DEA reports, as well as a December 10, 1987, case memorandum produced by DEA-Atlanta.

65 "The ledger did not give..." Information on the ledger comes mostly from a DEA report, supplemented by interviews with Ferrari and DEA analyst Gail Shelby.

66 "In Colombia, the incident left Ospina steaming." A DEA report and interviews with Costello.

66 "The luckless Serrano..." Serrano told me he had bought the toys for his son.

66 "The Atlanta investigation kept sputtering and stalling..." Various DEA reports and interviews with Latson, Diaz, and Parker provided this information.

66 "As bad as business was..." The information about Operation Pisces and Attorney General Edwin Meese's announcement comes from reports aired May 6, 1987, on CNN, supplemented with information from former Assistant U.S. Attorney Russell Hayman.

67 "The smuggling part of the Atlanta probe..." Interviews with Costello, Latson, and Parker, as well as DEA reports.

67 "Finally, in June, they found..." Information about Carlos Restrepo's appearance in the Atlanta case and his meetings with Costello comes from interviews with Latson and Costello.

67 "On Friday, June 12..." The account of Costello learning of Restrepo's arrest comes from Costello and a CNN report. Details on Operation Cashweb-Expressway come from a June 12, 1987, Justice Department press release, reports on CNN, and a story by Stephen J. Hedges and Jeff Leen, "FBI Arrests 41 in Drug Money Sting," *Miami Herald,* June 13, 1987.

68 "He called Skip at home." The conversations between Costello and Latson were recounted to me by them.

68 "As soon as Skip hung up..." Interviews with Latson and Parker.

Chapter 5: Glimpsing a Gold Mine

70 "Finally, in the summer of 1987..." Interviews with Latson and Parker; DEA reports.

70 "Stepping up a rung, Ramón met Nicolás Ramírez..." Background on Ramírez comes from Costello and Serrano, as well as a DEA report.

70 "Ramírez told Ramón the air route..." Interviews with Parker and Latson.

70 "He took Ramón to meet him." The trip to the brokerage house is based on interviews with Costello, a DEA report, and Skip Latson's affidavit of September 7, 1989, offered as the government's Proffer of Evidence in Support of the Government's Prosecution of Eduardo Martínez and filed in the case of *United States* vs. *Pablo Emilio Escobar-Gaviria, et al.,* Indictment No. 1:89-CR-086-WCO (N.D.Ga.)

71 "It looked like the load would fly..." Information about the trip to Atlanta and the California partner comes from interviews with Latson, DEA agent Michael Moren's testimony, June 30, 1988, in the case of *United States* vs. *Alvaro J. Echavarría-Olarte, et al.,* Indictment No. CR 89-0598-CAL (N.D.Cal.), and DEA transcripts of conversations from that trip.

71 "and DEA–San Francisco soon learned the truth..." This and information about the case in California come from interviews with Latson and Parker.

71 "John Featherly knew the Sevilla well." Featherly and Diaz provided the information in this paragraph.

72 "Traveling in separate cars..." Interviews with Diaz and Featherly and a DEA report provided information about the meeting at the Sevilla.

73 "Two weeks later, that call came." Information about this money delivery and the two following pickups comes from interviews with Diaz; a December 10, 1987, memo by the DEA-Atlanta office; and the Latson affidavit.

73 "Jimmy Brown's laundry was great..." The fact that the laundry was slow, irritating its customers, comes from interviews with Costello, Diaz, Featherly, and Latson. The chain of events the slowness triggered was reported to me by Latson.

74 "The Atlanta laundry was taking a week..." This comes from interviews with Latson and Diaz and from DEA reports.

74 "The money had to go through Atlanta for venue purposes..." Interviews with Latson, Parker, and Ed Guillen provided details as to the money's route.

75 "Real money laundries, if they are big enough..." Interviews with Guillen.

75 "Juan Ospina was plenty hot..." Interviews with Featherly and Diaz and a DEA report gave information about Serrano's conversation with the agents at the Sheraton Grande.

75 "The following month in Medellín..." Details of the meeting with Martínez come chiefly from interviews with Costello, although Serrano, a DEA report, and Martínez's indictment in Atlanta also provided information.

76 "Black market money exchanges..." Interviews with Latson, Guillen, and Serrano.

76 "Only the world's biggest traffickers..." Interviews with Latson.

76 "At the wholesale U.S. price..." A DEA report at the time put the wholesale price of cocaine at $14,000 a kilogram.

76 "It seemed incredible..." Interviews with Latson and DEA-L.A. supervisor Tony Ricevuto.

77 "Perhaps sensing disbelief, Martínez pulled out a ledger..." Interviews with Costello and the Latson affidavit.

77 "The group, said Martínez..." What Martínez said about La Mina comes mostly from interviews with Costello and Latson, supplemented by the Latson affidavit, interviews with Serrano, and DEA reports.

77 "Ramón and Serrano accepted Martínez's offer..." Interviews with Costello, Serrano, Latson, and Parker.

78 "Nicolás Ramírez was steaming..." The accounts of Ramírez's anger and embarrassment come from interviews with Costello, who had firsthand knowledge of his reaction, and Latson and Parker, who were told about Ramírez by Costello and Serrano.

78 "Ramírez knew everyone..." Interviews with Costello and Serrano.

78 "It was time to visit the compound..." Interviews with Costello; DEA reports; the Latson affidavit in Support of the Government's Prosecution of Eduardo Martínez; and *United States* vs. *Pablo Emilio Escobar-Gaviria, et al.,* Indictment No. 1:89-CR-086-WCO (N.D.Ga.).

78 "As the man in charge..." Gaviria's importance to Escobar is based on interviews with Costello, Latson, and Parker, and the testimony of DEA agent Michael Moren, June 30, 1988, in the case of the *United States* vs. *Alvaro J. Echavarría-Olarte, et. al.,* Indictment No. CR 89-0598-CAL (N.D.Cal.)

79 "On Wednesday, October 21..." Costello described this trip in interviews. The date came from a DEA report and the Martínez indictment.

79 "At the house..." Costello described the house, what took place inside it, and his thoughts at the time. Separately, Serrano described the house the same way Costello had, and I also drew from the Latson affidavit.

80 "Ramón had met Ochoa twice before." Information about those meetings comes from DEA reports and interviews with Costello and Parker.

80 "In fact, Ramón's ability..." Interviews with Parker and Latson.

80 "Nodding to his associate..." The conversation between Costello, Ramírez, and Ochoa has been reconstructed based on Costello's recollection.

81 "Now Ramón knew he was in trouble." Interviews with Costello. Serrano said in interviews that he was angry once Costello told him.

82 "Ramón did not want to call..." Interviews with Costello.

82 "In his room, he was still..." The telephone conversation was reconstructed based on Costello's recollections, with the basic tone confirmed by Serrano, who gave slightly different details.

82 "Over breakfast..." In interviews, Serrano confirmed this meeting and the gist of the conversation; Costello gave more details.

83 "Finally, Serrano agreed..." In separate interviews, Costello and Serrano described the trip to the compound. Some details come from the Latson affidavit.

83 "The men shook hands..." Most of the account of this meeting is based on Costello's recollections and the Latson affidavit, with Serrano supplementing and confirming key elements. Both men, in separate interviews, said Gaviria brought Escobar into the meeting.

83 "Excuse me, Don Pablo..." The account of Serrano bailing out Costello comes from Costello.

84 "But in the account Ramón gives..." Interviews with Costello and the Latson affidavit. The numbers and details of the proposal come mostly from the Latson affidavit.

84 "Maybe it would be better..." Interviews with Costello and Serrano; Latson affidavit.

84 "No, that would not do..." The discussion between Serrano and Escobar is based on Costello's account and the Latson affidavit.

84 "Escobar turned to Ramón." Interviews with Costello; Latson affidavit.

84 "Ramón told him . . ." This, as well as the rest of the account of this meeting, comes from the Costello interviews and the Latson affidavit. Serrano said he recalled few of these details, but did confirm the use of the map.

85 "That this package was rejected . . ." Interviews with Costello.

85 "All the way back . . ." Costello described the conversation in the ride back to town and at the Inter-Continental; Serrano did not discuss the conversations, but did describe his feelings after the meeting.

85 "He hopped in his car . . ." Interviews with Costello.

86 "The conversation started as usual . . ." I base my account of this conversation on Costello's and Latson's recollections.

Chapter 7: Revelations

87 "Skip flew Ramón up . . ." Information about the debriefing comes from interviews with Costello and Latson, and the Latson affidavit of September 7, 1989, which was based on the DEA report Latson wrote at the time of the debriefing.

87 "Caffrey knew he had . . ." Interviews with Ron Caffrey.

87 "Flamboyant, Louisiana-born Barry Seal . . ." Information about Seal comes from Guy Gugliotta and Jeff Leen, *Kings of Cocaine* (New York: Simon & Schuster, 1989), pp. 146, 234–36.

87 "Caffrey was especially familiar . . ." Ibid., p. 168.

88 "Caffrey figured Ramón would be rendered useless . . ." Interviews with Caffrey and Parker.

88 "So, while he would brief the head . . ." Caffrey, Parker, and Jack Lawn interviews.

88 "Ramón noted the excitement . . ." Interviews with Costello, Latson, and Featherly.

88 "With or without a microphone . . ." The discussion of luring Escobar out of the compound is based on interviews with Latson, Caffrey, Parker, and Costello.

89 "Skip was talking to a Colombian . . ." Interviews with Latson; DEA report.

89 "Ever since the Pisces takedown . . ." Interviews with Latson and Diaz, as well as a DEA report on Serrano's attempts to drum up business.

89 "In an ostensibly routine traffic stop . . ." Information about Ochoa's arrest comes from Gugliotta and Leen, *Kings of Cocaine,* pp. 309–10.

89 "The United States wanted Ochoa . . ." Ibid., pp. 275–78; interview with Parker.

89 "The chance for extradition was slim . . ." Interviews with Parker and Chuck Saphos, then Chief of the Justice Department's Narcotic and Dangerous Drug Section.

89 "It was the Monday after Thanksgiving . . ." The dates and sums of money pickups come from a DEA-Atlanta memo prepared for a December 12, 1987, meeting; an interview with California Bureau of Narcotic Enforcement agent Orlando Lopez; and the indictment *United States* vs. *Pablo Emilio Escobar-Gaviria, et al.,* Indictment No. 1:89-CR-086-WCO (N.D.Ga).

89 "Jimmy Brown's laundry was just too slow . . ." Interviews with Serrano,

Costello, Diaz, and Featherly, with specific complaints and details of conversations coming from a DEA report of a meeting with Serrano.

90 "As a Glendale police officer..." Information about Lopez comes from an interview with him.

90 "Serrano had missed him." A DEA report contained this information, as well as the remaining details of that conversation with Serrano.

91 "Ramón says they had no plans..." Interview with Costello.

91 "No matter what Serrano said..." The lack of improvement in the Atlanta laundry is based on interviews with Latson, Featherly, and Costello, and on the fact that Martínez still complained about the slowness, according to DEA reports.

91 "Still, the money kept coming." Information about the money deliveries comes from an interview with Lopez, from several DEA reports, and from the Martínez indictment.

91 "some of the biggest drug lords in the world." That Martínez counted them as his clients comes from interviews with Diaz, Latson, and Parker, as well as DEA reports and the Martínez indictment.

91 "Serrano loved getting all that money." Interview with Lopez, and a DEA report about that conversation.

91 "but *Forbes* had just come out..." A DEA report and *Kings of Cocaine,* p. 337.

91 "Ochoa, and José Gonzálo Rodríguez Gacha, among others." Serrano would later say he had never met drug kingpin José Gacha, although Lopez says Serrano had boasted about knowing three of the men *Forbes* listed. Interview with Serrano.

91 "Serrano kept bragging..." From interview with Lopez and a DEA report about the conversation.

92 "Though outwardly cheerful..." Interview with Lopez.

92 "To do that, the L.A. agents and cops..." From interviews with Lopez, Latson, Romero, and DEA group supervisor Tony Ricevuto.

92 "But in Atlanta, Buddy Parker wanted..." Parker, Caffrey, Featherly, Latson, and Diaz all told me in interviews they wanted to make as comprehensive a case as possible.

92 "In the United States, federal officials..." Interviews with Joe D. Whitley, then an assistant attorney general; Saphos and Parker provided information about the government's review of the cases against Ochoa.

92 "He found himself at a conference table..." Sign-in sheet from the December 10, 1987, meeting. Parker, Latson, and others described the accomplishments of the people on the list, some of whom are also named in *Kings of Cocaine.*

93 "As impressive as the cartel indictment had been to Buddy..." Interviews with Parker.

93 "Gregorie and Schnapp, for example, wondered uneasily..." Interview with Mark Schnapp, now a private defense attorney in Miami. Dick Gregorie, now a state prosecutor in Miami, did not mention this concern when recalling the meeting.

93 "The focus of their uneasiness..." Interview with Schnapp.

93 "Saphos and others from main Justice..." Interviews with Parker and Saphos.

94 "Atlanta was first up." Agenda of the December 10, 1987, meeting.

94 "Featherly gave the group an overview..." The agenda; interviews with Featherly and Latson. A December 10, 1987, memo DEA-Atlanta prepared for the meeting provided more detail about Atlanta's presentation.

94 "Miami's case against Ochoa..." General information on the Miami indictment comes from interviews with Gregorie and Schnapp, but details come from *Kings of Cocaine*.

94 "But as Saphos pointed out..." Interviews with Parker. Saphos did not recall details of this meeting.

94 " 'I went berserk'..." Interviews with Parker.

94 "This was the opening to disclose..." Interviews with Parker. Featherly, Latson, and others said La Mina was discussed.

95 "The CI, who had met with Martínez again..." Latson interviews and DEA reports.

95 "From the Los Angeles delegation..." That there was skepticism came from interviews with Parker, Caffrey, Whitley, Featherly, and Ricevuto.

95 "No, the money launderer had shown..." Interviews with Parker, Featherly, and Latson.

95 "By this time, the Atlanta group was certain..." In interviews, Parker, Featherly, Latson, and Caffrey told me they were sure of the CI.

95 "Ricevuto believed nothing Atlanta's CI said." Interview with Ricevuto.

95 "The Atlanta delegation sensed condescension..." Interviews with Parker and Latson supplied that. Parker also told me the thoughts I attributed to him in the next few sentences.

95 "Skip described it further..." Interviews with Parker.

95 "The idea of gold imports..." That Fred Duncan laughed at the idea comes from interviews with Parker, Latson, and Ricevuto.

96 "Gregorie, who had heard evidence..." Interview with Gregorie.

96 "neither was anyone eager to surface Ramón..." Interviews with Parker.

96 "The Atlanta group was washing..." The December 10, 1987, memo and the Martínez indictment.

97 "In the investigations department..." This segment comes primarily from interviews with the banker, who agreed to talk on the condition I not disclose the name she uses now. (She suggested I use her maiden name, Drusilla Leightner.) The contour of her story was confirmed by DEA agents Michael Orton and David Barkett.

99 "In all, the documents showed..." The $25 million figure comes from the February 1989 search warrant affidavit of FBI agent Bruce R. Stephens and DEA Agent Lance C. Williams's affidavit of November 1, 1988, in support of a petition for electronic surveillance.

99 "The telephone message..." Interview with Barkett.

Chapter 8: A Million-Dollar Ticket

101 "Eduardo Martínez was sending so much money..." DEA reports and an interview with Detective Orlando Lopez.

101 "Nearly a year had passed..." Based on seizures reported in a February 23, 1988, agenda prepared by the Atlanta DEA team for a meeting on Operation Fis-Con.

101 "There was no need to check..." Interviews with Latson and Featherly.

102 "The chance seemed to come on January 5, 1988..." The account of the events of this day is based on interviews with Lopez and DEA agent Alex Romero, a California Bureau of Narcotic Enforcement report, and a DEA report.

103 "'Just over one,' came the answer." The BNE report, which Lopez wrote, contains this direct quote.

103 "Officer John Enriquez said he spotted..." The Garden Grove Police Department's arrest report of Ramier Restrepo provided details on the traffic stop, and what transpired at the police station.

104 "Back at the Carl's Jr...." The interview with Lopez and the BNE report provided information on the wait for Alvarez and the resumption of money pickups that day.

104 "That the cops in L.A. had taken $1 million..." Interviews with Costello and Latson.

104 "At 1:00 P.M. on the day after the seizure..." Latson and Costello told me how the calls were placed. The time and the content of the two conversations come from government transcripts of the taped telephone calls. (The transcripts included the original Spanish and the government's English translation.)

106 "That was the name Serrano used..." Interviews with Serrano and Costello.

106 "That night on the phone..." A government transcript.

106 "But Ramón realized that at the moment..." Interview with Costello.

106 "The first reaction in Medellín..." The account of the questioning Serrano underwent comes chiefly from my interviews with him.

106 "'He had to answer for that money'..." Interview with Serrano. The importance of the car in placing blame for the $1 million loss was told to me by Latson and Serrano.

107 "When Martínez was done questioning Serrano..." Interviews with Serrano provided details of his further interrogation. The fact of the questioning is corroborated by a DEA report and a government transcript of a telephone conversation between Costello and Serrano that night.

108 "an engineering degree..." Interviews with Serrano; DEA report.

108 "Here in Moncada's office..." Serrano described the questioning.

108 "A couple days later, Martínez called..." Interviews with Serrano.

108 "Martínez took Serrano to a different location..." Interviews with Serrano. The description of Moncada comes from Serrano, Costello, and a DEA drawing of him.

109 "Losing $1 million was not something..." Martínez's reaction to the loss is based on his conversations later that month with Costello and Diaz, who recounted them to me. Latson, Diaz, and Parker discussed the dynamics of the situation and why it would continue to trouble Martínez.

109 "Martínez asked Serrano to hire a lawyer..." This is based on a translated government transcript of a January 11, 1988, conversation between Costello and Martínez.

109 "he wanted to meet the men behind the business." Interviews with Costello, Latson, and Parker. The DEA report of their eventual meeting said Martínez repeated several times that he had wanted to meet them.

109 "This struck the agents in Atlanta as good news and bad news." Interviews with Caffrey, Latson, and Diaz.

110 "The business meeting was set . . ." Government transcript of the January 11, 1988, telephone conversation between Costello and Martínez provided details on the planned meeting, as did interviews with Latson and Diaz.

110 "A grand jury in Miami was poised to indict General Manuel Noriega . . ." Noriega was indicted February 4, 1988, according to Kevin Buckley, *Panama: The Whole Story* (New York: Simon & Schuster, 1991). Buckley wrote that newspapers had been reporting the possibility for months.

110 "In Panama at that point, a drug agent . . ." Interviews with Caffrey, Parker, and Latson. However, DEA personnel who worked in Panama at the time —Country Attaché Fred Duncan and his second in command, Rene De La Cova—told me they did not feel uneasy about drug enforcement in Panama at that point. De La Cova said he sensed corruption in Panamanian drug enforcement only after the Noriega indictment.

DEA's relationship with the Panamanian government before the indictment has been the subject of controversy. Duncan has maintained Noriega and his Panamanian Defense Forces cooperated with DEA until the indictment. In fact, at trial, the Noriega defense offered a letter from Duncan praising Noriega's anti-drug efforts and even brought Duncan to the stand as a defense witness. However, prosecutors proved to the satisfaction of a jury that Noriega allowed his country to be used by Colombian drug lords as a transshipment point for cocaine and as a hiding place for dirty money —while keeping up the appearance of cooperation with the DEA.

110 "If Caffrey was going to send agents . . ." Interviews with Caffrey.

110 "Skip wanted four . . ." Latson says he recalls asking for at least four, and probably five agents for the assignment. Caffrey says his recollection is vague, but he believed the request was for three or four agents.

110 "Caffrey pleaded with Washington . . ." Interviews with Latson. Caffrey, too, said he asked for the backup.

110 "Two agents only . . ." Interviews with Latson, who also described why he and Diaz would be those two agents.

111 "But Cesar was still green . . ." Diaz discussed his experience at that point.

111 "Caffrey worried about Cesar . . ." Caffrey discussed his concerns. Diaz discussed his relationship with Stastny's widow.

111 "Caffrey told Cesar he did not have to accept . . ." Interviews with Caffrey and Diaz.

That Featherly had been transferred out of Atlanta comes from Featherly; the difficulty of getting him involved in this comes from Caffrey and Latson.

111 "it was important for Skip to be there." Interviews with Latson.

112 "For Ramón, the trip . . ." Interviews with Costello.

Chapter 9: Panama

113 "It was night when Ramón and Cesar reached . . ." Information about their arrival in Panama comes from interviews with Diaz and Costello; the details on time and date from a DEA report. That Costello took the wheel comes from both men.

114 "It was also where the DEA . . ." That U.S. agents stayed at the Marriott comes from Michael Levine, *Deep Cover* (New York: Delacorte, 1990).

114 "From the time they stepped off the plane . . ." Interviews with Diaz.

114 "In fact, when he and Ramón . . ." That the two were being watched comes from a DEA report, and interviews with Diaz and Costello.

114 "Ramón and Cesar checked into rooms . . ." The DEA report and interviews with Diaz and Costello.

114 "Ramón was walking down . . ." Costello and Diaz recounted the events of that evening early the next morning when they slipped away to meet Skip Latson. Latson recorded their recollections that morning. Later, I copied and transcribed that tape.

114 "The men exchanged greetings." This conversation has been reconstructed based on Costello's recollection as told that morning to Latson and later to me.

115 "The trio arrived at Room 1018 . . ." The account of this meeting comes from the Latson tape and from interviews with Costello and Diaz.

117 "When the other two joined them . . ." Details of the gathering at the Marriott bar come mostly from the Latson tape, with some information—mostly about what they were thinking—from my interviews with Diaz and Costello. The anecdote about the vote in Colombia on the extradition treaty appears in Gugliotta and Leen, *Kings of Cocaine*. They report that the Supreme Court voted 12–12 on May 28, 1987, and that a specially appointed "alternate justice" broke the tie in June, killing the treaty—p. 304.

119 "It was still dark when . . ." Details of this early morning meeting were told to me by Diaz, Costello, and Latson.

119 "Skip pressed for anything . . ." Details of what Costello and Diaz said that morning, including all direct quotes, come from my transcript of the tape.

120 "Cesar and Ramón were late . . ." Details of this conversation came from my interviews with Costello and Diaz.

120 "In Panama, international banking ranks . . ." Information about banking in Panama comes from several sources, including interviews with Panamanian bankers; Clifford Krauss, *Inside Central America* (New York: Summit Books, 1991); and Kevin Buckley's *Panama: The Whole Story.* The number of banks and size of assets came from a 1989 brochure from the Panama Banking Association, which cites as its source the National Banking Commission.

121 "A longtime Panamanian banker . . ." This banker spoke to me on the condition of anonymity.

121 "Banco de Occidente's home office is elsewhere . . ." Interviews with the bank's lawyers, William Richey and Kirk Munroe of Miami.

121 "When Eduardo Martínez strolled into . . ." Details on what happened in the bank come from interviews with Diaz, Costello, and the DEA report.

123 "the letterhead called the company..." I have a copy of the paper on which Martínez drew that day, which became evidence in the case against him.

124 "The DEA laundry was taking..." DEA reports; interviews with Diaz and Latson.

126 " 'Oh, man,' Cesar would later remember." Interview with Diaz.

126 "As the three men drove away..." Interviews with Diaz and Costello.

126 "Skip was waiting anxiously at the apartment..." Interviews with Latson.

126 "Ramón drove Cesar around town..." Interviews with Diaz and Costello.

126 "Finally, it rang..." Interviews with Diaz and Latson. The direct quote comes from Latson's recollection of the telephone call.

127 "Ramón drove the length of the causeway..." Interviews with Costello and Diaz.

127 "You look tense..." The reconstruction of this conversation comes mostly from Costello's recollections. Latson and Diaz's memories of their conversation after the meeting were vague, although they confirmed Diaz's uneasiness.

Costello, Diaz, and Latson each had different memories of the chronology and location of their secret meetings with each other, which were not included in the DEA report. To resolve the differences, I constructed a chronology using the Latson tape and the meetings with Martínez that were recorded in the DEA report as certainties. From there, I chose whoever's recollection of the secret meetings (as told in a series of interviews) best fit with the known events and with the other men's recollections. Latson and Diaz said the chronology seemed accurate.

128 "As Cesar and Ramón recounted the details..." Interviews with Latson.

128 "Cesar was back in his room..." The knock at the door and the conversation there and in Serrano's room come from the DEA report and interviews with Diaz.

128 "Yeah, what would happen?" That Ospina turned threatening comes from the DEA report and a second Latson tape. Latson dictated the tape on Wednesday, January 20, 1988, to record what Costello had told him when they met secretly that afternoon.

129 "Cesar agreed." The rest of this conversation is based on the DEA report.

129 "Ramón took Cesar to one of..." This account of their dinner is based on what they each told me in separate interviews.

130 "Once the case was over..." The content of this conversation is based mostly on Costello's recollection. However, Diaz confirmed its accuracy.

131 "Everyone else was staying, but Cesar..." Interviews with Diaz.

131 "That morning, Cesar and Serrano went to..." This conversation is based on the DEA report and interviews with Costello and Diaz.

131 "Once they all reconvened..." The location and conversations over breakfast and in the meeting afterwards come mostly from the DEA report, with Costello and Diaz recalling some of the same information.

131 "Ramón drove him to the airport." DEA report.

132 "Cesar left Panama eager to go..." Interviews with Diaz.

132 "Ramón and Serrano—and Skip, too..." Interviews with the three men.

132 "This seemed the right thing to do..." Interviews with Serrano.

132 "Martínez was satisfied with keeping Serrano . . ." Interviews with Serrano, Costello, and Latson.

Chapter 10: Surfacing the Mine

133 "In the three weeks following . . ." A DEA report says Martínez gave Serrano the $24 million figure, and Serrano passed this along to Diaz.

133 "Serrano desperately wanted to get back on track with Martínez . . ." Interviews with Diaz and Costello; DEA reports.

133 "So in mid-February, Featherly met Serrano . . ." Information about these meetings, including details of the conversations, comes mostly from DEA reports.

135 "Big cases, big problems . . ." Interview with Doug Ross of DEA.

135 "Some $12.8 million in drug proceeds . . ." The indictment in the case of *United States* vs. *Pablo Emilio Escobar-Gaviria, et. al.,* Indictment No. 1:89-CR-086-WCO (N.D.Ga.).

135 "about $1.7 million had been seized." Package of materials prepared by DEA-Atlanta for an August 1988 meeting.

135 "spinoff investigations had brought in . . ." Ibid.

135 "On Tuesday, February 23 . . ." The agenda and sign-in sheet for the meeting.

136 "The DEA sent it from one cooperating bank to another . . ." Interviews with Ed Guillen and Skip Latson.

136 "the Atlanta contingent wanted to coordinate and streamline . . ." Interviews with Parker and Latson.

136 "Each jurisdiction told the others . . ." This is my synopsis of what a number of people at the meeting told me, including Parker, Latson, Diaz, Dan Ortega, Tony Ricevuto, and Ed Guillen.

138 "The Atlanta group bristled . . ." Interviews with Latson and Diaz.

138 "From New York, one of the higher-ups said he knew . . ." Interview with DEA analyst Gail Shelby.

139 "the alleged La Mina sums brought more skepticism . . ." Interviews with Ricevuto, Latson, Diaz, Parker, Ortega, Ferrari, and Craig Gillen.

139 "Ricevuto stated emphatically that no $8-million . . ." Several people who attended this meeting said they remembered this emphatic statement from one of the L.A. representatives—either Ricevuto or Hayman, but they were unsure which. Ricevuto said it was probably he; Hayman said he has no recollection of making that statement; Ortega said he remembers Ricevuto as the one.

139 "A fissure had developed . . ." This is based on interviews with Parker, Latson, Diaz, Ortega, Ferrari, Guillen, Gillen, and Stock.

139 "The La Mina story did not surprise . . ." Interviews with Russell Hayman.

139 "DEA-L.A. was in fact homing . . ." Interview with agent David Barkett; November 1, 1988, affidavit of DEA agent Lance C. Williams.

139 "it was $25 million over three months." The Williams affidavit; the February 1989 affidavit of FBI agent Bruce Stephens.

140 "Barkett was operating on the belief . . ." Interviews with Barkett.

140 "Barkett was having trouble getting the resources . . ." Interviews with Barkett and DEA supervisor Vincent Furtado.

140 "At 4:30 A.M. on Sunday, February 21 ..." Details of what these informants told Devlin come mostly from my interviews with Phil Devlin and his former supervisor, Elaine Harris.

140 "Devlin wasn't sure what he had." Interviews with Devlin.

141 "The early morning meeting would be ..." Interviews with Devlin and Harris.

142 "Devlin and other DEA agents began watching ..." Interviews with Devlin and Harris. Information about what they saw comes from Devlin.

142 "The drug agents and prosecutors meeting in Atlanta ..." Interviews with Parker, Latson, and Russell Hayman.

142 "One month before the Atlanta meeting ..." The details of the box containing $800,000 come chiefly from the September 9, 1988, affidavit of FBI-L.A. agent Bruce Stephens, supplemented by interviews with Barkett, Harris, Stephens, FBI-L.A. agent Fred Wong, and FBI-L.A. group supervisor Ralph Lumpkin.

143 "Loomis reported its suspicions to the FBI in New York ..." Stephens affidavit.

143 "no one from New York contacted the FBI in Los Angeles ..." Interviews with Lumpkin, Stephens, and Wong.

143 "Meanwhile, on Thursday, February 25 ..." Stephens affidavit of September 9, 1988.

Chapter 11: Back to Aruba

145 "In a series of telephone calls ..." DEA transcripts of telephone conversations between Cesar Diaz and Eduardo Martínez beginning February 24, 1988.

145 " 'Wherever he wants to go ...' " February 24, 1988, transcript.

145 "They finally settled on Aruba." A DEA report.

145 "This time, there was no question ..." Information about setting up the meeting comes mostly from Latson, but also from Featherly, Diaz, and Caffrey.

146 "The idea of returning to Aruba ..." Interviews with Costello.

146 "On Tuesday morning, March 8 ..." Interviews with Diaz and Costello.

146 "If Eduardo Martínez harbored anger ..." Interviews with Diaz and Featherly; author's viewing of videotape of the meeting.

146 "Ramón offered Cokes and beer ..." DEA transcript of the March 8, 1988, meeting.

146 "Ramón directed Martínez to the two-seat sofa ..." Videotape of the meeting.

146 " 'Doesn't Jim speak any Spanish at all ...' " DEA transcript of the meeting, translated by a government interpreter. The dialogue from this section comes entirely from that transcript. Thoughts attributed to people in the meeting were described in interviews with those people.

146 "Skip Latson and the DEA technical expert ..." Interviews with Latson, who also described the location of this room, the *"Do Not Disturb"* sign, and the bank of electronic equipment.

147 "He was monitoring ..." This comes from what Martínez told the men at that meeting. More details on the banking situation come from Buckley,

Panama: The Whole Story, and from my interviews with bankers in Panama.

147 "The first of several U.S. indictments . . ." The first BCCI indictment came down on October 8, 1988, in Tampa, Florida, according to James Ring Adams and Douglas Frantz, *A Full Service Bank: How BCCI Stole Billions Around the World* (New York: Pocket Books, 1992).

151 "Martínez picked up the briefcase . . ." I saw this gesture, and others, while viewing the videotape.

151 "Martínez had the clear impression . . ." Martínez was not interviewed for this book. My assumption is based on the conversation up to this point and his reaction to what had been said.

152 "Using initials to indicate people's first names . . ." The description is based on a copy of the paper on which Martínez wrote, which became a government exhibit.

152 "the Atlantans had no idea Martínez was buying . . ." Interviews with Latson and Diaz.

153 "At first, Skip didn't know . . ." Interviews with Latson.

153 "After a late lunch at a mediocre . . ." Interviews with Featherly and Diaz.

153 "Featherly went to see Skip . . ." Interviews with Featherly and Latson.

153 "All Cesar wanted to do was nap . . ." Interviews with Diaz.

153 "He hadn't rested for long . . ." This conversation is based on what Diaz and Featherly told me.

154 "Daytime resort wear had given way . . ." DEA videotape of the evening meeting. The tape and a translated transcript of it provided details for this account of that meeting.

158 "The five men dined at the hotel . . ." Interviews with Diaz and Featherly.

158 "Everything had gone so well . . ." The assessment of what the tape showed comes from Latson, Featherly, and Parker.

159 "At five thirty in the afternoon . . ." The translated transcript of this conversation noted the time.

159 " 'Jimmy . . . told me to tell you . . .' " DEA transcript.

159 "The guys in Atlanta wanted badly to resume . . ." Interviews with Latson.

160 "If they had asked, they would have heard . . ." In interviews with me, Ed Guillen discussed the impact lower fees would have on other federal investigations.

Chapter 12: Linking the Dots

161 "While the others argued . . ." Interviews with Gail Shelby.

161 "Such was the job of the intelligence analyst . . ." The description of this job comes from interviews with Mike Orndorff and Keith Baudoin, to whom Shelby reported, and with Shelby.

161 "The Atlanta group had asked headquarters . . ." Interviews with Latson and Shelby.

161 "Drawn to the agency at the dawn of the war . . ." Interviews with Shelby.

162 "At that, Shelby was diligent . . ." Interviews with Orndorff, Baudoin, Latson, Featherly, and Parker.

162 "When she returned to Washington . . ." Interviews with Shelby; a DEA report she filed.

162 "As she worked, Shelby recalled something..." In interviews in 1992 and 1993, Shelby tried to recall what triggered her call to New York. The account told here is the best of her recollection.

162 "She reached Mancini." Shelby wasn't sure whether she reached Mancini or Phil Devlin, but Kevin Mancini testified in his July 9, 1990, testimony in Los Angeles in a hearing in *United States* vs. *Wanis Koyomejian, et. al.,* Indictment No. CR 89-189-CBM [C.D.Cal.]) that he took the call. The New York office of DEA denied my requests to interview Mancini. By telephone, I interviewed Phil Devlin, who by then had been transferred overseas, but Devlin did not remember receiving a call from Shelby.

162 "Yeah, three Colombians had walked in..." What Mancini told Shelby comes partly from her recollection. I have included information Devlin and his supervisor, Elaine Harris, said DEA–New York had at the time of the call, but I exclude information which did not also appear on reports Shelby wrote in May 1988. Shelby says she reported every link among the cases she knew about.

162 "In Spanish, that would be 'Kiko'..." The spelling the New York office gave the name comes from reports the agents filed and interviews with Devlin.

162 "It struck Shelby as too much of a coincidence." Interviews with Shelby.

162 "She told him she believed his case..." Interviews with Shelby; Mancini testimony of July 9, 1990.

162 "Until recently, Mancini had been helping..." Mancini testimony; interviews with Latson.

163 "Mancini already knew about Martínez..." Mancini testimony.

163 "Mancini had attended the December 10, 1987, meeting..." The sign-in sheet for the meeting.

163 "Mancini says he called Skip..." Mancini testimony.

163 "but Skip remembers being the one..." Interviews with Latson.

163 "By this time, Mancini and Devlin had written..." In her interviews, Harris told me about these reports.

163 "Shelby and the Atlanta agents say..." Interviews with Shelby, Latson, Diaz, and Parker.

163 "Even when processing works..." Billy Yout, then a public information officer for DEA, told me this.

164 "Part of the reason why neither Shelby nor Atlanta..." This is my analysis, based on what the New Yorkers said about links between the two cases.

164 "By early April, Shelby had flown..." Interviews with Shelby and Ferrari; DEA reports.

164 "Cops had found the 'pay and owe'..." This term comes from Michael Ferrari of the West Covina Police Department.

164 "The confiscated ledger was kept..." Shelby provided details of finding and reading the ledgers.

164 "The three entries in the ledger showed..." Interviews with Shelby and Ferrari; DEA reports; a copy of that page in the ledger.

165 "As soon as she spotted it..." This account of Shelby's interaction with agent Dan Ortega is based on what she told me. A DEA report says Ortega called Diaz after Shelby pointed out the link.

165 "In meetings he had attended in Atlanta ..." Interviews with Ortega.

165 "Ortega called Cesar ..." The DEA report.

165 "Shelby learned something else ..." Interviews with Shelby.

165 "By this time, bank records were showing ..." November 1, 1988, affidavit of DEA agent Lance C. Williams; interviews with banker Drusilla Leightner and DEA agent David Barkett.

165 "He gave her the few case reports ..." Interviews with Shelby.

165 "he had never said Armenians were running La Mina." Interviews with Shelby, Latson, and Diaz; DEA reports.

165 "Dave Barkett had become increasingly convinced ..." Interview with Barkett.

165 "But supervisor Tony Ricevuto says his group was too busy ..." Interviews with Ricevuto.

166 "So Barkett did something considered heretical ..." Barkett said he made these calls; supervisor Vincent Furtado confirmed this.

166 "FBI personnel say that the banker ..." Interviews with FBI agent Fred Wong and FBI supervisor Ralph Lumpkin.

166 "An L.A.-based DEA agent defines the difference ..." Interview with Michael Orton.

166 "The people at FBI like to say ..." Interviews with Lumpkin and FBI agent Bruce Stephens on the FBI's long-term approach; Wong on the buy-bust mentality; DEA agent Cesar Diaz on the typical DEA case.

166 "More important, according to the widespread attitude at DEA ..." This is based on interviews with many people at DEA, including Barkett, Michael Orton, and Vincent Furtado.

166 "With five times the agents of DEA ..." From DEA and FBI public information offices.

166 "But Barkett knew the FBI was already on the case." Interview with Barkett.

166 "In addition to the banker ..." Stephens affidavit of September 9, 1988; interviews with Stephens, Wong, and Lumpkin.

166 "Within DEA, Barkett set out to get the case ..." Interviews with Barkett and Furtado.

166 "He remembers Barkett telling him ..." Furtado described how the case came to him.

167 "By March, FBI agents from Los Angeles ..." Stephens affidavit of September 9, 1988.

167 "At the meeting the agents learned ..." Stephens affidavit of September 9, 1988. Agent Wong also told me some of this.

167 "the Koyomejians had also referred another family ..." Williams affidavit; interview with Barkett.

167 "Like Ropex, the Andonians ..." The description of the Andonians' shipments comes from the Williams affidavit.

167 "Agents had started rummaging ..." Williams and Stephens affidavits; interview with Barkett.

167 "One Thursday in April, a discarded box ..." Williams memo of June 22, 1988.

168 "It was rather shocking." Interview with IRS-L.A. agent Carl Knudson.

168 "Back in Washington, Gail Shelby..." Interviews with Shelby and chief of DEA's Financial Intelligence Unit Michael Orndorff.

168 "The Ropex ledger contained lots of first names..." I have seen the ledger itself.

168 "Knudson told Orndorff about Raoul..." The account of this telephone conversation is based on what Orndorff and Shelby told me, my viewing of the ledgers, and a report Shelby filed at the time. A few key elements were confirmed by Knudson and Doug Ross.

169 "His boss agreed." Interview with Ross, who called the meeting in Los Angeles.

169 "In a two-day meeting in the middle of May..." The description of this meeting is based on interviews with Latson, Shelby, and Keith Baudoin, as well as a DEA memo reporting the event.

170 "Shelby pulled it all together..." Shelby told me this when she discussed the events of the meeting. Many other people (including Latson, Orndorff, Baudoin, Furtado, and Orton) told me more generally that Shelby was the person who found and reported the links in the case. The state of the investigation at that point is based on DEA memos and reports written at the time.

170 "Furtado threw all of his group's ten agents..." Interviews with Furtado; a DEA memo.

170 "This was the first acknowledgment..." Interviews with Latson and Shelby.

170 "L.A.'s Barkett realized..." Interview with Barkett.

170 "At roughly the same time as this meeting..." Interviews with Barkett and Ortega.

171 "New York's Kevin Mancini, for example..." I base this on what he said during a July 9, 1990, hearing in Los Angeles in the Wanis Koyomejian case. The description of Mancini comes from several people who know him, including Latson, Orton, and Wong.

171 "But headquarters wanted to coordinate..." Interview with Ross.

171 "Two days after the meeting of DEA personnel..." A DEA memo; interviews with Shelby and Orndorff.

Chapter 13: Peering Down the Mine

172 "Ramón traveled back to Colombia..." DEA reports.

172 "He and Serrano had something of a reputation..." Interviews with Costello and Serrano.

172 "In his rounds, Ramón kept hearing..." Interviews with Costello; DEA reports.

172 "For all his rumored success, neither Chepe..." My account of Costello's meeting with Chepe is based on interviews with Costello and DEA reports written after agents debriefed Costello.

173 "the $1 million seizure had scared Jimmy Brown's..." Interviews with Costello, Latson, and Parker.

173 "Martínez was sending his business to La Mina." Martínez's remarks to Costello are based on a DEA report.

175 "Plenty of cops and agents had tried to make cases..." Interviews with

DEA agent David Barkett, West Covina Police Detective Michael Ferrari, and others.

175 "That business was Ropex..." That Ropex was receiving near-daily shipments comes from FBI agent Bruce Stephens's September 9, 1988, affidavit; interview with Russell Hayman.

175 "agents rummaging through Ropex's trash had found..." The findings in the trash mostly come from the Stephens affidavit.

175 "Supplementing these clues were Loomis records..." Ibid.

175 "But a straight jeweler whom the feds used..." Ibid.

175 "The legitimate business these companies claimed..." For the Ropex information, the Stephens affidavit; for Andonian Brothers, DEA agent Lance Williams's November 1, 1988, affidavit gives the information agents gleaned from Dun & Bradstreet, utility records, and other documents referred to in this paragraph.

176 "Koyomejian, forty-six, had arrived in the United States..." Most of the personal information about Wanis Koyomejian and his family comes from the Stephens affidavit.

176 "Preliminary checks into Andonian Brothers showed..." Information about the Andonians comes from the Williams affidavit, with additional background from Stanley Greenberg, Nazareth Andonian's attorney.

176 "The feds were learning not only who these people were..." Information on the methods agents used comes from the Stephens affidavit, the Williams affidavit, and interviews with agent Michael Orton.

177 "Loomis and bank records were showing astounding sums..." Stephens affidavit; Williams affidavit; DEA reports; Third Superseding Indictment, *United States* vs. *Wanis Koyomejian, et al.,* No. CR 89-189-CBM (C.D.Cal.).

177 "Loomis not only delivered boxes to Andonian Brothers and Ropex..." Williams's memo of June 22, 1988, gave me the information in this paragraph.

177 "They needed to see and hear..." Interviews with Orton, Vincent Furtado, Russell Hayman, Stephens, and Ralph Lumpkin.

177 "But there was nothing to stop them from installing..." Interview with Hayman.

177 "The FBI rented office space in the Jewelry Mart..." Interviews with Stephens and Furtado.

177 "A Loomis guard usually came between 9:00 and 10:00 A.M. ..." Interview with Stephens; Stephens affidavit; Stephens's September 17, 1990, testimony; FBI videotape.

178 "To follow these people to their destinations..." Interviews with Stephens, Lumpkin, Orton, and Furtado.

178 "But even with all that manpower" The difficulty of surveillance comes mainly from Stephens's testimony of September 17, 1990, and from the interview with Hayman.

178 "keeping up with him in the heavy pedestrian traffic..." In interviews, Orton and DEA agent Selby Smith told me of the difficulty of street surveillance.

178 "surveillance crews organized by the FBI..." Stephens affidavit.

178 "Later, the feds would match their observations . . ." Williams affidavit.

179 "Loomis would also arrive regularly for afternoon pickups . . ." Stephens affidavit.

179 "Later in the summer, as if to dispel all doubt . . ." The Stephens affidavit had the account of the man carrying the money counter.

179 "They needed an informant . . ." Interviews with Stephens, Lumpkin, and Orton.

179 "At DEA in Los Angeles, the group supervisor . . ." Furtado described his views of the FBI's involvement.

179 "The FBI began with fifteen agents . . ." Interviews with Furtado and Lumpkin.

179 "The investigation focused on Ropex . . ." Interviews with Furtado, Barkett, and Lumpkin.

179 "To replace him, Furtado picked . . ." Interviews with Furtado and Orton.

179 "Orton was happy to be back in the States . . ." Interviews with Orton. The explanation of Operation Snowcap comes from Linda Robinson and Gordon Witkin, "America's Deadly Drug War in the Jungle," *U.S. News & World Report,* April 30, 1990.

179 "One of Orton's first acts as case agent . . ." Interviews with Orton.

180 "Furtado had to keep his agents in line . . ." Interviews with Furtado.

180 "Orton set up a watch post . . ." Interviews with Orton and Furtado.

180 "The DEA wanted to install hallway cameras . . ." The account of this installation comes from Orton.

181 "That office served as a staging ground . . ." Agents Orton and Selby Smith both described how they watched and tried to follow their targets.

181 "Sometimes the people would take the suitcase . . ." Information on what the targets were doing comes from the Williams affidavit and interviews with Orton and Smith.

181 "That's how it was for Selby Smith . . ." Smith told me details of this anecdote, which was also reported in the Williams affidavit.

182 "DEA agents were watching the homes . . ." Interviews with Orton; DEA reports. Orton described the garbage collection.

182 "The other agencies—the FBI, the IRS, and Customs—were assisting . . ." Interviews with Furtado, Orton, Lumpkin, Stephens, and Hayman.

182 "In fact, a lot of information, but not all . . ." Different agents, supervisors, and prosecutors had quite different accounts as to the degree of cooperation among the agents. One federal source who stayed out of the fray told me interagency squabbling was much worse than anything I could have possibly been told about; others said the cooperation was tremendous, with only occasional outbreaks of jealousy. I concluded that undoubtedly agents cooperated, but undoubtedly they also competed, sometimes to the detriment of the investigation.

182 "That is a preposterous allegation . . ." Interviews with Lumpkin and Stephens.

183 "He acknowledges slacking off . . ." Interviews with Orton.

183 "By June, the mysterious 'Raul' . . ." A DEA report written by Shelby. That Vivas refined gold in Uruguay comes from the April 10, 1990, affidavit of

DEA agent David C. Panek in Atlanta, filed in *United States* vs. *Pablo Emilio Escobar-Gaviria, et al.,* Indictment No. 1:89-CR-086-WCO (N.D.Ga.).

183 "The IRS subpoenaed Vivas's bank..." June 20, 1988, letter to Republic National Bank from the U.S. Attorney's Office in Los Angeles.

183 "but it also sent a copy of the subpoena to Vivas." June 28, 1988, letter from Republic International Bank to Mr. and Mrs. Raúl Vivas. Republic National Bank, to which the U.S. Attorney's Office addressed the June 20 letter, was a subsidiary of Republic International Bank of New York, which, on June 28, responded to that letter. The correspondence shows the same address for Republic National and Republic International.

183 "Suddenly, trashed records at the jewelry store..." Interviews with Orton, Hayman, and Knudson.

183 "News that La Mina was under IRS scrutiny traveled..." What Francisco Serrano told Cesar Diaz comes from a DEA report of that conversation.

Chapter 14: Pulling Together, Pushing Apart

185 "At DEA headquarters, Gail Shelby compared reports..." Interviews with Shelby, Michael Orndorff, and Keith Baudoin; Shelby's reports.

185 "Now, Shelby was trying to match up phone numbers." Interviews with Shelby; a report she filed.

186 "The number was 32-44-67." DEA transcript of the conversation between Ramón Costello and Francisco Serrano's wife, Sol.

186 "She remembered the CIs in the New York case..." Interviews with Shelby. She told me about the call to New York; agent Phil Devlin didn't remember it, and Kevin Mancini wasn't available for interview. That other numbers were called out before the matching one is based on the order of the numbers as listed in the DEA report.

186 "It was one of the numbers the CI..." DEA reports; interviews with Shelby.

186 "But out in the field, memos are only words..." Interviews with Orton and Furtado; testimony of Kevin Mancini, July 9, 1990, in a hearing related to *United States* vs. *Wanis Koyomejian, et. al.,* Indictment No. CR 89-189-CBM (C.D.Cal.).

186 "Buddy Parker remembers..." Interviews with Parker.

186 "Shelby's boss, meanwhile, was going up..." Interviews with Baudoin and Doug Ross.

186 "At the same time, Ron Caffrey in Atlanta..." Interviews with Ron Caffrey and Jack Lawn.

186 "They both wanted to push this case..." Interviews with Baudoin and Caffrey.

187 "David Westrate... called a meeting..." Memo from the meeting; interviews with Westrate and Ron Caffrey.

187 "At 2:00 P.M. on July 14, 1988..." The description of this meeting comes mostly from the memo. The location given is where DEA used to be; it has since moved.

187 "The reason for gathering these far-flung DEA agents..." Interview with Furtado.

187 "John Featherly... remembers it differently." Interview with Featherly.

187 "Through surveillance and records checks..." Interviews with Furtado. The figures came from a memo written by Lance Williams.

187 "From Atlanta, Caffrey volunteered..." Memo from the meeting.

188 "The New York office, which was just now installing..." Ibid.

188 "Working a case without an inside source..." In interviews, several agents talked of the difficulty of working a case without an informant; Russell Hayman compared it to working blindfolded.

188 "New York reported its main CI had patched..." Meeting memo; DEA report on the agents' debriefing of the CI.

188 "In Houston, the DEA had fended off..." Meeting memo.

188 "And now, a new report from Customs..." Meeting memo; interviews with Latson and Parker; report by U.S. Customs Service entitled *Gold Bullion Importation into the United States.*

189 "Half of the gold shipments from Uruguay..." The Customs report; a DEA report Shelby wrote discussing the Customs report.

189 "For nearly three hours, agents and DEA managers..." The meeting memo; interview with Westrate.

189 "to talk to the top man at DEA..." Interview with Jack Lawn.

189 "Each of the different DEA offices needed to coordinate..." Interviews with Furtado, Barkett, Caffrey, Ross, and Featherly; the meeting memo.

190 "Their main CI had just returned..." DEA reports; interviews with Elaine Harris and Phil Devlin.

190 "The agents had already come up with..." Interviews with Harris and Devlin; DEA reports.

190 "The DEA agents checked various government offices..." Information about the photograph comes from interviews with Harris and DEA reports.

190 "Yes, this is the man I know as Chepe..." Interviews with Harris.

190 "Until now, Atlanta agents had not been certain..." Interviews with Latson and Parker; DEA reports.

190 "DEA had a description of Luis Garces-Restrepo..." A DEA report gives the various descriptions of Luis Garces-Restrepo and the Chepes.

191 "The photo ID had to be bad..." Interviews with Latson and Parker.

191 "The New York office stood firm..." Interviews with Harris, Devlin, Latson, and Parker.

191 "Almost everything the New York CI said..." The list of characteristics the two Chepes had in common comes from a DEA report Latson wrote in October 1989, which was based on information from earlier DEA reports.

192 "That same week in July 1988..." Interviews with Latson, with date provided by a DEA report.

192 "Alvaro was acting as the trafficker's representative..." Interviews with Latson and Francisco Serrano; DEA report.

192 "From the suburban airport, Skip drove..." Latson told me about the lunch, the beeping, and the conversation with Diaz; a DEA report confirmed details.

192 "Skip made it a quick lunch..." DEA report.

193 "Serrano had been negotiating..." Details of his negotiations come from DEA reports.

193 "A memo to Westrate spelled out . . ." Details come from that memo.

193 "so Featherly traveled to Los Angeles . . ." DEA report; interviews with Featherly, Serrano, and Costello.

193 "The tab would be paid from the commission . . ." Interviews with agent Dan Ortega. In addition, Skip Latson and Ed Guillen explained in general how the commission paid for investigative costs.

193 "So on this particular Wednesday night in July . . ." This walk and the dinner were described in DEA reports.

193 "But Featherly, stationed . . ." Interviews with Featherly.

193 "They talked about setting up bank accounts . . ." DEA report.

194 "By meal's end, it was time for a fine cognac." Interviews with Costello, Serrano, and Ortega.

194 "At about 10:00 P.M., Featherly picked up the check . . ." The time comes from a DEA report; the rest from the Ortega interview.

194 "But Serrano was in a superb mood . . ." Interviews with Serrano and Ortega.

194 "Serrano gazed through the small park . . ." Interviews with Serrano, Featherly, Costello, a DEA report.

194 "Francisco Serrano had connections . . ." Interviews with Latson, Costello, Parker, and Ortega.

195 "Serrano was becoming ubiquitous . . ." Interview with Ortega.

195 "By mid-August . . . Carlos 'Junior' Guarin . . ." DEA report.

195 "Serrano had unwittingly introduced Guarin to the DEA . . ." Interviews with Latson; DEA report.

195 "Dan Ortega, figured the time would come to pop Guarin . . ." Interviews with Ortega.

195 "The cops surveilled the house at 9763 Yolanda . . ." Ortega interviews; transcript of his November 9, 1988, testimony before a federal grand jury in Atlanta.

195 "They punched the address into the Narcotic Information Network . . ." Interviews with Ortega, and his testimony of September 17, 1990, at a hearing in the case of *United States* vs. *Wanis Koyomejian, et. al.,* Indictment No. CR 89-189-CBM (C.D.Cal.).

195 "Arresting Junior Guarin was simply a matter of timing . . ." Interviews with Ortega.

195 "But on Monday, August 15 . . ." Documents filed in *California* vs. *Alvaro Mejia Ruiz, et al.,* No. A973754 (Municipal Court of Los Angeles).

195 "The L.A. Sheriff's Department had gotten wind . . ." This account comes mostly from interviews with Ortega and Serrano, court documents, and sworn testimony given by Ortega and detective Joe Nunez, whose versions differed. Conflicts were resolved in favor of Ortega. Neither Nunez nor Stephens would consent to an interview. Additional information was provided by Deputy District Attorney Carole Chizever and Buddy Parker.

196 "But in the meantime, Nunez took five other deputies . . ." Transcript of Nunez's February 10, 1989, testimony in the case of *California* vs. *Alvaro Mejia Ruiz, et al.*

196 "Such was Yolanda Avenue, where at 7:30 P.M. . . . ." In Nunez's February 10,

1989, testimony, he described watching the house, seeing cocaine, and making the arrests. The description of Guarin comes from a DEA report.

197 "The second woman, whom a defense lawyer would later accuse . . ." This accusation came from defense attorney Thomas V. Johnston at the February 10, 1989, hearing, according to a transcript; interviews with Serrano; Ortega's testimony before the Atlanta grand jury on November 9, 1988.

197 "Serrano would later insist . . ." Interviews with Serrano.

Chapter 15: Operation Polar Cap

199 "Ortega could not believe . . ." Interviews with Dan Ortega.

199 "Ortega called Cesar . . ." Interviews with Ortega and Cesar Diaz.

199 "Skip and Cesar in turn rang up Buddy." Interviews with Parker.

200 "Skip had just written his higher-ups . . ." This comes from the memo itself. Skip Latson said in interviews he was not that concerned about Serrano's arrest; Parker and Diaz said they were angry about it.

200 "The Atlanta group had been preparing to reveal . . ." Interviews with Parker.

200 "Set for August 24–25, the conference . . ." Information about the conference comes from many interviews, as well as a DEA memo outlining what occurred there.

200 "Until now, the guys in Atlanta had eagerly anticipated . . ." Interviews with Parker, Diaz, and Latson.

201 "On August 24, 1988, close to a hundred federal agents . . ." The date, place, and number of participants come from a DEA memo. (The name of the hotel, Marina Beach Hotel, was later changed to the Doubletree Hotel.)

201 "For this conference, the meeting room . . ." Interviews with Parker.

201 "The man in charge of the FBI's Los Angeles office . . ." The DEA memo gave me an account of what was said. Several agents who saw the memo and attended the conference said it was accurate.

201 "a name that caused hilarity among agents in the field." Interviews with Furtado and Orton.

201 "The IRS man called for unity . . ." Details of what was said come from the DEA memo, with various participants confirming some elements.

202 "Out in the audience, the call for unity . . ." Interviews with Furtado, Orton, Phil Devlin, and others.

202 "New York, where all-out war had broken out . . ." Interviews with Furtado, Devlin, and Parker.

202 "as the two agencies raced to petition . . ." Interview with Orton and Latson. FBI agent Fred Wong acknowledged some degree of competition, but said it wasn't great. He said FBI agent Bruce Stephens helped the DEA write its affidavit; Orton said that's not true.

202 "permission before taking a significant step didn't sit well . . ." The DEA memo gave me this and the other details of what was said, with various participants confirming some elements.

203 "For the rest of the afternoon, and into the next day . . ." DEA memo; interviews with Parker, Latson, Furtado, Orton, Devlin, former Assistant U.S. Attorney Jonathan Liebman of New York, and others.

203 "This was the first time anyone in the Atlanta delegation..." Interviews with Parker and Latson.

203 "He pointed out that the Atlanta Fis-Con investigation..." DEA memo provides the details of what else the Los Angeles delegates said.

204 "With the IRS presentation, 'everybody was astounded...'" Interview with Orndorff.

204 "I think we scared everybody...'" Interview with Carl Knudson.

204 "The FBI came next..." DEA memo.

205 "The Atlanta agents knew they had been on the right track..." Interviews with Latson and Parker.

205 "much of the business of the conference was taking place..." Interviews with Parker.

205 "the delegations from New York and Los Angeles..." Interviews with Furtado, Harris, Parker, and Arthur Donelan, Customs Special Agent.

205 "toughest district in the country, New York." Interviews with Devlin, Parker, Ed Guillen, and Jonathan Liebman.

206 "The New Yorkers opened the conference's second day..." The DEA meeting memo provided most of the information about the New York presentation.

206 "blown-up charts showing men carrying suitcases..." From copies of those charts and handouts.

206 "The petition had been filed and granted the day before..." DEA memo about the conference.

207 "A search warrant issued in a seemingly unrelated money-laundering case..." DEA memo; interview with Elaine Harris.

207 "In yet another initially unrelated investigation, undercover Customs agents..." DEA meeting memo.

207 "During the lunch break, New York DEA agents and prosecutors..." The interview with Furtado provided most of the information about this meeting, although Parker had some knowledge of it. In separate interviews, Harris, Devlin, and Liebman said they did not remember this specific meeting, but each confirmed serious tension between DEA–New York and FBI–New York. And Devlin confirmed that there were side meetings at the conference.

208 "The next delegation up was Atlanta..." DEA meeting memo.

208 "For weeks he had been pumping his contacts..." Interviews with Parker.

208 "Skip Latson and Cesar Diaz had been organizing..." Interviews with Parker and Latson; the handout Latson wrote.

208 "But the centerpiece was Skip's list of twenty-one characteristics..." The list; interviews with Parker and Latson.

209 "Buddy began by telling the agents about Ramón..." DEA meeting memo.

209 "As for Atlanta, Buddy said the piece of the case he wanted..." The DEA meeting memo; interviews with Parker.

210 "Whatever he said...'" Interview with Knudson.

210 "Likewise, Hayman says, 'We had already scrubbed...'" Interview with Hayman.

210 "Some of the participants believed the Atlanta group..." Interviews with Devlin, Knudson, and Furtado.

210 " 'Anyone who's in this business . . .' " Interview with Arthur Donelan.

210 "FBI agent Bruce Stephens from Los Angeles said the Atlanta presentation made him realize . . ." From Stephens's September 17, 1990, testimony at a hearing in the case of *United States* vs. *Wanis Koyomejian, et. al.,* Indictment No. CR 89-189-CBM (C.D.Cal.).

210 "Dirty money brokers interact . . ." Interview with Lumpkin.

210 "As for that part of Buddy's presentation . . ." Interview with Furtado.

211 "By 5:15 P.M. of the second day . . ." DEA meeting memo.

211 "For all the rancor in the other delegations . . ." Interviews with Parker and Latson.

Chapter 16: A Man in Between

213 "A few miles from Marina del Rey . . ." A DEA report and interviews with Cesar Diaz.

213 "Through Francisco's lawyer, Ramón sent word . . ." DEA tape of the conversation between Ramón Costello and the lawyer.

213 "When the conference was over, he took a ride . . ." Interviews with Diaz.

214 "Francisco told him what had happened . . ." The conversation between Serrano and Diaz is based chiefly on a DEA report, but also on interviews with Diaz and Serrano.

214 "through Buddy Parker, he and Skip were doing . . ." That the Atlanta group worked to keep Serrano in jail comes from interviews with Parker, Diaz, and Latson.

214 "bail was set at $2 million . . ." Magistrate's order setting bail.

214 "the case against Francisco was turning to mush." Interviews with Deputy District Attorney Carole Chizever.

214 "The Sheriff's Department's informant, the woman inside the house . . ." That the woman did not want to testify comes from agent Daniel Ortega's grand jury testimony of November 9, 1988, in Atlanta.

214 "The state crime lab checked the packaging . . ." Interviews with Chizever.

214 "Buddy, Cesar, and Skip tried to predict . . ." Interviews with Parker, Diaz, and Latson.

215 "Long before Ramón had become a confidential informant . . ." That Serrano helped Costello broker cocaine loads comes from interviews with Latson and Parker and from Parker's statements at Serrano's sentencing hearing, October 26, 1990, in Rome, Georgia.

215 "Buddy appeared before a federal grand jury . . ." Interviews with Parker.

215 "and came out with a sealed indictment . . ." Interviews with Parker and Latson; Parker's statements at the October 26, 1990, sentencing hearing.

215 "On the morning of October 18, 1988, a cheerful Francisco . . ." The date and location of this hearing come from statements made by Chizever and Judge Elva R. Soper during the February 10, 1989, hearing in municipal court. That Serrano was cheerful comes from my interviews with agent Daniel Ortega.

215 "He knew the local prosecutor . . ." Serrano told me in an interview what he had expected that day.

215 "Present in the courtroom . . ." Details of this hearing, including all direct quotes from it, come from court records.

216 " 'We didn't want to give him ...' " Interview with Ortega.

216 "Francisco's lawyer, John Taussig, stood." Court records.

216 " 'I've got an arrest warrant ...' " Interviews with Ortega.

216 "That night Junior Guarin's lawyer called Cesar ..." Information about this call comes from a DEA report.

216 "Cesar had just come back from Panama ..." I relied on a DEA report of this trip for information about it.

217 "Ramón kept trying to get business going ..." Tapes of his conversations with Martínez.

217 "But since Serrano's arrest ..." That neither the smuggling nor the money-laundering ventures were working comes from interviews with Diaz, Latson, and Parker, and DEA reports.

217 "As for Francisco Serrano, Atlanta was in no hurry ..." Interviews with Latson.

218 "they made sure he had a way to flip ..." Interviews with Latson and Parker; Ortega's November 9, 1988, grand jury testimony in Atlanta.

218 "When the feds moved Francisco to Atlanta ..." Specifics of his relocation come from DEA reports.

218 "He had been in this Georgia jail ..." Details of Diaz's jail visit come mostly from a DEA report, supplemented by interviews with Diaz.

218 "What Francisco did not say ..." That Serrano called Ortega came from a DEA report; Ortega confirmed it.

219 "To Ortega in L.A., Francisco sounded like a man ..." Interviews with Ortega.

219 "Francisco told Ortega ..." DEA report; Ortega interviews.

219 "So Ortega came to Atlanta ..." The time, place, and participants in this meeting come from a DEA report; Ortega confirmed the gist of what occurred that day.

219 "waiting in a holding facility in the U.S. Marshal's Office." Interviews with Parker.

219 "Buddy told the lawyer a little ..." What Parker told the lawyer and what Parker wanted out of the meeting are based on my interviews with Parker.

219 "Buddy wrote out the standard immunity statement ..." DEA report; interviews with Parker.

220 "In the middle of all this, Cesar ..." Specifics of this message come from a DEA report and my interview with Diaz.

220 "He must have gotten Cesar's number ..." Interviews with Parker.

220 "Cesar knew the Atlanta lawyer ..." Interviews with Diaz.

220 "The main risk in Cesar's returning the call ..." Interviews with Parker.

220 "Cesar returned the call, tape recorder running." DEA report; interviews with Diaz.

220 "The lawyer said he was calling ..." Contents of the conversation come from a DEA report.

220 "it felt like an awkward attempt at a shakedown ..." Interviews with Diaz.

220 "Cesar and his supervisor went upstairs ..." Interviews with Diaz and Parker; DEA report.

220 "Cesar had barely arrived when the magistrate called..." DEA reports.

221 "Maybe Francisco would call Los Angeles..." DEA report, which also contained specifics on the message Serrano left for Ortega.

221 "Buddy and Craig had no reason to believe the lawyer's ties..." Interviews with Parker.

221 "Buddy and Craig decided they must try again..." Interviews with Parker; DEA report.

221 "At 4:45 P.M., Francisco and Ortega finally met..." DEA report, with Ortega confirming what happened.

Chapter 17: Breaking the Gold Code

222 "The FBI beat the DEA..." The dates that each agency began electronic surveillance come from several affidavits, including Bruce Stephens's affidavit of December 22, 1988.

222 "The scene inside these boring rooms..." Interviews with Assistant U.S. Attorneys Russell Hayman and Jean Kawahara and FBI group supervisor Ralph Lumpkin.

222 "They saw people nonchalantly breaking open boxes..." From the September 21, 1988, tape of the Ropex counting room and descriptions by Stephens and Kawahara.

223 "The DEA agents, whose wiretap affidavit..." Interview with Michael Orton.

223 "The hard part was finding interpreters..." Interviews with Orton and DEA-L.A. agent Tony Coulson.

223 "And so in a small room at DEA-L.A. headquarters..." The description of the wire room comes from interviews with Orton and Coulson.

223 "At the same time, the agents would make..." Interviews with Selby Smith.

223 "On the first day, they heard conversations..." Orton's February 21, 1989, search warrant affidavit supplied details of the conversations. I have used quotation marks for exact quotes as given by the affidavit; otherwise, I paraphrased.

224 "If Wanis Koyomejian's lack of business frustrated him..." Interviews with Orton, Furtado, and FBI agent Fred Wong.

224 "At the end of the business day, the men and women..." Interviews with Orton and Coulson.

224 "A pattern soon emerged..." This pattern came from the Orton affidavit of February 21, 1989, and interviews with Furtado.

224 "But the agents did not understand..." Interviews with Furtado, Coulson, and Selby Smith.

224 "In one conversation they monitored..." The details of this conversation come from the Orton affidavit. Nazareth Andonian's attorney, Stanley Greenberg of Los Angeles, told me agents misunderstood his client's statement about the danger and risk associated with his work. Greenberg said Andonian ordered the gold before he received the cash, so if the cash did not come, then he would have to find a way to pay for the gold out of his own pocket.

225 "On the morning of December 7..." The account of events that morning is based mostly on what Orton told me. Where other sources confirmed details, I have indicated below.

225 "Orton and the DEA agent in charge ..." Interviews with Orton and Coulson.

225 "Seresi called in to Andonian Brothers to talk to Saini ..." Quotes and details of the telephone calls come from the Orton affidavit.

226 "Whatever it was, it was not the sort of thing ..." Interviews with Orton and Coulson. Lawyers for Seresi and Saini, who maintained their innocence at trial, told me their clients did not suspect law enforcement officers but were nervous about being followed when there was money in the trunk.

226 "Eventually, DEA learned who was behind the tail." Interviews with Orton, Furtado, and Coulson.

226 "The court order permitted hidden cameras ..." Orton affidavit.

226 "but installing video was considerably trickier." Orton described in interviews the problems with installing video cameras.

226 "The Polar Cap 'working group' in Washington ..." The account of the camera installation comes from interviews with Orton and Furtado.

228 "When DEA agent Manny Figlia arrived ..." Interview with DEA-L.A. agent Manny Figlia.

228 "The FBI had installed the camera bottom up!" Interviews with Figlia, Orton, Furtado, and Bruce Stephens. I have also viewed videos the camera recorded.

228 "Figlia crooked his neck." In an interview, Figlia described looking at the monitor. Videos from that camera, including a video from that day, showed me the view of the room and what transpired.

228 " 'I'll be honest with you,' says DEA supervisor Furtado ..." Interviews with Furtado.

228 "People would come into the room ..." From the DEA videotapes.

229 "On December 20, interpreters and agents ..." Information about this telephone call comes from the Orton affidavit of February 21, 1989.

229 "One day not long after the counting-room camera ..." Figlia told me about this incident.

229 "Figlia called the wire room ..." Interviews with Figlia and Orton. In separate interviews, Furtado and Coulson each claimed to have taken Figlia's call, but Figlia said it was Orton. Since there is no dispute that Figlia was the agent who placed the first call, I base the account of what happened on his interview.

229 " 'What do you want me to tell you?' ..." I have used quotation marks because these are the words Figlia said he used.

229 "As long as there's money on the table ..." Interviews with Orton and Figlia. Furtado said that was the rule, too.

229 "agents would soon realize was a regular afternoon habit." Interviews with Orton, Coulson, and Figlia.

230 "They talked about 'kilograms' and 'grams' ..." Orton affidavit; interviews with Coulson and Selby Smith.

230 "The drug agents naturally first suspected ..." Interview with Orton.

230 "The Andonians talked frequently with Ronel ..." Orton affidavit.

230 "In addition, Orton suspected . . ." Interviews with Orton.

230 " 'We knew they were committing a crime. . . .' " Interview with Selby Smith.

230 "Smith, the green agent who . . ." Interviews with Smith and Coulson.

230 "So one morning a few days before Christmas . . ." My account of how Smith and Coulson broke the gold code is based on Smith's telling of the story. I took the dates, the telephone conversations, and the numbers from the Orton affidavit. After writing this account, I showed it to Coulson, who confirmed it as an accurate reconstruction.

Chapter 18: Shutting Down the Mine

233 "Says prosecutor Russ Hayman . . ." Interview with Russell Hayman.

233 "Meanwhile, the agents were watching the Andonian brothers . . ." The $5 to $10 million a week comes from Hayman.

233 "Over a year's time, they would spin hundreds of millions . . ." From interviews with Assistant U.S. Attorneys Hayman, Steven Clymer, and Richard Rathmann, as well as the resulting indictments and press release from Attorney General Richard Thornburgh.

233 "That had to stop, and soon . . ." Interview with Hayman. Also, several case agents and supervisors said Hayman was pushing for an early takedown, including Vince Furtado, Tony Coulson, and a participant in the meeting who did not want to be quoted by name.

233 "At a mid-January 1989 meeting of key L.A. personnel . . ." That there was a January meeting where a takedown date was set comes from interviews with Hayman, Furtado, Coulson, Bruce Stephens, and a participant who did not want to be quoted by name. Others, including Ralph Lumpkin, remember the discussion but did not say when it occurred.

233 "DEA–Los Angeles was more than eager . . ." Interviews with Furtado, Coulson, and Orton.

234 "The FBI's cooperating cops had followed a Ropex courier . . ." FBI agent Bruce Stephens's affidavit of December 22, 1988.

234 "but so far the DEA had no strong drug connection . . ." Interviews with Furtado and Orton.

234 "Not so at the FBI." That the FBI wanted the investigation to continue comes from Lumpkin, Stephens, and Wong of the FBI, as well as Furtado, Orton, and Coulson of the DEA.

234 "FBI agents were up to their necks in telephone conversations . . ." Interviews with Wong, Furtado, and a participant in the January meeting who did not want to be quoted. Others, including Hayman and Assistant U.S. Attorney Jean Kawahara, confirmed that translating foreign-language tapes posed a problem for the FBI, but said that was not necessarily related to the FBI's position on a takedown date.

234 "You'll never catch up . . ." Interview with Furtado.

234 "The FBI supervisor said he needed six months." Interview with Coulson and the unnamed participant. Lumpkin says he does not recall asking for that much time.

234 "Hayman, in the words of one of the men there . . ." The unnamed participant. Others, as noted, confirmed that Hayman was firm in wanting an early takedown.

234 "Finally they settled on a takedown at the end of February." Interviews with Hayman and Furtado.

235 "This time even more agents, supervisors, and bureaucrats..." Interviews with Parker and Furtado.

235 "By now, the matter of which jurisdiction would get which piece..." Interviews with Jonathan Liebman, Parker, Charles Saphos, and Furtado.

235 "This view infuriated agents..." Interviews with Elaine Harris and Phil Devlin.

235 "Liebman calls that charge ridiculous..." Interview with Liebman.

235 "The La Mina storefronts changed name..." Interviews with Hayman, Customs–New York agent Arthur Donelan, and Furtado.

236 "The animosity between the FBI..." Interviews with Devlin, Hayman, Harris, Furtado, Parker, and a source who did not want to be quoted by name.

236 "But the worst problem in New York..." Interviews with Harris, Donelan, and Latson.

236 "The U.S. Attorney's Office insisted the government bring charges..." Interviews with Harris, Devlin, and Latson.

236 "Without a conviction to show a jury, prosecutors were wary..." Interviews with Liebman and Hayman.

236 "Along with protecting their CI from prosecution..." That DEA–New York kept the CI from other agents comes from interviews with Devlin, Latson, and Orton.

236 "When the time came..." That New York prosecutors made no pitch for the case comes from Furtado, Parker, and Saphos.

237 "Hayman wanted to indict..." The part of the case to be indicted in L.A. comes from interviews with Hayman, Parker, and Furtado, and from the indictments that resulted.

237 "the man at the Justice Department coordinating the case..." The Saphos admonition comes from Furtado, with confirmation from an agent who declined to be quoted by name.

237 "Says Liebman..." Interview with Liebman.

237 "The Atlanta contingent had no bid..." The piece of the case Atlanta would prosecute comes from interviews with Parker and Latson and from the eventual indictments.

237 "Buddy was pleased..." Interviews with Parker.

238 "Craig Gillen and Buddy Parker had aggressively pursued..." Interviews with Parker and Gillen, as well as the court record in several cases.

238 "Using the forfeiture law against Banco de Occidente..." Interviews with Gillen, Parker, and Miami attorneys Kirk Munroe and William Richey.

238 "Craig and Buddy saw an opportunity..." Interviews with Gillen and Parker.

238 "Occidente had no U.S. offices..." Interviews with Parker.

238 "An American company buying Colombian coffee..." The explanation of correspondent bank accounts comes from Eduardo Martínez's Aruba tape, as well as from interviews with Parker.

238 "Before this case began, Buddy Parker and Craig Gillen..." Interviews with Parker and Gillen.

239 "At the Marina del Rey conference in mid-January..." Interviews with Parker.

239 "To some in the audience, he sounded like a wild man." From an agent who did not want to be quoted by name.

239 "The prospect of pulling this off..." Interviews with Parker.

239 "The FBI won more time." Interview with Furtado.

239 "Takedown date was finally set for March 8, 1989." Interviews with Furtado and Coulson.

239 "Within the restless DEA..." Interviews with Coulson, Furtado, and Orton.

239 "A week after the Marina del Rey conference..." Details of this call come from the Orton affidavit of February 21, 1989.

240 "In the DEA-L.A. wire room, an interpreter alerted..." Interview with Coulson.

240 "The men on the phone talked about..." The conversation and events in the wire room come from the Orton affidavit and interviews with Orton and Coulson.

240 "The way Orton tells it, he called up..." Orton interview. (DEA–New York denied my requests to interview Mancini.)

240 "Orton had consulted no one before acting." Interviews with Orton and Furtado.

240 "In New York, his call led to a hastily arranged meeting..." Interview with Elaine Harris, DEA group supervisor in New York at the time.

240 "They contacted the U.S. Attorney's Office..." Interview with Coulson. Then–Assistant U.S. Attorney Jonathan Liebman of New York declined to discuss the matter of a search warrant.

241 "The agents had learned that Loomis had taken the boxes..." Interview with Elaine Harris.

241 "Customs routinely sent a drug-sniffing dog..." Interview with New York Customs Special Agent Peter Noonan, Jr.

241 "Customs could take a dog there..." Interviews with Orton and Noonan.

241 "At a West L.A. restaurant, a beep on FBI supervisor..." Information about this call comes from interviews with Lumpkin.

241 "The way Furtado of DEA–Los Angeles tells it..." Interview with Furtado, who described this conversation to me. In his version, Lumpkin was angrier than Lumpkin said he was.

241 "The truth was, Furtado was annoyed..." Interviews with Furtado and Orton.

241 "Hayman, too, called Furtado demanding an explanation..." Interview with Furtado.

242 "Orton remembers Hayman's fury..." Orton interview. Also, Tony Coulson said in an interview he remembered Hayman's anger over the incident.

242 "The debate reached the Justice Department in Washington..." Interview with Charles Saphos, then of Justice.

242 "There would be no seizure, everyone agreed." Interview with Saphos.

242 "Furtado called DEA in New York . . ." Interview with Furtado.

242 "By that time, seven or eight federal agents . . ." Interview with Noonan.

242 "One of the boxes had a hole in it . . ." Interviews with Noonan and Harris, and photographs of the boxes.

242 "When DEA–New York called Furtado back . . ." Furtado interview.

243 "Orton, on the other hand, felt great." Orton interview.

243 "Nazareth Andonian arrived early at work . . ." Orton affidavit of February 21, 1989, which provided details of the following series of telephone calls.

243 "The pen register showed each telephone number . . ." Orton interview.

243 "At 9:10 A.M., Andonian called New York." Orton affidavit.

243 "In the basement . . ." Interview with Customs agents Noonan and Deborah Ladomirak.

244 "Using tables covered with brown wrapping paper . . ." From photographs of the counting; interviews with Noonan and Ladomirak.

244 "This was very good evidence." Interviews with Furtado, Orton, and Hayman.

244 "FBI agents say the seizure in fact scared off a couple . . ." Interviews with Lumpkin and Stephens.

244 "But Furtado insists the seizure was worthwhile." Interview with Furtado.

244 "Suddenly, Eduardo Martínez was calling again." DEA transcript of the telephone call, translated into English.

244 "Ramón had tried to resume business . . ." DEA tapes of conversations between Ramón Costello and Martínez.

244 " 'When could we start?' " DEA transcript.

245 "No one had expected Eduardo Martínez to reappear . . ." Interviews with Parker and Diaz.

245 "The feds had thought that the La Mina gang would react . . ." Interviews with Orton, Hayman, and Wong.

245 "Polar Cap agents in Los Angeles and New York watched . . ." Interviews with Orton, Wong, and Hayman.

245 "The money had stopped coming from New York . . ." Orton interview.

245 "Wanis Koyomejian told Nazareth Andonian in a monitored conversation . . ." Orton affidavit.

245 "From Buenos Aires, Avo . . ." My account of this conversation comes from the Orton affidavit.

245 "It came on February 21 over a Ropex telephone . . ." Interviews with FBI agents Wong and Stephens, as well as Hayman and Orton.

245 "Hello, a male caller said . . ." This comes from Wong, who heard the call.

245 "Sergio Hochman, believed to be a major power . . ." Interviews with Wong, Lumpkin, Stephens, Hayman, and Parker.

245 "He had been out of the country and living in Montevideo . . ." The story of why Hochman fled New York comes from interviews with Assistant U.S. Attorney Jean Kawahara, Orton, Wong, and Hochman's attorney, Errol Stambler.

245 "Now he was back in the country, and he was telling Koyomejian . . ." Interviews with Wong and Stephens.

245 "The feds believed panic over the $5 million . . ." Interviews with Wong, Orton, and Furtado.

245 "Hochman had been out of the business for months..." Hochman would later testify at the Andonian trial that he had gotten out of the business, according to his lawyer, Errol Stambler, as well as Assistant U.S. Attorneys Steven Clymer and Richard Rathmann of Los Angeles. That he said he intended to start up again came from the prosecutors. Stambler said he was in the States for a social visit.

246 "They were also wrong about Hochman's importance..." Clymer, Rathmann, and Wong told me about confusing Hochman with Merkin, with most of the detail coming from Wong. Orton said the feds believed Hochman was more important than he was.

246 "By February 1989, the feds had realized their mistake..." Interviews with Wong and Stephens.

246 "In the four weeks since the seizure..." Wong described how he learned of Hochman's whereabouts, and how the feds followed him.

246 "The Polar Cap agents didn't know who the other man was..." Interviews with Wong, Lumpkin, and Stambler.

246 "but with Hochman, they believed they had..." Interviews with Wong, Lumpkin, Stephens, and Hayman.

247 "Hochman would be returning to New York that evening..." Interviews with Wong and Stephens.

247 "A surveillance team followed Hochman..." Interviews with Wong and Hayman.

247 "Wong peeled off for a meeting..." Wong interview. Others, including Hayman and Furtado, told me about interagency discussions.

247 "Hayman alerted the Polar Cap lawyers..." Interviews with Hayman and Parker.

247 "When the call came, Buddy Parker was in the kitchen..." Interviews with Parker.

247 "Chuck Saphos was on the line..." Interviews with Parker. Hayman said he did not remember this specific call but confirmed the issues under discussion. The others either did not remember or were not available to discuss it.

249 "When Sergio Hochman showed up at a gate..." My interviews with Wong provided most of the details of Hochman's arrest, with confirmation of the key elements coming from Stambler.

249 "But he didn't tell anyone that the man he was with..." Interviews with Wong, Stambler, and Lumpkin.

249 "All night long, Polar Cap agents, cops, and prosecutors worked..." Interviews with Hayman, Kawahara, Wong, Furtado, Orton, and others.

249 "... Hochman's mysterious traveling companion was forgotten." Interview with Wong.

249 "And sometime in the early morning hours..." Interview with Orton, Hayman, Kawahara, and Stephens.

249 "On Wednesday morning, February 22, they began bursting..." Interviews with Hayman, Orton, and Furtado; DEA videotape of the Andonian Brothers' raid.

250 "The same thing was going on at the Ropex offices..." Interviews with Furtado, Hayman, and Lumpkin.

250 "At Ropex, the raiding agents found a stack . . ." Interviews with Rathmann and Clymer.

250 "Sixteen businesses in L.A.'s jewelry district . . ." The number of places raided is based on a list of search warrants the agents used.

250 "while agents in Miami moved in on the Ronel Refinery." Interview with Lumpkin.

250 "Luxury cars were seized and buildings . . ." Interview with Stephens.

250 "In the suburbs flung out from L.A. . . ." List of search warrants.

250 "The case got big news treatment in the La Mina cities . . ." Videos of various newscasts, newspaper stories.

250 "But the announcement from Washington took place on paper . . ." Department of Justice press release dated February 22, 1989.

Chapter 19: Cranking Up the Old Laundry

251 "The day La Mina was shut down, Eduardo Martínez learned . . ." I base that on what Martínez said to Cesar Diaz in a February 23, 1989, telephone conversation, as recorded, transcribed, and translated by DEA.

251 "In the two weeks since Martínez had renewed contact . . ." What DEA had been doing comes from interviews with Latson and Diaz.

251 "He asked Cesar whether Jimmy Brown's laundry . . ." DEA transcript of a February 24, 1989, conversation between Diaz and Martínez.

251 "Martínez told Cesar to caution his people . . ." Transcript of February 23, 1989, call. The direct quotes come from that transcript.

251 "The operation would work much as it had before . . ." The discussion about using another bank instead of Banco de Occidente comes from a DEA transcript of a February 22, 1989, conversation between Diaz and Martínez. The eventual indictment, *United States* vs. *Pablo Emilio Escobar-Gaviria, et al.,* Indictment No. 1:89-CR-086-WCO (N.D.Ga.), which includes Martínez, shows they used the other bank.

252 "On Monday, February 27, undercover drug agents . . ." The account of these pickups in Los Angeles and New York is based on DEA reports detailing them and on *United States* vs. *Pablo Emilio Escobar-Gaviria, et al.,* Indictment No. 1:89-CR-086-WCO (N.D.Ga.).

252 "Every working day that week, drug dollars poured . . ." DEA reports; *United States* vs. *Pablo Emilio Escobar-Gaviria, et al.,* Indictment No. 1:89-CR-086-WCO (N.D.Ga.).

252 "Cesar and Martínez were constantly on the telephone . . ." Interviews with Diaz; DEA transcripts of telephone calls.

252 "At week's end, more than $4.3 million in cash . . ." *United States* vs. *Pablo Emilio Escobar-Gaviria, et al.,* Indictment No. 1:89-CR-086-WCO (N.D.Ga.).

252 " 'We need to speed up the payments . . .' " DEA transcript of March 6, 1989, conversation.

252 "That afternoon, a grand jury would vote . . ." *United States* vs. *Pablo Emilio Escobar-Gaviria, et al.,* Indictment No. 1:89-CR-086-WCO (N.D.Ga.).

252 "By this time, Buddy had taken Cesar, Skip, Ramón . . ." Interviews with Parker.

253 "He also introduced the jurors to La Mina . . ." *United States* vs. *Pablo Emilio Escobar-Gaviria, et al.,* Indictment No. 1:89-CR-086-WCO (N.D.Ga.).

253 "By now, Francisco had reluctantly agreed to cooperate..." Interviews with Parker.

253 "Buddy brought Francisco and his public defender..." Interviews with Parker.

253 "In walked Jimmy Brown and a grinning Alex Carrera." Interviews with Parker, Diaz, Featherly, and Serrano.

253 "It was on that day that Francisco Serrano decided to roll." Interviews with Parker and Serrano.

253 "But one thing he did give them was Chepe's name." Interviews with Parker and Latson.

253 "That was the name under which Chepe..." *United States* vs. *Pablo Emilio Escobar-Gaviria, et al.,* Indictment No. 1:89-CR-086-WCO (N.D.Ga.).

254 "The resumption of business with Eduardo Martínez..." Interviews with Parker.

254 "A March 15 takedown was planned..." March 7, 1989, memo from Parker to Saphos at Justice.

254 "and on Monday, March 6, even as Martínez was continuing..." That Martínez was still sending money comes from DEA reports. The date and description of the indictment comes from the indictment.

255 "In fact, on the day of the indictment..." That money continued to come through comes from the September 7, 1989, affidavit of Skip Latson.

255 "In New York, Ed Guillen's group kept surveilling..." DEA reports.

255 "In Atlanta, plans were being made to lure Martínez..." Parker, Latson, and Diaz interviews.

255 "while bosses in Washington planned a major public announcement..." Parker interview; March 8, 1989, memo to Saphos from U.S. Attorney Robert L. Barr, Jr., in Atlanta.

255 "Memos and cables flew from city to city..." This is based on copies of some of the memos and cables, and interviews with Parker and Latson.

255 "While tracking that activity, Craig Gillen and Buddy Parker..." In interviews, Parker described their preparations to move against the bank, the substitute-asset theory behind their action, and the mechanics.

255 "What made this idea so unusual—and so incredibly unfair..." Interviews with Miami attorneys William Richey and Kirk Munroe, who represented Banco de Occidente.

256 "But under federal law, the funds represented bank assets..." Interviews with Parker.

256 "Through Martínez and the business DEA-Atlanta had conducted with him..." March 1989 affidavit of Skip Latson and IRS Special Agent Jack Fishman.

256 "These were added to the undercover bank accounts..." March 28, 1989, restraining orders signed by U.S. District Judge Marvin H. Shoob, in *United States* vs. *Pablo Emilio Escobar-Gaviria, et al.,* Indictment No. 1:89-CR-086-WCO (N.D.Ga.).

256 "The problem was setting a date..." Interviews with Parker, Latson, and Diaz.

256 "Martínez and Cesar had been talking for weeks..." DEA transcripts of their conversations.

256 " 'I need your help with the payments . . ." DEA transcript of March 8, 1989, conversation between Diaz and Martínez.

256 "By the end of the second week . . ." The sum comes from Latson's September 7, 1989, affidavit.

257 "Cesar gave Martínez all sorts of excuses . . ." Transcripts of telephone conversations; interview with Diaz.

257 "Guillen had decided to slow down the laundry . . ." Interviews with Guillen, Diaz, Latson, and Parker.

257 "Skip and Cesar tried hard to keep Martínez happy . . ." Interviews with Latson and Diaz.

257 "No, we are not going to do it that way . . ." The back and forth between Latson and Guillen comes mostly from Latson, with Guillen confirming the gist of the running debate.

257 "Meanwhile, Martínez was calling Cesar every day . . ." Diaz interviews; transcripts.

257 " 'Why is it so slow this time?' . . ." DEA transcript of a March 14, 1989, call.

257 "He hung up and put in a call to New York." Diaz interviews.

257 " 'Did you talk to the boss?' he asked." Transcript.

258 "Eventually, Guillen let a little bit of money go . . ." Interviews with Diaz; transcript of conversations where Martínez refers to this.

258 "but Martínez wasn't satisfied." Transcript of a March 14, 1989, call.

258 " 'Listen, I think we have to talk,' . . ." Transcript of a March 15, 1989, call.

258 "Still, plans to meet kept evaporating . . ." Transcripts of more conversations.

258 "Some very serious men were squeezing him . . ." Transcript of March 21, 1989, conversation.

258 " 'Why don't you pay the account?' . . ." The transcript of March 23, 1989, call gave me this and the remainder of the conversation in this segment.

258 "Time and place were set for 9:00 A.M., Wednesday, March 29 . . ." Transcript of a March 27, 1989, conversation; interviews with Diaz.

258 "Martínez's agreement had sent . . ." Interviews with Parker; the affidavits and orders previously mentioned.

259 "Cesar would go with two other Atlanta-based agents." Interviews with Diaz.

259 "On Tuesday, March 28, as scores of federal agents . . ." Interviews with Parker; DEA reports.

259 "Shoob nonetheless signed a set . . ." Copies of the restraining orders.

259 "So while federal law enforcers were organizing agents . . ." DEA reports of the activities of March 29, 1989; Shoob's seizure warrant of March 28, 1989.

259 "The idea was to hit all of them as close to 9:00 A.M. . . ." Interviews with Latson and Diaz.

259 "Buddy called each of the agencies . . ." Interviews with Parker.

259 "For his task on takedown day, Skip would go . . ." DEA report; interviews with Latson.

259 "Buddy was feeling the pressure." Interviews with Parker.

260 "Word came back that Thornburgh would hold . . ." Interviews with Parker.

Chapter 20: Return to Panama

261 "Cesar and his two backups flew into Panama..." Interviews with Diaz.

261 "To make an arrest in Panama, U.S. officers had to work..." Interviews with De La Cova and Diaz.

261 "De La Cova accompanied Cesar and the other two..." Interviews with Diaz and De La Cova.

262 "Nonetheless, the DEA was still getting help..." Interview with De La Cova.

262 "Quiel and De La Cova, who had worked many cases together..." Interview with De La Cova.

262 "seemed to get along." Interviews with Diaz, on whose account of the meeting with Quiel I base my account. De La Cova confirmed a few details.

262 "while Cesar, the other two DEA agents, and the three PDF officers headed to the Marriott..." Interviews with Diaz and De La Cova.

262 "Cesar would be carrying his briefcase..." Interviews with Diaz. He provided the details of his attempt to meet Martínez at the Marriott, and his telephone conversation with Martínez.

264 "Thornburgh would be holding his press conference soon..." That CNN would cover it came from CNN tapes.

264 "On the way to the bank, Cesar used the mobile phone..." Interviews with Diaz and De La Cova.

264 "The plan was this..." My account of what occurred at Banco Ganadero is based on what Diaz told me.

266 "He told De La Cova what had happened..." Inteviews with Diaz and De La Cova.

266 "reporters from major U.S. news organizations had gathered..." Videotapes of the press conference. Stories appeared in *The New York Times, The Washington Post,* and on television networks.

266 "Live on CNN..." CNN tape of the coverage.

266 "Thornburgh unveiled Operation Polar Cap..." The CNN tape, a tape produced by the Justice Department, and Thornburgh's press release of March 29, 1989.

268 "The press conference would further inflame jealousies." Interviews with Parker and, in Los Angeles, Lumpkin and Furtado.

268 "Thornburgh stepped up to the mike..." Justice Department videotape.

268 "By the time the other agencies' roles were mentioned..." CNN videotape.

268 "Lawn announced that the PDF..." Videotape produced by the Justice Department.

268 "Although De La Cova in Panama was communicating..." Interviews with De La Cova and Saphos.

268 "Reporters questioned Thornburgh and Lawn..." Tape of press conference.

268 "Cesar's call to De La Cova brought..." My account of what happened next at Banco Ganadero and Diaz's thoughts about it is based mostly on what Diaz told me.

268 "De La Cova was still getting calls from Washington for updates." Interview with De La Cova.

269 "but Quiel's version of things was passed along . . ." De La Cova interview and Michael Isikoff, "U.S. Sues Nine Banks in Drug Money-Laundering," *The Washington Post,* March 30, 1989.

269 "In Atlanta, U.S. Attorney Robert L. Barr, Jr., waited till noon . . ." Interviews with Parker.

269 "Alongside him were Buddy Parker and Ron Caffrey . . ." CNN story that included footage from the Atlanta press conference.

269 "Barr's staff handed out statements . . ." This is based on my recollection of the press conference, which I attended, and the documents themselves.

269 "But the normally talkative U.S. Attorney refused to take questions . . ." Barr's March 29, 1989, press release.

269 "Craig and Buddy . . ." Interviews with Parker.

269 "Meanwhile, the PDF officers were now inside . . ." Interview with Diaz.

269 "Cesar returned to the DEA office . . ." Diaz interview.

270 "*La Estrella de Panamá* carried an Associated Press account . . ." William M. Welch of the Associated Press, "Arrestos en Estados Unidos/FFDD, contribuyen desmantelar banda," *La Estrella de Panamá,* March 30, 1989.

270 "On Friday, two days after the failed arrest attempt . . ." Antonio Dudley, lawyer in Panama representing Banco de Occidente, described the bankers' arrests.

270 "Using information Cesar provided, Panamanian authorities . . ." Interviews with Diaz and Dudley.

270 "Cesar had returned to Atlanta with an unused plane ticket . . ." Interviews with Diaz and Parker.

Chapter 21: The Big Freeze

271 "By the time takedown happened, Ramón was well out of the way . . ." Interviews with Costello and Latson.

271 "It was clear from the indictment . . ." *United States* vs. *Pablo Emilio Escobar-Gaviria, et al.,* Indictment No. 1:89-CR-086-WCO (N.D.Ga.).

271 "None of the Colombians knew Ramón's real name except for Francisco . . ." Interviews with Costello and Serrano.

271 "Buddy and the agents blame Francisco Serrano . . ." Interviews with Parker, Latson, and Diaz.

272 "The only way the money handlers and drug traffickers . . ." Interviews with Costello and Latson.

272 "A month or so after the takedown, he started getting odd calls . . ." I base my account of these calls on a DEA report.

272 "On the day of the takedown . . ." DEA reports of the takedown activities; U.S. District Judge Marvin H. Shoob's March 28, 1989, restraining orders.

272 "Parker's telephone rang steadily . . ." Interviews with Parker and Gillen.

272 "But within forty-eight hours, $22 million had collected . . ." Interview with Banco de Occidente lawyers William Richey and Kirk Munroe. (I interviewed them and their colleague Clemente Vazquez-Bello in Miami together, along with Antonio Dudley, who came in from Panama.)

272 "Most of that ($17.5 million) . . ." A DEA report.

272 "The frozen funds represented almost double the amount..." The sum of money sent through the Atlanta laundry is based on information in *United States* vs. *Pablo Emilio Escobar-Gaviria, et al.,* Indictment No. 1:89-CR-086-WCO (N.D.Ga.).

272 "Between La Mina and Jimmy Brown's laundry..." The $412 million figure comes from the transcript of Banco de Occidente's sentencing hearing, August 14, 1989.

273 "The only drug proceeds the feds froze that day..." The sum comes from the plea agreement between Martínez and the U.S. government.

273 "Within twenty-four hours of the Thornburgh press conference..." Interview with Richey.

273 "Incredulous that the federal government would move on money..." Interviews with Occidente lawyers Richey, Munroe, and Clemente Vazquez-Bello.

273 "That Friday, two Miami lawyers and an Atlanta lawyer..." Munroe and Parker interviews.

273 "From Miami came Kirk Munroe..." Munroe gave me biographical information.

273 "Buddy Parker, Craig Gillen, two assistant U.S. attorneys..." Munroe and Parker told me who attended and where they sat.

273 "Banco de Occidente is a good bank..." I reconstructed the discussion in Barr's office according to the accounts given me by Munroe and Parker.

274 "As the meeting broke up and the visiting lawyers..." Munroe told me this parting remark by Gillen.

274 "Craig remembers it differently." Interview with Craig Gillen.

274 "Cesar came back from Panama that weekend..." The account of the documents Cesar Diaz brought is based on what Parker told me and on Diaz's April 4, 1989, affidavit.

274 "The bank's lawyers would later say the bank shifted the money..." Interview with Richey and Munroe.

274 "Still, the transfers included $8.6 million..." Diaz affidavit.

275 "At least two U.S. banks reported to authorities..." DEA reports.

275 "When Buddy looked at the papers..." Interviews with Parker and Gillen.

275 "Buddy and Craig pulled out a decision..." *United States* vs. *Bank of Nova Scotia,* 691 F.2d 1384 (11th Circuit, Nov. 29, 1982), cert. denied, 462 U.S. 1119 (1983).

275 "As for the murkey way they got the documents..." Interviews with Parker.

275 "On Tuesday, April 5..." Interviews with Parker, Munroe, and Richey.

275 "Agents served Shoob's orders at the U.S. offices..." Interviews with Parker.

275 "Cesar and Skip, who were in Miami..." Interviews with Latson.

275 "the bank and its lawyers were trying to react..." Interview with Richey, Munroe, and Vazquez-Bello.

275 "After the meeting in Atlanta, Kirk Munroe, his partner Bill Richey..." This account of the meeting in Colombia is based on what Richey and Munroe told me about it, with Dudley discussing Panamanian law.

276 "The $22 million hit hurt badly, but the bank could manage ..." Interview with Richey and Munroe.

276 "had already explained to Panama's National Banking Commission ..." This according to Dudley.

276 "The lawyers were planning motions, plotting strategy ..." Interview with Richey, Munroe, Dudley, and Vasquez-Bello.

276 "The frozen funds included, for example, a $2 million payment ..." Munroe and Richey, Parker interviews.

277 "No way. Assets are assets ..." Parker interviews.

277 " 'The United States is expected ... to seek out crime ...' " Gillen interview.

277 "At midday on Wednesday, April 5 ..." Munroe described this.

277 "Still reeling over the U.S. accounts, the bankers now ..." Interview with Munroe, Richey, and Dudley.

278 "At the same time, the Banking Association of Panama ..." Interview with Edgardo Lasso, president of the association.

278 "Not wanting the case to further sully ..." In separate interviews at separate banks, two Panamanian bankers expressed these opinions to me but insisted that I not use their names.

278 "Banco de Occidente could not go on in this condition." Interview with Richey and Munroe.

278 "As predicted, Craig was fielding telephone calls ..." Gillen interview.

278 "Posturing aside, nobody wanted to go to court over this." Parker and Gillen interviews.

278 "The Atlantans, Justice Department officials in Washington ..." Interviews with Parker, Gillen, and Latson.

279 "In Wiesbaden, near Frankfurt ..." Parker and Latson described the meetings in Wiesbaden and Bern.

279 "told him the government of Colombia had now weighed in ..." Parker told me this, and Peter Djinis confirmed it.

279 "Moreover, Colombian President Virgilio Barco, an anti-drug president ..." Interviews with Parker, Djinis, and Saphos.

279 "Buddy was relieved to hear the U.S. State Department was already on board ..." Parker interviews.

280 "The hours that Bill Richey and Kirk Munroe ..." Interview with Richey and Munroe.

280 "But by Monday, April 17 ..." Interviews with Munroe, Richey, and Parker.

280 "Just because Occidente has $82 million in foreign deposits ..." The conversation at this meeting is based on my interviews with Richey, Munroe, and Parker.

281 "The following week they went at it again." Munroe, Richey, and Parker described these talks.

281 "On Saturday morning, April 29 ..." The account of this meeting is based on what Munroe, Parker, and Jerome Froelich, the bank's Atlanta attorney, told me.

282 "Meanwhile in Germany, bank lawyers had managed to dissuade ..." Interviews with Parker, Munroe, and Richey.

282 "The bank's certified audit from a Big Eight accounting firm..." Transcript of August 14, 1989, sentencing hearing in CR 89-086.

282 "In June, the prosecutors made their final offer..." Parker, Munroe, and Richey interviews.

282 "But when they traveled to Colombia to present the offer..." Munroe and Richey interview.

282 "For the prosecutors, it proved more than embarrassing..." Parker interview.

282 "U.S. government lawyers kept chipping away at the barriers." Munroe, Richey, and Parker interviews.

282 "In Panama, Antonio Dudley portrayed the U.S. turnabout..." Dudley interview.

283 "But the prosecutors insisted on a guilty plea or a trial..." Parker interviews.

283 "No one had predicted how complicated..." Parker, Munroe, and Richey interviews.

283 "Finally, in August 1989, it all came together." Details of the plea agreement come from that agreement, dated August 14, 1989, as well as from interviews with the lawyers.

283 " 'Call the matter of *United States of America* vs. *Banco de Occidente*...' " The transcript of the August 14, 1989, proceeding gave me the details and direct quotes from the hearing.

287 "In Panama, we had a legal problem..." Interview with Dudley.

287 He presented letters from Buddy Parker... Dudley interview and an August 16, 1989, letter Parker wrote to Richey.

287 "Dudley finally persuaded the banking commission..." Interviews with Dudley and Lasso.

287 "The seven-member ethics committee had already voted unanimously..." I base this on information from a banker I agreed not to name.

287 "The guilty plea and the U.S. treatment confused..." Interviews with Dudley, Lasso, and a banker who did not want me to name him.

287 "The association and its committees held hearings..." Dudley and Lasso interviews.

288 "Sending $412 million in drug funds through Occidente..." I base my account on the issues debated at the meeting on my interviews with Lasso, Dudley, and the two bankers who asked me not to name them.

Chapter 22: A Prisoner of War

289 "the bank's guilty plea satisfied Buddy." Interviews with Parker.

289 "Thornburgh issued another press release..." Press release dated August 14, 1989.

289 "Skip had viewed Martínez's arrest..." Interview with Latson.

289 "Still, they all had hoped to bring in..." Interviews with Parker, Diaz, and Latson.

289 "As for the two bankers, Panama had released them..." Interviews with Parker and Dudley.

289 "On Friday night, August 18, just four days after..." Details of the murder of Senator Luis Carlos Galán come from the following news stories: Associated Press, "Colombia Arrests 4,000 After Slaying," *The New York Times,* August 21, 1989; Lucia Newman, CNN, August 22 and 23, 1989; James Brooke, "Drug Traffickers in Colombia Start a Counterattack," *The New York Times,* August 25, 1989.

290 "Galán had advocated a get-tough policy..." AP, *The New York Times,* August 21, 1989; Brooke, *The New York Times,* August 25, 1989.

290 "The day before Galán's death, the provincial police commander..." These two murders were reported by AP, *The New York Times,* August 21, 1989.

290 "The murderous month had begun August 1 when Judge Helena Díaz..." Newman, CNN, August 28, 1989.

290 "Since 1981, 220 Colombian judges had been slain." AP, *The New York Times,* August 21, 1989.

290 "This was why traffickers feared extradition so much." Brooke, *The New York Times,* August 25, 1989; Robert Pear, "Thornburgh Gives Colombia a List of 12 Drug Figures the U.S. Wants Most," *The New York Times,* August 23, 1989.

290 "For two years, since the Supreme Court lifted Colombia's extradition treaty..." Pear, *The New York Times,* August 23, 1989.

290 "The assassination became a rallying cry..." Pear, *The New York Times,* August 23, 1989; James Brooke, "Bogotá Says It Plans to Extradite Major Drug Financier to the U.S.," *The New York Times,* August 23, 1989.

290 "President Barco declared the country to be in a state of siege." Decree No. 1860, Office of the President, Republic of Colombia, English version as translated by the U.S. Department of State. The fact that this was the most concerted government attack on drug traffickers in years comes from Brooke, *The New York Times,* August 23 and 25, 1989.

290 "That Friday night, word of Barco's emergency orders..." From a source in Colombia who did not want to be quoted by name.

290 "All weekend long, Colombian police raided ranches..." Associated Press, *The New York Times,* August 21, 1989; Brooke, *The New York Times,* August 23, 1989.

290 " 'They were hitting all the *fincas*...'" Interview with DEA agent Javier Pena.

290 "By Sunday night, nearly four thousand people had been rounded up." AP, *The New York Times,* August 21, 1989.

290 "and the raids continued Monday, a national holiday..." Brooke, *The New York Times,* August 21, 1989.

290 "Still, no kingpins." Pena interview; Pear, *The New York Times,* August 23, 1989; Brooke, *The New York Times,* August 25, 1989.

291 "At DEA-Atlanta, on Monday afternoon, Ron Caffrey took a call..." Interview with Latson.

291 "Caffrey passed the news to Skip and Cesar..." Interviews with Latson and Diaz.

291 "Surprised as the Atlantans were..." Interviews with Latson, Diaz, and Parker.

291 "They had never heard of Eduardo Martínez." Interviews with Pena and Bruce Stock, who ran DEA's Colombia office at the time.

291 " 'We are consulting with the government of Colombia . . .' " The statement by Richard Boucher comes from CNN, August 22, 1989.

291 "The networks showed footage of Martínez . . ." Newman, CNN, August 22, 1989; Jeff Levine, CNN, August 24, 1989.

291 "the traffickers were mounting a bloody counteroffensive . . ." Brooke, *The New York Times,* August 25, 1989; Newman, CNN, August 28, 1989.

291 "CNN was calling Martínez 'the cartel's main treasurer . . .' " Newman, CNN, August 22, 1989.

291 "while a front-page *New York Times* story tagged him . . ." Brooke, *The New York Times,* August 23, 1989.

291 "In Atlanta, he was 'Finance Minister' . . ." Gail Epstein, "Estates of Drug Kingpins Raided," *The Atlanta Constitution,* August 22, 1989.

292 "In Colombia, Martínez denied it all." Stephen Labaton, "U.S. Hopes to Try Colombian in Laundering Plot," *The New York Times,* August 23, 1989.

292 "In Atlanta, Buddy, Skip, and Cesar feverishly prepared paperwork . . ." Interviews with Parker, Latson, and Diaz.

292 "If it came off, this would be the first extradition in two years . . ." Pear, *The New York Times,* August 23, 1989.

292 "Meanwhile, Colombia's foreign minister and, later, its justice minister . . ." Michael Wines, "High-Level Officials of U.S. and Colombia Meet on Drug Issue," *The New York Times,* August 25, 1989.

292 "and Attorney General Thornburgh called for . . ." Peter Arnett, CNN, August 23, 1989.

292 "Pressure built as President Barco delivered a televised plea . . ." CNN, August 28, 1989.

292 "Washington responded with a $65 million emergency aid package . . ." Arnett, CNN, August 29, 1989; Joseph B. Treaster, "U.S. Sending Wrong Equipment to Fight Drugs, Colombians Say," *The New York Times,* September 12, 1989.

292 "But as for extradition, there were still so many kinks . . ." Interviews with Parker and Latson. Also, Pear, *The New York Times,* August 23, 1989.

293 "Skip and Cesar wanted to make sure . . ." Interviews with Latson and Diaz.

293 "One of the suggestions was to get the pair of agents to Bogotá . . ." Interviews with Diaz and Parker.

293 "No, Colombian police would fly Martínez from Bogotá . . ." Interviews with Latson and Diaz.

293 "But where in Atlanta would the plane land, and how could the marshals . . ." Interviews with Latson, Diaz, and Parker.

293 "In Colombia, the 'Extraditables' had pledged to kill . . ." Michael Wines, "U.S. Giving Colombia Names of Possible Narcotics Figures," *The New York Times,* September 12, 1989.

293 "For Ramón, hidden away . . ." Interviews with Costello.

293 "On Monday, August 28, a week after Martínez's capture, the U.S. government . . ." I took the date from the Acknowledgment of Conditions of Extradition of Defendant Eduardo Martínez, filed August 23, 1990, by U.S.

Attorney Joe D. Whitley in *United States* vs. *Pablo Emilio Escobar-Gaviria, et al.,* Indictment No. 1:89-CR-086-WCO (N.D.Ga.).

293 "Pounds of documents were submitted." Interviews with Parker and Ron Caffrey.

294 "Skip and Cesar flew to Miami . . ." Interviews with Latson, Diaz, and DEA pilot Kelley McCullough.

294 "On Tuesday, the twenty-ninth, President Barco granted extradition." Resolution 108 of 1989, the President of the Republic of Colombia, as translated and included as an attachment to Whitley's Acknowledgment of Conditions of Extradition in 1:89-CR-086 (N.D.Ga.).

294 "Proceedings had hit a further snag in Colombia." The facts of the appeal come mostly from Resolution No. 113 of September 6, 1989, the Department of Justice, Republic of Colombia, as submitted, in English, in Whitley's August 23, 1990, Acknowledgment of Conditions of Extradition. That resolution, which denied the appeal, gives the date of the appeal.

294 "Skip and Cesar flew back to Atlanta . . ." Interviews with Latson, Diaz, and McCullough.

294 "The case seemed to be swirling above the agents . . ." Interviews with Latson and Parker.

294 "But the Atlantans needed to know what was happening . . ." Latson and Pena told me of the unofficial line of communication.

294 "Buddy had felt the eyes of the world . . ." Parker interviews.

294 "Finally, two weeks after Martínez's arrest, Skip and Cesar were told . . ." Interviews with Latson and Diaz.

294 "At this point, with anti-drug and anti-trafficker sentiment reaching a pitch . . ." My description of U.S. anti-drug sentiment was based on two stories: Richard L. Berke, "Poll Finds Many in U.S. Back Bush Strategy on Drugs," *The New York Times,* September 12, 1989; and Joseph B. Treaster, "Some Think the 'War on Drugs' Is Being Waged on Wrong Front," *The New York Times,* July 28, 1992. Colombian sentiment was reported in Pear, *The New York Times,* August 23, 1989; Brooke, *The New York Times,* August 23, 1989.

294 "Bush would address the nation in his first televised speech . . ." September 5, 1989, speech as released by the White House; story by Peter Arnett, CNN, September 6, 1989.

295 "(Within days, *The Washington Post* would report . . ." Michael Isikoff, "Drug Buy Set Up for Bush Speech," *The Washington Post,* September 22, 1989.

295 "Under the new emergency extradition agreement, the United States . . ." Decree No. 1860 from the President of Colombia, August 18, 1989, English version by U.S. Department of State.

295 "Within the administration, there was fear . . ." Arnett, CNN, September 6, 1989.

295 "Martínez's lawyer was already challenging the legality . . ." The grounds for the appeal as well as the timing of it come from Resolution No. 113, Department of Justice, Republic of Colombia, September 6, 1989, which denied the appeal.

295 "In Miami, Skip and Cesar and the DEA pilots..." Interviews with Latson and Diaz.

296 "That same day, in Bogotá, the day after Bush's faux pas..." That the appeal was denied and the date it happened come from Resolution No. 113, Department of Justice, Republic of Colombia.

296 "Skip and Cesar took a phone call about 4:00 P.M...." The account of their wait in Miami comes from interviews with Diaz and Latson.

296 "The pilot flew the Marlin 3..." Interview with DEA pilot McCullough.

296 "around Cuba to avoid Cuban air space, but Cesar was watching..." Diaz interviews.

296 "The agents waited..." Diaz interviews.

297 "After arresting Martínez and reading him his rights..." Diaz and Latson interviews.

297 "Analysts had been poring over bank records..." Latson interviews; DEA report.

297 "This was their chance, facing him in this small, six-seater..." The account of the flight back to Atlanta is based on what Latson and Diaz told me in separate interviews.

298 "It was nearly 5:00 A.M. and still dark when the plane neared Atlanta..." The time comes from a DEA report, as well as interviews with the agents; McCullough described the visibility problem.

298 "As the plane rolled in..." Diaz, Latson, and McCullough interviews.

Chapter 23: Truth and Consequences

300 " 'It was long before sunrise that federal marshals...' " Larry Woods, CNN, September 7, 1989.

300 "One man could be seen, and then three more..." CNN footage of the helicopter's arrival.

300 "For Martínez's first appearance in federal court..." Interviews with Parker.

300 "while photographers and camera crews..." CNN footage, September 7, 1989.

300 "To an American Legion convention in Baltimore, he said..." Charles Bierbauer, CNN, September 7, 1989.

301 "In fact, the extradition had set off..." Lucia Newman, CNN, September 7, 1989.

301 "Judge O'Kelley called him into his chambers..." Transcript of September 8, 1989, meeting in O'Kelley's chambers.

301 "That was just fine with Buddy and Craig..." Interviews with Parker.

301 "Accused of headline seeking..." Ann Woolner, "Does Bob Barr Talk Too Much?" *Fulton County Daily Report,* December 22, 1988.

301 "throughout Fis-Con and Polar Cap, the prosecutors had purposely held back..." Interviews with Parker.

301 "soon began attacking almost every aspect..." Based on the numerous defense motions filed in the case.

301 "Skip had asked Captain Oscar Naranjo, chief of intelligence..." DEA report.

302 "Skip decided to pull together everything he could . . ." Latson interview; DEA report. That report gave me the information that follows about Moncada.

302 "The more Buddy and Skip looked, the more drug probes . . ." Latson and Parker interviews.

302 "On October 3, 1989, Skip wrote a sixteen-page DEA-6 . . ." Details come from that report.

302 "If Moncada was extradited, he would be the most significant drug baron . . ." Moncada's importance is based on what I've already reported about him, the fact that the DEA listed him among the twelve most wanted Colombian drug traffickers in 1989, and several stories that have been published since 1989. Among them are: James Ring Adams, "Medellin's New Generation," *The American Spectator* (December 1991); Andrew and Leslie Cockburn, "On the Trail of Medellín's Drug Lord," *Vanity Fair* (December 1992); and Alma Guillermoprieto, "Exit El Patrón," *The New Yorker,* October 25, 1993.

302 "Bombings and terrorism continued as police rounded up . . ." I base this account of violence in Colombia on interviews with Bruce Stock and Javier Pena of DEA in Colombia, as well as the following news stories: Associated Press, "Ambush Kills Former Medellin Mayor Who Fought to Drive Out Drug Lords," *The Atlanta Journal and Constitution,* September 12, 1989; James Brooke, "For Children, Colombia Is a Scary Place to Be," *The New York Times,* September 26, 1989; Joseph B. Treaster, "Colombians, Weary of the Strain, Are Losing Heart in the Drug War," *The New York Times,* October 2, 1989; unsigned world briefs, "Colombia Finds Bomb Caused Airliner Crash," *The Atlanta Constitution,* December 6, 1989; Guy Gugliotta, "Beating back the cocaine kings," *U.S. News & World Report,* February 19, 1990.

303 "Finally, on December 15, Colombian and U.S. authorities . . ." Joseph B. Treaster, "A Top Medellín Drug Trafficker Dies in a Shootout in Colombia," *The New York Times,* December 16, 1989.

303 "The next day, December 16, in a suburb of Birmingham . . ." Gail Epstein and Joe Drape, "Mail Bomb Had Return Address of Vance Colleague," *The Atlanta Consitution,* December 18, 1989.

303 "Buddy didn't think so." Interviews with Parker.

304 "Nonetheless, the U.S. Marshal called Buddy . . ." Interviews with Parker and U.S. District Judge Marvin Shoob.

304 "Two days after Vance's murder, authorities intercepted another mail bomb . . ." "Events Leading to Moody's Indictment in '89 Bombings," *The Atlanta Constitution,* November 8, 1990.

304 "Buddy was worried enough . . ." Interviews with Parker.

304 "The bombs would turn out to be the handiwork of a strange fellow . . ." Bill Montgomery, "Moody Convicted on All Counts," *The Atlanta Journal* and *The Atlanta Constitution,* June 29, 1991.

304 "Noriega had stolen the presidential election in May . . ." My account of the events in Panama comes mostly from Buckley, *Panama: The Whole Story,* and from several stories that ran in December 1991 in *The Atlanta Constitution* and *The New York Times.*

304 "Riding back on a military plane to Miami . . ." Interview with Rene De La Cova.

304 "With Noriega gone from Panama . . ." Information about the freezing and defrosting of the 700 bank accounts comes from interviews with Parker; the April 17, 1990, press release of Attorney General Thornburgh; interview with Tony Cheng, deputy manager of Chang Hwa Commercial Bank in New York; and the following stories, all of which appeared in the *Fulton County Daily Report:* Ann Woolner, "Feds Freeze 700 Alleged Medellin Bank Accounts," April 18, 1990; Ann Woolner, "Thaw Ordered on Frozen Accounts," April 26, 1990; "400-Plus Accounts Defrosted," April 27, 1990; Jane Okrasinksi, "Access to Thawed Accounts Removed," May 4, 1990; Ann Woolner, "Atlanta Freeze Order Takes Heat in Miami," June 13, 1990; Robert Kuntz, American Lawyer News Service, "After 2 Years, Operation Polar Cap Melts," July 30, 1992.

306 "June 22, 1990, when Eduardo Martínez signed a six-page letter agreeing to plead guilty . . ." A copy of the plea agreement gave me the terms.

307 "he still could be a valuable source." Interviews with Parker.

307 "But he agreed to cooperate only after getting permission from Colombia . . ." Latson said Martínez got permission from Moncada; Parker said he got it from Escobar.

307 "he did not want it widely known he was cooperating." Interviews with Parker, who told me of steps taken to minimize news coverage of the hearing.

307 "At 8:10 A.M., Judge O'Kelley's clerk called the case . . ." The time of the August 23, 1990, hearing, the lawyers there, and what was said come from a transcript.

307 "Just twelve days earlier, Colombian police had tracked . . ." Gustavo Gaviria's death was reported in a news release from U.S. Attorney Joe D. Whitley, August 23, 1990.

307 "Judge O'Kelley accepted Martínez's guilty plea . . ." Transcript of hearing.

308 "For months after his arrest, Francisco had been telling . . ." Serrano declined to discuss his interactions with his wife. The following is based on what Parker said.

308 " 'Mr. Serrano has suffered more than any one man can . . .'" I attended the sentencing hearing; the account of it here is based on my notes and a story I wrote, "Cartel Convicts to Stay Behind Bars," *Fulton County Daily Report,* October 30, 1990.

309 "Sol's suicide shook Francisco to his soul." Interviews with Parker; attorney Jake Waldrop.

309 "He would have just as soon avoided his day in court . . ." Interviews with Costello.

309 "That day came on January 16, 1991." Transcript of the hearing.

309 "As the date approached, Ramón recalled his first trip . . ." Interviews with Costello.

310 "Through his lawyer, Mark Kadish, Ramón tried to persuade Buddy . . ." Interviews with Parker and Costello.

310 "Buddy was willing to sing Ramón's praises . . ." The conversation between

Parker and Mark Kadish is based on Parker's account. (Kadish declined to be interviewed for this book.)

310 "Ramón's efforts, Buddy told U.S. District Judge Robert H. Hall . . ." The following account of the hearing is based on the transcript.

312 "Ramón had planned a little speech . . ." Interviews with Costello.

312 " 'I think you've said it for me . . .' " Transcript.

312 "Ramón had never come to terms with the fact . . ." Interviews with Costello.

312 "Skip insisted to Ramón that Francisco's problems . . ." Interviews with Latson and Costello.

312 "To Ramón, that seemed like rationalization." Interviews with Costello.

Index

About the Author

Ann Woolner is currently Associate Editor with the *Fulton County Daily Report,* and was previously a reporter for *The Atlanta Journal* and *The Atlanta Constitution.* Her work has appeared in *The American Lawyer, Atlanta,* and *Southpoint* magazines. She lives in Atlanta, Georgia.